Privileged

Jeanne Selander Miller

Copyright © 2015 Jeanne Selander Miller
All rights reserved.

ISBN: 069247224X
ISBN 13: 9780692472248
Library of Congress Control Number: 2015944586
Pebble Path Printing, Vero Beach, FL

For the wounded healers–

*Who can take away the suffering without
entering it?*

–Henri Nouwen

I offer my love and gratitude to my writing coach,
my editorial crew, and my first readers
I couldn't tell my stories without you

David Hazard, Susan Rimato, Jeanne Whyte,
Samantha Salsbury, Jacqueline Foley, and Denis
Naeger

DESTINY

February 2015

At certain times in my life I've ended up places and really wondered what the hell I was doing there.

A couple of years ago, I had moved to this quiet little beachside community in Florida after my children had grown up and flown off into their own adult lives. I knew I was living a life that others only dreamed of. I had been told how lucky I was often enough. I was living in a place where by comparison I was still a youngster. I liked the sunshine, and the peace and quiet, but this had never really been my dream. In my heart I knew I had never consciously chosen this.

This was my default position. I was here because my sister lived here. Had I really fled my old life seeking the safety and protection of my sister? How pitiful, absolutely pitiful was that?

What did I want? I didn't know. So many people know exactly what they want and what will make them happy. They seek it out. They *run* to it, moving heaven and earth to find a way to claim their treasure. The question that lingered wasn't what should I be running *to*, but rather, what was I running *from*.

One day in the afternoon mail I had received an invitation to attend a workshop on *Learning to Read your Natal Chart*. My neighbor had extended the offer to attend. She was a children's author and also an astrologist. I had met a number of other authors, but I'd never had the pleasure of knowing an astrologist. And quite frankly, I was uncertain what I thought about astrology.

However, I'm forever the student and a curious cat by nature, so once asked I could see no reason in the world not to accept the invitation, and learn a little about this very ancient study of astrology.

I persuaded my sister to join me. When the evening came, with the aid of the map on my cell phone, we made our way to the little art gallery where the class was being held. The space was intimate and the dozen people attending were warm and welcoming. Immediately, I felt at ease. I sensed I would like them.

The students were given a folder containing a whole slew of papers, including a copy of their chart based on their date of birth, as well as the exact time and place of their birth. The chart provided information on the positions of the planets and a lot of other things I did not yet understand. I ruffled through my papers and it didn't take a wizard to see there was a whole lot more to this than the daily horoscope that appeared in the newspaper.

I had spent my life trying to be a person who did the right thing. It was deeply ingrained within me. There had been plenty of times when others laughed at me because of my serious nature. Yet there it was in my astrological chart. The moon was in Capricorn at the time of my birth. I was destined to be serious for it was written in the stars.

As the teacher went described people with their moon in Capricorn as serious, I thought about my life. I believed my serious nature had served me well. I had a great deal of responsibility at a young age. I worked as an emergency room nurse right out of college, and went on to experience enough trauma and tragedy in my personal life to send the strongest of souls to their knees.

My sister, who knew me so well, told the others in our astrology class, "She hates comedies. She always has."

I protested, "That isn't true." At first I took offense feeling typecast as humorless in the presence of these congenial strangers.

She responded, "Name one. Really, name just one that you like."

The truth was in the moment. I couldn't think of one. Wow. I really had no interest in lighthearted comedy, I found it witless and it bored me to tears.

My late husband used to go to the video store long before the days of Netflix. He would come home with a period piece, a drama and say, "I looked for the longest, most boring movie I could find and I knew it would be right up your alley."

"Perfect."

I wasn't offended then. But there among strangers who didn't know me and certainly didn't love me, I felt classified as humorless. This wasn't exactly the case. I had a sense of humor. It was just that the humor must be rooted in wit and clever repartee. It was the lowbrow humor I had no time for. So maybe I'm a bit of a snob. Was that in my chart too?

But my serious essence was more pervasive than in just my choice of movies.

I was serious. I had worked as a nurse, a teacher, and a counselor for most of my adult life. I had been widowed in my early forties, which left me a single mother. I didn't have the luxury of being empty-headed or lighthearted. No, I gravitated towards people and situations that needed to be mended, healed, and made stronger.

Over the course of the week while I studied my chart and prepared for the next week's lesson, I reflected on what it meant to be a serious person.

What else was in my chart? What other secrets were inscribed upon my path by the place and time of my birth? I entered into the study of astrology as a skeptic. I'd been looking for a way to connect with some interesting people in my new community. I was in *yes mode*. So that was how it started, but it wasn't the reason I continued. I continued because of the truths that I came to see. Right there in my chart were my strengths, my weaknesses, and where I carried my past hurts and life lessons.

The week passed and it was time for the next lesson.

Leslie, the teacher, described the comet Chiron or the wounded healer. I was perplexed about why Chiron was in my first house. My first house was where I met the world. What did this mean?

I sat in silence while Leslie proceeded with the lesson. She was moving on, but I could not. There was something she said about Chiron that needed greater exploration.

"Once the wound has been healed, then the healer will be operating from a position of strength and be stronger."

Wounded? Yes, I knew I had been wounded, too many times. I counted and recounted the litany of losses, betrayals, and injustices that had been the hallmarks of my life. But I had dealt with my deepest personal wounds and no longer chose to let them define me. God knows, I wasn't the only one who had been beaten up by life. I met people every day carrying pain from past hurts.

Was the placement of Chiron in my first house related to issues I had already healed? I so wanted this to be the truth, but it didn't feel like it. There was a reason I had turned away from the healer's path.

Deep within I wanted to be off the hook, but from what?

I wondered, was there something in my life that needed to be opened up and looked at? Did I still have a festering wound that needed healing? Without much need for prodding or reflection, in that moment I knew what it was. I just knew.

Oh dear God, it happened so many years ago. Why did it still feel so unresolved? Perhaps it was because I had been juggling so much at the time. Perhaps it was because I had felt so powerless. Perhaps it was the damn golden handcuffs that kept those of us who knew better from being courageous enough to do the right thing. No, I looked the other way and turned my back. I was still haunted by my inability to right the wrong and heal the injured. Thus I took that injury with me.

Could I, at long last, bring energy and light to this darkness? Could I possibly return to the role of healer, where my gifts might be put to good use?

Whoa. What was that?

It came to me like a download from somewhere deep inside of me.

Was *this* the reason I was sitting here tonight? Was it time I looked at *this* ... *this*, which had been swept under the carpet? *This*, which had never really been discussed? Was *this* one of the reasons why I had left my chosen work as a nurse? Was I still wounded and needed to heal?

Was there something to this astrology stuff?

I had an indwelling knowing. I couldn't just let this be. It was like the healing scab that itched and called out for attention. There was a part of me that admonished myself– *let it be*, and another part that knew, really knew, at a deep soul level that something still festered beneath the surface and if it was not cleaned out it would never heal.

The class ended and I knew I had missed some important information while I'd been wandering around in my past. No doubt I would need to do some self-study to catch up.

And yet, this wandering had unearthed questions that needed to be looked at, with all the clarity that hindsight could provide.

What really happened so many years ago? Unlike religious zealots who seemed to have all the answers about right and wrong, truth and lies, guilt and innocence, for me, the answers to this personal quandary still eluded me. Or perhaps more aptly put they still haunted me.

The years had turned into decades. The situation happened so long ago now that the edges of the memory had softened and some of the specifics had gratefully been lost. There were times when I still woke up feeling something I can only describe as a soul sickness. Perhaps this was an indication there was some soul work that needed to be done around the incident.

Mine had been a bit role. If I hadn't played it, someone else would have. That was what I told myself. I wanted to believe it. But still, I carried feelings of guilt. The tragic outcome could never have been predicated. There wasn't any overt exercise of malfeasance. No, I was just doing my job. We all were. Perhaps, just not very well. So much had been left unspoken for so many years.

The notion that I was not alone whispered in the stillness. Were there others who remained haunted by the tragedy? I wondered what stories they'd told themselves to fill in the gaps between what was known and what was conjecture. How had they spun the tale so they could at last put it to rest?

CHAPTER 1

August 1995

I wasn't actively seeking employment when a friend of my husband's had called to say the school where she taught was looking for a health teacher and a nurse while the woman who held that position was out having surgery. Was this serendipity? Fortunate happenstance? A sign from beyond? Those in my inner circle knew– although I had been dragging my feet, the truth was I needed to find a job, a good job that paid a livable wage.

My husband, Elliot, was battling an aggressive form of bone marrow cancer that had a very poor prognosis. Less than a year ago he had relapsed and was back on chemo again. He had already exceeded all predictions for his life expectancy. It seemed a prudent and wise thing for me to get back in the job market.

The issue was that we had two young children, an 8-year-old son and a 6-year-old daughter. Ian was pretty independent, Shea had just started school, and I had been a stay-at-home mother for the last ten years.

When the job at the Academy of Halcyon Heights was offered to me, I seized it. If the scenario regarding Elliot's health played out as everyone in the medical community expected, my future would involve widowhood and single parenting. I did not want to add *unemployed* to this dreary forecast.

So I took the job fully expecting to find something else at another point in time. Something better suited to my skills and dreams.

What were my skills? I had been a trauma center nurse. My clinical skills and expertise had been refined with years of practice caring for the critically ill.

What were my dreams? I didn't dare dream. My future frightened me. I tried not to look too far down that road.

In some ways, the job suited me far better than I could've imagined. It was a Godsend in so many ways, yet in other ways, maybe less so.

I had grown up in this wealthy community and had attended the public schools. I had friends in high places in the medical, legal, and business communities. I was not a child. I took this job at the ripe old age of 39. I was connected socially and thought I had been around the block enough to know what was going on. However, what I encountered at Halcyon Heights and in the prep school world took me by surprise.

Mens Sana in Corpore Sano or translated from Latin– a sound mind in a sound body. This was the school's motto. It was emblazoned on the flags and banners that graced the entrance and was even inlaid on the floor in one of the three school gymnasiums. The school prided itself in its athletics and academics. This combination of world-class academics and athletics was meant to justify the $25,000 annual tuition. The marketing slogan that the school traipsed about the media was "The right school will change your child's future." The school even went so far as to guarantee that every student who graduated from this fine establishment would be admitted to a four-year college. This was the return on the investment. A place among the privileged was what the school was selling, and that was what the parents were buying.

The headmaster referred to our students as our customers. These parents were indeed buying their children's futures.

I entered both naïve and grateful for the opportunity to teach at this prestigious institution. I was so thankful to have found a good job, within an hour drive from home, with working hours that allowed me to be home in the evenings and on weekends with my husband and my children. I *needed* this position in every sense of the word.

But even early on there was something unsettling. Perhaps it was the arrogance that I detected in the interview process when I mentioned I had gone to the public high school just down the road, and was quickly informed that The Academy of Halcyon Heights was nothing like Chesterfield High.

Lesson number one—remember to never mention my alma mater. There was an obvious disdain for that perceived as inferior or common among the elite. I was now rubbing shoulders with the well born on a daily basis, even if in truth I was only a functionary performing a job that needed to be done.

Even when given an enormous financial incentive to bring my children to The Academy, I opted not to. Call it honoring my intuition. There was something being offered there that I was not interested in partaking in. Thanks, but no thanks.

I remember the early years taking attendance in my classes, struggling with the pronunciation of my students' first and last names. The student body resembled the United Nations. This was really a beautiful thing and over the years I taught there I would learn so much from the diverse student body. I would learn to see our common ground as members of the human family. I had students of every race, religion, ethnicity, sexual orientation, financial, and family circumstance, each bringing something uniquely theirs to the school. I would come to see that this was the school's real strength.

However in a multicultural community with over 600 teenagers gathering daily and testing the limits of their teachers and parents, there were also conflicts that weren't always so easily resolved.

I took my job as teacher very seriously. I had children of my own and I knew how wonderful young people could be. I wanted to play a role in helping my students see the beauty and wonder of creation, and that included the beauty and possibility in their own lives. Succinctly put, I believed it was my job to help them grow and blossom into all that they had been created to be. Our Creator filled the world with vast diversity, each beautiful in its own way, each fulfilling a different and extraordinary function in this life. I saw my students this way too.

Besides, teaching high school was often like being a daily participant on Comedy Central.

There was this beautiful young girl who had been asked to the prom by dozens of the young and eligible prom gods. She was a catch, and the boys all knew it. Yet, she turned the boys down left and right. Word got out that she was going to the prom with someone who didn't attend The Academy.

She arrived in a Mercedes convertible with the top down accompanied by a male blow up doll dressed in a black tux. He was anatomically correct and even his male anatomy had been fully inflated for this auspicious occasion. Her companion even had elastic straps on his shoes that she attached to her own while dancing. Some of the administrators were aghast that she had made a mockery of such a glamorous affair, but I had seen the photos and they were hilarious.

Some days the hijinx and hilarity filled my life with joy and laughter, but not every day. No, certainly not every day. What was funny to some was not funny for all.

Walter was a student of mine who had a peculiar type of learning difference.

Some people would use the label *learning disability* but I preferred *learning difference,* as it was often really only a matter of learning to work around these differences to find a unique way to solve a problem.

Walter was smart in so many ways, but he didn't always appear to be in the classroom. Walter had a word-finding difficulty. He would substitute one word for another and be oblivious that he had done so. This often set him up to be the butt of the joke, and all too frequently his classmates had a few laughs at his expense.

I taught a class on sexually transmitted infections and Walter asked a question about nasal sex. Initially, I went slowly, trying not to embarrass him and told him there was no such thing as nasal sex, but he was insistent. He thought this was something new that his generation had come up with. "Mrs. Duncan, you may not know about this, but kids in my grade are having nasal sex, lots of kids."

When it dawned on me he was referring to oral sex, I tried to substitute one word for the other, but by then the ninth grade boys were going crazy with the very notion of someone putting their penis into someone else's nostril. Some of the girls smirked, covering their mouths and turning away in laugher, but the damage had been done. Walter had been cast as the fool.

I got the class under control and continued with the lesson, but after class Walter waited for me. He wanted me to know that he had just used the wrong word. He didn't want me to think he was a fool. It mattered to him that I didn't see him in such a light. I assured him that I did not. My heart went out to him. It's never easy to be the butt of the joke and the object of ridicule. We've all been there; or at least I knew that I had. There were lessons to be learned. Learning to laugh at yourself is an important lesson, but Walter was not there yet. He just felt the pain.

It didn't help that the buzz around the school was in full force. Students from other classes arrived having heard the story and wanted to know if what they had heard was actually true. I knew if this was happening in my class, it was happening elsewhere too.

Over the years Walter learned to trust and rely on me. Occasionally, he would stop by to chat. When Walter was a senior he told me about working as a volunteer over the summer. His job had been delivering candy, flowers, and cards to patients at a local hospital. He informed me he'd worked as a *candy swiper* rather than a *candy striper*. His word-finding difficulty continued, and I was certain when he misspoke, his classmates continued to have a good laugh at his expense.

But there were some days the sun refused to shine. Those days were overwrought with drama and tragedy.

One night I received a call at home that Simon, another student, had been in a horrible accident.

Simon was a senior. He'd been honored to receive an offer of early admission to MIT, but had stayed out late working on some final calculations for a research paper he was submitting for the Westinghouse Science Talent Search. He was known to be a contender for first prize, a $100,000 scholarship.

Heading home from an all-night coffee shop, he'd fallen asleep and swerved into another lane. No one else was hurt, but Simon had sustained a head injury and was in a coma in the Intensive Care Unit.

You could almost hear a pin drop in the hallways during the next few days while we held our collective breath awaiting word about one of our own, one of our best and brightest. It was not the loss of his yet untapped intellectual prowess we feared losing, but Simon, dear

Simon had an inherent goodness in his sweet, gentle soul.

When the word came down that Simon was awake and hadn't sustained any permanent brain damage, tears of joy filled the hallways while students and teachers hugged one another with no regard for position or policy.

There was a wonderful truth in that moment– we were a community, a diverse multicultural community, where people knew one another and cared about each other. Yet we were different from other communities because most of our members were teenagers.

Teenagers are caught in a place between childhood and adulthood. Some days that could be a very difficult place to be– you're too old for this and too young for that. There was a time when the worst insult that could be thrown at another was that he or she was "*so immature*" and yet that was exactly what they were– not yet mature. To expect otherwise set these kids up for failure.

The teenage years are a time to be trying out new things, to see what fits and what needs to be discarded. The insular life where family once shaped most of one's opinions and attitudes about everything from music and fashion to what was happening in the contemporary world was now up for debate. To watch this unfold could be painful as students were often at odds with their parents and were frequently in transition as they moved from one group of friends to another. It was a time where every move and comment was scrutinized by a jury of their peers or by their *wanna-be* peers. Students jockeyed for position in the social hierarchy of high school as if their ranking would somehow predict the ultimate success or failure of their life.

It wasn't uncommon for me to return to the clinic to find a student who had stopped by for a cough drop or a Kleenex, only to watch them break down into tears because they'd had a fight with their mother on the way to school. All too frequently, I would find a student sobbing because one student had sharpened their tongue at another's expense only to be told, "*It's just a joke.*"

The way I saw it was that children were like flowers. Given enough love, nourishment, and support they would all bloom in time. Some flowers bloom in the spring, and some bloom in the fall. Some would be roses and some would be tulips. The rose is not better than the tulip; they are just different manifestations of the love of the Creator. You cannot make a rose into a tulip or the other way around, each needs to be loved and honored for their uniqueness.

This philosophical perspective was often at odds with the goals and objectives of some of the parents, and some of the administrators. *The Academy* placed great value on winning and winners. There were unending competitions in all facets of school life: State championship sports teams, National Merit Scholars, Gold and Silver Keys for artistic endeavors, Quill and Scroll awards for writers, and ultimately the graduation parade of scholarship opportunities. Honors and college admittances were flaunted like the crown jewels for all to see and pay homage to.

Sadly, those who brought different gifts to the table were often overlooked. Those with a predetermined destiny to be a late bloomer were often seen as not quite measuring up. For these children high school could be very difficult, particularly when they were put in the hot house of a college prep school and forced to bloom and blossom before they were intellectually, emotionally, physically, or spiritually ready.

Some children were just not ready. The emphasis was on the word children. When children were forced to grow up too soon the results could be devastating.

Yet the parents were paying over $25,000 a year to send their children to this fine academic institution. There was an expectation and an implied promise. For the magnitude of this financial investment, many believed the return would be substantial and their next generation would be secured. Their children would take their rightful place in the hierarchy of economic and social leaders. Indeed, this school would secure their children's future.

The Academy was a day school, but in the dark recesses of the hallowed halls everyone knew it was a night school too. When a child was admitted– or committed– to the school, the faculty assumed responsibility for helping to raise these children. We filled their every waking hour with obligations: sports, clubs, volunteer work, academic contests, fine and performing arts. The belief was truly that idle hands and idle minds would become the devil's workshop. School life was filled with mandatory obligations and students were only released to their parents for school holidays and summer vacation. But we could fill that time too if their parents had a prior obligation, or were just too busy to be bothered.

But sometimes these little hot house flowers were just too tired and worn out, and just needed a little space and time in their young lives to just be. After all they were still growing children, little human *be-ings*. They were not human *do-ings*. But time and again this was overlooked. Heaven forbid if one of these children needed a little more time to grasp some of the teachings and was falling behind in this marathon of achievement.

We had options. We could and would help them to succeed.

Parents could seek and find a pharmaceutical amphetamine to improve their child's concentration and help them stay up to all hours of the night completing their homework. Then, when unable to sleep due to pharmaceutical stimulants the child could be put on a light sleeping pill that had the potential to evoke nightmares, and when they awoke in the morning we could start again with amphetamines—speed or a stimulant, as they are all the same things. And when the child's heart began to race and they began to hyperventilate we could always provide an anti-anxiety medication and perhaps a little something for depression. The number of students walking around on some combination of this pharmaceutical cocktail was mind blowing.

As a nurse, this concerned me. Deeply.

In the middle school, the nurse was responsible for distributing prescription medications, but by the time students arrived in the upper school they were deemed *old enough* to take their own medications. It was a tough call as age is really just a number and looked so different on different kids. The school's written policy was that students on prescription medication were required to bring any and all medications by the clinic so the nurse would know what the students' health issues were and who was taking medication.

But then there was the issue of stigma. There were parents who didn't want the school to know that *Junior* was on medication, because then they might appear flawed or somehow less than perfect. Their budding little protégé who was spawn from two high achieving perfect parents could not be seen in their humanity as it may reflect poorly on them. So *Junior* had his pockets filled with medication before leaving home and was told with a kiss good bye, "admit to nothing."

There was the morning Andrea found her way to the clinic on the arm of another student. Andrea was a second semester sophomore. She was a pretty blonde who was normally well groomed and pulled together, but not that day. That morning she looked like she'd been dragged behind the bus or at least just dragged out of bed after sleeping in her school uniform.

"What's the matter, Andrea? You look a little rough this morning," I said as she sat down in front of the computer station.

Leaning on the arm of the sofa she cradled her head in her hands. "I was up all night working on my history paper," she said.

No more explanation was offered or needed. The research paper in sophomore World History was legendary. Kids had been knocking themselves out for weeks trying to complete this paper. "I finished about three this morning, but I was so wired on Adderal that I couldn't sleep." Her eyes were glazed over and she looked like she could hardly focus. "Can I just get some sleep?"

Before I consented I said, "I didn't know you were on Adderal. Do you have ADD?"

Perhaps it was her lack of sleep or perhaps she trusted me, but most likely it was just her naïveté. "No, but Melissa does."

Melissa was her known compatriot.

"She has a prescription and she gave me a few so I could finish the paper. When I finished I was so wired. I couldn't sleep so I took some of my mom's Ambien, and now I can't stay awake."

She was clearly exhausted and drugged. I helped her over to the bed to lie down, "How often do you take these medications?" I asked, as I pulled a blanket up and around her shoulders.

"Only when I can't get all my work done. Maybe a couple of times a week," she said.

So this was a common occurrence for her. And apparently she felt she had done nothing wrong and thus had nothing to hide.

"I'm a little too warm," she said.

I helped Andrea sit up as she took off her cardigan letter sweater, exposing her stained blouse. "Oh, I forgot I spilled my coffee this morning. My windshield was all iced over, but I was late so I poured my coffee on the windshield, and the wipers let loose and splashed it all over me." She laughed. "Seemed like a good idea at the time but now I'm all stained and sticky thanks to the cream and the sugar."

"Oh my dear," I sighed. "You *drove* to school today?" I was far more concerned that she'd been behind the wheel like this than I was about the condition of her blouse, as she could not keep her eyes open.

The main issue now was that she had competing drugs in her system. Adderal is a stimulant. It was available by prescription and a controlled substance used for the treatment of attention deficit disorder. Basically, it's prescription speed. Ambien, on the other hand, is a hypnotic sedative or a sleeping pill. It's also only available by prescription, and should never be taken unless someone can sleep for seven or eight hours.

According to Andrea she'd taken the Ambien about five hours before, and she'd probably only slept for three hours after she took it or she couldn't have been to school on time.

I checked her pulse, respirations, and blood pressure. Thank goodness they were normal.

By then she had settled back under the covers and was ready to sleep. "Will you wake me before lunch?"

"Mrs. Arlington gave you a pass for this class but you can't stay here all morning and sleep. I'll have to call your mom or dad to come and pick you up."

This was the school policy, if students were not well enough to be in class they needed to go home. And Andrea was in no condition to be in class, and it was highly unlikely she would be any better in 45 minutes. More likely, she would be sound asleep. There were consequences to staying up all night and taking other people's medications. I wanted Andrea and her mother to know this.

"I'll be fine. Melissa has some more Adderall. She'll be bringing me some later. Please don't call my mom, I'll be okay," she pleaded. She struggled to keep her eyes open as she negotiated for leniency, but even as we spoke her eyes were drooping and in less than a minute she was out.

I would have given Andrea my lecture on substance use, misuse, and abuse, but she was in no condition to receive it.

Despite her protest, I called her mother. When I informed her mother that her daughter was taking Melissa's prescription medication for ADD, she politely responded, "Thank you for your concern. I guess I'll just have to make an appointment with her pediatrician and get Andrea a prescription of her own. My husband and I have noticed an improvement in Andrea's grades and we are most pleased about this."

And then she became indignant that I'd implied there was something wrong with providing her sixteen-year-old daughter her prescription sleeping pills and then allowing her to drive to school four hours later while she was still under the influence of the drug.

Things went from bad to worse when I insisted, "Your daughter needs to be taken home. She is in no condition to be in school."

"I can't come and get her right now. I have commitments this afternoon that I simply must honor." Then she sighed deeply and added, "How on earth would I get her car home? She still has play practice this afternoon and she'll need her car in the morning to get back to school."

After a moment when I didn't respond, she added, "Let her stay there and sleep. There's no possible way I can pick her up."

With that the phone went dead.

I blinked in disbelief. She had hung up.

Asked and answered. I looked over at Andrea and she was sound asleep.

I wished this was an isolated occurrence, but the truth was this kind of thing happened more often than I could count.

I knew that according to the most recent statistics from the Center for Disease Control that 9.5 % of all children and 13.5 % of all boys between the ages of 13 and 17 years old in the United States were medicated for attention deficit disorder. As outrageous and pervasive as this seemed, amongst the wealthy and privileged class the access to medical care was unimpeded and the pressure to perform and excel was unrivaled. My best guess was that among 14 to 18-year-old students, the use of legally prescribed psychotropic pharmaceuticals was closer to 25 percent, to say nothing of what was being shared among students without any medical reason or supervision. As someone well acquainted with the ins and outs of western medicine I knew this was just the tip of the iceberg.

And we were left to wonder why our children suffered from depression. They were not allowed the luxury of growing up and learning in a way that was in alignment with their inner nature and personal developmental timetable.

No, we, the responsible adults, felt compelled to hurry life along, for we feared there were only so many pieces of the pie. If we didn't get ours now, then we might get the inferior piece or perhaps none at all. So hurry, hurry, hurry, before it was all just too late.

Another option to help struggling students was to provide intensive tutoring during their study halls and directly after school before their mandatory hour and a half of athletic practice would begin. Fortunately or unfortunately, depending who you asked, some of our students were prodded, dragged or carried through their classes all the way to graduation.

No doubt for some of the students, particularly those whose gifts and talents resided in areas outside of academics, The Academy of Halcyon Heights was absolute torture, every waking minute.

CHAPTER 2

August 1999

The alarm rang and I reached over and hit the snooze button. Ugh. The room was still dark. The clock said 5:30. 5:30 AM. It couldn't be. But it was. I pulled the covers up around my shoulders and rearranged the pillows. Sleeping alone in a king size bed. Elliot's side of the bed was undisturbed. He hadn't slept there in over ten months now. My first thought every day carried both the grief and anxiety: *I'm a widow and a single mother.*

Today was the first day of school and my summer vacation was over. The teachers were just as upset about this as the students were, maybe more so. It was hard to believe this was the start of my third year at The Academy. I was grateful to have meaningful work that allowed me time to spend with my children.

It had been a good summer. Shea turned 10 a few weeks ago and Ian would be 13 later in the fall. Where had the time gone? I must have spent the entire last year wrapped in a blanket of haze. Elliot died last October and the remainder of this year was still a blur.

I'd never planned to be a single mother, and now I needed to come to terms with it. It had been over ten months since Elliott's death. The people closest to me expected me to get on with my life. I knew I had better find a way to do just that. Teaching was a good diversion.

Thank God for my job, I thought. What would I do without it? I could only imagine.

Elliott had made certain we would be taken care of financially. The kids were doing pretty well, all things considered. I didn't want to compound their losses by changing their school. Yet, I knew if we continued on the trajectory we were on, I would need to continue to work if we were going to be able to keep up.

Keep up with whom?

I guess we were just *keeping up with the Joneses*, whoever they were.

The snooze alarm rudely buzzed through. I snatched the clock up off the bedside table and pushed the off button. *How could that have been nine minutes?*

I climbed out of bed, pulled the sheet straight, rearranged the duvet, and fluffed the pillows. Task one completed, the bed was made. Some days, just getting everybody up, fed, dressed, and off to school was the most difficult part of my day.

But not today, the kids wouldn't be back in school until next week.

By the time I had showered, dressed, and the kids had walked next door to spend the day with my lovely and generous neighbor, it was 6:40 AM. I needed to make haste. My morning drive in from the country took an hour on a good day, but if there was an accident or a train it, could take even longer. There were reasons I chose to drive this far and live in this little rural town. We lived on a small lake with an ordinance that prohibited boats with motors. It was peaceful, and in many ways it felt like the town that time forgot. People here truly knew each other and cared for one another. I felt at home here and so did my kids.

I also liked my job. Or rather, I liked my students. At least most days, I liked most of them. There was something about being in the company of young people that helped me laugh, get out of my own head, and generally feel younger. There was something about the work and the job that made me feel like what I was doing mattered. Maybe not the kind of work that matters in the big scheme of things, but the kind of work that matters in the moment, in the interaction between two human beings on the planet.

Besides, it worked with my family. My family was what mattered most to me, and my job allowed me to be home when my children were home: after school, in the evenings, on the weekends, and during the summer. Yep, I liked my job and I was glad to have it. Although I really didn't like the commute, this arrangement was a necessary piece of the puzzle called *my life*.

I pulled the car out of the driveway. Two weeks before he died Elliot bought me a new car, a silver GMC Blazer. It was the first new car I'd ever owned. I couldn't get into it without thinking about how much he had considered the welfare and well being of his family. He wanted to be certain we were all well taken care of. I glanced over my shoulder as I backed down the driveway. I knew Elliot wouldn't be happy to see how the kids had trashed the car with their soccer cleats, shin pads, and dirty socks still thrown in the back. I took note. I needed to be better about making them pick up after themselves. This was part of my job as a mother, but there were so many things that were my responsibility now that I had to be both mother *and* father to Shea and Ian.

Before I'd even realized it, I was off the highway and driving through the suburbs. I had been lost in my own head for nearly an hour. I wondered, *was this common when people were grieving?* I could lose hours, wandering around in my own daydreams.

In a few more minutes, I turned up the long driveway towards the Winsome Winds Country Club with its lush, meticulously trimmed lawns of the golf course that had been just barely visible from the road. The clubhouse and the stables in the distance resembled a gracious plantation of the Old South. African-American and Hispanic workers in uniforms attended to the horses, drove the lawn equipment and worked in the manicured gardens. The flowerbeds filled with annuals were in full bloom in their end-of-season glory, for they had been tended, watered, and fertilized after a long warm summer. Members walked the grounds towards the clubhouse in their tennis whites or pastel golf ensembles.

The membership was conspicuously white.

Late summer beckoned, the start of school was just around the corner, but it still felt like summer and it would for about another month. I wondered whose idea it had been to let the academic calendar take precedence over the wisdom of the natural world? Here in Virginia it was still summer, and yet students and teachers everywhere were returning to school. Before too long the summer vacation would be just a distant memory.

Pulling up to the gatehouse, I informed the uniformed attendant, "I'm Elise Duncan. I'm supposed to pick up something here from Mr. George Walker." The headmaster had finally signed off on the addendum to my contract the day before and left it for me to pick up at his country club.

"Good morning, Mrs. Duncan," the elderly black gentleman in the gatehouse smiled. "Mr. Walker left this for you. He said you can leave it with his secretary and he will receive it when he gets in." He continued smiling as he handed me a document envelope engraved with the school crest and addressed to me.

"Thank you very much," I responded, then pulled through the circular driveway and exited out onto the street.

I wondered why I couldn't just sign this at school later that afternoon. I suppose he wanted to be certain he had dotted all the I's and crossed all the T's before the opening of school. I understood this. The contract protected him as much as it protected me. I couldn't help but note that the faculty was reporting back to work, while the head was still out on the links. It was a beautiful day. Lucky him. He must have started early.

I knew he would be back to school before too long, because today was the annual Welcome Back Breakfast.

I drove past the Starbucks, a new Thai restaurant, the Whole Foods grocery emporium and then the shopping district with a couple dozen designer boutiques: Ralph Lauren, Burberry, Chanel and Tiffany's to name a few. It was one of *those* neighborhoods.

Turning left into the school's long driveway, I waved to Mr. Jones, the security guard in the guardhouse. He knew me and recognized my car. He smiled and waved back. I wondered if his diabetes was under control. He had been diagnosed last year and didn't want anyone except his wife and me to know about it.

I'd come to realize I was the keeper of a lot of people's secrets.

People have a right to their privacy; some of this was not any of our employer's business.

But I knew my employer, the headmaster, Mr. George Walker wouldn't agree with me. It didn't matter that the HIPPA privacy laws had been enacted about 3 years before. If you worked at The Academy, you could forget about a right to privacy. If you wanted to keep something private or confidential you'd best not discuss it here.

There were already some cars in the student lot. Most of the upper classmen and women didn't need to report until next Tuesday. School officially started the Tuesday after Labor Day. But most students had been coming and going from the campus since the August 15th when the fall sports teams officially started to practice. The parking lot was peppered with late model vehicles both domestic and foreign since most of the upperclassmen drove themselves to school.

Many students at Halcyon Heights got a new car when they turned 16 and passed their driver's test. Just last spring Stephanie's father had a brand new white Hummer H-1 delivered to the school with sixteen multi-colored helium balloons tied to the antennae. This was a massive 4-wheel-drive utility vehicle. Daddy wanted to be certain his little darling would be *safe*, but I wasn't certain the rest of the driving public in Virginia was the least bit secure with Stephanie behind the wheel of the street-legal equivalent of a military Humvee. The purchase price of this vehicle was somewhere in the neighborhood of $80,000.

The trend at The Academy was that when students reached their sixteenth birthdays, their parents arranged to deliver their sons' and daughters' amazing new cars to school– Mercedes, BMWs and the like. And then only the best of the best friends were invited for the first ride to the club for the birthday dinner. "When I get my car I'm going to invite *so and so* and *so and so . . .*" the conversations would unfold. Some girls were always invited, and some never were. Feelings were hurt, but never acknowledged.

Affluenza was a disease in a class by itself.

I angled around the parking lot looking for a space. The teachers' lot was nearly full this morning.

The Academy required our students to wear uniforms. It was supposed to be the great equalizer so students weren't compelled to compete about insignificant things like what you wore. Instead, the stakes were elevated to what kind of a car you drove, what kind of shoes you wore, and what kind of watch, cell phone, and handbag you had. The competition based on material possessions had not gone away, it was just shifted to higher ticket items. For the most part, the faculty was oblivious. I didn't know the difference between a Louis Vuitton handbag and the $50 knock off, and I wasn't all that interested in learning. But trust me, my students knew. They really cared about these things and were continually assessing where they stood and whether they were rising or falling in the pecking order.

I had noticed some of the girls never carried a purse. Many of these were young women of color who were attending on scholarship. Some had been recruited to play on the women's basketball team. Many carried only their backpacks. There was a reason for this: if your handbag didn't quite measure up, it was better not to carry one at all. I'd also noted that these same girls didn't wear coats into the school, even on the coldest days of winter.

The dress code helped, but it was not the great equalizer. Not by a long shot.

After a nice summer break from this place, I was already feeling consumed by these insidious thoughts–and I wasn't even out of my car. Some of my colleagues were already here. *The student lot vs. the faculty lot*, now here was a contrast worth noting. Some of my colleagues drove cars that were at least 10 years old. But none of the students did. In its own way, this spoke to me about the career choices that were acceptable for these students. How could you consider a career as a teacher or a coach or any number of other careers, when you might work for decades and still not be able to afford a car that was as nice as the one you'd been given for your sixteenth birthday? This kind of affluence brought different concerns than the ones children growing up in poverty faced. But I knew they should not be dismissed as irrelevant, as they created a different kind of prison.

As I climbed out of the car I reminded myself: yes there were parts of my job that I loved, but not all of it. Maybe it was just like that in the world of work. Maybe there always were compromises that had to be made when you had to make a living. I wanted to be here, and in many ways I needed to be here, but I didn't always *like* being here. Sometimes I felt like a cog in the wheel that perpetuated an inequality that I disdained.

I tried to snap out of it. After all, these children of the wealthy had no more of a choice about the families they'd been born into than did the children of the poor. If I could and did feel compassion for one group, then I must also feel compassion for the other. So many of these children of privilege were the benefactors, as well as the victims, of their parents' affluence. Maybe in some important way, I was needed here, to help these kids learn some balance and provide perspective.

It was now 8:30, and the faculty had gathered in the dining room. They were catching up with one another and sharing stories about their summers. The school year always started with the Welcome Back Breakfast followed by an afternoon of meeting with the freshman and new students. It felt a little like a pep rally for the faculty and staff. *Ra Ra Sis Boom Ba!* Same old, same old, there was nothing new here. Three years in and I knew the drill.

Three years, I thought: *this was supposed to be a temporary stop on my career path, and yet I'm still here.*

Grabbing a cup of coffee, I headed over to the breakfast buffet. Casey from the science department came over and wrapped me in a warm embrace. She was expecting and just starting to show.

I hugged her back and asked, "How are you feeling?"

"Okay. But we need to talk."

There was something in her tone that told me this was personal. Casey was edging-in on forty, and this was her first pregnancy. She had been around the block and back with the infertility specialists. I knew how much she wanted this child. All last winter I'd been giving her the medications prescribed by her infertility doctors. She'd asked me if I would help her out because they needed to be given by injection and her husband couldn't, or perhaps he just wouldn't.

Casey headed back to her table, and a group of friends waved me over to an empty seat at their table. The room was abuzz with friendly chatter. Maybe being back was going to be okay after all. My colleagues treated me with a gentle deference, as they knew this had been my first summer without Elliott. Leaving much left unasked, and thus unanswered, the conversation shifted to my vacation to Yellowstone and the Grand Tetons with the kids.

Someone asked, "How *are* you?" Did she really think I wanted to bare my soul right then and there? Not a chance. There would be a time and place to provide a real answer and this wasn't it.

"We'll catch up later," I offered. It was partly a stall tactic. Did I really want to go into how sometimes I felt an overwhelming sense of anxiety about raising and supporting my children all on my own?

"It's so hard on the students to get back to school after being off all summer," one of the history teachers said.

"The students?" I laughed. "What about the teachers? I'm coming back kicking and screaming."

I'd gone for the laugh, but the reality was that I'd hoped to be in a better place emotionally than I currently was. I knew I was still grieving the loss of Elliot, but I wondered if there was something else too?

One of my colleagues leaned over and whispered, "I wouldn't say that too loudly. You know how things are taken out of context and how gossip is traded when it offers an advantage and serves the agenda." She nodded towards the front of the room.

George, the headmaster had rushed in and gone directly up to the podium. The room went respectively quiet. "Sorry for starting a few minutes late," he offered, but then ruined the apology by recounting a couple of stories about his morning golf game over at Winsome Winds. There was not another person in the room who could afford a membership. I had to keep telling myself: *You're here– for now. You're here– for the kids. Chill out. Just do your job.*

Before long I had completely tuned him out and was off wandering about in my own head.

Fundamentally, it was true. I had a problem with this place. Some of my friends thought I was totally mad not to send my children to school here. It was rated *The Best Private School in Virginia.* I had considered the faculty tuition program but decided against it. Given the nature of my position, I found myself involved in a few fairly gnarly situations every year. If my children were here and their friends had difficulty I would likely be drawn in, and it might not play well for my kids. I had also seen how some of the faculty kids had a rough time with the economic and social disparity. I didn't need to bring this influence into my home. Besides, I couldn't imagine going to high school and having my mother present every day, let alone have her be my teacher, worse yet, the sex ed teacher. Even though Ian and Shea were only 12 and 9, I could understand their relief that they were going to school elsewhere.

And there was something more . . .

I couldn't quite put my finger on what I was protecting my children from, but I trusted my intuition on this one.

There were reasons I felt unsettled. Most members of the faculty in the upper school were not certified teachers, including myself. Most of the faculty was indeed outstanding, with little or no interference from the administration, the teachers excelled in the classroom and the students were the beneficiaries.

But since the school took absolutely no state or federal funding, there was no obligation to follow any of the state or federal mandates. So they didn't. Instead The Academy was governed by its own policies. The faculty could only teach classes where they had academic expertise, and that meant they must have earned either a Master's or Doctoral Degree. I had a Master's Degree in Public Health from Georgetown, therefore I was deemed qualified to teach health.

Underneath this policy was a hidden truth: this was a hiring strategy that bred compliance. After years of teaching without a teaching certificate, and after honing the skills of a teacher as opposed to the other skills that might be valued in one's field, you had seriously compromised your viability in the job market. So if you got frustrated with a policy or the governance you were left with little recourse, except to do your job and keep your mouth shut or risk being terminated.

The truth was I'd gone into this with my eyes open. It was just that I hadn't intended to stay this long, as it had never been a lifelong dream of mine to teach high school. It was sort of a stopgap job to help me through the years when Elliott had been ill, and it bought me some time to get back on my feet after he died. But here I was, and it was likely I would stay for a while longer, in spite of the fact this really wasn't the best use of my skill set. This just wasn't my dream. It never had been, but I justified it by telling myself it worked for my kids. For now. So there I was, my contract had just been signed for another year.

George was reviewing the strategic plan and the ongoing results of the capital campaign. I'd heard this all before. It may have been more interesting if I thought any of that money might trickle down my way, but I had long ago given up that illusion.

I focused my mind on some of the benefits of working at The Academy.

Year after year The Academy was at capacity, with a waiting list of qualified students ready to fill a seat if one should become available. This was a good indication that our students and their families were satisfied with the academic and athletic programs that were being bought and sold here. Perhaps this was the master plan.

I looked around the room. My colleagues' eyes had glazed over as George continued. He was completely oblivious that he had lost his audience. Did he even *notice?* If he had, did he even *care?* We all knew he liked to hear himself talk.

I glanced from table to table. We were an awesome collection of diverse individuals. I truly thought well of most of my compatriots. There were a few teachers who pushed the curriculum without regard for the needs of the individual student or understanding of their family circumstances. But there were many teachers who worked diligently with students to help them understand complicated concepts that they themselves found easy, but some students found difficult to grasp.

And there were teachers who showed great patience and compassion towards their students. But students, like everyone else sometimes needed to rant and rave about their perceived injustices. It wasn't unusual for students to find their way to my office when they needed to unburden themselves about one thing or another. And although adolescents could spin the slightest incident into a major catastrophe or drama, I knew if I heard the same thing over and over again from a wide variety of people, no matter how wild the tale, I suspected there might be a bit of truth there.

Such as the math teacher who explained the same material the same way over and over again and was continually surprised when the students still didn't understand. When 30 percent of the class failed the geometry test, this said more about the teacher than it did about the students.

The kids from wealthy families hired private tutors while the kids without the wherewithal to do so often failed and had to repeat the class.

I'd heard it all, over and over again.

Then last May there was the incident with Dr. Edwards, a teacher in the English Department. He prided himself on teaching only *the academically talented*. But every now and again, due to a scheduling snafu, some unfortunate soul, who Dr. Edwards felt did not quite measure up, was seated in his classroom.

Unfortunately, Dr. Edwards wasn't the only member of the faculty who was infected with this mindset. It was just a little less obvious in some, but it still resided just beneath the surface.

Rodney was a scholarship student from a working class family in East Richmond. He was diligent, hard working, and had made great academic progress while at The Academy. He would be the first member of his family to go to college, but he was not destined for the Ivy League.

A battle of wills ensued as Edwards repeatedly tried to get Rodney dismissed from his class, but Rodney, who needed this class to graduate, wasn't easily dissuaded and persevered. By the end of the second semester, he was frustrated and angry because every paper he wrote was deemed unworthy by Dr. Edwards and received a D or worse.

Rodney was not to be denied this time. He took it upon himself to have a paper conference with the chairman of the English Department prior to submitting his final paper.

He worked and worked on the paper. He was bound and determined to show his teacher that he had not been misplaced in this English class, that he understood the assignment, that he was capable, and could write a paper that met the requirements for a passing grade.

Leaving nothing to chance, Rodney also submitted the paper to another English teacher, who taught a different section of the same literature class, for an unofficial grade and critique.

There was a great deal riding on this paper, far more than just Rodney's fulfillment of a graduation requirement. This had evolved into a battle to expose Dr. Edward's underlying prejudice and injustice.

Predictably, Rodney's very crucial, final paper was deemed inadequate and he received a failing grade by Dr. Edwards. The very same paper was graded and received an 89 from the other teacher from another section.

So there it was, out on the table.

Word spread like wildfire, and students throughout the school cried racism. Rodney was black and Edwards was white. Before the students had whispered that Edwards was a racist and an elitist, but now they were openly outraged. The faculty and students waited and watched to see how this would play out. The students spoke amongst themselves and so did the faculty, though we spoke more cautiously. We knew who our allies were and where we could speak freely, and likewise when to hold our tongues.

This was a powder keg.

There was speculation on whether Rodney had been advised by someone to have his paper independently evaluated or whether he had decided this course of action all on his own. The administration began to question the faculty, but no one was talking. Either way, it had been a brilliant, tactical move as both teachers used the standard grading rubric that had been sanctioned by the English Department.

Ultimately, the situation was resolved behind closed doors. No one was talking. Concessions had been bought and sold by an agreement of silence.

There had been some kind of buy-off.

Rodney walked at graduation and ended up with his diploma.

Dr. Edwards was a legacy of The Academy. He had been educated through his PhD in the Ivy League. He was old money and well connected. A letter of recommendation from Dr. Edwards was worth its weight in gold.

And so the esteemed Dr. Edwards would be back in his classroom this fall subjecting yet another group of students to his deeply entrenched ideas and barely-concealed prejudices. From his podium and position of authority he would continue to subject impressionable students to his own brand of poison as he pontificated on issues of intellectual elitism, race, class, and gender.

I'm sorry to say that Dr. Edwards would not be going anywhere.

And the students were learning how conflicts were resolved and deals were made in the real world. This was the kind of life-lesson our students were being taught. Nice.

I glanced across the crowded dining room. The English Department was seated together, and it looked like Dr. Edwards was holding court as others sipped their coffee and feigned interest. Perhaps I was interjecting myself into the situation, but I'd had lunch with this pompous pig often enough to know that if he was talking, as he always was, that I would need to be a darn good actress to convince anyone that I gave a rat's ass about anything this old bigot had to say.

At that moment Millie rushed into the room.

Thank goodness someone in his or her infinite wisdom had gone out on a limb and hired Dr. Millie Holmes. She graced this school with a new level of compassion and a breadth of understanding of learning differences that had been missing here. She was a bright light and we were so lucky to have her.

I caught her eye and she smiled with genuine warmth and waved enthusiastically in my direction.

I waved back. Now there was a good woman and a wonderful teacher.

As I smiled at her I recalled how she had worked with the Taylor twins. These boys were both over 6'5", and had played on the championship basketball team the previous year. A rival school had actively pursued them as freshmen, but they had decided to stay at The Academy. Unfortunately, their skills on the basketball court were not matched academically. Both boys had been offered full athletic scholarships to play basketball in college, even though neither of them could pass the NCAA clearinghouse standards, which mandated that college athletes meet a minimum standard for high school grades and SAT scores. If you had higher grades, you could get by with lower scores on your SAT. Likewise, the lower your grades, the higher your SAT scores had to be. By the time it came to someone's attention that both of the Taylor twins were in academic trouble and were ineligible for the scholarships, their low grade point averages were beyond repair. They had already accumulated too many low grades and had too few classes left to significantly move their averages. The only hope that remained was to improve their SAT scores.

Millie worked and worked with those boys tirelessly, giving countless evenings and weekends of her own time. As a direct result of her selflessness, both Taylor boys were at university, with a newfound confidence as students, as well as confidence as athletes.

Millie Holmes was an angel in human form. Just the fact that she was here made my job easier.

"Health will no longer be taught in the junior year. It has been decided that students need this information earlier than they did in the past." That brought me around as I focused momentarily on Will, the Director of the Upper School. Mercifully, he had taken over the podium from George. He went on to explain that the mandatory health class, which I taught, was going to become a class for freshmen.

Heads turned, and a few teachers smiled at me in a congratulatory way. Some knew I'd been lobbying for this. Based on what I had learned about our students, I knew that by the time they were in their junior year they thought they knew more about sex, drugs, and rock 'n' roll than I did.

How did I know, maybe they did.

Besides it also allowed me to interact and get to know the students earlier in their high school experience. Millie and I had spoken about this, and she supported me. I was the only teacher in the school who had every student in class. If someone was in trouble I had a pretty good sense of things. Sometimes, I felt like I had an indwelling radar system or maybe I was just paying attention.

I had a sense of pride in my work, even if teaching hadn't been part of my long-term career plan. I had written the text, created and compiled the curriculum for my class. Apart from being able to provide good reliable information about health, sex and sexuality, drugs and alcohol, and mental health, I also had the chance to spot kids who were having academic trouble.

To help me spot learning difficulties, the text I'd written included a couple of readings I used early every semester. I had each of my students read a couple of paragraphs aloud. It wasn't difficult to determine which students were not reading at grade-level. If they were having difficulty in my class, they were going to be having difficulty in their other classes. The sooner these kids were identified, the sooner we could intervene. This was important in so many ways. When a student struggled academically it impacted their sense of self, and a deteriorating self-concept could begin to show up negatively in so many other aspects of their life.

I also had my students write in their journals. There was a daily writing assignment. I used this as a way to get a handle on other language-based differences, like the kids who couldn't spell. If you can't spell in English, your native tongue, you were going to have a heck of a time with the mandatory four-year foreign language requirement, which required speaking, reading, and writing in another language.

I learned a whole lot more than whether my students could spell or not when they turned in their journals. Rather, soon I found that quite often I had been entrusted with a glimpse into their sacred inner worlds, filled with their daily struggles, joys, and sorrows.

One girl of fifteen wrote about how her prestigious and powerful father, whose daily escapades with other women, had turned her once-loving mother into an alcoholic. The pages of her journal were filled with the horrors and abuse she endured at home. All the previous year I'd found myself drawn into this young woman's family drama. I was her confidant and her safety net. And much to the dismay of the administration, I was also the one to contact Child Protective Services.

There were those I worked with who felt the one who needed to be protected was *me*. Protected from what? Protected from all that had become my responsibility.

Maybe, I needed to be protected from myself. Although working with these young people had its rewards, maybe I needed protection from the strain of my workload. Maybe carrying their secrets and listening to so many soul-wrenching personal agonies was just too much to put on the shoulders of a grieving person.

I was coping as best as I was able. I was aware enough to know that dealing with the cares and concerns of others was a tactic I used to keep myself from dealing with my own inner devastation. I couldn't save my husband, so let me serve my purpose by saving and protecting the innocents.

I guess I'd zoned out for a bit. George had returned to the podium. What was he going on about now?

Ah– the annual service awards.

One by one, my colleagues stepped forward and then to my surprise the headmaster called my name.

As I walked up to receive my gift, George said, "Here she is, the nurse, the health teacher, and the Director of Health Education. But most importantly, in our times of need, she has been mother to us all."

Dear God, was this really how he saw me? I knew he meant well, but the very notion overwhelmed me. How could I possibly keep this up?

When I returned to my place at the table I unwrapped the gift. It was a beautiful crystal clock etched with the school's crest. I should've felt grateful, but instead I thought of the minutes, hours, and days of my life I had already spent here.

The real question was, did I have the stamina to continue? And yet, just that morning I had signed my contract. Here I was again, back in the fire.

Within thirty minutes, the Welcome Back Breakfast was over for another year. I made my way to the dish depository when I heard Millie call out, "Elise!"

Freeing my hands of my china plate and coffee cup, I leaned into her and gave her a hug. "Hi, my friend, how are you?"

She responded with a smile and a twinkle in her eye. I truly liked and cared about so many of my colleagues, but Millie was one of my favorites.

"I'm heading over to the copy center. Are you going to your chambers, m'lady?" Millie asked.

"My torture chamber is more like it. And yes, I'm afraid I am." I chuckled. Then the conversation turned to our families, while we made our way from the dining room along the brick pavers behind the six new tennis courts. Over the summer the twelve older courts had all been resurfaced and outfitted with new nets and windscreens.

"Looks like the tuition checks have already been cashed and spent," Millie added as we took in some of the more visible expenditures that had been made by the Athletic Department. "I hope they have saved a few bucks to replace the space heater in my office before winter," she continued with a good-natured laugh.

We often met in Millie's office, and although it didn't have central heating or air conditioning, it did have privacy. Given the nature of the issues we both were dealing with, privacy often trumped the need for climate control, at least most days. But I didn't have to sit in there hour after hour and day after day like she did.

Looking over the improved athletic facilities, I recalled the words of my professor in grad school,

"How you spend your money and your time is the true indication of what you value." It didn't take a rocket scientist to realize neither Millie nor I were among the school's most favored.

As we rounded the corner to the upper school and headed for the athletic corridor, I paused briefly to take a breath of air and soak in a moment of the glorious sunshine before entering the building. Millie paused with me.

"We had better enjoy this moment, because you and I both know what awaits us," I said.

And with that I opened the door and held it for Millie as we walked into the dimly-lit corridor. It took just a moment for my eyes to adjust as it always did when going from bright sunlight to low light. Students dressed in sports clothing were sitting on the wooden benches that lined both sides of the hallway.

Bart was in the laundry room that was also known as *The Cage*. He was collecting the dirty practice uniforms he would launder before the afternoon practice. I called hello to him and Millie waved.

"Welcome back ladies," he called out.

A band of football players were gathered around The Cage. Male students were placing their sweaty, dirty clothes on the Formica countertop.

"Come on, Bart," one boy called out too loudly given his proximity to the older man. "Put a little more elbow grease on my grass-stained knees. I can't have everyone thinkin' I'm fixin' this fairy's joystick," the first hurly burly Neanderthal said. He laughed loudly and elbowed his mirror image.

It took me a moment to put it together– more homophobia, alive and well in the hallowed halls of Halcyon Heights.

Seeing Millie and I approaching, Evan Hedges, one of the senior football players said, "Hey knock it off Jordan, or you'll be back in the weight room pumping iron."

The boy quickly changed his tune. "Sorry Ms. Duncan and Dr. Holmes, I meant no offense," he said, dropping his chin and turning away in an attempt to cover his grin. The others laughed that he'd been caught being inappropriate in the presence of women faculty and school hadn't even started yet.

Others would've written him up and issued a detention on the spot, but neither Millie nor I were about to do that. Nor did we need to. Evan had threatened to discipline Jordan, and Jordan had apologized. Clearly the other boys on the football team respected Evan or at least his position. They'd elected him their captain, and apparently the captain he could require more training time. I didn't know that was how it worked.

I looked towards Bart and he shrugged his shoulders, as he stood behind the counter of *The Cage*. It was interesting, I thought, that they called this *The Cage*. It had a metal door that went up and down like a garage door. Perhaps it was Bart himself who referred to his work environment as *The Cage*. Hadn't I just referred to mine as a torture chamber?

Once this space had been used as the bookstore, but now the school provided laundry services for these children or more likely for their families. I doubted whether these kids ever did their own laundry. I, for one, was glad we offered this service. I couldn't imagine having the clinic, my classroom, and my office here without it. Without the laundry service this place would smell like a sweaty, old gym sock.

Still there was something that bothered me. I didn't know why it bothered me. Many of their mothers worked and paid for goods and services such as housekeeping. It wasn't a gender thing. Certainly both men and women were capable of doing laundry.

No, I think it was that they called him Bart. That was his name, but he was about 50 years old. He wasn't their peer. They referred to their teachers as Dr. or Mr. or Mrs. but referred to this gentleman who did their laundry strictly as Bart.

It was a class issue again. They never would've been so brazen to openly tell an inappropriate joke in the presence of a member of the faculty. No, this was an issue of respect. What had become of *respect your elders*? Had this been lost and replaced by respect that was conferred based on position, as in *respect your betters*? I was irritated.

Who was training these kids? I don't know if it bothered Bart, but it certainly bothered me.

We walked a little further down the hallway.

"Looks like you have your first student," Millie said under her breath as we approached the clinic.

Sitting on the wooden bench outside of the clinic, which was also my office, was a young girl. I didn't recognize her, which meant she was either a new student or a freshman. I assumed the latter. She was wearing a scarf around her head. It wasn't a hijab. I knew, because I'd had Muslim girls in my classes over the years that chose to wear one and this wasn't a hijab. No, this girl was wearing a scarf tied under her chin, like an elderly woman might wear a rain scarf. She was dressed in her school uniform, but there was something about her posture and the way she held her head that suggested she wanted to disappear and not be seen at all.

She called out, "Are you Mrs. Duncan?"

I nodded.

"Mrs. Duncan, I need to see you. You're finally here. I've been waiting for you. Where have you been?" A flood of words spilled from her with no regard for the fact that I was in conversation with another adult. I could see she lacked awareness and concern for social protocol.

"And so it begins," I heard Millie say as she continued down the hall without me.

"What can I help you with?" I asked. There was wildness in her dark eyes and I took note of this. My initial assessment: this was a child in crisis.

She nodded, but strangely, said nothing more.

"Come in with me," I invited. She stood close behind me. Too close, while I unlocked the door to the clinic and turned the lights on.

I looked around the clinic and could tell that people had been coming and going from here all summer. The place needed a little tender loving care. I'd planned to clean it up this morning, but it would just have to wait. I put my purse, the clock, and my papers on my desk, and turned to this young girl.

"Sorry, this place is in a bit of disarray. I haven't been in much this summer. So tell me, dear, what's your name?" My excuses had been offered, and now it was time to get down to business.

"My *name*?" The inflection of her voice rose, answering my question with a question, and then for a moment her face went blank as if she'd forgotten what I'd just asked her.

"Yes. Please tell me your name," I said, as we walked passed the two beds and the bathroom to an adjoining private consultation room. Opening the door, I turned on the light, and allowed her to enter ahead of me.

The tiny consultation room was about six by six feet square. It was just large enough for a loveseat and two upholstered chairs. The walls were made of cinder block and had been painted a light blue color. There were two doorways allowing entry and exit from the hallway as well as from the clinic. This young girl paused, scoping out the room before deciding to sit on the love seat. I sat in the chair in front of her and leaned in with my elbows on my knees. The door closed slowly behind us. There was something about this small space that made students feel safe. Sometimes they felt safe enough to give voice to their deepest, darkest, most heart-felt concerns.

We sat for just a moment as this young girl settled in. I waited. I knew she'd heard my question. When she was ready she would tell me what was on her mind.

The minutes hung there while I sat and waited, just breathing. Clearly, something big was troubling her. Would she decide to trust?

At last, she took a deep breath, and began, "My name is Amirah. Amirah Masood. I need to know if you can make arrangements for me to take a shower in the girl's locker room during lunch. Every day during lunch."

Once she'd started, her words were delivered rapid fire. She was clearly agitated. Her eyes darted from one doorway to the other.

"Okay, Amirah. Let's slow down just a little bit. Are you a new student here?" I asked, hoping to get a little more information, and a chance to observe and assess this young girl who was obviously in acute distress.

"No, I went to the middle school. I have been at The Academy since pre-K3." She sounded offended that I didn't know whom she was and that she was a *lifer.*

"Okay, but you're new to the *upper* school, right? You're a ninth grader?" I asked gently and her head bobbed up and down, almost like a tick.

"Help me understand your request. Can you tell me why you want to take a shower every day during lunch?" I proceeded slowly and kept my voice soft and low. I didn't want to add to her visible distress.

"Can't you smell it? I smell awful, noxious, and disgusting," she said.

She didn't wait for a response. She reached up with one hand and removed her floral scarf from her head. Her hair had been completely shaved off. She was shaved bald and there were signs of recent wounds where the razor had been dragged too close her scalp.

I'd been curious about why she was wearing a scarf. I was certain the reason would be forth coming, but I'd not expected this. High school was difficult enough with insecure teenagers continually comparing themselves with their peers: their appearance, their clothes, their grades, their social status, and everything else. The rigor of measuring up at The Academy of Halcyon Heights was like an Olympic event complete with the pageantry, the score keeping, and the 24-7 running commentary. This was going to draw a great deal of unkind attention to this girl. No, this would not play well for her even if everything else were going in her favor. And clearly, it was not.

I paused and waited for Amirah to explain.

"I shaved my head yesterday. I thought the odor was coming from my hair. I washed it and washed it, but I couldn't make it to go away. So I shaved it all off and I can still smell it. It's making me sick. Can't you smell it? The other girls on my field hockey team can smell it. They're all talking about me and how bad I smell." She was so clearly upset.

"Amirah, you smell just fine to me. You don't smell bad. When did you hear the girls talking about you? What did they say?" I asked as slowly and as quietly as I could.

"After the pre-season field hockey tournament at Maryknoll. We were coming back on the bus and I could hear them. They said I was a lesbian. Mrs. Duncan, you must believe me, I'm not a lesbian. I had a boyfriend last summer. Well, not a boyfriend really. I'm not allowed to date. More like a pen pal. I'm not like that. I don't do those things. I'm going to be a virgin when I marry, but not before I go to medical school and go into practice with my father. I'm taking all the honors courses. I don't know why I have to play sports. My dad is going to try and get me out of it. Do you know if you can get a blue point by competing in the Science Fair?" she asked.

Ah . . . the blue point dilemma surfaced yet again. School policy dictated that all students were required to participate in a minimum of two seasons of athletics every year. The rationale for this mandate was rooted in an underlying philosophy that espoused the following values and virtues– competition produced winners, leadership required a strong mind and a strong body, and competition helped to separate the wheat from the chaff. At the completion of every season a blue point was granted for those who participated and met the attendance requirements. This was not optional. It was a requirement for graduation.

But before I had a chance to tell her how the blue points were allocated, she was onto something else. "Dr. Benton is the chairman of the Science Department and he is my advisor. I bet he can get me out of field hockey. It's just such a waste of my time and talents to be chasing a little ball up and down the field."

She paused and looked up towards the ceiling adjacent to the door leading to the hallway. In a forced conspiratorial whisper she said, "Did you hear them? They're outside in the hallway. They're saying I'm a lesbian."

I paused to listen. The hallway was perfectly quiet. There was no one outside of the door. "Amirah, I don't hear anyone or anything," I said while I tried to reassure her. She had bigger issues than how she would earn a blue point.

"They're out there right now. Can't you hear them? Is there something wrong with your hearing? Listen," she demanded emphatically, "they're just outside the door."

Then, without any confirmation or transition she changed the topic. "But I just can't wash away the stink," she shuddered as if in complete disgust. "This is why I *must* shower at lunch."

"Did you have a shower this morning before school?" I asked.

"Yes, yes, and last night too. I don't know why I smell so bad." She hung her head.

My heart went out to her. She was really suffering from deep anxiety and possibly something more. She needed help. I made eye contact with Amirah and held her gaze momentarily.

"Have you talked with your mom or your dad about any of this?"

"You can't tell my mother. She hates me. She's jealous of me. All she ever does is wash the dishes and clean the house. She will beat me if she finds out I told you about the voices," Amirah looked away and did not elaborate. "May I use your bathroom?"

And again, without waiting for a reply, she got up from the couch and headed back into the clinic and into the restroom. I heard the door lock and the water in the sink was running and running. Then I heard reams of paper towel being ripped from the dispenser.

I waited and worried. I tried to think of what I would do if she didn't emerge in the next few minutes. This young girl wasn't safe to be in school. If she were having this much difficulty right now, what would it be like when the academic pressure cooker heated up?

In about five minutes she exited the bathroom. Her face was red. Her hands were chapped, red, and raw. She had put her scarf back on her head, but it no longer covered her shaved scalp completely. Her scarf and her blouse were wet and bits of brown paper towel clung to the stubble on her head where a shadow of regrowth had already begun to appear.

"See if you can work this out for me, okay?" she asked, in a tone that sounded more like a command than a request.

"Amirah, I want you to stop back after lunch," I responded, leaning back against the side of my desk.

She was noncommittal and was already making her way out the clinic door and down the hallway into the sea of humanity.

"Oh dear God," I uttered audibly. In my own way, I too was asking for help.

I opened the door to the lavatory. There was soap and water slopped all over the floor, the toilet, the sink and the mirror. Paper towels were in the sink and on the floor. Here was a clear, outward sign of this young woman's inner chaos.

I tidied up, left the clinic and locked the door. I needed to see the Director of the Upper School and my supervisor, Mr. William Warwick. I hoped he was in his office.

Will was hedging in on sixty, but retained a youthful appearance despite his salt and pepper gray hair. He was tall, lean, and had the physical presence of a much younger man. He was kind, thoughtful, and could be counted on to do the right thing.

I stood outside Will's office window and he waved me in. No appointment necessary. It was a great arrangement. He knew when I showed up it was always for something that couldn't wait.

"Welcome back, I saw you across the room this morning, but I didn't have a chance to say hello. How was your summer?" Will was seated behind his desk in full uniform– the navy Brooks Brothers suit, white shirt, and red striped tie. He inquired with all the kindness and courtesy I had come to expect from this man.

I felt a sense of relief in just seeing him. Will Warwick was my boss, but I also considered him my friend. He had been very good to me when Elliot died. He went out of his way to check in on me and always asked about my kids.

"Do you have a few minutes?" I asked.

Will nodded and gestured towards the chair.

"Good thing as this may take a little time. I have just spent the better part of the last hour with Amirah Masood. She's a ninth grade girl from our middle school, and she's actively delusional with auditory and olfactory hallucinations."

Will looked confused.

"Sorry– nurse speak. She's hearing voices and smelling noxious odors that have been created completely in her imagination."

Will's eyes widened, "Tell me more."

"Amirah's on the JV field hockey team. The girls traveled to the other side of the state for a tournament and on the bus ride home she thought the other girls were talking about her. She said she heard two girls say that she smelled bad. Amirah believed the smell was coming from her hair. When she arrived back home she washed and scrubbed herself and her hair in an effort to remove the odor, but she was convinced she could still smell it. So, believing she had no recourse, she shaved all her hair off. She was sitting outside the clinic this morning wearing her school uniform and a floral silk headscarf tied under her chin. And according to Amirah some of the faculty has already confronted her because she's out of dress code, and she's been told she can't wear a headscarf. She undoubtedly feels self-conscious, as she now has no hair."

Will looked at me and slowly shook his head from side to side. "Let me get this right. She shaved off all of her hair because she *thought* it smelled bad? And there is no odor. Is that correct?"

I nodded, "That's right."

"Is there more?" He asked as he brought his left hand up to cradle his forehead.

I nodded, "One moment she was telling me of all her academic achievements and expounding on her own intellectual prowess, and the next she was tearing up because she feels the other students don't like her and are gossiping behind her back. She told me she hears people whispering about her in the hallways. They're saying she's a lesbian, but she is adamant she is not."

"What do you make of this?" Will asked.

"Vacillating between grandiosity and paranoia, the flight of ideas and tangential thinking are textbook signs of mental instability," I answered. But I had not finished painting this picture. I needed Will to have a complete understanding of this morning's interaction with this young girl. "She asked me if I could still smell her noxious odor. I assured her I could not. When I suggested we call her mother, Amirah was adamant that her mother didn't like her either and that her mother would beat her if she found out she had spoken to anyone about *the voices.*"

I sat quietly for a moment as Will tried to decide what to do next.

"Other than that, I'd say its been just another day in paradise, you know, business as usual." I smiled.

Will took a deep breath and sighed, "Like I said, welcome back. Do you have any free time later today?" he asked.

"No, I need to meet with my advisory group, and then with all my freshmen classes. I won't be free until after school," I replied.

"I'll see if my assistant can set up a meeting with the parents. I know this father already. I met with him multiple times over the summer regarding Amirah's schedule. This is going to be a rough one." He looked dejected. I knew him well. He was always looking for the best possible outcome and sometimes there just wasn't one.

The meeting was scheduled for 3:30 PM in the director's office.

❦

I hurried back to the clinic. It was time to meet with my advisory. Halcyon Heights had an advisory system. All the teachers were also advisors and they acted as advocates for their students in all academic and school-related concerns. My advisory was almost always chosen for me by the faculty in the middle school, and my groups tended to distinguish themselves as needing a little more hand holding or closer supervision. I was okay with this. I'd had some great kids roll through my door.

Since this would be the first meeting with my advisees, I was grateful only the freshmen were coming by today. I had brought some fresh fruit and lemonade for this auspicious occasion. There were other teachers, who routinely put on a lavish spread for their crew, but unfortunately these kids had drawn the health teacher and I wasn't about to fill their bellies with toxic junk food, if it even qualified as *food*. If they chose to eat that way it would be their choice not mine.

The kids wandered in and found a seat as their guides stuck their heads in the doorway to say hello. The upperclassmen were acting as guides today, helping the new students get the lay of the land and figure out their schedules. The guides earned a quick and easy four hours of community service. There were plenty of volunteers because every student needed ten hours of community service each year. Community service was mandatory for graduation.

I looked at the combination of wide-eyed innocents and their seasoned ambassadors and I wondered what else they might be learning today. Yet with about 150 new freshmen and 150 guides, the school was about half full today. I was that kind of a person– I chose to see the school as half full.

The morning agenda was very short. We only had about ten minutes together before there would be a brief run-through of the schedule. My responsibilities included: making a face-to-face connection with each of the students to help them feel welcome, explaining what the role of the advisor was and the purpose of the advisory, explaining the dress code, distributing the combinations to their lockers, and exchanging contact information. I had created a little form for them to fill out, and in exchange each student was given my business card with my name, title, office phone number, email address, cell phone, and home phone numbers.

Yes, Halcyon Heights was a day school, but there was a clear expectation that we would be available to our students both day and night.

Just as I was about finished and ready to dismiss my advisees, in waltzed Laurel Winton on the arm of Jordan Stone, one of the senior football players. "Wait for me, I'll only be a minute," she called out to the man-child who waited for her just outside my door.

She was laughing loudly and was overly animated as she flung herself onto the couch and dropped her backpack on the floor. My initial thought was– how could this girl only be 14? She looked like she could be 25. Her thick, curly blonde hair hung nearly to her waist, her skirt was already too short and out of compliance with the dress code, her blouse was untucked and pulled so tight across her full breasts that the buttons gapped. This was not an uncommon look for a junior or a senior who was embracing their blossoming sexuality, and still wearing uniforms that were purchased when they were freshmen. But for the first day of school as a freshman, most kids were buttoned up tight and wanting to make a good impression. She wanted to impress someone all right, and it certainly wasn't me. This was a train wreck just waiting to happen.

With that, the bell rang and my advisees went off to find their lockers. "Have a good weekend and happy Labor Day," I called out after them. I would see them all again on Tuesday. Between now and then I needed to find out a little more about them.

Given my position as the Director of Health Services and Chair of the Crisis Team I had administrative privileges that included access to the students' permanent records. I didn't always read them. All too frequently, I'd found them to be prejudicial. After all, this was high school, a new school year, and students change a great deal as they grow up and mature. However, these students had been hand-selected to be my advisees and I wanted to know a little bit about what they were struggling with and why they'd been placed with me.

Maybe later during a *free period* I'd have a chance to read their files. That was a laugh. None of my time was ever free. I felt as hemmed in by the demands of the day as the students did. I liked it that way. I was less likely to fall apart if I kept wrapping myself in emotional duct tape. Nothing got out and nothing got in. Perfect.

The remainder of the afternoon was a series of brief, ten-minute *meet and greet*s with my classes. By the time all the students found the classroom there was barely enough time to say hello, good-bye, and pass out their textbook that I had written and revised over the summer.

I taught five classes of Health Education every semester. It was the only class that was mandated by the state and I was the only one who taught it. Therefore, by the time the year was over, every freshman had rolled through my classroom. The class size would make most public school teachers green with envy for my average class had 15 students. Like it or not, we were stuck with one another. It was a good opportunity for me to assess first hand their intellectual capabilities and learning style, as well as their social skills and emotional well being. Over the course of the year I would come to know these students and they would come to know me. This also helped if they ran into difficulty when they became upperclassmen.

When the final bell rang at 3:20 I stopped by the clinic briefly to deposit my teaching paraphernalia. I took a moment to regroup before I made my way down the hall towards the Academic Office. This had been a hell of a first day and it wasn't over yet. I needed to shift gears. I now needed to function in a different role.

My official title was Director of Health Services, which encompassed the role of health teacher, nurse, and public health administrator for The Academy of Halcyon Heights. There could be inherent conflicts in the blending of these roles. The role of the nurse/ teacher was to seek the best possible outcome for the individual student and that may or may not be in line with the thinking of the parents. Opinions could differ about the best way to help a child.

However, the Director of Health Services was also the public health administrator for the whole institution. The primary responsibility in this role was to make decisions that safeguarded the health and well being of the entire community. When conflicts arose, the safety of the community must take precedent over what may be deemed best for the individual student. There had been countless tragedies in numerous schools across the country when people did not understand the priorities or see the conflict. In my head the words were already taking shape– *Not on my watch.*

By the time I arrived, about 3:25 PM, both of Amirah's parents were already seated in Will's office.

"Elise, these are Amirah's parents, Dr. and Mrs. Masood," Will said, "Mrs. Duncan is the Director of Health Services." They remained seated when I reached over to shake each of their hands.

Dr. Masood exhaled audibly as he shook my hand with a weak grip that further revealed his indifference. "Mrs. *Dun*-can," he repeated my name slowly like he had just tasted something foul. His lip curled into a smirk.

Mrs. Masood was wearing a traditional Muslim headscarf and a floor length skirt. She took my hand silently and gently before her eyes fell to her lap and she folded her hands.

I wondered what Will had told them before I arrived?

Perhaps it was merely a cultural difference, but in the culture of this academic institution, men generally stood when a woman entered the room and when introductions were made. It was a sign of respect. This was an environment where manners mattered and were drilled into the youngest children. The adults were expected to use them. This simple lapse in etiquette was not lost on me.

I got the clear impression that Dr. Masood felt there was little I could add to the conversation. I had encountered this arrogance before: doctor trumped nurse, and man trumped woman. He wasn't interested in my perspective, and if he had been the one to call the meeting he would have dismissed me on the spot. But this was not his prerogative, and I took my seat.

Will turned his gaze towards me, "Mrs. Duncan met with your daughter this morning. Why don't you tell Dr. and Mrs. Masood about your conversation with Amirah and your concerns?"

I had just begun to describe my interaction with Amirah that morning and explain why I was concerned for her mental and emotional fragility, and my fears for her safety, when Dr. Masood interrupted, "Excuse me, Mrs. Duncan, but are you a licensed psychiatrist or perhaps a psychologist?" he said with a sneer.

Without waiting for my reply he added, "No, of course not. You are the *nurse*, am I right?"

"Yes, I'm a Registered Nurse." I straightened up and I confirmed my credentials. I wasn't about to let this arrogant man disrespect me. Instead, I attempted to turn the conversation back to his daughter's behavior.

Again Dr. Masood interrupted, "I don't believe you are qualified to speak about my daughter's mental health," he said in a tone that left little room for any further discussion on my part. "My daughter Amirah is a brilliant scholar. She and I have just finished writing a book, an elaborate tome really, on the etymological origins of Latin and Arabic root words. We have plans to continue our work on words of Germanic origins."

I was beginning to see how her father had laid the foundation for her grandiose thinking.

"She could not possibly participate in such scholarly pursuits if she was not of sound mind. To imply she is mentally defective in any possible way is a grave insult to me and to my entire family," he finished. Then he turned and glared openly at me.

There was something about the way he protected and defended his daughter without really listening to the concerns that were being raised. He was defensive, and outright hostile towards me.

I'd sat through enough of these meetings to know when a parent was unwilling to discuss a matter any further. We had reached that point. As far as Dr. Masood was concerned, there simply could not be anything wrong with their daughter. Problems were viewed as defects, and defects were not permitted.

I had seen this kind of parental refusal before. There was an unwillingness to acknowledge their child's distress. But this situation was different. This girl was quite likely psychotic.

I turned away from his angry stare and in my silence I thought, *something is amiss here.*

William had heard enough. "Dr. Masood, you are right, neither Mrs. Duncan nor I are licensed psychiatrists or psychologists. We both have worked with thousands of adolescents however, and are well aware that intellectual ability and mental illness are not mutually exclusive. A child can be both."

The decision was Will's to make and thankfully he made it without hesitation. He decreed, "Amirah may return to school only after she's had a psychiatric evaluation. We will let a psychiatrist decide if she is safe to be in school."

"This is *ridiculous*. You will have your signed document on Tuesday morning, and I expect my daughter to be welcomed in her classes, which I have bought and paid for." In the moment of silence following this tirade, Dr. Masood held his breath to keep from saying anything more. His face reddened, and deeply entrenched wrinkles on his nose and between his eyebrows appeared. He looked like he might explode with anger.

My impression was that he was used to having his own way.

There it was. He was buying not just an education, but also a child who came out of this *leader-mill* as a perfect specimen, ready to attend a prestigious university, and prepared to step into a top-ranked position among the *Who's Who of America*.

Then, Dr. Masood stood to leave and Mrs. Masood followed his lead.

Mrs. Masood appeared slightly embarrassed and powerless. I suspected this was also an ongoing state of affairs in their marriage. He commanded and everyone else acquiesced.

When they left Will closed the door, and returned to his desk. I stood to leave, but he motioned for me to stay.

"You know she'll be back in here Tuesday morning, don't you?" Will asked.

I nodded my head. "Getting psychiatric clearance in this town is as easy as getting booze on prom night. You just need to know who to ask. But the real issue is who is going to help this delusional child?"

Will shook his head. He knew, as I did, that this child was mentally unstable and her grasp on reality was precarious.

We sat for a moment in silence.

"Dr. Masood was clearly furious at the mere suggestion of a psychiatric evaluation and therapy for his daughter. But Amirah had shaved her entire scalp for God's sake. This is hardly *normal* behavior for a fourteen-year-old girl. This wasn't a distress signal that I'd fabricated in my imagination. And where does her mother stand in all this? Why did she not speak up?" I started to process aloud.

Will listened while I continued.

"He was so dismissive of me and of his own wife. His anger was way out of proportion to the situation. Which begs the question– what's behind this? What is Dr. Masood so afraid of? Why was he so resistant to having his daughter receive the help she so desperately needs? This whole encounter did not sit well with me," I finished.

"If someone suggested that my child was exhibiting signs of mental illness, would I be so quick to shoot the messenger?" Will asked aloud and then answered, "Not a chance. No, I would be doing everything in my power to keep her safe and well."

And then he addressed the elephant in the room. "I was thinking about what you'd said about your conversation with Amirah this morning."

I waited. I was pretty sure I knew where this was going.

"You said that Amirah had been adamant she wasn't dating and that she was a virgin."

"That's right, and the issue of her dating and her virginity came out of left field. We had been talking about something completely different. We'd been talking about the girls on the field hockey bus." I recalled the way Amirah had been insistent that she was protecting her virginity and her virtue until she was married. The comment had been totally out of context with the flow of the conversation we'd been having.

"Remember last fall when Geoffrey, the goalie on the soccer team, came to school with a black eye and a concussion?"

Will nodded.

"Do you remember the first thing he said to me when he came into the clinic?" I asked and then answered, "*My father didn't hit me.* That possibility hadn't crossed my mind, nor had I even asked how he got the black eye." I paused and took a breath.

The unspoken question hung in the silence between us.

Then just above a whisper Will asked, "Do you think there's some kind of incestuous relationship between this guy and his daughter?"

"Do you mean child abuse, criminal sexual misconduct, and statutory rape? I have no idea." I responded. "Dear God, I hope not."

"At least for now, let's leave this to the psychiatrist and see what unfolds," Will said as he let out a deep breath. "I think we've done our part for today."

If I had learned anything in my days on earth and trips around the sun it was this:

—Do not disregard your intuition.

When I stood to leave I thought about how quickly the day had turned. Only eight hours earlier we had been at the Welcome Back Breakfast, and now this heavy sense of sadness and worry invaded Will's office. From the look on Will's face I knew he felt it too.

"I need to go home and be with my own children," I said.

Will shook his head. "What can I say? Some people just have no business being parents."

"Even if there is nothing evil going on here, the good doctor doesn't seem to know that his daughter is a person in her own right. She is more than just an extension of him. She is more than just another entry on his resume or lifetime list of achievements. I'm not certain who is more delusional, Amirah or her father. She needs help," I said standing in the open doorway.

There would be no easy fix. Especially, if we could not get the parents to set their egos aside and care enough to do the right thing for their own child.

"Look, try to have a good weekend. I'll see you Tuesday," Will offered.

I let out a long slow breath, and Will gave me a sad smile that acknowledged we were already back in the thick of it . . . and the school year had barely begun.

First Semester

CHAPTER 3

September 1999

Monday was Labor Day, but on Tuesday before the first bell had rung Will Warwick had a letter on his desk. It was signed, sealed and hand-delivered by Dr. Masood while Amirah waited in the chair just outside of Will's office.

A colleague of Dr. Masood's, a psychiatrist, had written the letter. The Masoods had complied. They had produced a letter from a psychiatrist indicating that Amirah was safe to be in school. It was brief and devoid of any helpful information, but succinctly stated that Amirah Masood was fine and perhaps just a little stressed.

There was no indication that the psychiatrist had even evaluated her, nor any indication she would be receiving ongoing therapy.

Before the first class, Will was standing outside of my classroom. He told me, "Amirah's back in school.

I informed her father that Amirah's readmission was contingent on her meeting with you every day so you can assess her ability to cope with the stress of school."

"Really?" I caught his gaze and held it. We both understood the weight of the burden he had just placed upon me.

"I'm sorry. It was the best I could do in the moment," he said as the first bell rang.

No therapy or medication had been prescribed for this young woman who was hearing voices, feeling paranoid, had delusions of grandeur, believed she had a noxious body odor that no one else could smell, her remedy being to cut off all her hair and to spend hours every day bathing until she had rubbed her skin to the point of bleeding . . . how could anyone believe this was a normal and healthy transition to high school? How could anyone expect her to be well when her parents required her to get straight A's? This young girl was on an impossible trajectory. Her father expected her to attend an Ivy League Medical School. This was the prerequisite to becoming a person of value, just like her daddy.

Great, now even my own internal chatter had become tainted with a sarcastic edge. How could I ever be the calm and loving presence I sought to be when my observations and opinions felt so devalued?

Yet, the ongoing care of this delusional child rested with me.

"Okay," I said with a smile that I'm certain more closely resembled a smirk. Will knew I wasn't happy with the outcome. When you'd worked with someone long enough and closely enough, you just knew.

The specifics differed, but the underlying issues were repeated over and over again.

When I closed my classroom door the cynical chatter played on in my head. Should I do this before or after I taught five classes every day? Should I rely on Amirah to stop by and see me in the clinic? That was never going to happen. She would avoid me like a drug addict avoids the cops. No, I would need to hunt her down and find her.

But I knew if this kind of craziness continued, her teachers and coaches would come looking for me. Amirah was not a well child and that would soon be apparent to even the least interested.

∾

At the Academy of Halcyon Heights, meeting with your advisory was the equivalent of going to homeroom. Attendance was encouraged, but there was little consequence for missing. In my advisory most of the students were freshmen and had yet to figure this out. The handful of upper classmen usually came to see if we had any food to share or just because they liked hanging out together. But today was the first full day of school, and all my advisees were in attendance. Who were these students that had been entrusted to my care?

Over the course of the year I would grow to know them better. But for now, all I had to go on was the report from the middle school dean shared with me last spring when these former eighth graders matriculated into the upper school. They wandered in one by one. I could read the looks on their faces. Some were comforted to have found a safe place to land, but others sized up the group. The least, the lost, and the forgotten were amongst us.

There was a brother and a sister who were both brittle diabetics. Monica was a junior and had been my advisee the last two years. She was absolutely lovely, and now her brother Michael was joining us. I knew if he was anything like his sister then I would like him too. They looked like they could be twins. They were both statuesque– tall, thin, blue-eyed blondes.

Then there was Adrian, who was an openly gay young man of color. He was on the cheerleading squad and was wearing eye make-up. I suspected he didn't want there to be any confusion about his sexual orientation. Had he been a young woman I might've counseled him that sometimes when it comes to eye make-up, less is more. But I wasn't going to go there.

Theodore P. Rogers the III, otherwise known as Trip, arrived all buttoned up tight with his briefcase. He looked like a junior executive at a Fortune 500 firm rather than a high school freshman, except that Trip was about five feet tall. According to the middle school, he liked to hang out in the library and read books about military battle strategies.

Mohamed was the class clown in eighth grade. Schoolwork was difficult for him, so more often than not, rather than struggle through the class work, he chose not to do anything. I suspected it was easier to be thought lazy by your peers than stupid. Kids can be really rough on anyone and everyone who falls outside the very narrow parameters of what others find acceptable.

Hesha was Indian. She sat quietly among the others, nervously twisting and twirling a lock of her long dark hair between her fingers. All I knew about her was that she had an anxiety disorder, and a history of self-mutilation. She was a cutter.

There were also two new students who arrived without any commentary from the middle school. All the others I knew as they were returning from last year. This year I had 15 students. Over the course of the school year we would learn a great deal about one another, but today we were just exchanging information and beginning to deal with issues related to schedules, classes, and textbooks.

Again Laurel Winton was the last to arrive. She was the young, blonde bombshell whose wealthy parents were in the throes of a nasty divorce. According to the middle school she had been diagnosed with oppositional defiant disorder. She was a very bright student whose behavior was beyond the pale. She'd been in the room for less than five minutes and nearly everything that came out of her mouth was snarly and said to shock the wide-eyed innocents. She was going to be a challenge.

When the bell rang and we all hustled off to our first class I wondered, how would I ever keep them safe while they were under my tutelage?

∾

My classroom was in the athletic corridor. It was one of the few classrooms in the building that had not been renovated. The room itself was a pretty good size but there was a cinderblock wall that divided the room in half. This was once a biology classroom before the $10 million renovation of the science department was completed, and all the science classrooms were moved to the second floor. Still, it worked fine for me because I believed that teaching and learning took place between students and teachers and had very little to do with bricks and mortar.

But given the fact it was located in the athletic corridor, there was a never-ending parade of kids going back and forth from the locker rooms to the gyms. Kids who had early dismissal for sporting events were always hanging around just outside my classroom door. Initially, it had been more than a little distracting to have students peering through the windows in the doors, waving, and generally fooling around in the hallway outside of my classroom. So I'd obstructed the view into my classroom by putting posters over the windows of the doors. Problem solved.

Over the past few years, I had arranged and rearranged the furniture in my classroom until at last I had it where I wanted it. The student desks were placed in two semicircles, one within the other. This arrangement worked well. It allowed me to walk among my students while teaching and also allowed the students could look into the faces of their peers. I found that students learned as much from one another as they did from me. It was important that students learned to find their voices and be comfortable expressing their own opinions. I could offer up the factual information and bait them with issues I wanted them to think about, but for any real learning to take place the students needed to debate the issues and make up their own minds. They needed to be open and honest. They needed to have their questions answered. So much of health education wasn't about the recitation of the facts, but whether or not the young people could and would make conscious, healthy decisions when there was so much pressure in the outside world to do otherwise. I hoped if they could talk about the issues within the safety of my classroom, they might be able to act in a wise and informed manner once they were out on their own.

When I arrived in my classroom some of the students had already taken a seat, and others were still clustered about in the center of the room, uncertain where to sit or by whom.

Ah … and so it began.

"Take a seat, any seat. In this class you may sit anywhere you choose to sit unless that proves to be too great a responsibility for you to handle," I said as the students scrambled to find a desk. It rather resembled a game of musical chairs as they negotiated who would sit next to whom.

"How will I know if this is too much responsibility? You will continue yammering on when I need you to be listening. If this proves to be the case then you will have the privilege of sitting right up here next to me," I said, indicating the empty chair right next to the teacher's desk that no one was seated in. Once they had turned their eyes towards the empty chair,

I gesticulated as if I could reach out and backhand a mouthy kid right within my arm's reach.

I got the laugh I was hoping for. This was The Halcyon Academy after all, and not a parochial school in the 1950s. These children knew the faculty here would never lay a hand on them no matter how far out of bounds their behavior was.

The students quieted down as I reached for my reading glasses, which as usual, were hanging on the front of my blouse. I looked over the class list then peered out over the top of my reading glasses. These were the children of the world, and their families' heritage was reflected in their faces as well as their names. "Bear with me as I start to learn your names. Please correct me if I mispronounce your name and continue to correct me until I get it right. You have a right to have your name pronounced correctly and if you prefer to be called something else let me know."

I only butchered about half the names, but I expected these kids were used to it. There were very few girls named Mary or boys named Bob. One young boy of Ethiopian parentage named Eremias suggested, "Call me *Huggy*. That's what my grandmother calls me." He smiled brightly.

"Hmm…*Huggy*? I'm not certain I can do that, I think I can remember Eremias," I assured him.

The world of a ninth grader is a whole different world. Their bodies were changing right before their very eyes. By the age of 14 most of the girls had begun to show signs of physical development. Their biological clocks were on average two years ahead of the boys. There were boys in my class that were well over six feet tall, and yet some were still less than five feet tall. Some looked like full-grown men and needed to shave every day, and some could have been mistaken for sixth graders. Some were emotionally and intellectually wise beyond their years, yet still were living in child-like bodies. Others appeared full grown and still reasoned and behaved like little children. It was never easy to be first or the last to go through puberty. Part of my job was to alleviate their fears and make everyone feel okay no matter where they fell on the continuum, without causing any embarrassment. This growing up thing wasn't easy in the best of circumstances.

During my first years teaching I learned a few things from the seasoned veterans and the master teachers, and one was to engage the students in establishing the classroom rules. Never really one to be dictatorial, if the students set the rules they were much more likely to follow them and would play an active role in calling out the rule breakers. So it had become part and parcel of the opening day agenda. The students already understood one of the rules that governed my classroom when I allowed them to choose their own seats.

I asked for a volunteer, "Who would like to write on the board?"

Eremias was up and out of his seat like a shot. He stood at the whiteboard with a red marker in his hand. Someone called out a suggestion– "Raise your hand and wait to be called on." It was clear to everyone that this comment was directed at the young man at the board. I smiled because I knew the other students would help me rein in his behavior.

So before too long the list was completed and had been written on the board. The list varied very little from class-to-class or even over the years.

1. You may choose your own seats, unless you are disruptive.
2. Raise your hand if you want to speak.
3. Everyone must participate in the discussion.

This warranted a little further discussion and so we talked about the importance of finding your own voice. "This is a safe place to practice speaking your mind and expressing your opinion. Remember that we will be discussing a wide variety of sensitive issues and you may have some deeply held beliefs. You have a right to express yourself, but there may be others in this classroom that also hold beliefs every bit as deeply as you hold yours. They have the right to disagree with you. They also have a right to be heard. Chances are that you will not change anyone's mind no matter how impassioned you are, and they will probably not change yours, but maybe we will gain some understanding of the issues, and then we must learn to agree to disagree," I paused a moment and then we continued with the list.

4. Be respectful.

"Be respectful to yourself, to all members of the classroom, and this includes the teacher. Be respectful of the material. Students may ask any question, but may not use street language. If you don't know the appropriate words, go slowly, I'll help you out. If you have the question probably others do too," I added.

Welcome to the Upper School.

The first unit was on human sexuality. How was that for grabbing their attention? I opened with the origins of gender, first from a biological perspective and then we talked about how children are socialized into gender and sex roles, which led to a lengthy discussion about sexual orientation.

The students learned pretty quickly that I could and would talk with them about sex and sexuality. It seemed to sink in that they could probably talk with me about just about anything. And they did.

The bell rang and the class was dismissed. Some said thank you and others smiled and said good bye. We were off to a good start.

One class down and four more to go, in some ways it was good to be back. I really did like being with the students in the classroom. I recalled other teachers saying this student or that one fell asleep in their class, but that didn't happen in my classroom. Sex, drugs, and rock 'n' roll, okay, maybe not too much about rock and roll, but for the most part my students were interested in the subject matter.

My boss, Will Warwick, had told me early on that when I was in my classroom I was the *Queen of my Kingdom*. I was responsible for establishing the curriculum, writing the text, establishing pedagogical strategies and evaluating learning. He was available to talk things through with me but the responsibility for what went on in my classroom was mine.

While taking attendance in my last class of the day, I noted that Amirah Masood was absent. I was suspicious. I had seen her earlier in the day. Where was she now? I marked her absent and left the attendance form in the envelope outside my door.

After class, one of the other students stopped by my desk. "Amirah is the girl who shaved her head, right?" he asked.

I nodded.

"I overheard her in the hall saying that her father was going to get her out of health and that her advisor had put in for a schedule change." He whispered like he was imparting a secret to a trusted friend.

"Thank you, Jacob. If that's the case I'm certain Mr. Warwick will let me know."

When he'd left I sat at my desk and continued to struggle with an uncomfortable feeling about Amirah and her father. This was not the first time that a student had tried to be excused from my class. Health Education was mandated by the State of Virginia for a high school diploma and I was the only person that taught it at Halcyon Heights. Over the course of my teaching career there had been only one young lady who was given a reprieve for the human sexuality component of the course. Her parents were Christian fundamentalists and they were trying to protect their daughter's innocence. But she was required to attend the rest of the class. I thought it was highly unlikely that Dr. Masood, given his only objection was his willful disregard for me, would be seen as having an adequate reason to allow his daughter a reprieve from the mandates of the state. I didn't need to be a soothsayer to know he wanted to keep his delusional daughter out of my presence. Good luck with that.

Most of the students actually liked my class, but there were a few who treated the class and me with disdain as if what I had been hired to teach was a waste of their precious time. Usually their attitude and arrogance was deeply rooted in their upbringing. And as I had been known to say, "That said more about them than it did about me."

By the end of the day, Will had left me a voicemail message. "Amirah's father has requested a schedule change. Dr. Masood wants his daughter to drop health. He said he would home school her in the content area, since as a physician he was clearly capable. I denied his request and he was very unhappy. So as a last resort he requested that she at least be able to postpone the class until the second semester. This request I granted. I don't know what this father is up to, but he is clearly threatened by you. Call me later if you need to discuss this." The line went dead.

Great, I had planned to see Amirah and assess her mental and emotional stability when she came to class and now that plan had just gone up in smoke.

Be that as it may, it was still my responsibility to determine if she was well enough to be in school. Her father had just made it that much more difficult, but not impossible. Now I would need to track her down for a little *tête-à-tête*, as well as to enlist the eyes and ears of her teachers.

Meanwhile, I had 75 freshmen passing through my class every day, not to mention the other 600 students who at any given moment might need some assistance, regarding their own health and well being or lack thereof, while living in the pressure cooker of the Halcyon Academy. There were times when it felt like things might blow apart at any given moment.

This was certainly not the image of the place projected by our headmaster. Mr. George Walker had once compared my job to that of the Maytag repairman, from the old television ads. In the ad there was an older gentleman who spent every day just sitting around hoping something would break so he would have something to do.

How little George understood about a whole lot of things that were happening at The Academy.

Later, George commented about the line of students waiting outside the door to the clinic. He mocked me, "My wife and I are having a little trouble. Could I come by and see you?"

I didn't laugh or smile. I didn't think he was funny.

So he continued, "Do you really think these students have problems? Or do you help them make some up? We both know how adolescents love drama."

I ignored the personal dig. I didn't know if there had been any sexual undercurrent to his comment, but if so, I didn't take the bait. Instead, I replied, "You've seen the line. If you're having trouble take a number."

The Maytag repairman indeed.

There were truly some very ignorant people in the world. This had little to do with education or lack thereof, but as my mother had often said, "It was not my responsibility to tell them."

Welcome to my world.

∾

As the first week turned into the second, additional faculty responsibilities began to fill in any gaps in my schedule. There were lunch meetings scheduled. Monday was the Freshman Support Team, Tuesday was the Sophomore Support Team, and Friday was the Crisis Team meeting. On Wednesday and Thursday I made a point to try and be available to meet with students or faculty members who had concerns. Those concerns would run the gamut: eating disorders, drugs and alcohol, sexual orientation, harassment, loss and grief, difficulty with their parents, relationships or issues with other students to name just a few. We were dealing with teenagers and rest assured wherever there are teenagers, there are teenagers with issues. It is part and parcel with growing up.

I had looked over the textbooks that were available for teaching health education prior to my first semester at The Academy. Across the board they had reduced the content to the least common denominator. There was no way I could or would teach from any of these books. I was passionate about the subject matter and I wanted my students to embrace the content and believe it was relevant to their lives. From the beginning, I'd decided I would use a different approach.

So we started with the biology of gender.

"What was it or more accurately, who was it that determines the sex of a child?" I asked. Hands went up around the room.

I started with the basics– the sperm and the egg, the somatic chromosomes and the sex chromosomes and how children are born either male or female.

"Simple enough– until we begin to look at genetic aberrations in both the somatic chromosomes or the sex chromosomes and errors in embryonic development."

I used the scientific vocabulary associated with human reproduction and my students began to take notes and ask questions. It's a joy for a teacher to have students who are intellectually curious.

"You mean some people can be born with both boy parts and girl parts?" A kid seated on the right side of the class asked.

"Yes. When that happens the condition is called a hermaphroditism," I responded, and wrote the word on the board.

"How do they decide if they will raise the baby as a boy or a girl?" another student called out, forgetting to raise his hand.

"Well, at one point in time, those children were usually changed to little girls. Why? Because the surgery is simpler," I said.

I waited a moment as they visualized why this might be so. Then I continued, "Can anyone think of a reason why this might be a problem?"

Again the hands went up around the room. I called on the tall boy on the left. I was still learning their names.

"What if the kid is supposed to be a dude? What happens if the girl starts to grow a beard and never grows any titties?" He asked.

The class giggled and they turned at me to see how I would respond.

"Did you mean breasts?" I asked, as I looked him in the eyes.

He nodded, "Sorry, Mrs. Duncan, breasts."

I smiled and using some of their newly acquired vocabulary I addressed his question. "You're right. That could be a problem. So now, since our scientific understanding has caught up, instead of doing surgery and changing these children into girls, we draw some blood on the baby, and send it off to a lab to do a karyotype. The karyotype will determine the genotype of this child and then we do the surgery so the external genitalia match the genotype, which is present in every cell of the body."

Students began to see that even the issues of biology were not always straightforward.

Once the students began to grasp the biologic components of gender, we discussed the societal and cultural aspects of gender, and how as young children we were socialized into our gender. Infant girls were dressed in pink and infant boys in blue. Clearly the selection of color was not determined by our biology.

Little girls were given dolls and tea sets to play with and little boys were given trucks and sporting goods as preparation for adulthood where women became the homemakers and boys the auto mechanics. None of this was prescribed by our biology, rather it was all prescribed by culture. And down the garden path we went, laying the argument one stone at a time for an understanding that gender was much more complex than initially thought.

And then it was story time . . .

"Let's pretend it's Thanksgiving Day," I began. It was always a safe bet, in a multicultural school where different holidays were celebrated, that pretty much everyone celebrated Thanksgiving.

"You've been helping your parents prepare for the day, the invitations have been extended, your brothers and sisters are home from college, your aunts, your uncles, your cousins, your grandparents on both sides of the family, even that neighbor who everyone calls Uncle Joe, but he's really not your uncle, they're all there."

The class was nodding and I could see in their eyes that they were remembering their own family gatherings.

"The table has been set, the food has been brought forth from the kitchen and the blessing has been said, and before anyone has a chance to begin eating you decide this would be a good time to make an announcement." The students are quiet and I wait until their eyes turn up towards me.

"You say, 'Since everyone has gathered here together I think this would be a good time to tell you, that after a great deal of soul searching I have determined that I am gay.'"

Momentarily the class went silent, and then all the students wanted to talk at once.

So I asked, "How would your family respond?"

Hands went up around the classroom. I surveyed the class and everyone was asked to consider how this announcement would be received in their home. The responses ran the gamut from, "My Aunt Isabelle is gay and she always brings her partner so I don't think it would be a big deal" to "My mother would cry and my father would throw me out in the street," and every other conceivable reaction from acceptance to violence.

"These are the people who are supposed to love you best in the whole world and some of you can't imagine ever having this discussion with your family because you wouldn't be accepted. There are gay students who live in families just like yours. Some have supportive parents and some will never tell for fear that their families would stop loving them." I added my own commentary to the class discussion.

One young lady stated, "We are Christian and homosexuality is a sin. My parents would never allow this." As if her parents' judgment could really control the sexual preferences of anyone.

To further stir this already boiling cauldron I asked her, "Do you know what Jesus said about homosexuality?"

"Yes, it's a sin," she answered with conviction.

"Now I must admit that I'm not a Biblical scholar but my understanding is that Jesus, the one whom Christians follow, never said anything at all about homosexuality." I paused to let the magnitude of that sink in.

"I do know that Jesus did say, 'Love your neighbor as yourself.' If I have this wrong I welcome your correction." I added this gently. I looked around the room and then caught the eye of the girl who had just issued this proclamation. I didn't want to cast her in the role of a fool. I wanted her to feel free to enter in and find her voice, and truly stand by the tenants of her faith. But I also wanted her to look at what it was that was informing her choices and decisions.

"Feel free to check with your pastor."

Then we went on to discuss what it would be like to have your best friend, someone you have known for years, tell you that they're gay.

"I'd be okay with it unless they tried to hit on me," one young man said and some of the others nodded their heads in agreement.

Soon a few other voices began to pipe up around the room.

"No more sleepovers."

"It would change things for me."

"If they were my best friend, they'd still be my best friend."

I could see my students were looking at this issue in a way they'd never considered it before. This exercise asked them to consider what it would be like to be in another person's shoes, to make it personal and real, to put a face on the nameless, faceless other. They were learning it was easier to pass judgment when we allow ourselves to see people as different and faceless. When able to put a real face on someone they began to develop empathy and understanding of how difficult it might be to be cast as an outsider, and as I expected, a stirring of compassion began to follow.

So it was time to shift things up again. Teaching high school was like putting on a dog and pony show. The teacher needed to keep it interesting or something else would grab or vie for the students' attention.

"Okay who wants to play?" I asked.

I looked for the most *macho macho* man. There was always one. Randall was a big, confident, and handsome kid of African and Asian descent. He was practically jumping out of his seat with his arm raised to indicate his willingness to participate.

"Okay, Randall." All the other kids who hadn't been chosen lowered their hands with a collective sigh of disappointment.

"Let's assume that you are heterosexual. You like girls." He smiled broadly. "Oh yes sir, you're a ladies man. Is that right?" Again he smiled and nodded.

"Do you know what happens when we assume?" I asked him and he shrugged. It was one of the joys of teaching 14 and 15 year olds; they hadn't heard all of the old jokes yet.

"Go ahead and spell assume." I smiled at Randall.

He looked at me suspiciously, like this was way too easy.

"Is this some kind of a trick question?" he asked, and then he said each letter aloud, "A-S-S-U-M-E."

"That's right Randall, when you assume you make an *ass* out of you and me," the class laughed along with Randall. "Come on, you said you wanted to play," I cajoled good-naturedly, and Randall smiled.

"Okay, so I am going to assume you like girls," I stated again.

To which Randall responded with a smile, "Yes ma'am."

"Oh I know. I get it. So that means you like, and are attracted to, and want to be affectionate with all the girls. Right?"

Randall looked confused so I continued, "Tall, short, old, young, heavy, thin, white, black, green, geeks, hippies, and beauty queens, you are attracted to them all. Right? After all, you are a heterosexual. Right?"

"No," Randall said while shaking his head, and then again with more emphasis, "No."

"No?" I said seeking clarification. "Oh, do you mean you are discriminating about the girls you find attractive and want to spend time with?"

Randall nodded his head and smiled a big smile, showing off his perfect white teeth, "That's right, I'm discriminating."

"So even if your best friend is gay, what makes you think that your friend is attracted to you? I hate to break this to you, but as charming as you are, you just might not be his type." The whole class laughed as Randall just got played. He dropped his head and laughed because he hadn't seen it coming.

"So, let's assume– and you already know how this goes when we assume," and the whole class continued laughing along with Randall. "You ask this girl out who you think is hot, hot, hot, and she says in the kindest and most gentlest of ways, '*Sorry, big boy, but you're just not my type,*'" I altered my voice to sound like a sweet young thing.

"Do you continue to pursue her?" I asked Randall and he was already shaking his head no. "No, of course not. Most of us do not have the ego strength to deal with rejection more than once. You asked; she answered. If you have any good sense in that head of yours you'd move onto someone else who just might be interested in you, someone who is more likely to say yes." The class was with me on this. They may or may not be dating, since most of them were only 14, but they already understood what this felt like for they'd been negotiating friendships since early childhood.

"If you continue to pursue this person after you have been turned down, well maybe you're a stalker and that's a lesson we will cover another day."

A couple of kids started talking under their breath naming students they thought were either stalkers or had been stalked.

"And just because you are attracted to someone, does that give you the right to act on that attraction, whether you are gay or straight? Can you imagine if we all acted on every sexual attraction we had? Heaven forbid, that would be mayhem. Get yourself under control." The students laughed at the very notion.

Time to shift gears again as I focused in on the point of the lesson.

"Let's assume being gay isn't a choice. Really, why would someone choose this? When as we have just seen, in some families you would be kicked out of the house, unloved, and seen as sinful by others. For some people, even their best friends would no longer invite you over to hang out and certainly not for a sleepover."

I used all of the exact language that my students had been using to drive home my point. This was what they had just said themselves.

Now the kids were talking among themselves, debating about whether people choose to be gay.

So I asked, "Do you think we choose our sexual orientation?" Hands went up, the kids wanted to weigh in on this one.

I called on Yousef. "Yousef, do you think this is a choice?"

Emphatically he said, "Yes."

Another one took the bait. "Okay, let me assume." He started to smile as I added, "You know the drill. A-S-S-U-M-E. I am going to assume as a male you are attracted to females. Right?"

"Right," he affirmed.

"So this morning as you stood in front of the mirror admiring your handsome mug and brushing your teeth you said to yourself, 'Yousef, you handsome dog, today I'm going to choose to be attracted to the ladies. Tomorrow, I might choose something else, but today it's the ladies.' Right?" I asked. "Was that how it was?" Now he was laughing.

"No, I can't help it. I'm just attracted to girls," he replied.

"My point exactly," I said.

He nodded his head as he began to see the world a little differently.

"Do you really think it's any different with gay people?" I asked. "You don't have to have all the answers here, but please just try to imagine what it would be like to walk the walk of another."

And then we shifted again.

"What kind of things do we hear when we walk these hallowed halls here at The Academy?" I asked. "How often do we hear people say, *'that's so gay.'* I paused and watched as my students began to process the impact of those three little words.

Someone tried to defend himself. "People don't mean it like that. They're just saying that something is stupid."

Others in the class turned on this boy. Their awareness was increasing right before my eyes.

"It's a terrible thing to say, it's hurtful. Can't you see that?" One student said to another and I began to feel the energy in the room shift.

It was my turn to speak. I wanted to draw the attention away from this poor kid who looked like he wanted to crawl in a hole and disappear.

"So what would happen if I substituted my own ethnicity for the word *gay*? What would it be like for me if I walked down the halls of The Academy and around every corner someone was telling Irish jokes, where the Irish person was always the butt of the joke or people were saying *'that's so Irish'* when what they really meant was *'that's so stupid?'* Do you really think I would show you the last dance steps I'd mastered in my Irish dance class or tell you about my big Irish family reunion where my 42 first cousins would be gathering? No, I don't think so. No, you would not get the benefit of knowing me as a person. I wouldn't show or tell you who I am and what it's like to be me. You are also limiting your ability to know and be known when you are acting out of prejudice." I took a deep breath and waited a moment before continuing.

"But when I feel the bigotry and prejudice here at school, I can go home to my big Irish family and feel their love and support. The gay student may or may not have that kind of support at home." Again, the students were silent.

The lecture was winding down, but not before I made my final point.

"One of the major problems that gay teenagers face is social isolation. Many may feel there is nowhere that they can just be themselves. Not at home, not at school, and not even with their dearest friends. Suicide is the second leading cause of death among young people between the ages of 10 and 24. And lesbian, gay and bi-sexual youth are four times more likely to attempt suicide than their straight peers, and young people questioning their sexual orientation are three times more likely to attempt suicide than their straight peers. This is your health class and this is your school. Your behavior and your words can help make this school a good place for all students to live, learn and grow. What you think and what you say matters." And with those final words the bell rang.

But the students sat silently in their seats until I said, "Go and be the good, kind person you are intended to be."

୬

As I packed up my belongings I thought about how grateful I was to have my job and what it meant to be a teacher. In many ways it was less than perfect, but I relished the personal freedom I'd been granted in my classroom. My goal wasn't to provide definitive answers because this particular body of knowledge was ever changing, and not stagnant. Rather, I sought to begin the inquiry process. I wanted my students to ask the questions, and to seek answers that resonated with truth, as they knew it.

I passed through the athletic corridor. The hallway was filled with students getting ready for their afterschool sports. The hallway was still abuzz and I could hear kids talking about what had gone on in health class. This was good. If they were still talking about it, then they were still thinking about it.

By the time I got back to the clinic Dr. Greg Benton and Amirah Masood were waiting for me. Greg was Amirah's advisor and the chair of the Science Department. Greg asked, "Is there somewhere we can meet privately?"

I pointed towards my little consultation room.

He said, "Amirah, I want you to wait here on the couch. Mrs. Duncan and I will be right back."

She did not respond, so he looked her in the eye and repeated, "Wait here and do not go anywhere," his voice was stern. He waited for her to acknowledge what he had said.

In response she nodded her head, and sat down on the couch. She looked down at her shoes as the wig she was wearing slipped down over her forehead nearly concealing her eyes.

I led Greg toward the consultation room. With our backs turned to Amirah I whispered, "I've been seeing her nearly every day, for at least a couple of minutes."

Earlier in the month she had taken to wearing a wig to school to cover her bald head while her hair grew in. This was probably a good idea for she appeared a little less odd. Sadly, her behavior was not. Some days her wig fell forward and the bangs covered her eyes, just like they did now. Still, she seemed to be oblivious.

Last week she had confided to me that the other girls were still talking about her. I was uncertain if this was a paranoid delusion or perhaps it was true. Fourteen year-old girls could be cruel or at least unkind.

I'd spoken with Amirah's teachers about trying to protect her from the unkind comments of others. Some of the faculty found this difficult, if not impossible. She was known to spout off in class informing her classmates how she was so much brighter and well read than any of the other ninth grade students. It didn't help that most of the time the comments she made during class were often only partially rooted in fact and were often just wrong. Her arrogance and condescension weren't helping with her ability to make and maintain relationships.

Greg followed me into the consultation room and the door closed behind us. He didn't sit down indicating this was going to be a very short meeting. "I don't know if she's medicated or if she's off her medication but she is not thinking clearly. Her grades are awful, and right now that's the least of my concerns."

I could read the worry and apprehension written all over his face.

The last letter I'd received from Amirah's psychiatrist indicated she was no longer in need of medication or therapy, and that she was safe to return to school. I didn't believe that for a minute and clearly neither did Greg Benton.

"What happened? What did she say or do?" I asked, trying to get a grip on what I was being asked to deal with.

"When I asked her for her lab report in biology she went off on a tangent about some obscure theory of genetic evolution. She informed her classmates and me that she is the lead researcher in a study on population genetics. She would have turned her lab report in, but that she was waiting to hear from her research partners at Johns Hopkins and the University of Chicago." Greg's voice was infused with frustration.

"I'm assuming that this is beyond the scope of the assignment and couldn't possibly be true," I said. I smiled as I tried to defuse the situation.

He blew out a big breath and relaxed a little. "You could say that. The lab was on the external anatomy of a frog." And with this Greg started to smile. "I'm way too far outside my field of expertise to have any idea how to help this young lady. So I'm handing her over to your capable hands," he said with a shrug. "I'm sorry. I've heard some crazy excuses when students don't have their homework. But they're lying and they know it. I'm concerned that Amirah really believes all of this to be true. I had planned to call her parents to suggest that this might not be the right school for her, and she might do better in a therapeutic environment," he concluded.

"You and I are in agreement on this one, but good luck getting her father to see it," I responded. "Thanks for bringing me into the loop. I'll talk to her."

When we opened the door Amirah didn't look up. In the short time that Greg and I had been in consultation, her wig had fallen even further over her eyes leaving the back of her bald head exposed.

I said a silent prayer for this young lady. She had to be in such emotional pain. Greg said, "Amirah, I'm going to leave now, but I want you to talk with Mrs. Duncan." And with that Greg let himself out of the clinic door. In the partially closed doorway, he paused and I read his lips as he mouthed the words, "Thank you," before closing the door completely.

I pulled up a chair, sat and faced this young lady. In a low, soft voice I asked as gently as I could, "Amirah, tell me why you think Dr. Benton brought you down here to see me."

"I didn't have my lab report," she said.

"Is that all?" I asked hoping that she would elaborate.

"No, it's not my fault," she said, and tears welled up in her eyes. "I'm just so sad. I don't have any friends and now I'm starting to do poorly in my classes." With this moment of honesty the floodgates opened and she began to sob. "I've never had any friends, but at least I've always done well in school. I'm just so tired now. I can't keep up and I'm getting confused."

I reached behind me for the box of tissues on my desk and handed it to her. She blew her nose a half a dozen times and placed the used tissues in her lap. Then a little more controlled, she took a deep breath and began to rummage through her backpack until she found a prescription bottle from a pharmacy. "My father is giving me these," she said, extending her trembling hand in my direction.

I reached out, and she allowed me to take the bottle. I turned the bottle in my hand until I could read the label, *Risperdal 3 mg–1 capsule every 12 hours.* Dr. Fatif Masood's name was on the bottle as the prescribing physician. Great. He was giving her a drug that was used to treat schizophrenia. I held onto the bottle.

"Why did your father prescribe these for you?" I asked.

"He thought they would make me feel better," she responded.

"Do they?" I asked.

"No. I'm so tired all the time and sick to my stomach too. And now my hands are all shaky. In fact, I feel shaky all over, even on the inside. So I stopped taking them last week. Please don't tell my Dad, he'll be so mad at me. He forbids me to talk to you about this or anything else. If he finds out, I'm in big trouble." Her eyes grew wide with fear.

The symptoms she described were common side effects of this medication.

"Please don't worry about that. Your dad and I want the same thing, we just want you to feel better. Okay?"

With this small bit of reassurance she seemed to relax just a little. She sat up a little straighter and readjusted her wig so she could see me.

"Amirah, have you been seeing your psychiatrist or a therapist?" I asked, but I suspected I already knew the answer.

"No, I only saw him once. My father says I don't need a psychiatrist." And with this confession something shifted in Amirah's psyche. "I have to go. I need my biology book. I'm in big trouble now. Where's my coat? My mom's picking me up. I'm already late." Her words were delivered quickly, in a disconnected jumble of ideas, and then just as abruptly she stood up, adjusted her blouse, and walked out of the clinic.

As I had suspected, if she was under the care of the psychiatrist who'd determined she was safe to be in school, then her own father would not be the person prescribing anti-psychotic medication. This was just wrong on so many levels.

It was moving on towards 4:00 PM. I knew if I didn't act quickly I would miss Will, if I hadn't already. Amirah had left in such haste that I still had her bottle of pills in my hand.

Will was in his office. He saw me through the window.

"You can run, but you cannot hide," I said entering his office.

"Do I need to hide?" he asked.

I handed him the prescription bottle. As he looked at it he said, "What is this?"

"Dear Dr. Fatif Masood is now prescribing anti-psychotic medications for his own teenage daughter. Risperdal is prescribed for schizophrenia and for people with delusions associated with severe cases of bipolar disorder, autism, violence, and self-mutilation. It's not generally prescribed for high school stress. Isn't that what we were told Amirah was suffering from– a bit of ordinary high school stress? Risperdal is prescribed by psychiatrists, not urologists, and certainly not by one's own father. It is used in combination with therapy, and oh by the way, Amirah's not in therapy.

She only saw the psychiatrist once when she needed the note to return to school."

I stopped to take a deep breath and to give Will time to catch up.

But I was on a roll, and had some things I needed to say, "Greg Benton brought her to the clinic because she's actively delusional. She now believes she's the head researcher collaborating on a human genetics project with researchers from Johns Hopkins and the University of Chicago. So she's actively delusional as well as experiencing side effects from the medication. She's tremulous, fatigued, and sick to her stomach. So in the last couple days she's taken herself off the medication without any medical supervision, which is probably why she's having break-through delusions again."

Again, I paused wanting to be certain Will understood just what it was we were dealing with here.

"Actively delusional people can hurt themselves or hurt others. This is not like the doctor who prescribes antibiotics for his own kid when they may have strep throat. This is medical misconduct. And then of course there is the school policy, which is delineated in the parent-student handbook that states students on prescription medication are required to inform the clinic and the nurse. Students may carry and self-medicate at school *only* after it has been cleared by the nurse, who just so happens to be me. Shocking that no one thought to keep me in the loop that Amirah has been self-medicating with antipsychotic medications, which are prescribed to keep hallucinations and delusions at bay." I paused and met Will's eyes. "Okay,

I'm done. Your turn." I offered a little half smile. I knew I'd just been on a bit of a rant.

Will held the bottle and rolled it around in his hand. "Where is Amirah now?" Will asked.

"She fled the clinic when it dawned on her that she'd said too much. She said her mother was waiting to pick her up."

Will picked up the phone and called the guardhouse. In a moment, Mr. Jones confirmed that Amirah had indeed left with her mother.

"When is your free period tomorrow?" he asked.

"Just after lunch," I responded as Will called the headmaster's assistant and scheduled a meeting.

"Thanks for being on top of things," he said as I stood to leave.

I smiled, "See you tomorrow."

CHAPTER 4

October 1999

It was a beautiful fall morning with just a hint of freshness in the air. The leaves on the maple trees were in their full autumn glory. This was forecasted to be the kind of day we once thought of as Indian summer. I still thought of these last warm days of autumn in this way, in spite of the fact it was no longer politically correct. I doubted that native people would object if their culture and way of life were associated with such a glorious day.

By the time I arrived at school, the young men on the football team were already walking the halls sporting their game day jerseys and all the cheerleaders were in uniform. If I didn't know any better one might think that this was just a high school. Any High School, USA. Maybe it was, maybe all high schools across the country were dealing with the same issues we were dealing with here at Halcyon Heights, but it just didn't seem like it.

It was autumn and just a month into the school year the academic pressures were already building. The seniors were busy working on their college applications and cozying up to former teachers hoping they'd put a good word in for them while they labored over their letters of recommendations. God help the teachers who taught the honors classes because every student needed at least one letter from someone who would speak to their outstanding brilliance. Luckily for me, very few students felt that a letter from their freshman health teacher could sway anyone in any admissions department.

The juniors were spending their weekends and evenings in SAT prep classes. Every unaccounted-for moment was spent memorizing the vocabulary and improving the speed of their mathematical calculations as they hoped and prayed for a score that would guarantee them a position in the university of their choosing.

I suppose it was the trickle down effect, for as the upper classmen ruminated about colleges and concerned themselves with life beyond high school, the freshmen and sophomores began to feel the pressure as well. In a world where millions of children are dying from hunger every year, the concerns of our students at the Academy of Halcyon Heights rested in collecting honors and awards that would distinguish them as the best and the brightest, and guarantee them a bigger piece of the pie.

I tried to shake it off. These kids were suffering too; it just took on a different form.

I hadn't slept very well in anticipation of my meeting with the headmaster. He had his agenda and I had mine. I knew from past experience that when our agendas conflicted I didn't stand a chance. But just last spring the massacre at Columbine High School occurred. The whole country had watched in horror. The student perpetrators were dead, along with 13 of their classmates and teachers. What had set them off? We could only speculate, but those of us who worked with students learned a lesson that day– if it could happen there, it could happen anywhere. For the safety and well being of all the young people under our care, we had better be paying attention.

There had been warning signs at Columbine and there were warning signs here. We also had students who were emotionally unstable and mentally ill. Besides Amirah, there was Patrick, Raúl, and Durgya to name a few. When people are in emotional pain, sometimes they turn that pain and anger inward and are a danger to themselves, and sometimes they turn it outward and are a danger to others. It was our obligation to keep them safe until the crisis passed. At least this was my perspective; I hoped I wasn't going to be left singing solo.

I had voiced my concerns to the headmaster that I felt we were ill prepared should a disaster strike our school. Other schools across the country were getting prepared. In response to my concern I was asked to chair another committee and develop a plan to deal with traumatic incidents. Great, here was another unfunded mandate from the front office.

Teaching could be a great distraction. I had back-to-back classes all morning and a meeting with the Crisis Team over lunch. Will and I were on the same page; we would bring the Crisis Team up to speed on the latest craziness with Amirah after we'd met with the headmaster. Our colleagues had a long list of concerns about other students that needed to be addressed. I took notes during the meeting and made plans to meet with teachers, students, and to follow-up with parents as needed.

This meeting really should have been rescheduled for a day other than Friday. There was no possible way I could get a handle on all of this before dismissal at 3:20. I would do my best. It was all I could ever do. I hoped to God it would be good enough.

Will and I left the Crisis Team meeting and walked directly to the headmaster's office. His assistant Martha ushered us in and we took our seats around the long mahogany table in the conference room. In less than a minute George entered the room. Will and I both stood and shook his hand before he took his seat at the end of the long table. After exchanging a moment or two of idle, friendly chatter, George got down to business. "So, what brings you to my office on this beautiful fall afternoon?" I sat quietly while Will recounted the latest issues that had transpired with Amirah. George's whole demeanor changed. He leaned back and folded his arms across his chest as he listened.

Will spoke for both of us when he said, "I think that Amirah is actively delusional and needs psychiatric help. The fact that her father is prescribing psychiatric medications and that she is not under the care of a psychiatrist troubles me greatly. We expressed our concerns a month ago and Dr. Masood, by being less than forthcoming, has thwarted our attempts to help his daughter. I fear for Amirah's safety and the safety of the others in this building. I think she needs to be dismissed until she is psychologically healthy enough to meet the rigor of The Academy. I believe this young lady would be better served in a therapeutic school."

George shook his head slowly. "Amirah is Dr. Masood's minor daughter. He is a medical doctor and clearly he has his own daughter's best interest at heart," he said before he got to the real heart of the issue. "He is also a major donor here at Halcyon Heights. In fact, he made a $100,000 donation to the biology program just last week. But . . . " his eyes flashed with an unsettled awareness as he looked first to Will and then to me, "you didn't hear that here. I think that was supposed to be an anonymous donation. Anyway we will not be interfering."

Then he stood up to signal the meeting was over.

Maybe this was what people with executive power did. They made decisions easily. In this situation there had been no real inquiry, concern or space made to discuss the pros or cons of what might be the best course of action for Amirah. There was no discussion of what the inherent risks for this child were or the risks for the school and everyone in it. There was no discussion.

The decision had been made.

As I walked towards the door to the outer office George said, "Keep up the good work Elise. Just keep an eye on her. I'm sure she'll be fine."

Right-O Buck-O. Money talks and the bullshit walks. I wonder if the timing of Dr. Masood's substantial donation was purely coincidental to the very real possibility that his mentally-ill daughter may not be allowed to continue at Halcyon Heights? A coincidence? No possible way. I wonder what else is for sale at this prestigious institution?

The voice in my head was running at full force saying all the things I dared not. Perhaps I had more in common with Amirah than I cared to admit. The difference was I still knew enough not to speak these thoughts aloud.

Will walked beside me and as I turned to head down the athletic corridor he said, "We tried."

I nodded and kept walking.

One more hour before school would be over. I had three kids I needed to touch base with before they'd leave for the weekend. School could be a safe place for some of these kids, at least when their time was accounted for and the faculty kept an eye on things. Weekends, however, could be a crapshoot. Anything could happen– some of it good, and some of it not so good. I wanted to be certain some of the most vulnerable of this tribe knew that someone was checking in on them, that someone cared enough to ask about their plans. The number of students who had my home phone number was growing. Very few ever called, but it was a safety net.

By the time I'd found all three the final bell had already rung and chaos ensued. The athletic corridor was filled with student athletes and others who were hanging out, making plans for a weekend rendezvous. But the real buzz in the air was about *The Game*. Friday night football under the lights, and the undefeated Falcons had a home game.

I made my way to my classroom to put a few things away. The football teams or the coaches often used my classroom, because it was right across the hall from the men's locker room. There were a few things I used during class, like electronics and anatomical models that I wanted to be certain didn't grow legs and walk away. The cheerleaders, their faculty sponsor Nina Dominion, as well as a dozen mothers were already in my room rearranging the furniture in preparation for the *team meal.*

My desk had been covered with a tablecloth and would be used to hold the silverware, paper plates and paper napkins in the team colors of green and gold. The table at the front of the classroom had been turned into the buffet table. It looked like a feast befitting an Italian wedding with a variety of salads and lasagna, meatballs, sausages, cheeses, and a sweets table. The only thing missing was the wine.

"I hope you don't mind," Nina smiled.

What could I say? Plenty, but instead I bit my tongue and smiled. "Just let me get a few things and I'll be on my way."

"Will we see you at the game tonight?" Nina asked as I moved the vase of long stem yellow roses and locked some papers in my desk drawer.

"No, I'm headed home to spend some time with my children. I'll have enough spectator sports tomorrow as both Ian and Shea have soccer games." I smiled. I knew I had just stepped into it.

"You're not going? I haven't missed a single game in 23 years. You just can't teach here and not go to the games." Her tone was sweet, but the message was not. Every Friday night in the fall, if the Falcons had a home game this prestigious college prep school took on the persona of a small Texas town.

"I guess I just bleed green and gold," she said and then giggled. "I guess I would do just about anything to support *our boys.*" It was positively coquettish and not in the least bit becoming on a grown woman in her mid-forties.

"I'm needed at home tonight to support my boy and my girl." I smiled as I put the new digital video projector onto a cart so I could lock it in the clinic.

I had already devoted enough of my life force to the raising of other people's children this week. I was unwilling to give up my Friday night too. I needed to have something left for my own children. We were approaching the one-year anniversary of Elliot's death and I was needed at home.

"You should bring your kids to the game!" She said. It was the glee in her voice that betrayed her; she was a former cheerleader.

Ah … now I knew whom I was dealing with. She acted as if she'd just solved this major dilemma for me. Just bring the kids. This was not a dilemma for me, major or minor. I had no interest in being at the game and neither did my children.

"And when are you going to bring your children here?" Now her tone had changed. She was deeply entrenched in the culture of The Academy.

After the week that I had just had– *when was I going to bring my precious and beloved children into this den of iniquity?* I asked myself. The voice within answered, *how about never.*

The fact that my children were not enrolled at The Academy of Halcyon Heights and the fact that I didn't attend the extracurricular events were a clear indication that I had not yet drunk the Kool-Aid. I was right, people *had* noticed.

"My kids are happy and doing well in school. Since their dad died they have been through a lot of changes. I'm trying to keep things as stable for them as I can. I don't think changing schools and leaving their friends is a good idea right now." All this was true, and really none of her business, but somehow I'd felt compelled to answer. Perhaps she would inform the powers that be.

I needed this job and I needed to remember that. "Maybe I'll bring them to the homecoming game. When is it?" I asked as I wheeled the cart out into the hallway.

"Two weeks. Be there. Remember *our boys* need us," she called out after me in her old school cheerleader voice. As I turned to look back I expected to see her doing a jump and shaking her pom poms.

I entered the hallway with my cart. Coach Sean Brogan was red faced and ranting on about something, and calling out one of his players, " . . . and I don't want to see you actin' like a little skirt tonight." He stopped talking as I negotiated the cart around the long legs of the boys sprawled out on the wooden benches on either side of the corridor.

I must have shot him a look of disdain.

"Sorry Mrs. Duncan, I didn't mean any offense," the coach said.

I became acutely aware of the little skirt I was wearing amidst the sea of testosterone and physical magnitude of these boys who lived in men's bodies. They pulled their legs in as I passed. They were waiting to gain entrance to my classroom where the elaborate spread awaited them.

I heard the door open behind me. "Dinner is served," one of the cheerleaders announced. The football players created a ruckus as they headed into the classroom for dinner. I wondered when the football team would be making and serving dinner for the cheerleaders. That's a good one. I think it's on the Twelfth of Never. I'd better mark my calendar.

I grabbed my purse and a stack of journals I needed to review over the weekend. I locked the door and headed for the parking lot. I was going home.

On the drive to pick up my kids I had time to replay the final incident of this very long day.

A little skirt, a little skirt indeed.

Was that how the great Coach Brogan referred to women? He was supposed to be a role model for these young men. He was a bully, he probably always had been. I knew his type. He meant no offense. That was what he'd said, but I was offended.

Why? I think it was because his tone was demeaning and derogatory, and the greatest insult he could come up with was to compare his players to a woman.

I was insulted.

What exactly were we teaching here at The Academy of Halcyon Heights?

By the time I'd retrieved my kids from the afterschool latchkey program, Ian and Shea were as ready for the weekend as I was. Quickly, I shifted into mother mode and they began actively negotiating sleepovers, where we should go for dinner, and if I would take them to the movies. It was a glorious feeling to be in the company of my own children. At this point in their young lives, what they wanted and desired was well within my ability to provide: the movies, pizza, and a sleepover. It was a time when it was easy to say yes and savor their gratitude. I felt like it was the first time I had satisfied anyone all day.

But the weekend passed all too quickly, as they so often did, and sadly in a blink of an eye it was Monday morning and we were all back in school again.

After the weekly Monday morning faculty meeting, which covered content that I either already knew or generally didn't pertain to my work or me, I headed off to teach my first class. When I arrived, I found the dirty dishes and leftover food from the football team's banquet had been sitting in my classroom and on my desk all weekend. I nearly blew a gasket. It was all I could do to refrain from exuding a litany of expletives.

Trust me, I knew all the words and I'd been known to use them. But my students were there with the wide-eyed innocence of youth. They were watching and taking note.

How do mature adults behave in such situations? They would learn by the example I would set right then and there. "Excuse me for a moment," I said as I exited the classroom and rounded the corner to the Athletic Department.

"Hi Elise, can I help you?" said Christine the bright and beautiful young woman who worked as the administrative assistant for Athletic Director and Football Coach.

"Hi Christine, is Sean in?" I asked.

"No, he doesn't usually get in until sometime in the afternoon. I know he won't be in early today, not after the big win on Friday night and all." She smiled.

Was this his some justification for working an abbreviated schedule when everyone else started at 7:30 AM day in and day out?

"Okay," I said and I turned to leave. "Will you have him come by and see me when he gets in?"

She nodded.

"Do you have a key to the training room? I need to get some garbage bags so I can clean up my classroom. Looks like the home team was in a little bit of a hurry to get on the field after their pre-game dinner last Friday." I stated and then I drew my lips together to keep myself from saying anything more.

With that Christine was coming around her desk and handed me her keys. She followed me into the classroom. She looked around the room and said, "They should be ashamed of themselves leaving your room like this. You should just leave this for the team to clean up," she stated emphatically.

To which I responded, "And where would I teach my classes today?" Christine and some of my students began to help pick up as I went across the hall to the training room for a roll of trash bags.

I was surprised to find four or five of the football players in the training room. "Excuse me gentlemen, but what are you doing in here?"

Evan Hedges spoke up, "Just getting some tape and ice for Jordan's ankle. He twisted it during the game on Friday."

"Are you okay, Jordan?" I asked.

"Yes, Mrs. Duncan I'll be fine," he said.

"Good, then I want all of you boys to give me a hand in my classroom," I said. Evan and Jordan and the other two boys followed me across the hall, where we spent the first 10 minutes of class time cleaning up the space, scraping the leftover food from crusty casserole dishes into the trash bag, stacking the dishes in the big sink in the training room, putting them to soak in some hot soapy water, before we washed down all the sticky desks with some spray cleaner that I kept in my drawer. Some of the students helped and some of them just watched. It wasn't difficult to see how differently some of these kids had been raised.

As we finished and took the trash to the hallway, I asked Christine, "Could you call housekeeping and ask them to pick up the trash bags outside my door?"

"We'll take the bags out to the dumpster, Mrs. Duncan," Evan said. Two of the boys grabbed the bags and the other two boys followed close behind.

"Thanks guys," I said.

"I'm going to tell Coach Brogan about this too," Christine said.

I smiled at her. "Just have him come by and see me, okay? Thanks for your help."

And with that I started class.

By the time lunch rolled around, word of how my classroom had been left was common knowledge. My students had described the mess to other students and their other teachers. Word traveled quickly. I thought I'd done a pretty good job of concealing my anger. Although I'd controlled my tongue, the students still knew I was seething. Coach Brogan finally stuck his head in the clinic at the end of the day before assembling his troops for football practice. Lucky for him I had cooled off considerably.

"Hey Elise, I'm sorry about the mess that was left in your classroom. I thought the cheerleaders and Nina would have cleaned it up. I'll talk with her. It won't happen again," he said.

I nodded to acknowledge that I had heard him. Typical. He assumed no responsibility for the conduct of his players. Instead he shifted the blame to the cheerleaders who'd provided and served the food before they'd been dismissed. Did he really think it was the women's responsibility to clean up after his players?

Before he headed back down the hall he asked, "Did you see the game? We're headed for the State Championship sure as shootin."

He didn't wait for a response.

Good thing, because I had nothing to say.

For the love of God, had I been transported back to the middle ages? In less than two months we would be celebrating the arrival of the new millennium, and yet right here in 1999 this Neanderthal still believed that these young women had been put on earth for the sole purpose of serving the needs of the young warrior princes who were doing battle on the gridiron for the glory of The Academy. I wanted to cry. How would I ever combat this pervasive culture of privilege?

The first Thursday Night in October was always Meet the Faculty Night. The program was scheduled to begin at 7:00 PM. The evening started where the parents met with the headmaster and the director of the school for a little socializing and what had come to be known as *The Ask*, as in, asking for an annual donation. Apparently the tuition payment of $25,000 per child per year wasn't enough. The headmaster was again asking parents to dig down into their deep pockets and find some money for the new capital campaign, money for our New World Campus.

Blah, blah, blah . . . I'd heard enough. It was time to slip out the backdoor and return to my classroom.

The parents were supposed to arrive as soon as George wrapped things up. The teachers were hanging around in the hallways talking in hushed whispers amongst themselves.

"He's running off at the mouth."

"The man has no regard for anyone's time."

"He has a captive audience and it looks like the dear old boy intends to make the most of it."

The only problem was that this wasn't a cocktail party and all the parents were supposed to be following their children's schedule. Classes were only ten minutes long to begin with. Now, we would be running late all evening.

"Take a deep breath. In just two hours this whole charade will be over for another year," one of the English teachers said as I passed him on the way back to my classroom.

It had already been a long day. The teachers had been at school since 7:30 in the morning, taught all day, and by the time we finished it would be well after 9:30 PM. Plus I had another hour to drive before I'd get home. Ah well . . .

The parents made their way to the first class. Instead of the ten minutes we are supposed to have we now had four. I had just enough time to pass out a copy of the syllabus, give the parents my email information, and a flyer on how to access the online grade book.

The online grade book was new that year. It was perfect for the parent who was interested in micro-managing their children's high school grades, and trust me, some of them did, to say nothing of writing their papers.

This was my third *Meet the Faculty Night* and I was beginning to feel like an old pro. The word among the seasoned teachers was to start on time, end on time, and just keep talking.

If you allowed the parents the opportunity to ask questions you would never cover anything about your class. Those who had been here for a while knew there were always one or two parents who would be pushing their own agenda. This was not the time to entertain questions. If you left an opening you would never get your time back.

No one ever covered everything they'd planned to cover. Parents wanted the syllabus. They wanted to know how grades were calculated. How could Junior get an A? How could I reach you if Junior didn't get an A? So the faculty shared their email addresses, phone numbers etc, etc.

I was pretty certain the geometry teacher wasn't under as much scrutiny as I was. I was teaching about sex and drugs and everybody was an expert, at least in the area of sex. They'd all had sex; after all they were parents. Their opinions ran the gamut as to what they wanted me to tell their little darlings so they didn't have to.

After one of the classes a woman stopped by my desk on the way out the door. "Do you know my son, Bobby Junior?" she asked with a sweet southern drawl.

I thought for a moment. The southern drawl gave her away. "Bob? Oh yes of course. You must be Mrs. Erickson." I surmised. He didn't go by Bobby Junior no matter what his mama called him. Bob was a big boy, a hockey player, and a funny kid.

"I'd like to be a fly on the wall in your classroom. My dear little Bobby is so shy and so sweet. He must be a blushin' and turnin' cherry red with all of this teachin' about the birds and the bees."

"Bob Erickson? Right?" We couldn't be talking about the same kid.

She smiled and nodded before she scurried off to the next class.

Huh, sweet little Bobby Erickson. The sweet little fella who'd asked about edible condoms. He wanted to know if they were safe and what flavors they made. Oh, he was so very shy and retiring. Mama here would get another look at her dear sweet little boy if she had been that fly on the wall. I think the only one who would be blushing would be Mrs. Erickson.

My next class of parents began to arrive. I wondered who was related to whom. Some had stopped at the reception table and were wearing nametags, but not everyone. It was always interesting to see who sat next to whom. The early arrivals chose their seats first and as others came in they sat where they were most comfortable. By the time the class was filled it was easy to see the racial and ethnic distribution.

There were the mothers who came to class dressed to the nines. They chatted and giggled through my entire presentation as they made plans with one another for some upcoming social affair at their country clubs, while their male counterparts, the fathers shook hands and talked sports.

There were the corporate parents, some traveling solo and others in pairs, who had raced to get here after work. Some with their careworn faces looked like they hadn't had a moment of leisure in decades.

Time was their most precious commodity. If they had allotted the time to be here, then this had damn well better be worthwhile. They sat in silence, checked their watches, took notes, and made no attempt to hide their disdain and annoyance with the giggling women in the back of the classroom.

Mine was a ninth grade class and there were always a large number of new students in the ninth grade, including kids on scholarship or financial aid. Their parents were as new to the social protocol at the Halcyon Academy as the children were. This was the first *adults only* evening and some of the new parents appeared like fish out of water. Some of the parents had dressed like they were going to church, and others like they had just run out to the grocery store for a gallon of milk. It was like a big social experiment with people of every race, religion, and national origin, to say nothing of culture, economic class, political ideology and expectations.

There was little doubt that all of these parents wanted the same thing: they wanted what was best for their children.

They hoped to find it here.

The question that was still unanswered was: could we deliver on what had been promised?

The array of parents in my classroom was not unlike the diversity of students that came to class every day. All the parents came to class: the reasonable and the overbearing, the quiet and the loud, the lax and the over-protective.

The apples didn't fall far from the trees.

It had been a long week and it was only Thursday. But at last it was time to drive home.

～

TGIF, Thank God It's Friday. The word among the teachers was– if we could make it to Thanksgiving, then we could make it. After Thanksgiving there were regularly scheduled breaks: Thanksgiving Break, The Holiday Break (formerly known as The Christmas Break), Mid-Winter Break, and Spring Break. But it was a long run from Labor Day until Thanksgiving, and Thanksgiving was still 6 weeks away.

At lunchtime on Friday I was at the Crisis Team meeting with a half a dozen of my colleagues including Will. There was a knock on the conference room door. Liz, Will's assistant, stuck her head in the room. This was highly unlikely, as these meetings were rarely interrupted, given the sensitive nature of what was discussed.

Liz's usual cheerful smile was gone. Something was wrong and it showed on her face. She appeared disturbed and with a short halting delivery she said, "Sorry to disturb you. Mr. Warwick and Ms. Duncan, I need to see you." She motioned for us to meet her in the hallway.

Both Will and I rose and met Liz in the corridor. "Amirah Masood has left campus. The police called. They found her walking down the median on Lancaster Avenue. She was miles from campus, incoherent, and crying about her bad grades. Initially, she wouldn't tell the officer her name, but she was wearing her blazer with the school crest on the pocket. Apparently, when Officer Maxwell threatened to call the school to find out who she was, she reluctantly provided him with her name. The police found a small silver packet in her blazer pocket. It had been opened and the contents were missing. She said she had taken and consumed some chemicals from Dr. Benton's science lab. They've taken her by ambulance to Chesterfield General Hospital." Liz sighed deeply. She had done her part. The message had been delivered.

"Dear God. We knew it was only a matter of time before Amirah would derail," Will said. He took a deep breath. "Now what?" he said. He was contemplating the next course of action.

"Do you know what she took?" I asked.

Liz shook her head. "The police officer told me what it was and I wrote it down, but it didn't mean anything to me. I have the note on my desk," she said.

"Would you go get Dr. Benton and have him meet me in my office? Can you find coverage for his class?" he asked Liz.

"Of course," she responded as she went off to the science wing to find Greg.

I followed Will back to his office and he closed the door behind us. He picked up the pink phone message that sat front and center on his desk. It was marked urgent. I sat with him while he dialed the phone number for Officer Maxwell.

By listening to Will's side of the conversation I was able to determine that Amirah was indeed in the

Emergency Room at Chesterfield General. Her parents had been called and her mother was already at the hospital. Her father was on his way and was expected shortly. The police officer was going on and on about how when he found Amirah she was jabbering incoherently. She exhibited signs of mental confusion and emotional distress. He continued to refer to this as a suicide attempt.

Will asked, "I know you told my assistant what it was that Amirah took from the lab, but she's not here right now. Can you tell me what it was?" he asked and he picked up a pen and wrote something on the pad of paper on his desk.

With that, Greg Benton walked in and took a seat next to me. We sat silently while Will thanked the officer and hung up the phone.

After Will brought Greg up to speed, Greg said, " I'm sorry. I knew she was upset because she failed her biology test ... miserably. Poor dear, her ego is so fragile. It's as if she has no personal value except as an academic, and when she does poorly she loses that too. I should've called her father. But I didn't. I'd planned to see him during conferences. He's such a prig. The truth is I was hoping to limit my exposure to him." Greg chastised himself. His voice was filled with remorse.

"Amirah was in my classroom studying while I was getting set-up for a lab. She left and I locked my door before I went to lunch. I can't imagine what she could have gotten into." Greg clearly was upset as he tried to recreate what might have happened.

Again I asked, "Do we know what she took?"

"She gave the officer a foil wrapper that was labeled," Will looked down at his notepad, "N-A-C-L."

I looked over at Greg and we both smiled as I said, "NaCl is sodium chloride or ordinary table salt."

Then we all laughed with relief.

Greg added, "She's delusional all right. NaCl won't hurt her but there are plenty of chemicals in our science labs that if she ingested could be toxic or worse. Some could be fatal if taken orally."

"I have a hard time figuring out what she actually knows," I said. "She's a bright girl even though she suffers with cognitive delusions. Did she know this was just salt and was just seeking attention or had she thought it was something else and intended to hurt herself?" I posed the question, not seeking any answers. "Either way, we always take threats of suicide seriously. We invoke the protocol. No student can return to school until they have psychiatric clearance," I said and Will nodded.

"You're absolutely right, Elise. Because of our protocol, a heavy dose of dumb luck, and blessings from above, we've never lost a student to suicide," Will said.

Both Will and Greg shook their heads. "I'd better get over to the hospital. The good Dr. Masood and I need to have a little tête à tête. I also need to talk with the headmaster before he catches wind of this latest development in the ongoing saga of Miss Amirah Masood. I'll call him from my cell phone. I'll call you both at home, when and if I know anything more."

Will left for the hospital and Greg and I went back to class. The three of us were of one mind on this– this young lady was unsafe to be in school. There was so much more that had been left unsaid. Why waste one's breath?

By the time I arrived home that night there was a message on my home answering machine from Will. "Amirah will not be returning to school this semester. I discussed alternative therapeutic schools with Amirah's parents, but it's highly unlikely that Dr. Masood will choose to exercise one of those options. He appears to be leaning towards home schooling his daughter and having her re-apply for admission next fall as a sophomore. Have a good weekend, Elise. Thanks for all you do. See you Monday," and with that he hung up.

This poor girl, I couldn't imagine what her life must be like. She was falling apart mentally and emotionally. She was not getting the care she so badly needed. Her father couldn't and wouldn't acknowledge that he had a mentally ill child. He somehow felt that her illness reflected poorly on him, and now he was signing up to be her one and only teacher.

I pinned what little hope that remained on the hospital psychiatric team. Perhaps they would keep her until Amirah was better equipped to cope with her dysfunctional home life, her pompous, overbearing father, and her spineless mother.

I knew it was a pipe dream. Health care for the mentally ill was like a revolving door. Law enforcement brought the mentally ill to the hospital, the doctors medicated, and the insurance companies, public and private, determined when it was time to release them, until their next psychiatric break with reality when law enforcement would bring them back to the hospital, and the cycle would repeat. When treating the mentally ill within our American health care system, we medicated for the symptoms, but all too often did little or nothing to address the root of the problem.

Poor Amirah, her problems were rooted in her home, and unfortunately she was probably too old to be adopted.

The problems were obvious, the solutions less so.

I wondered how it had all played out. Will was not in an enviable position. I knew in my heart that the school's very existence hinged on the donations of big bucks from the well-heeled parents and alumni. The headmaster was directly responsible for seeing that the endowment grew annually. I wasn't naïve enough to think otherwise. Dr. Masood was a big donor, and therefore he was catered to like a crown prince.

I also knew that the teachers and faculty were expendable and could be replaced without cause. My contract spelled that out clearly.

But now the police and social services had been brought into this, and Amirah was deemed a danger to herself. This could no longer be dealt with as a private matter.

The big donor could no longer purchase the desired response. It was no longer on the table. It was no longer up for sale.

I was certain if the police and social services hadn't been brought into this, it would have played out very differently. Teachers were a dime a dozen, expendable, and easily replaced, but a donor with full pockets didn't just come around every day.

How many times would the right and just solution be cast aside because someone with a self-serving agenda made a big donation? I was left to wonder–what else was for sale here at The Academy? Was everything negotiable if the price was right? How long before the rumbling of injustice would end with more than just surface cracks in the veneer? We had been lucky that this young girl hadn't been injured and didn't hurt herself, if that was indeed what she had intended.

The ground was shifting.

The earthquake had been diverted– this time.

Next time, we might not be so lucky.

But it was the weekend, and I wasn't about to let the drama of the day ruin it. It was time for me to think of something else, time to do something else.

I grabbed my coat and my kids, and we took our new little puppy for a walk around the lake at twilight. It was a beautiful October evening. The moon was full, rising golden and mystical up and over the lake. By the time we got home, my focus had shifted and I was once again in mother mode. And that was a beautiful place to be. I wasn't about to let my issues with the school impact my personal life and my family.

❦

It was hard to believe that in 1999 high schools across the nation were still celebrating homecoming.

Not that when people return to their hometowns or alma maters after being away for years or even decades was not worthy of celebration. Rather, it was the way it was celebrated with all the pomp and circumstance once reserved for victorious knights returning from a battle or arriving for a royal coronation.

Maybe homecomings were nothing more than the modern day equivalents. Had the knights of old been replaced by virile young men on the football field? The opponents for the big game had been carefully selected so that victory was assured. Were the homecoming queen and the dazzling young women on the homecoming court the closest thing we had to high school royalty? Followed by the homecoming ball where matches were made and fates were sealed, at least for the evening? Or was this nothing more than a little harmless teenage fun?

Yet, there were times when I saw life at The Academy through the eyes of singer-songwriter Janis Ian:

> *I learned the truth at seventeen*
> *That love was meant for beauty queens*
> *And high school girls with clear-skinned smiles*
> *Who married young and then retired*
> *The valentines I never knew*
> *The Friday night charades of youth*
> *Were spent on one more beautiful*
> *At seventeen I learned the truth*
> *And those of us with ravaged faces*
> *Lacking in the social graces*

Desperately remained at home
Inventing lovers on the phone
Who called to say, "Come dance with me"
And murmured vague obscenities
It isn't all it seems at seventeen
A brown-eyed girl in hand-me-downs
Whose name I never could pronounce
Said, "Pity, please, the ones who serve
'Cause they only get what they deserve"
And the rich-relationed hometown queen
Marries into what she needs
With a guarantee of company
And haven for the elderly
So remember those who win the game
Lose the love they sought to gain
In debentures of quality and dubious integrity
Their small town eyes will gape at you
In dull surprise when payment due
Exceeds accounts received at seventeen
To those of us who knew the pain
Of valentines that never came
And those whose names were never called
When choosing sides for basketball
It was long ago and far away
The world was younger than today
When dreams were all they gave for free
To ugly duckling girls like me
We all play the game and when we dare
To cheat ourselves at solitaire
Inventing lovers on the phone
Repenting other lives unknown
They call and say, "Come on, dance with me"

And murmur vague obscenities
At ugly girls like me at seventeen

Perhaps this was just the point of view of a cynical aging prom queen, but it appeared that all the broken hearts and hurt feelings could never be justified by this school-sanctioned circus. The competitions were based on an ill-conceived set of values.

Mirror, mirror on the wall who's the fairest of them all? Who's the strongest? Who's the fastest? Who's the most beautiful? Who's the most popular? Who are the winners and who are the losers? But I'd forgotten, it wasn't about the students, it never had been. No, homecoming was about bringing the alumni home. And oh, by the way, don't forget your checkbooks.

So during the entire month of October the question that occupied the students at Halcyon Heights was: whom are you going to homecoming with?

Most working adults have days when they loathe their jobs, but I counted myself among the fortunate, because there were days when I loved my job.

Most days there was an incident that could rival anything found on Comedy Central. You couldn't make this stuff up and yet it flowed out of the mouths of my students on a regular basis.

One afternoon before homecoming I was sitting in the clinic trying to get some papers graded before the weekend. Four juniors, three girls and one boy were sitting on the beds chatting. This wasn't uncommon as there were many students who preferred to hang out in the clinic rather than go to study hall, mostly because my colleague, Joanne, was the sweetest woman on the planet.

Maria, one of the four, was a big girl with an even bigger heart and a larger-than- life personality. She exuded confidence, generosity, and made us laugh almost every day. She was a member of our frequent flyer club as she was in the clinic at least once every day and usually more often. That afternoon she was bemoaning the fact that her boyfriend was angry because she'd accepted a date with a friend to attend his homecoming at another school. She had spent most of the hour berating her boyfriend as well as all other mammals with a penis. Her girlfriends sat around and added fuel to the fire when Maria decided to draw Hideki into the mix.

Now Hideki was also a junior and a bit of a bookworm and these girls liked him well enough. They thought he was funny, but they would never give poor Hideki a second glance when considering potential dates for the big homecoming dance.

Maria posed a hypothetical situation for Hideki to consider. "Let's say you have the chance to take a beautiful girl to homecoming. You've had a crush on her for months. It's absolutely confirmed that she will agree to go with you, however, it's also been confirmed that there's not a snowball's chance in hell that she'll sleep with you. Your alternative is to ask this other girl. The problem is that she's ugly but she's guaranteed to sleep with you. So, who do you ask?"

As this gaggle of girls sat around Hideki and awaited his answer, he looked so uncomfortable. He knew there was no easy way out of this one. Poor fella, he looked like he wanted to crawl under the bed and wait for the bell.

Not a chance, the girls pressed him for an answer.
At last Hideki responded. "Just how ugly is she?"

Everyone within earshot burst out laughing. Maria
yelled, "I just peed my pants," and darted into the
bathroom.

Just another day on the job.

Later that week, I found myself in a casual
conversation with a student I had in class last year.
Janelle sat with me in the clinic. She slumped onto
the couch and began talking about the homecoming
dance. It had monopolized everyone's attention for
weeks.

She clearly wanted to talk, so when I provided a
little time, space, and a listening ear, she opened up
and told me what was weighing heavy on her heart.
She'd been asked to the dance by a couple of guys,
and her mother had been encouraging her to go. But
she had turned both boys down and had decided she
wasn't going to go to the dance.

"Neither of the guys are talking to me anymore.
I thought we were friends or at least friendly. But
they want to be friends with benefits and I'm not all
that interested in losing my virginity on someone's
basement floor." She heaved a sigh of frustration and
I feared she might break into tears.

I handed her a tissue and got up to close my office
door.

"My mother can't believe I turned down Alex Paul
and Benson Bell. She knows their parents and they're
from such *good families*. Whatever that means. I could
just puke. Like she has any idea what she's talking

about." Janelle took a moment to dry her eyes. "When I told Benson *no*, he was unbelievably rude to me. That kid has a bad temper. I don't believe anyone has ever told him *no* before, about anything. Now that I've seen him for who he really is, I wouldn't go to the grocery store with Benson Bell. He scares me."

The door handle to the clinic rattled as another student checked to see if the clinic was open.

"I guess I'm just not interested in this debutante cotillion. I'm still a kid and I couldn't care less about making the right connections and the merging of family fortunes. I feel like I'm trapped in the middle ages." She took the tissue and blew her nose.

"Poor Mom, she went so far as to tell me how *hot* she thinks Alex is and that Benson is a great catch. A *catch*– what are we doing– going fishing?"

She didn't need any encouragement. She just needed to vent.

"I think Mom wishes she was going. Poor dear, I think she's starting to question my sexual orientation. Wouldn't that keep her up at night if her only daughter liked girls? How could she ever explain *that* to the ladies at the club? I tried to reassure her that I do like boys. I just don't want to go. She acts like I'm missing out on the best part of my entire upper school experience."

"Can you tell your mom the reason you don't want to go?" I asked.

"I've thought about it, but what if there comes a time when I do want to go?" She asked without expecting a response. "I just don't want to deal with all of her fret and worry about my personal business. I think I'm old enough to make these decisions on my own." she said.

"Okay, asked and answered."

"Nope, I'm going to the movies," she said. "I can't wait for homecoming and all of the hoopla to be over." She looked sad but resigned.

In all that had been left unsaid, I felt her wretched sorrow. She would have liked to go to the dance. She felt she might be missing out on the fun, but in other ways she had decided that the cost of participation was too dear. She wasn't going to put herself in that position. I admired her honesty, her strength and ability to hold fast to what she felt was right for her.

The Saturday before *the big weekend* I had been at the Farmer's Market with my daughter buying bags full of ripe tomatoes, peppers, onions, and mushrooms before the first frost. Shea and I planned to make our spaghetti sauce and put it up in canning jars for the winter. It was a ritual we participated in every year. I had done it with my mother and my mother with hers. The only difference was they'd actually grown all of the tomatoes in their own gardens. We were looking over the produce and it had been a good year for the gardeners. Everyone had more produce than they'd sell. My cell phone rang, interrupting our mother-daughter outing and our precious time together.

I didn't recognize the number. "Hello," I answered, not knowing who might be on the other end.

"Mrs. Duncan?" the voice on the other end asked as the woman tried to ascertain if she had indeed reached the right person.

"Yes," I responded.

"This is Louellen Briggs, Maribelle's mother. I am sorry to bother you on the weekend but I thought maybe you could help."

I held up a finger to my daughter Shea, indicating I would be with her in just a moment. "Yes, what can I do for you? Is everything alright?" I asked.

"Oh yes . . . well, no not really. I'm so sorry to bother you, but the kids are trying to decide who will be traveling with whom in the limo to the homecoming dance and we thought maybe you could help sort this out."

Was this woman for real? "What exactly is the problem?" I asked. I wasn't interested in any chitchat with this woman on my day off. Where was this delineated in my twenty-page contract? Come on, you're an adult and her mother, for God's sake, just deal with this.

Mrs. Briggs went on to explain. "Well, there are only 6 seats in the limo and 4 couples that want to go together. I'm afraid Maribelle and her date may be the ones left out," she said, her voice quivered and it sounded as if she might breakdown into tears.

I looked at Shea, she was ready to get home and get cooking.

"Perhaps Maribelle could ask two other couples to go with her and her date, and you could rent another limo or one of the parents could drive and act as the chauffeur?" I offered, because I knew Maribelle didn't have her driver's license yet.

"Maribelle will never consent to having her father or me drive her. Not when everyone else is traveling by limo. Do you know of any other kids who don't have a limo yet?" she asked.

"No, I'm not usually in the loop on these things. But why don't you have Maribelle stop by my office on Monday and we can do some brainstorming together," I suggested.

In response, Mrs. Briggs acted as if I had just found the cure for cancer.

Shea had overheard my side of the conversation. My nine-year-old responded, "You've got to be kidding me. They're calling you for stuff like this on a Saturday? Those people need to grow up and figure it out for themselves."

Wisdom proclaimed– out of the mouths of babes.

I thought about all of the mothers out buying evening gowns and making hair appointments for the deflowering of their virgin daughters. There was something unseemly about this entire homecoming ritual.

The adults who sanctioned this event were either closing their eyes or didn't care enough to look at what was really happening. We had offered up the vestal virgins and orchestrated sexual liaisons for both the boys and girls. Parents hired the limousines, opened their homes to all night parties, and provided the liquor or at least looked the other way.

The child in me still remembered what it was like to be young. I remember the anticipation of love and romance and a night of make-believe. We would make-believe we were all grown up. It was a night where dreams were bought and sold as if they were the crown jewels of one's entire high school experience. But, that was many years ago and maybe not all that much had changed, except my perspective. Now my adult observer saw things differently and wondered–

> *what's it good for . . . absolutely nothing*
> *–Edwin Starr*

Why did schools across the country continue to orchestrate such events? It may have made sense in centuries gone by, when the average life expectancy was between 30 and 40 years. It may have made sense when we married our daughters off right after their first menstrual periods so they could have babies and help work the fields. It may have made sense when having children provided an economic advantage.

Young people become sexually mature anywhere from 10 to 17 on the average. They were getting enough biological pressure from their own bodies to become sexually active without the school and their parents pushing them out of their childhood, and then shaming the girls as promiscuous or whores or sluts when they acted on their sexual desires.

I don't believe there was an equivalent name that was cast upon the boys for being their sexual partners. If there was, I was unaware of it.

I was not a prude or unrealistic when it came to teenage sexuality. I was just an adult woman who has had to help so many boys and girls pick up the pieces of their broken hearts when they felt they dishonored themselves and were left wallowing in shame. If the national statistics could be extrapolated to The Academy, it was likely that there were about 17 unplanned pregnancies every year among our female students. But there were zero live births. Because … well, that would be a problem. And we just didn't have *that* kind of problem at Halcyon Heights.

We, the adults, were the ones who should be ashamed of ourselves. We had set up our children, and for what end?

Where were the parents during all of this? They were taking the photos and writing the checks for the honor and glory of the Academy of Halcyon Heights and the privilege of being part of this legacy of grandeur.

But to be fair I must acknowledge the upbringing and family circumstances of the students at Halcyon Heights was vast and varied. One thing they had in common was that all the parents sent their children to The Academy because it was thought to be the best education– and the best future– that money could buy.

Many of the Hindu teenagers were not allowed to date until they were older.

Most of the Muslim boys and girls were not allowed to date at all, and certainly not outside of their own culture.

Old world values followed many of their parents as they immigrated to the United States and that included strict codes of conduct, particularly where their teenage daughters were concerned.

But these were teenagers whose bodies were changing as they reached sexual maturity. Many of their parents had forbidden any social interplay across ethnic, religious, and racial boundaries.

However the students met and interacted with one another in the classroom, in the dining room and on the playing field. They were classmates and they became friends and some of the socially derived and contrived barriers were broken down, in spite of some of their parents' vociferous objections.

Their parents could rant and rave and forbid all they wanted but we were talking about rebellious, sexually curious teenagers. The major developmental task for teenagers was to break free of the parental bonds of childhood, and break those bonds they did.

Suffice to say that many of the students were forming friendships and learning about love in ways that their parents were not all that welcoming of.

I was the Director of Health, and therefore the person responsible for teaching sex education. When issues arose, and they did, some folks liked to look for someone to blame.

Was I being too candid and too explicit? Was I putting ideas into the heads of innocents? Had I not been firm enough? Or should I have taken the moral high ground and quoted Nancy Reagan and said, "Just say no?"

We all just did the best we could. This was not a science experiment with results that could be replicated. In the world of human beings there were just too many variables, thus, the result of human interaction took on a myriad of unexpected permutations.

All the parents who sent their children to The Academy really wanted what was best for their own children. Whether rich or poor, Christian, Jew, Muslim or Atheist, white, black, yellow, red or brown or some other beautiful shade of humanity, enormous sacrifices had been made by all to ensure success for these children.

∾

But the big weekend came and went. The football team was victorious as was expected. The homecoming king and queen were crowned, the ball was held, and at the end of the weekend the alumni and the parents had written substantial checks to the endowment fund at The Academy of Halcyon Heights.

Although The Academy was a non-profit institution, all this meant was that it didn't return dividends to shareholders. This didn't mean The Academy didn't make money. Donations given to The Academy were deemed as philanthropic, and therefore really just another tax write-off for the wealthy. In some ways it seemed more like the donors were taking from one of their pockets and putting it into another of their pockets. The rich just kept getting richer and the coffers at The Academy were full.

CHAPTER 5

November 1999

The opening quarter of the academic year closed the first week in November. It was a busy time for faculty as there were papers to be read, exams to be graded, and grades to be calculated. But at Halcyon Heights the faculty was also required to write a personal note about the academic, behavioral, social, and emotional development of each of their students in every class.

For me this meant an additional 75 correspondences to the parents, and if done well it was a great deal of work. The parents had come to expect nothing less for their $25,000 annual investment per student.

Before the grades and comments were distributed to the parents, the faculty met all day for The Quarterly. This meeting was held four times a year, at the end of each eight-week marking period. We met to discuss all students who had received a C or lower in any class. Each teacher who *gave* a letter grade of C or lower was required to seek out the students' advisors and discuss what the problems had been that had led to the students' poor performance and have a clearly delineated plan for improvement. This was communicated through the written comments as a way to create the all-important paper trail. It was also communicated verbally as a way to convey a personal commitment to each student's success. Only grades of A or B were acceptable. I only wished that some of our students were as deeply invested in their futures as their parents and teachers were.

If a student had an overall average that was less than a C, then all of their teachers met for a round table discussion to determine why this student was struggling, and how we could help get him or her back on track.

Given my position, and the fact that I was privy to sensitive information, I attended all these meetings, whether I had the student in class or not. I attended to speak about any learning issues, health issues, and emotional issues that might impact the students' ability to be successful academically. I knew nearly all the students as they had either been in my health class or they would be. It was enlightening to spend the day in such a way. I found I gathered greater insight into the students, and into the faculty as well.

There were members of the faculty who led with their hearts and did everything in their power to help students be successful. Many of the students who were struggling were often dealing with other issues in their lives. Some had missed a great deal of school due to absences for illnesses both mental and physical. Some were grieving the loss of a love, perhaps a parent or a grandparent or a broken relationship. Some were self-medicating with drugs or alcohol or both, and there were many whose style of learning was frankly incompatible with the academic teaching style of their teachers.

Other students had been admitted without the academic skills necessary to be able to compete. There were areas where they needed re-teaching and re-learning in foundational areas if they were going to be able to move forward with more complex conceptual material. Often, these kids had been admitted from impoverished areas where their previous teachers had spent more time addressing the issues of poverty and therefore had less time to address the curriculum. The result was that many of these students arrived at Halcyon Heights reading below grade level, never having been exposed to a foreign language, having great gaps in their math skills, to say nothing of the social and cultural adjustment of going from an impoverished, over-crowded public school to an elite college prep school.

It was interesting how some of the faculty were quick to label some of our new recruits as *stupid* without ever acknowledging the effort they and their families had made to rise above their circumstances and their substandard grade school education. Rather than cheering on our new recruits, there were those who booed them and would have liked nothing better than to have dismissed them as inferior and incapable.

There were white supremacists hiding beneath the cloak of the respectable professor. It didn't take long to see just who they were.

Just keep talking so I can see who you really are.

It was only after the morning round tables were completed and information had been shared between teachers and advisors that we convened in the library for the Faculty Advisory Committee meeting.

Advisory was truly a misnomer. Trust me when I say that no one was seeking our counsel. Rather it was the forum, governed by Parliamentary Procedure and Roberts Rules of Order, for airing faculty grievances. Years ago under different leadership the administration had relinquished the illusion of absolute control and granted the faculty a voice in the school governance. This was it, a biannual meeting where the faculty had the opportunity to address the administration about their areas of concern. Attendance was mandatory and as I recall, the agenda was lengthy that day. No one would be heading home anytime soon.

Jonathon Douglas, my friend and colleague had first order of new business on the afternoon's agenda. He was going to talk about: Financial Aid. Jonathon was a lawyer and progressive English teacher. He was tortured by the lack of equity and justice apparent in the school's financial aid program.

It didn't take a wizard to figure out who was receiving financial aid and who our full paying customers were. There was a great racial divide. There was also a great geographical divide. Most of our financial aid students were African American and lived in East Richmond. There was a great disparity in wealth, as well as the quality of early education between our full paying customers of privilege and those on financial aid, who often arrived ill prepared for the rigor of The Academy. Then just to really unbalance the playing field we added an additional season of athletics to take away from these students' time to prepare for class or get the remedial assistance that they so sorely needed.

Students who had been benevolently gifted with tuition assistance were in return required to participate in the three seasons of competitive athletics, whereas students from families with the financial wherewithal to pay the full tuition were only required to participate in two seasons of sports. This had been the school policy as long as anyone could remember.

Jonathon was outspoken as he set forth his argument, "This policy is handicapping our financial aid students, many of whom have been reared in East Richmond. These students are mostly African American, many with single working mothers, and educated from kindergarten to grade 8 in the Richmond Public Schools which is financially bankrupt and proudly boasts a 28% high school drop-out rate. We all know who these kids are. These kids form the backbone of our state championship athletic teams. These students are not being provided the same opportunity to get the tutorial assistance because they are required to play three seasons of sports. So many of these kids are arriving in our ninth grade already so far behind the students who have grown up at Halcyon Heights. As educators we can do nothing to help them along academically because this policy has tied our hands."

I looked around the room. As usual the old boys club of well-honored coaches was seated together in the back of the library. Eight grown men in colored polo shirts, with an average age of about 55, stared across the room to the podium where Jonathon spoke. Each of them leaned back in their chairs with their arms folded above their ample bellies and across their chests.

There were certain things that were sacrosanct at the Academy of Halcyon Heights. The athletic program was at the top of that list.

Jonathon was no fool. He knew exactly what he was doing. He and I had discussed this more times than I could count. He knew who his allies were and where his detractors sat.

Bravely, he continued. "At graduation some of these kids can't even qualify for athletic scholarships. The combination of their grades and their SAT scores do not qualify them to meet the clearinghouse. We are kidding ourselves if we believe that athletics will be their ticket out of poverty. They will find their way out of poverty if, and only if, they are educated and employable. This magnanimous gift of tuition assistance in exchange for state championship teams is deplorable. We are using these kids for our own institutional gain."

Many of the faculty whispered to the person sitting next to them, covering their words behind an opened hand. Still, others had tuned their gaze away from the speaker and now appeared to be fascinated by something on their paper agendas. Jonathon had opened Pandora's box and God only knew what was going to be unleashed next.

He took a deep breath and continued, "These students may have talents and interests in other areas, but because of the three-season rule they are not allowed the opportunity to participate in the drama program, debate team, and a variety of other interesting programs that students from wealthier families can avail themselves to."

Jonathon was impassioned. He spoke eloquently and persuasively. He wanted a change in policy. Someone in the back of the room shouted, "I call the question."

To which Jonathon stated, "I move for a change in policy. The new policy being that all students must fulfill the same athletic requirements for graduation independent of the way their tuition has been paid."

David Ricci, who acted as the parliamentarian, called out, "Do I have a second?"

Hands went up around the room, including mine.

"Any discussion?" David asked.

At this point the room was rumbling as the headmaster stood. George Walker spoke with the authority that accompanied his position, "We need to move on." He looked directly at Jonathon and said, "If you want to discuss this privately with me later, please make an appointment."

Everyone in the room looked uncomfortable. This was a public admonishment. When decorum is the order of the day, to be cut off when one has the floor is the social equivalent of a slap in the face.

This was absolutely against protocol and the parliamentary procedure, which was always followed to the letter in formal meetings such as this one.

But again, we saw that those who held the power made the rules.

Jonathon had been airing the Academy's dirty laundry in a public forum. This went against an unwritten code of conduct for faculty members. Jonathon was not a new teacher. He knew the rules and he knew the risks. He had not just stumbled into this topic willy-nilly. No, he knew exactly what he was doing. He had sat silent too long and could no longer pretend to be in agreement with a policy that was inherently racist and classist.

A hush fell over the library. Now everyone looked down at their papers. Jonathon had been very brave or very foolish or both. Depending on whom you asked.

Jonathon stood and held the gaze of the headmaster for what seemed an interminable moment, and then he picked up his papers and walked out.

There was a collective sigh, but little relief.

Again– a problem exposed, and nothing resolved.

The remainder of the agenda was deferred for another day and another time. The headmaster called the meeting, and the biannual Faculty Advisory Meeting was concluded and we were dismissed. It had been a very long week.

I gathered up my belongings, once again feeling deeply unsettled about this institution and its priorities. No one was speaking to anyone as we left the library. The silence cast an eerie pall over the end of the day. It was gray outside. It was still early November. Only a week ago we had gone off daylight savings time, but as I walked through the atrium I noticed the light had already faded . . . and so had that light in my spirit.

As I walked towards my office I thought about the deeply rooted inconsistencies that were present in this place.

The student body had been selected with such rigor. Great care had been taken to determine what each individual student could bring to the party.

Over and over again the party line was repeated. "We do not recruit students."

That and, "There are no athletic scholarships, only financial aid." It didn't take a rocket scientist to determine that the Academy of Halcyon Heights had won multiple state championships in athletics year after year with the help of the students on financial aid.

The Academy prided itself in having won over 85 state championships. The athletic program was very important to the culture of the school and the State Championships were visible evidence that the athletic program was working. When the school won a state championship the parents and alumnae reached deep into their pockets and gold flowed into that ever-increasing endowment fund.

All of this was balanced on the backs of our student athletes.

No one wanted to hear it. Especially today as we were having a winning football season and in all likelihood our football team would again be going to the state championships– and state championships meant more money.

I'd heard Coach Brogan justify the three-season rule. He even quoted *The Bible*.

To whom much is given, much will be required.
Luke 12:48

Who could possibly argue with *The Bible?*

I unlocked the door to the clinic and slumped down on the couch. I needed to rest for a moment before I began my long commute home.

I was worried about Jonathon. This had not gone well for him. Jonathon and I had discussed the issues of class, race, and gender bias at length and we were allies in this battle for change.

When Elliot was alive I'd felt more confident taking on the powers that be. A year ago I hadn't really needed this job. Elliot had been the primary breadwinner in our family and the children and I were the benefactors. This was no longer the case. He had been gone just over a year now and I needed to work. I needed this job.

But so did Jonathon. He had two little boys and a wife at home that depended on his income. I feared for him.

We didn't work in a democratic environment; no, we served at the will of the powers that be. We could be terminated at any point and time, without cause. We didn't have the strength of a teachers' union to stand behind us.

Why did good people turn their heads and look away?

Sometimes it was out of the need for self-preservation. It wasn't that I was unemployable elsewhere, but in a very real sense I wore the golden handcuffs.

There was a knock on the clinic door. I thought about pretending that I'd already left and that no one was inside. Until I heard a familiar voice, "Elise, are you still here?"

I got up off the couch and opened the door. It was Sam. Samuel Fraser.

He stepped through the doorway, but kept his hand on the threshold as I leaned against the open door.

"Sam, is everything okay?" I was confused. He rarely came to see me in my office.

He whispered, "You need to be careful, Elise. These old dogs are the ones who butter your bread."

"What?" I said, truly confused. "Because I attempted to second Jonathon's motion. I didn't say anything to anyone."

"You didn't need to. Let's just say, you'd be a terrible poker player. The look on your face told it all."

"Oh, so I've already made my sympathies well-known?"

"It has long been suspected that you were Jonathon's confidant."

"So shoot me if the kids, the parents, and the faculty bring their troubles and concerns to someone who will actually listen to them," I said, as my ire and irritation grew. "Let me rephrase that, *don't* shoot me."

Sam turned and began to walk away. "I know what I'm talking about. This isn't a boat you want to rock."

I watched him retreat, his warning was ringing in my ears.

Sam had been one of the football coaches, but something had happened and he was no longer coaching. I didn't know why. Somehow I had missed that story. I'd been lost in my own world at the time. When all this was going on I'd been at home on a leave of absence because Elliott was dying.

Sam was a master teacher in all areas of mathematics. He taught and re-taught struggling math students using a wide variety of methods until each and every student that he tutored was able to pass. But his methodology required desire, time, and discipline, as well as $100 an hour. Sadly, not all the students in need possessed all of these necessary components.

I had always valued people who spoke their minds in a forthright manner. I wanted to be the voice piece for the voiceless. I, too, wanted to be that person who made decisions based on justice and fairness. I didn't think I was doing anything subversive.

Be careful?

I guess I had just been warned. I needed to think on this. Did I really want to work for an institution that didn't value my opinion? The Academy was purported to be a place where young people could grow and flourish in body, mind, and character to become healthy adults– but the leadership here did not seem to understand what that really meant. I sat back down on the couch, realizing I had some serious thinking to do.

∾

The following Monday night, the semi-annual Parent-Advisor Conferences were held. This was a time for the parents to meet for 30 minutes face-to-face with their son or daughter's advisor and get the scoop on how things were *really* going at school.

My first appointment was at 4:00 PM with Mrs. Ahmed regarding her son Mohamed.

Mrs. Ahmed knocked on my office door and I invited her in. Some of the parents were known to bring their children with them, but Mrs. Ahmed had elected to have Mo wait in the hallway with his younger brothers and sister. There were four children in this family.

In the early weeks of each academic year I spent some time learning about my advisees' families because it was often relevant to how they did at school.

Mo was the eldest. He had two younger brothers and a younger sister. He liked to be called Mo, so his classmates and I called him that, but his mother did not.

Mo was overweight and a bit of a slacker as evidenced by his poor performance his first semester. Last week, he was one of the kids whose poor performance had qualified him for an academic roundtable. I used that opportunity to see him through the eyes of his other teachers. He was the kid who was always cutting up and going for the laugh.

In response I'd reviewed a questionnaire that I'd given to my advisees when I first met them in September. Under the section entitled *goals and dreams*, Mo had written that he intended to become a comedian. I began to see how earning high marks in math and science might not be his highest priority.

I didn't know him well, as we were only eight weeks into the year, but I really liked him. However, I did know he wasn't the serious student his mother wanted him to be.

I wondered how much she understood her son when she asked, "How will he ever get into medical school with a C in Biology?"

Mo was bright enough to do anything he set his mind to, that was not the issue here. No, it was really more a matter of motivation to actually do the work.

He was a boy of privilege. This looked different in different homes. In this traditional Arabic home this mother was subservient to her son once he reached puberty. At 14 years old he was no longer considered a child. He was considered a man.

Mo's father was a first generation immigrant to the United States and a physician who worked long hours at the hospital. His mother was at home with four children, where she was without any authority to enforce the rules.

Mrs. Ahmed asked me to help her son. So we talked about how he used his free time, his study hall, if he had regular study hours at home, a quiet place to work and read, if she limited his television viewing, and monitored how much time he spent on the computer. I had a list of things I regularly discussed with parents when their kids were struggling academically. I always started with the obvious.

But she offered little insight into how Mo was studying at home. Instead, the conversation turned and she asked me about my diet. "What do you eat to have such a beautiful figure?" She said, as she smiled and looked me up and down.

Weird, weird, and weird– this woman was making me uncomfortable. There she was all covered up in her traditional dress and I felt like she was hitting on me.

I was so taken aback that I don't believe I even answered.

"It must be so distracting for my son and these young men to have a beautiful woman teaching classes about human sexuality," she stated, shaking her head. I felt her disapproval.

I was 42 years old for God's sake. As per The Academy's restrictive dress code I was all buttoned up in traditional business attire. I decided right then and there that I was not going to engage this woman in this discussion and I refocused the conversation on her son.

"What do we need to do" – I emphasized the word *we* – "to help your son be successful here at The Academy?"

"Please bring Mohamed into line. He must take his life more seriously. You must make him do his homework and get A's. He must go to medical school. His father requires it." She was nearly pleading with me, and once again, she was asking me to do what she could not.

This kid was a walking, talking squirrel. I was the advisor, not a miracle worker. So I offered her some suggestions of some things we might try at school, like a supervised study hall with teachers from every discipline available to tutor and answer questions. I also suggested some things she might try at home.

However, I understood her culture well enough to know that this woman lacked the authority in her life to implement any of the suggestions.

Her conference time was nearly up and there were other parents waiting in the hall for me. Before she left I asked, "Is there anything else I can help you with?"

To which she responded, "Perhaps you might be able to bring peace to the Middle East."

Then she nodded her head, smiled sweetly as again she perused my body before she left.

What was that all about? Was it me? Or was this place getting weirder every day? Or had we convinced the parents that we could work miracles if they just shelled out the big bucks? I wished I could've spent a few minutes pondering everything that had just happened in that conference, but I didn't have the time.

My office might as well have had a revolving door that night. As Mrs. Ahmed exited the next parent came right in.

My next conference was with the mother of Laurel Winton. Laurel was a stunningly beautiful ninth grade girl. She was the fourteen-year-old who looked like she was 25, and was frequently seen hanging on the arm of one of the senior football players.

This young girl was like ripe fruit, ready to be plucked from the branches.

But fruit that ripens too quickly ... also rots too soon.

I had concerns.

Mrs. Winton was a prominent attorney and she didn't like to be kept waiting. She extended her right hand to me. She had a firm handshake. "Carolynn Winton," she said, as she took the seat across the desk from me. I saw her glancing at the papers on my desk. I begged her indulgence as I put the papers from Mo's conference away in a manila file folder, which bore his name. Her daughter's file was waiting in a neat stack on the corner of my desk. These conferences were short so I had prepared.

Mrs. Winton looked to be in her mid-forties, perhaps just a few years older than I was. She was impeccably groomed and dressed in a skirted blue suit with a crisply ironed blouse. She looked like she might have come directly from court. Her blonde hair was shoulder length, coiffed, and sprayed into place. She clearly was a beautiful woman but she bore the telltale signs of her lifestyle– too much work and not enough exercise or fresh air and sunshine. Her careworn face had a grey pallor and she carried an additional 20 to 25 extra pounds. I suspected that the weight gain had been recent. Although her suit appeared to have been constructed of expensive gabardine wool, it was too tight on her.

I took a deep breath to clear my head from my last conference and reset my focus.

"Mrs. Winton, thank you for coming in tonight. I saw that Laurel is out in the hallway. Would you like to ask her to join us?"

"Please call me Carolynn," she asked. "And no, I think I would prefer to speak with you privately at first. If time permits perhaps we can ask Laurel to join us later."

Clearly this woman had things on her mind, so I deferred to her agenda.

"I don't know what you are seeing here at school, but Laurel is out of control at home. She is openly aggressive and angry with me."

"That's not all that uncommon with teenage girls," I offered.

"Her father and I were divorced two years ago and now her father is dating a woman in her twenties." She swallowed hard to keep her voice from breaking.

I could see how speaking about this was going to be very difficult for her.

"Last night I was confronting Laurel about her language. She drops the F-bomb every other sentence just to aggravate me. She even curses like a sailor around my elderly parents, her grandparents. And they would go to the ends of the earth for her. I'd had it when things between us really escalated and then she lost it. She was crying and screaming at me that if I hadn't *let myself go* and wasn't such *a matronly drill sergeant,* then Dad wouldn't have left."

Clearly, Carolyn Winton had been in therapy, as she went on to use words like narcissist and sociopath to describe her ex-husband.

"I think Laurel is punishing me. She blames me for the divorce. Maybe she's right. Things fell apart in our marriage, but I'm not the one who had an affair," she added, then quickly seemed to realize that we were not here to talk about her marriage or her divorce. I smiled gently as she reeled herself in and got the conversation back on track.

"Laurel was livid. She's doing everything in her power to sabotage her life, just to get her father's attention. Maybe some attention, even negative attention, is better than no attention at all." She pulled a tissue from her handbag and quietly wiped her nose.

"I've taken her to a therapist, who recommended she see a psychiatrist. Dr. Adams diagnosed Laurel with oppositional defiant disorder. Whatever that is?" she asked, without expecting an answer. "I just can't believe that this is my daughter, and that this is my life. I feel like I've lost her in the span of one year. She used to be such a dear, sweet girl," she said, and she sat up straighter.

"Anything else?" I asked. I needed to get a full picture of what was going on at home before I would begin to comment on what I'd seen at school.

"I'm afraid so. Now she's openly smoking pot at home. She looks like she's stoned every night." She dropped her head in shame. "I'm embarrassed to say that I've become the parent I vowed I never would be. Not only do I not recognize Laurel, but also I don't recognize myself either. I fear for my daughter and the choices she is making. I've read her diary. I know it is an invasion of her privacy, but this is what it has come to."

She took a deep breath before continuing. "I know she's having sex. She's only fourteen. She won't even be fifteen until June, and she's not being safe. I have been through her room, and her purse with a fine-toothed comb. She's not on any birth control. She's not even using condoms. Black boys, all upper classmen, and some who don't even go to school here, are calling her night and day. They take her out after school and it's not uncommon for her to be out past midnight on a school night. I call her cell phone, to find out where she is and when she will be home, and she turns her phone off. All I need is for her to get pregnant."

She dropped her head into her hands and began to cry.

My heart went out to this mother. She had her hands more than full with her daughter.

Within a few moments she had regained her composure.

"Perhaps we should invite Laurel into the conference," I suggested. "I want to talk with her about her academics. I think this discussion may go better if the three of us do this together. Let's try to keep focused on the grades and school while she is here. I need a little more time to think about what you've told me about her marijuana use and sexual behavior." I didn't want to speak or act in haste. Too much was at stake.

Carolynn Winton stood and went to open the door, "Laurel, please join us."

Once the door was open Laurel could be heard laughing and cutting up with other kids in the hall.

"Yes, Mommy dearest," she said snidely. This was followed by peels of laughter from her captive audience. "Hey guys, wait for me. I'll be right back," she issued the command that left little doubt who held the power.

I looked up from my desk and into the hallway. I wanted to see who these *guys* might be. I guess I was surprised, but there they were. Our star athletes were taking direction from this 14-year-old girl. Was this simply a matter of *boys wanting just one thing*? I didn't believe that for a minute. I knew these boys had sacrificed a great deal to rise up against all odds to be scholar-athletes, and men of honor and integrity. At least that was what we were striving for.

Laurel came into my office and slumped into the chair, sneering at both her mother and me.

"Hey, so what do you want?" she said to me.

Her mother came unglued. "Sit up straight and quit being such a punk. You speak to Mrs. Duncan with the respect that she deserves." Then she grabbed her daughter by her blazer and straightened her rumpled collar.

"Good evening, Mrs. Duncan," Laurel said, the sarcasm was dripping from her lips.

I felt a knot developing in my stomach as I thought about this girl, barely a teenager, acting out sexually with multiple partners. What was going on inside her head, to make her behave with such a lack of self-respect?

"Would you like to see your grades and comments?" I asked Laurel. I handed both mother and daughter a copy to look at and sign. This girl was clearly not working up to her potential, and it was reflected in her first quarter grades. She had to know I was in her mother's corner on this one.

Laurel was headed for big trouble if she stayed on this path, but how to remedy the problem? I had seen kids get their act together with a firm hand at home. Mrs. Winton was a single parent who worked long hours at a prestigious law firm. She lacked the wherewithal to monitor her daughter's every waking move and there was no guarantee that even if she did this she would be able to keep her daughter safe until adulthood, when God willing some reason might kick in.

Laurel grabbed a pen off my desk and scrawled something that resembled her name on the bottom of the report card, then tossed the pen back on the blotter. "Can I go now?"

"Yes," I said. "I'll talk with you tomorrow during advisory. Please come to that meeting with a written plan on how you intend to improve your performance before the end of the semester or you can rest assured that I will have a plan for you. Right now I need a few more minutes with your mother."

"Of course, Mrs. Duncan," she said exuding her lack of respect.

"You will be waiting for me outside this door. I don't want to have to go looking for you," her mother said. It was terrible to witness the tension between them.

Laurel was only two years older than my son, Ian. I couldn't imagine how wounded I would be if he ever spoke to me in such a way. She was a pip.

And while she may have looked like a full-grown woman, inside her mature body was a 14-year-old little girl who was angry, hurt, and actively rebelling.

The conference was supposed to have been about Laurel's academic issues, but most of the time was spent in a lengthy discussion about her anger and acting-out behavior.

Before too much more time had passed, and much to my relief, my next advisee's parents were knocking at the door. I pulled out a business card and wrote down both my cell phone and home phone numbers for Carolyn Winton. We were both single mothers. We were in this together. I would do my best to help keep her daughter safe while she was here at school. Laurel's academic issues were really just a symptom of a much larger problem. She was making one bad decision after another.

Thankfully, my other conferences that evening must have gone smoothly as they have long been erased from my memory.

Only later, as I drove home, would I begin to understand the comment made by Mohamed's mother, Mrs. Ahmed.

Clearly, I lacked the power, position, and authority to make any change that would bring peace to the Middle East and likewise she lacked the power, position, and authority to bring about the changes I had suggested in her own home.

In this moment of clarity I saw her as the bright and clever woman that she was, but I also felt a deep compassion for her. There was something in her life circumstances that had robbed her of her rightful place as a capable adult who could make decisions in her own life, in her home, and in the lives of her minor children. Her eldest son was 14 years old and floundering. Yet, as his mother, by virtue of her gender alone, she lacked the authority to lower the boom, set the boundaries, and make him straighten up and fly right.

By then, I knew many Islamic students and families, and they were as diverse as the families that identified as Christian or as Jews. Some were progressive in their interpretation of the Quran, and they embraced gender equality and allowed modern, although modest, dress, while others were much more extreme followers. Few true Muslim extremists chose to send their children to Halcyon Heights.

I knew I would not have fared well in such a male-dominated culture. I could be feisty and outspoken, and resisted anyone's attempt to control me. I got myself in enough trouble by forgetting my place in *this* academic bastion of manhood. Perhaps our Creator in his or her infinite wisdom had spared me the lessons this poor sister was learning.

༄

The next Friday night it was confirmed. The football team from The Academy of Halcyon Heights would be going to The State Championships. Someone, somewhere, had pulled some strings and the game would be played on The FedEx Field on Thanksgiving

Day. Let there be no doubt that the school was abuzz. The school hired fan busses to take students and their families up to Maryland for the game. Those who were driving were busy orchestrating tailgate parties and extending invitations. The game was going to be televised on ESPN so even those who were staying home were rearranging their Thanksgiving Day dinners so they wouldn't miss *the game.*

There was a lot of chest banging and chatter about who was going to the game.

Everyone was falling all over themselves making plans.

Everyone, except me. I gave enough of my lifeblood to the raising of other people's children. Thanksgiving was a family day, and I was thankful to be spending it with my own children and my extended family.

I was not a football fan, so I could really only feign excitement, but on the other hand each and every one of the young men on the team had been my student and many were part of the *frequent flyer club*– which meant they hung out in the clinic during their free periods. This game was important to them and for that reason alone I cared about the outcome because I cared about them.

For some of these young men, this would indeed be their ticket to college scholarships, and that had the potential to improve the quality of their lives. In my heart of hearts, I hoped and prayed for their success, on the field on Thursday, and off the field in life. Many of the kids on the football team were among those receiving financial aid to attend school at The Academy.

We didn't offer any athletic scholarships and we certainly didn't recruit athletes to play sports at our school. Why? Because that would just be wrong. Yeah right. I could quote the party line, but I didn't believe it for a minute and neither did anyone else. Winning teams and state championships drive college admissions and big donations for the alma mater. There was nothing altruistic going on here. I didn't believe that for a minute.

Historically, the school was always closed on the Monday after Thanksgiving. This must have been a throw back to when The Academy was an all boys' school and the faculty was all men.

The school was in session all day Wednesday, the day before Thanksgiving. It always had been. Things changed very slowly around here. I could still hear my male colleagues talking about how much they loved Thanksgiving. I'd love it too if all I had to do was show up. But that was not the case. Elliot had been my equal partner in the preparations for this feast, but now, I carried the lion's share of the tasks alone.

The faculty had once been all male and their wives and/or mothers stayed home to prepare the Thanksgiving feast, and all they needed to do was to put on a clean shirt and carve the turkey. So there was no consideration given to the fact that many faculty members would be hosting Thanksgiving dinners in their own homes and had very little time for preparation. Even though I'd been shopping and cleaning the house all week, I knew that I'd still be out the night before picking up the fresh produce for out Thanksgiving Day dinner.

Still, when that Monday rolled around and I would have the day off, I was grateful for it. My children would be back in school and I planned to use the day to change the house over for Christmas, and begin a little Christmas shopping.

As a single, working mother, planning was critical.

Thanksgiving was always my favorite holiday. Everyone in the family, both families, all families, were invited and included. Somehow, it just went without saying that these traditions would continue.

As I set the table on Thanksgiving morning I acknowledged the empty chairs at the tables. I had my own losses to struggle with. Each year the number of people coming to dinner was getting smaller. First we lost Gram, and then Elliot's mom, the next year his dad was gone, and now Elliot had passed on too. Parents are supposed to pass on before their children. Gram and my in-laws had lived good long lives but Elliott had been only 48, and that was just way too young.

Dear Lord, I missed my husband. When would this get easier or at least bearable?

I wondered if Laurel Winton would be missing from her mother's table this Thanksgiving. Perhaps she would be at *the game* and her mother would be dining alone. I found no solace in knowing that there were other families that were struggling too.

In the past year I'd begun to struggle with my own children as they tried to break the bonds of enmeshment all the while I was holding tight. I was trying to keep my family together, yet I knew it was my children's developmental task to break those bonds, stand on their own two feet, and walk out into the world. Oh dear God, I didn't want to let them go.

As I placed the good china and the crystal at every place setting I could hear Ian and Shea conspiring upstairs. Most of their conversation was reduced to whispered mumbling followed by laughter.

I heard Ian say emphatically, "Don't tell Mom."

It hurt. I saw it every day at school. I was everybody's confidant; everyone's except my own children's. I could rationalize and intellectualize. My brain knew it was necessary, but my heart still ached.

Ian was turning thirteen this weekend and I knew that the tighter I held on, the more he would push and pull away to distinguish himself from me as separate and different. Shea wouldn't be far behind. I understood what my students' parents were dealing with; I was dealing with some of the same issues in my own home.

My heart was breaking. My children shared their closely guarded secrets with their friends and with one another– the secrets that they had once shared with me.

Now I was the one who could not know. I was just like Carolynn Winton and every other parent who was struggling to give their kids a better life. In that moment, I felt great empathy for these people.

What I felt was a sense of loss. I thought that this must have been what some of the parents were feeling as their children were growing up, especially the mothers. Everyone was moving on and I was being left behind. I did not have an empty nest, but I could see that the winds of change were coming and my children were trying their wings in preparation for flight.

The day was coming, and I knew I'd better be prepared.

I had to shake myself out of this. The day was lovely and I needed to move beyond this moment of temporary gloom. Both kids came downstairs and I put them to work helping in the kitchen and by noon our most beloved guests– the members of our family, began to arrive, and the festivities began.

Sometime in the afternoon before we sat down at the table, my brother-in-law Brian announced, "The Academy of Halcyon Heights has won the Division 4 Football State Championship and defeated the Jesuits of Holy Redeemer by a score of 38 to 32. Congrats, Elise. Your school is the big winner. Your quarterback Evan Hedges threw an amazing pass for the winning touchdown in the last minute of the game. They just interviewed him on TV. What an outstanding young man."

The word was out and *we* had won. But "Congratulations?" Which part of this *we* belonged to me? Trust me I was nowhere near FedEx Field on Thanksgiving Day. I didn't suit up or throw a football. I did not like the overemphasis I saw on sports and did not count myself as a part of this winning team. That honor belonged to the young men on the field. It was they who had won the State Championship and brought the fame and glory to their school. I was happy for *them*.

But I also knew what this would bring. There would be even more importance placed on athletics, the distinctions between winners and losers, and scholars and athletes would be bandied about, and the unfortunate kids who never wore those crowns of glory would be trampled in the celebratory parade.

So, with that, my empathy had gone and again my thoughts returned to all of the ongoing institutional irritations and injustices.

I retreated into the kitchen to check the bird one more time, as dinner would be ready in about 30 minutes. I thought about Coach Sean Brogan. If you were building a stereotype of the macho Irish Catholic middle-aged football coach, Coach Brogan would be the prototype. I could almost visualize his red-faced exuberance. He must have been just beside himself.

I didn't know him well and perhaps what I thought of him was all wrong, but he seemed to be such a one-dimensional human being who truly believed that winning at football was the most important issue to be addressed on the planet.

As I decanted the wine and poured water into the water glasses, I thought about the players. Who were these boys? What was their story? Why had they decided to attend The Academy and play for Coach Brogan? What dreams did they chase and at what cost?

But these were thoughts for another day. It was time for dinner, Thanksgiving dinner. As we said a traditional blessing over the meal I was overcome with gratitude, I had a warm home on this cold and wintery evening, plenty to eat, and a family that loved me.

CHAPTER 6

December 1999

When I arrived back to school Tuesday morning the place was stirring. Of course the halls were filled with students high-fiving one another for the State Championship victory, but there was an undercurrent of something else.

What had happened?

Students could be heard whispering in the hallways about, "What was the administration going to do?"

There was something going on here. Something I knew nothing about.

Before long the story made its way to my door. My colleague Joanne had been watching the game on television. There had been a clip of our student section on TV. The opposing team was from Holy Redeemer Jesuit located in East Richmond. Most Jesuit schools across the country were located in urban areas as it was part of their mission to serve the poor. When the boys from Holy Redeemer scored a touchdown, our students started a cheer. The whole student section was caught on television, standing up en masse and yelling:

"That's all right, that's okay, you're gonna work for us one day."

The media was having a field day with it, as the clip was played over and over again on the national news. What should have been a moment of glory for the school was being sullied and dirtied by the actions of its students. The school was officially "*embarrassed*," according to a statement issued by our high-priced public relations department.

My mind ran to one thought. Where had our students been taught this kind of arrogance? –at the knees of their parents and right here in the hallowed halls of The Academy of Halcyon Heights. Perhaps the words had never been spoken aloud, but the message was clear. These kids saw themselves as the elite, the privileged, and the leaders of tomorrow.

God help us.

By the next day at our regularly scheduled assembly, the headmaster was already standing at the podium as the students filed in. As expected, he congratulated the football team for the glory and recognition they had brought to the school, but then he went on to admonish the students involved in the now-renowned chant.

"You have brought shame upon yourselves and upon this institution. There will be consequences for your actions. Rest assured we know who you are," he stated, as his voice boomed through the microphone.

The auditorium fell silent. With nothing left to say he turned and left the stage.

The head of the student council approached the podium, and with the words that ended every assembly he said, "Seniors, you are dismissed."

This was the shortest assembly I could remember. Everything else on the typically lengthy agenda had been scrapped. The effect was dramatic. The seniors stood and exited in silence, followed by the underclassmen and the faculty.

The auditorium might have emptied in silence, but the chatter in the hallways was thunderous. The students had been threatened; God only knew what kind of punishment would be brought to bear.

Within a few hours every teacher had been sent an email with a list of students' names. These students were invited to a luncheon being held in the headmaster's private dining room. By now, everyone had seen the video clip of our students behaving badly, the list of invitees matched the kids visible on the film.

When their luncheon was dismissed a few of these students made a beeline to the clinic. They were laughing and joking as they entered.

"How did it go?" I asked as I looked up from the papers I was grading.

"Beef Stroganoff, baby, on china plates with white table clothes and cloth napkins," Jared replied, as he came through the door with his entourage of compatriots.

"Old George actually thought it was funny," another boy said.

"He wasn't real happy that we'd been caught on film, but he agreed with us. What did he say? 'Those poor pikers from Holy Redeemer would be lucky to work for us.' He was laughing," Kyle added.

I wanted to throw up. Yet again, our dear and revered headmaster showed the students the depth of his character. Was it any wonder our students exuded such arrogance?

"What are the consequences?" I asked.

"Oh, we have to do a community service project with some kids from Holy Redeemer. We're goin' slummin'," Jared said with a laugh. "But we will get our white points, so it's no big deal."

"Let me get this right, you're earning your community service hours as part of your punishment?" I asked. I was incredulous.

"Those are mandatory for graduation. You have to do those anyway. How is this a punishment?" I asked.

The kids in the clinic knew I didn't find this nearly as funny as they did.

"You should be ashamed of yourselves. Do you know what the phrase– *There but for the grace of God go I*– means?"

A blank look came over Jared's face.

"You are not any better than anyone else. You do understand that it was a simple twist of fate that you were born into your family, and that you don't live in an urban ghetto. This is a privilege, not something that you have earned. It would serve you well to learn a little humility. Now take your arrogance and get out of here, all of you."

It was rare that I lost my temper.

"Sorry, Mrs. Duncan," one of the boys called, as he gathered up his books and walked out into the hallway.

"I've heard enough. Go to class."

I was angry with the boys. But I was angrier with the headmaster. This could have, and should have been a teachable moment. But he blew it. He blew it right out of his white bread, country club ass. He was teaching these kids all right, but what was the lesson?

The privileged were not held accountable for their transgressions.

The rule of life that governs humankind, the rule that is the cornerstone of all the major religions of the world, the rule that mandates we treat one another the way we want to be treated– that rule had been violated. Here at The Academy and the sons and daughters of privilege had once again been absolved of their sins, and of any and all responsibility for their egregious and offensive behavior.

I locked the door to the empty clinic behind me and went to teach my class. I tried to take a couple of deep breaths as I made my way to my classroom. I was starting a new unit on nutrition.

Students were milling about the room, talking and laughing about the headmaster's luncheon and all the kids who would be doing community service in the city. I needed some time to think about what had just happened. Cowardice prevailed and I opted for avoidance. I didn't use this moment to teach my students. I didn't trust myself to speak for fear of what I might say.

"Take your seats," I said, and passed around a stack of plain white printer paper and new freshly sharpened pencils with erasers. "Start with one piece of paper and take a pencil. Some of you may need additional paper as this project unfolds." I informed the class.

"Today, we are going to begin to look at our family trees. We will be making a pedigree using a square for the male members of your family, a circle for the female members of your family, a horizontal line in between, indicating a mating."

And with that instruction I brought a copy of my own family tree up on the overhead as an illustration of what I expected them to do. "This circle here represents me. This square is my late husband. The line in between indicates we were mates. The line through the square indicates that my husband is deceased. This square and this circle represent my son and my daughter, and these symbols are my siblings, and these my parents and my grandparents."

I looked up from the overhead and my students' heads were down. They had already begun to draw their own family trees. These were bright kids.

Then the questions began.

"How do I draw my step-mother and my half-brother?"

"How do I draw my sister who was adopted?"

"What if my grandparents were never married?"

Every family was unique and everyone's chart was different. Some students knew a great deal about their family history and others very little at all.

Once most of them had some semblance of their pedigree drawn I asked them to indicate what health challenges the people in their family struggled with, and if anyone was deceased what the cause of death was.

Some kids completed this in class and others needed to consult their parents. "For your homework I want you to interview your parents to fill in the gaps in your family tree. Make a list of the health issues in your family, including things like obesity, alcoholism, smoking, depression, and death by violence. Tomorrow, we will look at how much our health might be affected by our genetics and how much is determined by lifestyle and under our control."

I'd found that students gained a great deal of information by sitting down and talking with their parents about the people in their family. Many students had never had this kind of intergenerational discussion with their parents. It was interesting how some of the students felt that this was the first really substantive conversation they'd had with either their mother or father. Students often returned to class with a wealth of information and found the project very valuable.

The flip side of that coin was there were some parents who had been extremely reluctant to share any of this information with their son or daughter, because they believed that this information was private and none of their children's business. These kids came back wondering, just what was the big secret that their parents thought they were too young to know? At an age when kids were typically growing up and separating from their parents, for some the project helped build a bridge from their world to their parents' and for others it only raised the height of the wall.

Along with the lesson on genetics, I took the opportunity to talk about the luck of the draw, about families, and the world, and the privilege they just happened to be born into through no action of their own. I needed to be careful not to lay it on too thick or take my anger that was born out of the headmaster's stupidity out on them. After all, here at The Academy we were a diverse community. The thinking and behavior of my students reflected the attitudes of the adults who were raising them, and hopefully the attitudes of some of their teachers.

By the second Monday in December we had begun a discussion on genetics and inheritance vs. lifestyle. This discussion helped students look at the diseases of affluence and excess vs. diseases of poverty and want.

In the late afternoon, I sat at my desk and revised my lesson plans for the remainder of the unit. The family tree project was part of a unit on nutrition. The following week all of my students were to keep a daily log of everything they ate. It surprised me to find how few families ate at home or had a family meal together in the evenings.

Some families ate out or brought home carryout every night. Some children's meals were prepared by their nannies. Some children, particularly those in single parent homes ate alone every night, and others were responsible for cooking for their younger brothers and sisters because their parent or parents worked to keep the roof over their head and the lights on.

A couple of years ago The Academy instituted a program called *writing across the curriculum*. Every member of the faculty needed to teach students to write in their given subject area. In my freshman health class all students were required to research a question on nutrition and write a paper that answered the question.

Research began with an inquiry– what did the student want to know? Students were required to write a five-page paper and make an in-class presentation on the results of their research.

When the papers came in, it was apparent which students had difficulty with the assignment. Some students are very good writers and had been doing this kind of assignment all through middle school. But others, in spite of lengthy instruction and hand holding, still didn't have any idea how to approach the work. Anyone who didn't earn an A or a B on the assignment had to see me for a tutorial and had to rewrite the paper.

The second round was always better, but for some, their inability to communicate in writing was a real handicap that needed to be addressed if they were going to be able to find their way in this world.

Millie Holmes and I discussed this at length as we identified kids who were struggling academically and interpersonally. We tried to formulate a plan to help them. Out of these discussions the freshman and sophomore support teams had been formed to help intervene with students who had learning issues. We needed to do this sooner rather than later.

The presentations were also very revealing as I assessed students for social confidence. What some lacked in their ability to communicate in writing, they more than made up for it in confidence and vice versa.

There was work to be done. If a student was not comfortable in my classroom, they were probably suffering other places where there was a lot more at stake.

I had my work cut out for me in these next few weeks before we broke for the holidays. I was finishing up my lesson planning and getting ready to go home, for it was already nosing in on 4:30, when there was a knock on the clinic door.

I got up from my desk to answer the door. Three of my students were there.

"Hi guys," I said in a tone that asked: what can I do for you?

Omar was the leader of this pack. "Sorry to bother you Mrs. Duncan. I know you must be trying to get home. You may or may not know that Ramadan begins tonight at sunset."

"Please come in," I said. I could see this wasn't a conversation any of these boys was interested in having in the athletic corridor, which was now filled with students who were milling around and waiting for their practices to begin.

The boys filed in and took a seat next to one another on the couch. Some of my 14-year-old students look like full-grown men, but these three were boys, good boys. I couldn't help myself as I thought– there they were: see no evil, hear no evil, and speak no evil. They were truly endearing.

I pulled up a chair and sat across from them. "Yes, I am aware that Ramadan starts tonight," I responded to their earlier question.

Rabah spoke next, "You may know that it's our tradition to fast from sunrise to sunset, and to pray five times during the day during this holy month. This is the first year we are considered men and are expected to abide by all the obligations of our faith."

He sounded so grown-up and well spoken. I nodded; as I thought how proud his parents would have been if they could hear him.

When at last Ghalib spoke, "We were wondering if we could use your classroom to pray during lunch."

They looked so nervous about approaching me with their request. They must have known that I would say yes, but still they looked apprehensive for some reason. I noticed it, but let it go.

"Of course," I said.

Their faces relaxed into smiles. Had it been difficult for them to approach their teacher, a woman not of their faith, with this request?

"May we keep our prayer rugs in your closet?" Omar asked.

"Certainly," I said, "Meet me in the classroom tomorrow during first lunch and I will show you where to put them. I will leave the door open for you when I leave, then just close the door when you have finished and it will lock behind you."

"Thank you so much Mrs. Duncan," Ghalib said as the other two boys smiled and nodded their heads and headed for the door.

I knew a bit about Ramadan, but not a lot. That night, after my kids had gone to bed, I did a little reading.

Ramadan was considered the holiest of season in the Islamic year. It commemorated the time when the Quran, the Islamic holy book was revealed to the Prophet Muhammad. Many Muslims abstained from food, drink, sex, and certain other activities in daylight hours during Ramadan. Fighting was also prohibited during this holy time. It was considered to be the most holy and blessed month, marked by prayer and almsgiving.

Ramadan was the ninth month in the Islamic calendar. The month of Ramadan traditionally began at sunset with a new moon sighting and ended 30 days later with the sighting of the next new moon. Eid-al-Fitr is the Islamic holiday that marks the end of Ramadan.

This year Ramadan began at sunset on December 9, and ended on Saturday January 8, with the celebration of Eid.

It must have been difficult for our Muslim students to play sports every day after school when they hadn't eaten or had anything to drink since before sunrise. This year should be easier as we approached the shortest days of the year. The sun rose later and set earlier in December and January. The students never complained, but some of the faculty thought it was cruel and unusual punishment to expect growing teenagers to abstain from food and water all day. The cultural divide grew wider as our good Christian coaching staff bitched and moaned about how our Muslim students' performance wasn't quite up to par during Ramadan. They just kept jabbering on until their lack of understanding of anything that fell outside of their own culture was obvious to even the most culturally illiterate.

There was an issue that arose when I granted their request to pray in my classroom. I was well aware that to leave my classroom unlocked was a violation of school policy. All classrooms were supposed to be locked unless a member of the staff or faculty was present. In a very real sense I had felt honored that these boys had trusted me enough to ask to use my classroom so they would have a private place to pray during Ramadan, and in return I trusted them. A core tenant of my personal beliefs was that everyone had a right to seek God in a way that was meaningful for them. Besides, I had lunch meetings four days a week and was therefore unavailable to supervise these boys. Yet, even if I had been available, I had no intention of hovering over and monitoring them while they were at prayer.

So at noontime on Thursday, December 9th, the first day of Ramadan, I gathered up a few papers that I needed to read during lunch and headed towards the faculty workroom, leaving my classroom unlocked.

It was a decision I would come to regret.

That weekend while I was at one of Ian's basketball games my cell phone rang. It was Carolynn Winton. It was half time so I stepped out of the gym and into the hallway to answer the call. As I answered the phone I thought, *This can't be good.*

Over the last six weeks Mrs. Winton and I had been in regular phone contact about her daughter. Things were not any better at school as her grades hovered in the 60s. It would be one thing if she was trying and this was the best she could do, but this wasn't the case. As much as things had been on a downward slide at school, they were even worse at home.

"Hi Carolynn, how are you?" I asked tentatively. Fearing the worst, I held my breath.

"Oh I've been better, Elise. Laurel didn't come home last weekend," she said. Then she went on to tell me, "I've become so concerned about Laurel's whereabouts that I've hired a private investigator to follow her. This is how I learned that a 25-year-old black man from East Richmond picked Laurel up after school last Friday. He took her to a drug house, had sex with her, and didn't bring her home until Sunday afternoon. She was hung over, dressed like a whore, and spewing venom at me for sticking my nose into her business."

"Carolynn, I'm sorry. Is there anything I can do?"

"I know who this guy is. I had a colleague in the prosecutor's office pull his record. He has a rap sheet as long as my leg for drunk driving, possession, sale of drugs, as well as violence against women. And now my dear sweet daughter tells me she loves him. She's only 14-years-old for God's sake. I should have him arrested for statutory rape. Good luck getting that to stick in Richmond."

"Tell me what you mean," I asked. I needed clarification. After all, Laurel was only 14.

"Come on Elise. You know as well as I do that it's highly unlikely they could assemble a jury of my peers in East Richmond, let alone 12 people who would find this rich little white girl, who just so happens to be my bad ass daughter, a very sympathetic victim."

I could hear her weeping now on the other end of the phone. Again I said, "I'm so sorry." I waited, as I was certain there was more that she wanted to tell me.

"I wanted you to know that I'm having Laurel picked up tonight. I've hired two big, burly men to come and take her from her bed at 2:00 AM this morning. They will be putting her on a private plane I've hired and taking her to an alternative school in Utah where she will be incarcerated for the next 18 months. It's a combination of boot camp and high school. You're the only person I've told," she whispered conspiratorially. "Please don't breathe a word of this to anyone."

"You have my word on this," I promised.

"I will notify you when she has landed and is safely ensconced in her new school in the middle of Nowhere, USA. Then if you would inform the school that Laurel has been withdrawn I would appreciate it. Please tell Will Warwick and the headmaster that she has been enrolled in an alternative therapeutic school but don't tell them where she is. I don't want anyone to know where she is. I can't risk it that someone will come looking for her." she said and exhaled loudly. "One more thing, Elise …"

"Yes Carolynn, what is it?" My heart was breaking for this mother and also for this young girl. How had their lives come to this in just a few short years? I'd been sick with worry for this girl and for her mother, too. There was no trust, no communication, and no respect between them. Too many hateful and hurtful things had been said. I didn't know who needed to get out of whose presence. Perhaps it was the mother who needed protection from her daughter as much as the daughter needed protection from herself. But I also knew that I would go to the ends of the earth to protect my children and that this woman was being so very brave and courageous. She was taking extreme measures to ensure her daughter's safety.

"Pray for me?" she whispered through the phone.

"Of course, my dear," I said.

"And pray for Laurel, too. God help us," she said.

"I will. Stay strong," I said, not knowing if that was even possible.

And with that the phone went dead.

As I returned to the drafty old gym to watch my 13-year-old son on the basketball court, I thought back on the incident with Dr. and Mrs. Masood who had been actively denying their 14-year-old's psychosis. For all these people I felt compassion. Parenting could be so difficult. There was no instruction manual or crystal ball to let us know when something was a big deal or just a minor blip on the trajectory of life. Growing up in a world of affluence may have looked like a picnic to people who lived in poverty, but it could be fraught with peril and danger for the unsuspecting youth who thought that the rules of life did not apply to them.

It was the last Monday morning faculty meeting of the year before we would break for the holidays. There was only one item on the morning's agenda– the dress code. The faculty was informed that *The Board* had decided to institute a change in the dress code.

There had been a great deal of scuttlebutt about the upcoming changes. Some feared the change of dress code was symptomatic of progressive or worse, liberal thinking that was infiltrating The Academy, which had long prided itself on holding firm to tradition and conservative values.

The school had been founded in 1814 as an all boys' school, and only twenty years before my arrival the first female students had been admitted. Yet, it wasn't until January of 2000 that the women faculty and the female students were allowed to wear slacks. Prior to that time all females wore only dresses or skirts. No, this was not a very socially progressive institution.

I sat and listened to the Director of the School fumble through a description of the new dress code and what the female students and women faculty would be allowed to wear. The women faculty had to wear a blazer and a tucked-in collared shirt whenever they chose to wear slacks. They could not take their blazers off unless they were granted permission by the administration. Women could continue to wear dresses of course, but all dresses and blouses needed to have a collar and the sleeves must cover their elbows.

Poor Will went on as he tried to describe women's shoes, stockings, ruffles, and hemlines. Clearly he was speaking about something he had little knowledge of: women's fashion. Only shoes with closed toes and closed heels could be worn and always with stockings regardless of the weather.

I guess the old boys were still afraid that it might be a little too much for our young male students to see a little flash of elbow or God forbid some toe cleavage on one of their female teachers.

Will was a really good man with an ability to laugh at himself. Good thing because it was two days before we were off for the holidays, and the faculty was having a field day with this.

Before too long, two of the women deans got out of their seats to help with the description of the changes. They had even coerced the women of the drama department to model in a fashion show depicting the *Fashion Do's and Don'ts*. As could have been expected they'd taken the *Fashion Don'ts* to an extreme. It had been a long time since we, as a unified faculty, had gathered together for a good laugh.

I knew Will; this had been his diversionary tactic. If he could get us to laugh, then maybe we wouldn't be so pissed off.

The real new change was that women were going to be able to wear pantsuits, right here and now at the dawning of the new millennium. This was big news as winters in this drafty old building could be mighty cold.

I sat back and listened as the Deans went on and on about what was acceptable and what clearly was not. I thought about the old men on The Board of Directors debating the merits vs. the pitfalls of allowing educated adult women to choose their own clothing. I could visualize them as they negotiated in agonizing detail the dos and don'ts of the new dress code. Whatever could be done if how we chose to clothe ourselves reflected poorly on the institution? Oh my, perish the thought.

If we couldn't be trusted enough to dress in a professional manner how could we ever be entrusted with the care and teaching of the next generation, the heirs to the *kingdom of gold*?

My mind drifted, as it often did when the point had long been made. I remembered they tried to send me home from school, back when I was in sixth grade, for having the audacity to wear pants. The temperatures were well below zero and we had to walk to the bus stop and wait for our ride. That had been back in 1969. I don't know how I ever convinced my mother to allow me to wear pants to school. Perhaps she was just being practical. Or was she a bit of a feminist herself? It was ridiculous to require girls to wear dresses and freeze when the weather dictated otherwise. Social convention could take a flying leap. I know that they called my mom from the office and told her to pick me up and take me home. Instead, she arrived at school with a skirt for me to wear and I was sent back to class. I don't believe she and I ever spoke about the incident afterwards.

But that was 31 years before the dress code was finally being changed at The Academy. For God's sake how we were still fighting these same battles on the eve of the new millennium? I could hardly believe my ears. It saddened me to think that so much time and effort had been spent on something of so little importance when there were so many bigger fish to fry.

What century were we living in?

But once again, as a widowed mother of two young children who needed this job and liked these kids, did I speak up? No, of course not and I was not alone. There were real reasons why people didn't object and confront the status quo and reasons why things didn't change.

It was disquieting and I felt miserable about it, but I knew that I was one of those reasons.

Instead, I laughed at the fashion show and quieted my feminist distain when the male power brokers told the women faculty how we would dress if we wanted to keep our jobs.

The meeting was over and we left for our classrooms for two more days of school before the holidays. Everyone was ready for an extended vacation. Here at The Academy of Halcyon Heights we celebrated *the holidays* as opposed to Christmas. The seeds of tension between Christians and a multi-cultural world had been sewn in this academic community a long time ago.

I was learning ... to wish someone a Merry Christmas was second nature to me, but I now considered how that might be received given the diversity of our student body. Hanukkah was over last week and I had already wished my Jewish students a Happy Hanukkah, my Hindu students had celebrated Divali, the festival of lights earlier in November. Many Indian students celebrated Christmas as well and called, "Merry Christmas," to all who celebrated.

I wished a young man, "Merry Christmas," as he left my classroom for vacation. He looked back and gently told me, "I do not celebrate the birth of Christ."

I felt small and foolish in the moment because I knew he was Muslim, and thus I apologized for my insensitivity. "Forgive me, Nabil, I knew that."

I think he spoke to me in this way, because if he could not get me to understand what it felt like to be him, what chance did he have to get some of the other faculty members to understand? His brown eyes met my blue ones as he nodded and acknowledged my apology, and I knew it had been accepted.

Then he raised his head and said, "A Merry Christmas to you, Mrs. Duncan. Enjoy this time with your family."

Ah, who was teaching whom?

That moment would stay with me for a long time. This boy was just asking to be seen for the individual he was and he had every right to ask me, his teacher, to acknowledge him and his individuality.

As instructed by my Muslim student, I did enjoy the holidays with my family. We were a family in transition now that Elliot was no longer here. The kids were still hurting and so was I. There was nothing like the holidays to feel the poignant loss when a beloved member of your family had passed on. So that year we mixed things up. I used a bit of the life insurance money and took the kids to the Caribbean. No Christmas tree, no midnight Mass, that year Santa found me on the beach, and the kids on their boogie boards in the crystalline waters of St. Maarten.

While others around the globe were actively stockpiling cash, bottled water, and canned food in their basements fearing the dismantling of the entire infrastructure of the world because of Y2K, I sat on the beach and watched my children play in the ocean. I couldn't help but think about the kind of world they would be inheriting. January 1st and the new millennium was less than a week away. Ours was the generation that was supposed to set things right, and yet the state of the world was anything but right.

I thought about my job. In so many ways I had felt better about the work I did when I worked in the inner city as an emergency room nurse than I did now in my job that many thought was soft and easy.

If I stayed and just did my job did I bear some of the responsibility for perpetuating the inequity that accompanied privilege and the status quo? The questions rolled around in my head: should I stay or should I go? Just as soon as I thought that I had worked out the answer, the voice within my head argued on with equally compelling reason to see my situation another way.

The truth was this job allowed me time with my children and that was precious. Besides, I was still under contract so I wasn't going anywhere, at least not right away.

CHAPTER 7

January 2000

There were students who were up to a week late when at last they returned to school. But it had nothing to do with Y2K, as it turned out all the bally-hoo about an impending technological disaster had been oversold by the fear mongerers. No, our students were delayed by the weather and the nor'easter that shut down the airports and blanketed the entire eastern seaboard with over a foot of snow, and diminishing visibility with its gale force winds.

So, we started the New Year as we always did-- with our Monday Morning Faculty Meeting. It was interesting to look around the library; nearly all of my female colleagues were dressed in pantsuits, looking just like our male counterparts, on this cold and snowy January morning of the new millennium. I now understood all the care given to the detail in the new and improved faculty dress code. The old guard wanted the women to dress just like the men. What the heck, did they fear our femininity?

Oh well, change came slowly around here. I was just happy to be dressed in something other than nylon stockings when the wind chill hovered below zero. We chatted over coffee while we waited for the meeting to be called to order.

Not only was I dressed in my new blue suit, but I was also sporting a bit of a tan from my trip to the Caribbean, as well as a swollen cheek and a black eye.

I had been in a minor boating accident on vacation. I had chartered a boat to take the kids snorkeling on a reef. I had just put on my sunscreen when the boat, which was not much larger than a rowboat, hit a rough wave and sent me sliding face first into the gunnels.

I had expected my colleagues to ask me what had happened. But they were silent. No one asked me anything about my black eye. I found this curious. Later in the day one of my students asked, "What happened Mrs. Duncan, were you in a bar fight?"

It was then that it dawned on me that my colleagues must've thought that someone had beaten me. But they never asked me about my black eye because they didn't want to pry into my private affairs.

This was a moment when the bright lights went on. If they weren't going to ask me about something as obvious as this, what else was happening in their presence while they were choosing to look the other way?

George Walker took the podium and everyone scurried off to find a seat. He started out with the usual welcome back chatter and then made some sexist joke, "I can see that change is in the wind here at Halcyon Heights," he said as the wind rattled the glass in the old library windows. "Looks like the women will be wearing the pants in this family during the new millennium," he chuckled at his own little funny. It might have been more tolerable if he wasn't such an overt sexist.

Before too long he switched over to glory mode.

"Our football team really did us proud over Thanksgiving by bringing home another State Championship. Our boys have been invited to a dinner given in their honor at the Richmond Club. So Thursday night is a *no homework night* and this Friday you will give no tests or quizzes." The decree had been given.

The rumblings of the faculty could be heard. To mess with the test schedule the last two weeks of the semester was problematic. We already had a policy that a student couldn't have more than two tests on any one day. People grumbled under their breath when at last Leo Jarvis, the Head of the Math Department, raised his hand.

Once acknowledged, Leo stood and spoke, "Why don't we just change the schedule for the students on the football team and still allow the other students to be tested according to the already established testing protocol? If we delay these tests we will not have time to review before mid-years." A large number of the faculty nodded their heads in agreement. There was dissension in the air.

"Well, we can't do that because the cheerleaders will also be in attendance. The Green and Gold Club has invited them to attend in their cheerleading uniforms and act as the coat check girls," George said with a smile as if this was some grand honor.

I raised my hand, was call on, and stood up. "Are the cheerleaders also being invited to the dinner?" I asked.

The room was silent and my question was left unanswered, as it was well-known that The Richmond Club had been a private club for white men only for over one hundred years. The first black man was admitted for membership in 1975 and the first woman in 1986. Prior to that time, women had to enter using the side door. But these were the outliers; the Richmond Club was and continued to be a gathering of rich, white men.

I still had the floor so I continued, "When is the Green and Gold Club going to invite the Women's Field Hockey Team down to the Richmond Club? After all they also won the state championship this fall." My voice was quivering and soft. Damn I hated that, but that was my voice. It always had been. I sounded like a frightened little mouse, but I was not. I had already opened the door, "Perhaps they would like to have the men's tennis team, dressed in their white tennis shorts act as personal valets, hold the doors, and check their coats."

The subject was changed. No response was given, but the look on the headmaster's face said it all– If you value your job, shut the fuck up. This conversation was over.

"Discuss this within your departments, but there is to be no testing on Friday for all students in attendance at the Richmond Club."

I sat there seething as I thought about the Green and Gold Club. It was an alumni club that consisted of only men. I opened my laptop and went to their website, where the Green and Gold Club was described as a collegial group of fathers and administrators.

What, no mothers?

What if a child didn't have a father who was active in his or her life, how would that impact their relationship with the coach? How would that impact their playing time, particularly in sports where playing time was discretionary and performance wasn't quantifiable like speed in track or swimming? The school's website went on to say that the purpose of the Green and Gold club was to pool resources, energy and talent to assure that The Academy of Halcyon Heights had a world-class athletic program.

Membership required a substantial financial contribution.

What if a student was on financial aid and their father wasn't able to pay the substantial dues?

I was completely preoccupied by my own thoughts as someone was filling time and yammered on about something. I continued to wander around on the Internet to confirm statistically what I already knew, 72% of black kids were raised in single parent homes, mostly by mothers who were the head of the household.

This whole institution was disrespectful to the fact that there were different kinds of families in the world and in our community. The single mother in me was raging now.

Was this a conspiracy to continue to promote white privilege and preservation of the status quo? The Green and Gold Club's newsletter was called *Traditions* and it included two old photographs where all the featured athletes were white males. I was outraged. These old goats planned and organized fund raising events that purposely excluded so many because they couldn't afford the price of admission. Really, what kind of a message were we sending here? The cheerleaders had been invited to act as coat check girls. What the fuck! What century were we living in?

Nina Dominion, the cheerleaders' sponsor, passed me a note across two tables. It was folded and had my name on it. Inside it read– the cheerleaders really don't mind that they will be coat check girls and have not been invited to the dinner.

I looked over at Nina as she smiled and shrugged her shoulders.

Again: what the fuck.

As the adult women in their lives, we needed to help these young women *to mind*. We needed to help them to understand that much of what they took for granted had been won only because of the voices and the hard work of their grandmothers and their mothers, and that this old boys' network would like nothing better than to dismantle the advancements and return to the good old days when white men ruled the world without question.

I am a feminist and I was unapologetic. The conservative powers had recast feminists and the feminine as some kind of radical movement. How radical could it possibly be to consider 50 percent of the population as equal citizens with equal rights?

The white male administration didn't see this as sexist; it never even crossed their minds because this was the way we had always done things here.

Did I have a moral and an ethical obligation, as a teacher in this school, to speak out when I saw injustice? If I was to be a teacher and a leader, then I must do so by example.

Rest assured this wasn't an institution that really liked to mix things up. They had a game plan that had been working for years and they weren't all that interested in disturbing the status quo.

Again, Sam Fraser was waiting for me in the hallway. "Please be careful," he whispered under his breath.

"I know, I know," I said. I began to nod my head and I fell into step beside him.

"No, you really need to know when to shut up," he said. "There is big money at stake here. Remember– you are expendable." He started to walk with me towards the clinic.

"I was once part of that inner circle. Remember, I was once a part of the elite football coaching staff. I attended all the Green and Gold Club's meetings and events. But that was before I spoke up in a coaches' meeting and said I couldn't endorse Preston Matthews and his scholarship to Notre Dame. There was a morality clause in the paperwork that I was supposed to sign. I couldn't and wouldn't sign it. My conscience wouldn't let me. That kid was pure evil. Mark my words we will hear of Preston again and it won't be for something good," Sam said under his breath.

Again I nodded, as I was certain we both recalled the incident of an alleged sexual assault that had taken place in the training room a couple of years ago. Preston had been implicated, but the young lady was discredited and basically told to keep her mouth closed as she was of limited standing in the school.

Gloria had entered the school as a full tuition student during junior school, but her parents had since divorced, and Gloria's life fell apart. By her sophomore year her daddy was no longer paying the full tuition and certainly not making any donations. Gloria had missed a great deal of school, thus her grades were barely passable. She was depressed, medicated, and had put on a great deal of weight. It had been in one of the Crisis Team meetings that her allegation of sexual assault had first come to my attention. Ben Schaeffer, one of the male members of the team had scoffed. Apparently, members of the male faculty and coaching staff had already discussed the assault and without any investigation had determined who was guilty and who was innocent. He even went on to quote one of the assistant football coaches, "Why would a boy with as much physical prowess as Preston be interested in a girl like Gloria. That girl would be *lucky* to spread her legs for him."

I remember being outraged and sickened. When I started to inquire into the status of the investigation, I was shut down and told in no uncertain terms that this would be handled administratively.

There was no need to speak in specifics. I knew why Sam did not endorse Preston, and he knew that I knew. We had both been at those meetings and we were allies.

"The next spring, my position as the assistant football coach was no longer in my contract. Essentially, that meant a 25% reduction in my salary. They were trying to push me out. They'd hoped I would be outraged and just quit. But my kids are still in school here, so now I tutor students at Starbucks to make up the difference. I know of which I speak, please Elise– be careful."

I knew that something had happened, but it never crossed my mind that it had anything to do with allegations about Preston and Gloria. As we walked further I remembered sitting in Will's office last spring and being told, "You need to drop this."

Before I could say anything I turned and Sam had disappeared into the sea of students moving towards their first class.

I reached into the pocket of my new blue blazer and pulled out the keys to my office, unlocked the door and went inside.

I had an hour before I was due in class. I sorted through the stack of mail that had accumulated during the winter break. There were some holiday cards that had been sent a little too late, but they were still gratefully received in the New Year. Included in the mail was a hand written invitation from Ghalib Ebrahim's father. It read:

Dear Mrs. Duncan,

I wanted to thank you for the great kindness you have extended Ghalib, Omar and Rabah by allowing them to use your classroom for prayer during the most holy month of Ramadan. It would mean a great deal to the boys and our families if you would join us as we break the fast and celebrate Eid on the evening of January 10 at sunset.

Their address and phone number was included. Followed by a closing–

In Gratitude,
Dr. and Mrs. Izaan Ebrahim

I was so touched by the generosity of this invitation. I really wanted to accept, and yet, being a single mother, I knew I must refuse. I needed to be home with my children. They were ten and thirteen. They didn't think they needed a babysitter, but still I wasn't comfortable leaving them home alone.

The week passed quickly as it often did when I was busy, and I was grateful that I heard no more about my outspoken comments at the faculty meeting. On Thursday, in the late afternoon, the students boarded the bus for The Green and Gold Victory dinner at the Richmond Club. The boys wore their color day attire– freshly pressed grey slacks, crisp white shirts, navy blazers with the school crest embroidered on the breast pocket and their green and gold repp striped ties were snug around their necks. And of course the cheerleaders were there in their full regalia.

I started my long drive home and I was left to wonder if I was the only one who had a problem with this. Maybe I was the one with the problem.

∽

I had been exposed to a slice of life here at The Academy that heretofore I was only vaguely acquainted with. There was a culture here that on one level appeared good and wholesome and righteous. We, the faculty, had been charged with the task of grooming the next generation of leaders. We were the educators of the modern day aristocracy and the privileged chosen ones. We did our best.

There was little doubt that the parents had the same goals in mind for their children. It was just that so often we were at odds on how best to teach those lessons and secure that outcome– good moral leadership for the next generation.

When privilege and need lived side by side, there were some people who were just trying their best to hold onto the good life, while others were striving with all their might for a piece of that pie.

The stakes for success ran high, whether real or overinflated or simply imagined. Too often there appeared signs of decay, like the subtle signs of rot on overripe fruit.

Could we trim it off and salvage what was good?

Deception could masquerade as truth, and when in the midst of a crisis, much was cloudy and unclear. Often those most affected lacked perspective.

Perspective was only granted by stepping away, and mercifully with time, came clarity. Or at least you could hope so.

It was a Friday afternoon in late January and it was hard to believe that only a few weeks ago we'd two weeks off for the holidays. It looked like everyone could use another few days off and away from this place. The mid-year exams had been taken and just been returned. Walking through the hallways, it was apparent on the faces of the students who had done well and those who once again, had proven to be a source of disappointment to their parents. God love 'em. This was not an easy place for some of these kids to grow up; emphasis on the word *kids.*

I had just left the weekly crisis team meeting. Post exams– today's list of kids we were worrying about had been long. I coordinated this team and at the end of each meeting I had some follow-up appointments to schedule and phone calls to make.

Again, it crossed my mind that we should schedule this meeting earlier in the week. Identifying kids in crisis on a Friday afternoon was a bit risky. Hopefully, these crises could wait until Monday and would not explode this afternoon as I hurried back to teach my class.

As I rounded the corner into the athletic corridor there were two girls waiting for me outside the clinic. "Mrs. Duncan, can we talk to you?" asked Catherine, as Libby held back and looked at the ground. Libby looked like she had been crying and was visibly upset.

I had gotten to know both of these girls fairly well during class this semester. Both girls played on the JV field hockey team. Both of the girls were slight in stature and beautiful in very different ways. Catherine was of Euro-Asian descent and Libby was a petite blue-eyed blonde.

I unlocked the door to the clinic and let them in. I closed the door and it locked behind me. With an upturned hand I motioned to the couch and both girls took a seat. I pulled up a chair to face them as I glanced at the clock. I took note. The second bell indicating the start of class would ring in less than a minute. Clearly, something was going on here and yet, I needed to teach my class.

"What class do you girls have right now?" I asked. They both confirmed that they were in study hall. Libby didn't look like she could or should go anywhere right now.

"Girls I need to be in class right now. Can this wait an hour?" I asked. "If not, I can get someone to cover my class." I waited as I assessed their faces. I wrestled with this real need to be in two places at the same time.

"No, Mrs. Duncan we can wait," Catherine said. They nodded in unison as Libby reached for a tissue to wipe her nose.

"You're certain?" I asked. I opened the private consultation space off the clinic and they went in.

"Okay, I'll see you right after class." I gathered up my attendance sheets and a pencil and hurried off to class.

Damn it. I hated when this happened and it happened all the time. What was I going to have to do to get some help for these kids? I think they just expected me to clone myself. Over and over, I had petitioned the administration for a school social worker, a school psychologist, or a counselor, and over and over again I had been told no. The rationale for the refusal was, "If we offered *those kinds of services* we would attract *those kinds of kids.*"

News flash, guess what, they're already here. We were dealing with teenagers, and teenagers have *those kinds of issues.*

I opened the door to my classroom and the students quickly rushed back to their seats and the room went quiet.

"I'm sorry I'm late for class." I started with an apology. I hoped to set a good example by being punctual and if I was late I felt an apology was in order. I expected nothing less from my students. I found that the best way to teach was to model the expected behavior. The whole level of respect was elevated when students felt they were treated with respect.

I took a stack of cards cut from red, yellow, and green construction paper and began to pass them out to the students as I gave the instructions for the day's lesson.

"The red card means no or disagree, the yellow is neutral and the green means yes or agree. Kendra will you write that on the board?" I asked. "Now, I'm going to read some controversial statements about drugs and alcohol that I want you to respond to. Once you have responded I am going to give you some facts that you may or may not be aware of. If one of your classmates or I say something that causes you to change your mind, please feel free to hold up a different colored card. Okay, Let's get started. The first statement is: adults are hypocritical when it comes to teenage drinking."

I looked out over the class and as expected there were red, yellow, and green cards.

"Bethany you raised your green card. Why?" I asked.

"I can't speak for all adults, but I know that my parents drink every night, but they would flip out if I had a beer," she stated.

"So, are you saying that there's no difference between teenage drinking and adult drinking?" I asked, and with that Denis was waving his hand wildly.

"Denis, what do you think?" I asked.

"Drinking is legal for adults and it is illegal for people under 21." He stated.

"Is that the only difference between adult drinking and underage drinking– the legal status?" I asked. We then went on to discuss the physiology and physical consequences of underage drinking as well as the impact of drinking and drug use in other areas of their lives.

By the end of the hour all the students were actively taking part in the discussion.

I found this was a great way to engage the students in talking about what they thought, how they felt, and to watch them learn by challenging their positions with facts. They had grown up so much since I first met them in September. They were no longer shy and reserved. It had been a delightful transformation in so many ways.

The bell rang and class was over. It was the last class of the semester. They sat in their desks for just another moment. "It has been my absolute pleasure and honor to have you in class. Stop by and see me anytime. Be well my friends, be well." I smiled, dropped my head, and bowed to them.

To which I received a heartfelt round of applause. Students called to me as they left the room, "Thank you Mrs. Duncan," and, "Have a nice weekend."

I quickly gathered up my things and returned to the clinic.

The girls were still in the backroom. I put the do not disturb sign on the door and locked the door behind me. Libby and Catherine sat on one couch and I sat in one of the chairs facing them.

"What's going on girls?" I asked as gently as I could.

Again Libby dropped her gaze towards the floor and Catherine slowly looked up and met my eyes. She took a deep breath and sighed.

Something had happened and these girls needed to talk. I knew that going to a teacher in a team of two was the last place these girls wanted to be. If they could have handled *this*, whatever *this* was, by themselves they wouldn't have been here with me. They were here because they were in over their heads.

I sat and waited a moment while Catherine collected herself.

"I don't know how to say this. I want to be sure no one will get into trouble if I tell you. Promise you won't tell?" Her eyes were pleading for a promise from me. But this was a promise I couldn't make, at least not without more information.

"Catherine, Libby," I waited until they both looked me in the eyes, "There are some promises I cannot keep. If you tell me that someone is hurting themselves or is hurting someone else, I have a moral and a legal obligation to get that person some help. You do understand this right? Remember we talked about this when you were in health class last fall?" The girls looked me in the eyes and nodded.

Libby leaned in towards Catherine, and whispered, "Go ahead, we have to."

Catherine nodded nearly imperceptibly and began, "You know Brooke?" she asked.

"Brooklyn Powell?" I confirmed. "Yes, of course." Quickly I tried to catalogue the few facts I knew about this young girl. All three of these girls had been in my class this semester, although they weren't all in the same section.

I knew her. I knew they were friends. I'd seen them together during school. I thought they played together on the freshman field hockey team, but I wasn't 100 percent certain.

Catherine continued, "Well, she's a pretty good student, but lately she's been falling behind in her classes. She doesn't have a study hall and she's taking both Bio and Chem this year."

"Two sciences? That's a pretty heavy load for a freshman," I commented.

"Her mother wants her to get into a really good medical school. So she is really pushing her and Brooke is starting to have trouble," Catherine said while Libby nodded her head in agreement.

Then Libby piped up, "Lots of kids struggle. She isn't struggling any more than a lot of us. It's just that her mom demands perfection. You know all A's."

"She can't get a B, you know the *Asian Fail,* and she's not even Asian," Catherine added.

I nodded. I'd heard this from students more times than I could count. Unrealistic parental expectations and yet they had loaded up their schedule so that success was unattainable, particularly with everything else that was expected here. But there was something in their demeanor that told me there was more to this story. I kept quiet as I let them tell me as much as they felt they could.

"You tell her," Libby said as she looked to Catherine.

"Do you know Evan Hedges?" Catherine asked.

"Yes, I taught him last year, when he was a junior," I responded. He was also an athlete, and therefore always in the athletic corridor after school. When others were fooling around and being fast and loose with the street talk, more than once I had heard Evan rein them in, at least when they were within earshot. He was a nice kid, as far as I knew.

"He's tutoring Brooke in Chemistry," Libby added.

"Is he taking chemistry?" I asked. Typically, most students took chemistry as a sophomore and Evan was a senior. Evan seemed like an odd choice for a tutor. "I know he's smart, but I would think with football and basketball that he wouldn't have time for tutoring." I said this aloud, not really expecting a response from the girls, but I got one anyway.

"Oh he makes the time to tutor Brooke. They have an arrangement. Evan is tutoring Brooke in exchange for sex."

The girls had let the secret out and tears began to run down their faces.

"It started in the fall just before a big chapter test and now he is pestering her all the time. She got herself into this thing, and now she doesn't know how to get herself out of it. Now, other boys have heard what she's doing and they want to tutor her too. She's even getting calls from older black guys in Richmond and some of them aren't even in high school any more. She's starting to make arrangements to see them on the weekends and even here at school."

The story was spilling out faster then I could wrap my head around what was happening.

The more they said, the more they were crying, and then Libby began to hyperventilate and gasp for air.

"Brooke and I were best friends in middle school. She's started to tell her mom that she's staying at my house. Now she's going into Richmond to hook up with these older guys. I know if my parents find out about this I'll be in big trouble, but mostly I'm just worried that something really bad might happen to Brooke. I don't know what to do." Libby looked up at me and her blue eyes were all red from crying and with traces of mascara beneath both of her eyes.

Catherine added, "I feel like such a rat for betraying Brooke, but she's out of control. I'm afraid for her and I'm afraid for us." Libby reached over and wrapped her arm around Catherine's shoulder in a show of solidarity and support. The girls held each other and cried as I bent in close and placed one of my hands on each of their shoulders giving them both a little squeeze.

I had a knot in my stomach. How could this be happening right here at school? We assume that our children and our students are safe when they're at school. In my mind's eye I tried to picture Brooke. She looked young and sweet just like Libby and Catherine. I tried to comprehend how this could possibly have happened; after all, she was still a young girl of 14. Some 14 year-olds look like they are 21 and some look like they are 12. All of these girls looked like young girls. If Catherine and Libby indeed felt afraid for their friend then perhaps their fears were justified. I sensed that there was more to this story than I was being told. I needed to take their fears and heartfelt concerns seriously. But first, I needed more information.

"Girls, let me assure you that you have done the right thing by bringing this to my attention. This was very brave of you, to care this much about your friend. Brooke is lucky to have two such good friends. Let me ask you a couple of questions. How old is Brooke?"

Libby answered through her tears, "She's 14. She won't be 15 until April."

"You said they've been having sex at school, where?" I asked.

"Well, in the fall they used to go out behind the field house during lunch, but it's too cold outside now, so lately they've been using your classroom."

My heart sank. Somehow, I felt complicit in this scandal. I had been leaving the classroom unlocked so the Muslim boys could pray during Ramadan.

"The door is unlocked, and they wait until Ghalib and his friends leave before they go in. Usually, someone is on watch for you to come down the hall, then someone knocks on the door, and Brooke and Evan go out the back door by the middle school gym," Catherine said.

"Oh dear God no, I feel terrible about this."

The questions came unbidden, followed by judgment: *Had I just been played? Was the request to use my room to pray really just a ruse? How had I allowed this to happen? You are such a fool, such a God damn fool.*

Then it was the girls' turn to comfort me.

"Please, Mrs. Duncan, this isn't your fault. It's just that there's no supervision in this hallway when you're at lunch. If it hadn't been in your room, they would've found somewhere else."

I felt sick about this, but it wasn't the students' responsibility to help assuage my guilt.

"Okay. How widespread is this knowledge? What I'm asking you is– do a lot of students know that Brooke and Evan have been meeting up to trade sex for tutoring?"

"Yes, Mrs. Duncan, a lot of the guys know, most of them are seniors. They're calling her all the time on her cell phone because now she's been having sex with *them* too."

I felt nauseous. I didn't ask the girls who *them* was. I didn't really want to know.

The girls went on and on for most of the hour filling me in on what they knew to be true and what they could only speculate on. The bottom line was that the girls were afraid for their friend. She had gotten herself into a situation that she didn't know how to get out of. They were afraid to bring this to the attention of an adult, but more than that they were afraid she might become desperate enough to hurt herself.

"We remember that you said, if someone was threatening to hurt themselves we should always take it seriously. To assume that they really didn't mean it when they said they wanted to kill themselves was way too risky," Libby said quoting me from health class.

Catherine continued, "So we decided to err on the side of caution."

I smiled. They had been paying attention in class. "So we will get Brooke some help to deal with the troubles she is facing," I said reassuringly to both Catherine and Libby as I handed them each another Kleenex to dry their eyes. "Okay girls, I want you to know that you have done the right thing. You have behaved in a way that is both loving and kind. I don't want you to say anything to anyone else about this. I don't want there to be any repercussions for the two of you. So go to your classes, attend to your studies, and if Brooke wants to discuss this with you just be a good friend and listen. I need to do some thinking about this. I'll let you know what I decide," I said as I wrote down my cell phone number and gave it to the girls. "Call me if you need anything okay? Night or day."

The final bell rang, the girls stood and I gave both of them a hug. I wrote them a pass for the class they had just missed and they headed down the hall.

It was officially the weekend. The first semester was over and it ended just as tumultuously as it had begun.

Second Semester

CHAPTER 8

Late January 2000

No, this was not going to go well. I didn't have a choice; I had to talk with Will.

I called his assistant. "Sorry, Elise. He's in a meeting now and will be tied up until about 4. Do you want me to interrupt him?" Elizabeth asked.

I hesitated and then said, "No, that's okay. Please ask him to call me, I need to talk to him before he leaves for the weekend."

"Will do," Elizabeth assured me.

I pulled the seniors' records. Evan Hedges turned 18 on September 9th. As I had feared, there were issues of consent. There were legal issues and criminal issues with the potential for criminal consequences. For according to the law, Evan was an adult, and Brooklyn was still a child of 14.

The laws defining the age of consent in Virginia were complicated, but it was clearly a felony for anyone over the age of 18 to have sex with a 14-year-old. Even if Brooke had begged Evan, this could be seen as statutory rape. Oh shit.

I knew the girls knew this. I had spent an entire class period on the state laws surrounding criminal sexual misconduct less than 6 weeks ago in health class. The students proposed a wide variety of possible scenarios to which my response had been, "Get a lawyer."

The issue was further complicated because Evan was black and Brooklyn was white. I knew that many of the students here at The Academy believed as I did: that race was an artificial construct and there truly was only one race– the human race. I also knew that *the school,* the board, and the affluent parents who sent their children here were anything but color blind.

Even at the dawning of this new millennium, here in Virginia there were many who were still fighting the Civil War. And this would be a big deal.

Evan was from East Richmond and on financial aid and Brooklyn lived on Riverside Drive. She was as close as it came to the American aristocracy.

There were lines that had been crossed based on age, race, and class. The law did not permit us, as teachers, to turn a blind eye to the issue of age.

I thought a moment about the well-worn slogan– Virginia is for Lovers. It did not apply here at Halcyon Heights. No, there were unspoken rules about social protocol, and those rules had been broken. The school espoused a welcome to all people. Or at least to the ones who could foot the bill. But the unstated rule was: do not touch our white daughters. When children dated across race and class lines, these were egregious affronts to the old vanguard.

While waiting I had a chance to think about all that had transpired. I felt sick to my stomach. Perhaps it was the mother in me who felt that something needed to be done to protect this young girl and her innocence. Libby and Catherine were still so young and shy and could barely bring themselves to talk about this sexual indiscretion with their teacher. They exuded embarrassment rather than bravado.

Again, I thought back on Laurel Winton and her impudence. She was also involved sexually with older boys and young men, but she felt no shame or need to apologize. No, Laurel had paraded her sexuality around like a badge of honor.

Maybe it had always been this way when young people felt the stirring of their blossoming sexuality and they crossed that boundary from childhood to adulthood. Why did some feel shame and others honored? It clearly had more to do with the social mores, than anything based in biology. We never saw the family dog slinking back into the house after it had been out for a romp with other dogs.

Perhaps it is only our conscience and that sense of guilt and shame that kept us from behaving like dogs. What was that line from the song by Paula Cole?

Call me a bitch in heat.

That's nice.

I had watched my advisee Laurel Winton flirting and carrying on with the upperclassmen. Laurel was also a freshman and also 14. Maybe it wasn't any different, but this seemed different and intuitively it just felt different. With Laurel it had all seemed so much more calculated like she was using her sexuality and her behavior as a weapon to hurt her mother. Even Carolynn Winton had characterized her daughter as an unsympathetic victim and a *badass*. No, maybe this situation wasn't really any different at all, but it certainly didn't feel that way.

However, these girls were not like Laurel. At least that was what they portrayed to me that afternoon. No, these girls were worried sick about their friend. I didn't have the impression that either of them felt that sex outside of marriage was immoral or sinful. But rather, there seemed to be a need for these fourteen-year-olds to believe in the promise of real love, and in romantic love. They were not jaded or cynical. They believed that sex should be shared within the confines of a loving relationship. They wanted nothing less for their dear friend Brooklyn.

They hadn't mentioned that there was a loving relationship between Brooke and Evan. Were they even friends? I had a hard time imagining that Evan would even invite Brooklyn to sit and have lunch with him or speak with her in the hall. Their ages and social circles just didn't seem to overlap. No, if he respected her, and if she was indeed his friend, he wouldn't have passed her off to the other boys. But if what Catherine and Libby said was true, Brooke was now sexually involved with a whole range of older boys inside and outside of school.

The girls felt this was wrong and they didn't know what to do. They'd tried to talk with Brooke, but she was too embarrassed and ashamed of herself to ask for help. She'd promised them that she was going to stop saying yes, when she wanted to say no. She vowed to break the pattern and stop the behavior, but she was being pressured everywhere she turned, and the more she repeated the behavior, the more requests for sex she received, and the more she complied.

The girls were worried that she might try and hurt herself as she became more entrapped by her own compliance. Her sense of self was changing as evidenced by her clothing and her language. Her girlfriends had taken a big chance by calling in an adult to help. This wasn't something that would be taken lightly. They feared their friendship would not survive this betrayal. But they could see the big picture and they feared if they did nothing, Brooke might feel so trapped and despondent that she would hurt herself. No one had said the word *suicide*, but that was what had been implied.

The girls were afraid. They had exposed their friend and a senior on the football team. They were seeking anonymity. I knew that Will would need to know the names of the girls who made these allegations and brought this to my attention. He would need to determine if they were credible, as these were serious allegations.

This had the possibility to blow the school wide open, as there could be punishments and legal consequences if the allegations were true.

I had no reason to believe otherwise.

When I'd dismissed the girls, I had tried to be reassuring. I did my best to convince them that they needed to keep a very low profile. "Stay close to home this weekend and don't bring any undue attention to this issue," I advised.

The last thing we needed would be for them to recant their story out of fear for the consequences. These girls had been very brave to come forward, and yet there was a part of me that feared for their safety. I encouraged them to talk with their parents, as they were both still children, not even fifteen years old.

Given Catherine and Libby's rendition of the facts, I assumed that Brooke had been the victim and these older boys were predators.

I sat at my desk and waited for my phone to ring.

Just after 4 the call came through. It was Elizabeth, "Will is ready to see you," she said.

I grabbed my notepad and keys and headed for his office.

I walked down the athletic corridor, the hallway that was filled with student athletes wearing and carrying all sorts of athletic paraphernalia. The students called out to me good naturedly, "See you on Monday," and, "Have a good weekend, Mrs. Duncan."

I rounded the corner into the academic office and nearly crashed into Elizabeth who was sitting on a stool with a stack of papers that she was filing into the infamous permanent records.

"Oh sorry, Liz," I said as I maneuvered past her.

"He's waiting for you," she called out over her shoulder.

I knocked on his door and Will responded, "Come on in Elise, the door's open.

I opened the door and closed it behind me. Will stood up from his desk as I entered. He was always a gentleman, with manners as natural as breathing.

"This can't be good," he said, "It's well after 4:00 on a Friday and I only saw you a few hours ago. We should both be packing up and heading for home. Dare I ask, what's going on?" He took his seat as he gestured towards a chair across from his desk.

As I sat down, it dawned on me that I had been here so frequently, that I had come to think of this as my chair.

I recounted the story as it had been told to me.

Will brought his elbows to his desktop and dropped his chin into his hands, and began to shake his head. His brow furrowed and I looked on while he began to process the issues. There were so many things that landed on his desk. There were so many difficult decisions he was responsible for making. I was just the messenger, and frequently the sounding board as we talked about the issues, and in this particular case there were many issues that needed to be sorted out.

Will sized up the situation quickly, fully understanding the implications of these accusations.

"You've had Brooklyn in class," he stated and then asked, "What's she like?"

"She's a good student, diligent, but not brilliant," I said. I'd had brilliant students in my classroom. You can pick them out by the questions they ask and the writing they submit. "She's 14-years-old and I've no doubt that her academic prowess will grow. She's quite capable and if she applies herself she can be and do whatever she sets her mind to. An A in chemistry in her freshman year will be inconsequential to her future success and happiness; however, being seen as a social and sexual reprobate at 14-years-old, well that's another story. This behavior will have far-reaching consequences long after her grade in chemistry has been forgotten."

"You've got that right," Will said.

"It's hard for me to fathom this young man getting involved in something like this or this young lady for that matter. He always seemed so courteous and respectful, and I thought Brooke was a sweet and serious student. Maybe all that counts for less than I thought. I do know this, even good kids make their fair share of mistakes, and the teenage years are a time for exploration. What students show to their teachers can be very different from the behavior they try out and try on with their peers," I continued. I needed to talk this out.

"Still, Child Protective Services has very clear reporting requirements and this kind of allegation whether true or not must be reported. There are legal implications for me as a nurse and a teacher, but there are also legal implications for this young man. She was only 14 and he is already 18. This is statutory rape even if it was consensual." There, I had laid the cards on the table.

Dear God, the storm clouds were hovering overhead and I had a very unsettled feeling that this was about to get ugly. Real ugly.

It was then and there that Will provided me with some additional information that I had been unaware of. "Brooke's parents are major donors to the school, her father and his father are legacies." This muddied the waters for him, less so for me.

Will said, "I need to know the names of all of the boys involved." This was not a request for information and I knew it.

I felt sick to my stomach. I hadn't asked the girls for names and I knew they wouldn't be interested in telling me. When I spoke with them, their fear had been palpable. The names had been so carefully guarded. They feared the fallout for Brooke, as well as for themselves.

"Will, they didn't tell me and I didn't ask them. They were so afraid just to be telling me what was going on. I wanted them to continue talking, and I felt if I pressed them for names they'd stop talking," I said.

He pursed his lips and then said, "Catherine and Libby trust you. I want you to ask them for the names. I understand their fears. I don't want anyone to see them coming into my office. This place is like a fishbowl; everyone knows what everyone else is doing. Or at least I thought I did. Anyway, offer the girls complete anonymity. I promise you, no one else in this administration will know the source of this information."

Will and I discussed the law and the legal issues of reporting. He and I had been around the block on this one more times than I could count. The law was clear and there were reasons for the laws. It was to protect against child endangerment. My late husband, Elliott, had been a prosecutor for over 20 years. I knew what the law said about this. I was the sex ed teacher for God's sake. Every student who had sat in my class had been taught about criminal sexual misconduct. The law was clear, I knew that criminal charges should be filed and this should be sorted out in the legal system. But I also knew if I wanted to keep my job that this was out of my hands.

This should've been out of Will and George's hands too. There was a reason this kind of issue went to trial and the determination of guilt or innocence wasn't left up to a well-meaning school administrator relying solely on hearsay. And in truth that was really all we had right now.

"Elise, talk with the girls on Monday. I'll ask security to look at the videotapes. There's a camera right outside your classroom, another by the stadium, and by all exits. That should give *Robo-Cop* something to do this weekend," he smiled.

I smiled a little, too. I should have known that William would call the Director of Security by the same little pet name that the students did. He had lightened the moment, and for this I was grateful.

"I need some time to think this through, and I need some solid evidence before going forward. We can't make this allegation based solely on the story of two freshman girls, in spite of the fact that the story is so far out of the box that I believe it to be true. I'll make an appointment with the headmaster. I'll need you to be there, too."

He looked so sad as I left his office for we both knew that the politics of right and wrong, and of guilt and innocence, would ripple through this whole community.

∾

All that evening and on through the weekend my mind was preoccupied with what I had just become privy to. I tried to wrap my head around the scenario and reserve judgment. I judged myself harshly, and my own culpability for leaving my classroom unlocked during Ramadan. I had talked this through with Will before he'd left for the day. He was kind, and far less concerned about where this had taken place than the fact that it had taken place. Still, I felt the remorse that came with poor decisions, specifically, my poor decision.

I still couldn't believe they'd used my classroom to have sex. I had been good to these kids and this felt like such a betrayal. I feared I might take the fall for this. This was a clear violation of school policy. And I had been the one who violated it: *all classrooms must be locked at all times if the teacher is not present.*

The underlying assumption behind the policy was that students could not be trusted. Trusted with what? Would they lie, cheat, steal or behave dishonorably? What would happen when trust was eroded? Perhaps this had become a self-fulfilling prophecy?

On the other hand, while we were prepping these kids for adulthood, they were still adolescents struggling to grow up. They were learning the rules, hating the rules, and sometimes breaking the rules just like we all did.

I tried not to take this personally. I had made a mistake, an honest mistake, and the truth was that this had nothing to do with me. I told myself this over and over again. I needed it to be true.

My students trusted me– often with their deepest, darkest secrets. The secrets they didn't tell anyone else. They needed to know that there was an adult in their lives they could talk to. It was a sacred bond.

In return I trusted them. So when the boys came to me and asked if they could use my room to keep their prayer rugs and pray during Ramadan, of course I'd said yes. This was absolutely consistent with my all-embracing philosophy that there is one Creator and these students had every right to pray and worship in accordance with their own beliefs. I had left the room unlocked for them.

I had trusted them, and yet it was really two others who had betrayed me. I was both sad and angry with them for their betrayal, but also for their lack of judgment. I was also angry with myself. I was the adult here. They were adolescents.

Still, tutoring in exchange for sex.

In the eyes of the law they were not just two adolescents. No, a crime had been committed because he was legally an adult and she was still a child.

One moment I chastised myself, and the next I tried to remind myself that I didn't do this out of negligence. Brooke and Evan, and their co-conspirators had violated my trust, and that said more about them than it did about me.

If the students involved were intent on procuring a place for a sexual liaison then they would've found a place, if not in my unlocked classroom, then they would have found another private place. Not only would they, but they did.

But would the administration see it that way? Would fingers be pointed and blame assigned? I had made a mistake, and a student had been compromised.

I already knew I wasn't one of the chosen few. I had been known to stir things up and question the status quo. Sam had tried to warn me. Sam had refused to compromise his integrity and in return he lost his coaching position. I wondered— what they would do to me?

I took a deep breath. I would have to own this. But I was fairly certain that the athletic director wouldn't be called on the carpet because he had not patrolled the bleachers in the football stadium. Neither would the band and orchestra teacher be reprimanded for not securing the auditorium and the orchestra pit. According to Libby and Catherine, these locations were also frequented during the lunch hour for sexual liaisons.

But again, did I really expect equity and justice? The others were men whose programs brought in substantial bequests and donations. I *just* taught health, and that was seen as unimportant. After all, the colleges and universities said it didn't count in calculating one's GPA. Therefore, why should anyone care if our students learned to care for themselves– body and soul? Even some of their own parents couldn't be bothered with such *minor* matters, as time and again, the real issues that impacted their children's health and well being were ignored.

Unlike the football, music, and theatre programs, my program was state mandated. It was just another unfunded state mandate. When the accounting was completed I contributed nothing to the bottom line. No, I was a cost, a liability. And when a school is run like a business and our students are seen as our customers, one goal of a profitable business is to cut costs.

I wondered if and when this all came to light, if there would be anyone who would speak for me and on my behalf?

Around and around I went as I tried to justify my decision to leave my classroom unlocked. What had been my intention? What were these students' intentions when they seized the opportunity to occupy my classroom after the Muslim students left and I was off at a meeting? Who should assume responsibility for what happened? Did the blame rest with me? I was the adult and the teacher. Or did the behavior of the students belong to them alone? Whom would the administration back and whom would they blame? The heat was on, and I knew I was in the hot seat.

∽

As I drove to school Monday morning I had a feeling of impending disaster. The week started as all weeks at Halcyon Heights did at 8:00 AM with the Monday morning faculty meeting. It seemed to be a kinder and gentler way to start the school week, at least for the students. There must have been some wise administrator who had considered the 16-year-old girl who shot up her school, murdered two teachers, and injured her classmates. The only rationale she offered for her behavior was "I don't like Mondays."

The hit song from the late '70s played on in my head. Maybe it was my intuition or maybe it was an omen or maybe it was nothing, nothing at all.

> *Tell me why?*
> *I don't like Mondays.*
> *Tell me why?*
> *I don't like Mondays.*
> *Tell me why?*
> *I don't like Mondays.*
> *I want to shoot*
> *The whole day down.*
> *-Boomtown Rats*

Per usual, I could barely focus during the faculty meeting. Could be that I'd attended so many over the years that they had begun to all run together, or equally likely was the fact that I was preoccupied with how the meeting with the headmaster would unfurl.

The bell rang overhead and the faculty meeting was concluded, finished or not. As I stood to leave the library, Will caught my eye and raised a finger. He was asking me to wait a moment.

I excused myself from my colleagues. "Have a good one," I called to Sally, and walked in Will's direction.

When the crowd around him had cleared, he moved closer to me and nearly whispered. "George wants to see us *now.*"

"Okay, let me take my coat and purse to my office and I will meet you there," I said.

Will nodded that this was okay with him.

Will and I arrived at the Headmaster's Office from different directions, but at about the same time. Will went in first and I was left to sit outside George's office in the vestibule. The minutes ticked by as my imagination created nearly every possible conversation they might be having. Finally, the door was opened and I was invited inside.

George asked my opinion, "I need to know a couple of things. First: do you find these girls credible?" There was something in the way he framed the question that I knew Will had been true to his word. George didn't know the names of the informants. I found comfort in that.

"I'm afraid to say that I do. I have had all these kids in class. The entire scenario is so far out of bounds that there is a part of me that still has difficulty believing these kids are trading sex for tutoring. But I also know the informants and I don't believe that they would make this up. There is nothing for either of them to gain. No, they are deeply concerned for the well being of their friend," I said.

I was the only one of the three of us who knew the students involved. I'd had all the students in my classroom. The girls involved were my students last semester and the boys were in my classroom last year when my class had been taught to juniors.

"I'm still having a hard time understanding this," George said. "Why would these girls tell *you* this?"

I spoke slowly and talked him through the facts again. "We don't have any guidance counselors here and the students who have been through my class have been told over and over again that there are secrets that we cannot keep. The first is when people are hurting themselves. The second is when they are hurting others. These freshmen girls had heard these things just before Christmas. They have had a chance to ruminate on it and are convinced that their friend is making decisions that are hurting her, and that she's in a position where other people are using and hurting her too. They think she's in over her head and doesn't have the courage or the backbone to get herself out of it. She's only 14," I stated, and then paused to let George catch up.

George looked like he would like me to disappear and take this thorny problem with me. Little did he know, I, too, would like nothing better than to disappear and leave this problem in someone else's lap, but that was no longer an option.

George folded his hands in front of him on the conference room table. He sat there silently staring at his hands, and so I went on. "In accordance with the state law, given her age she is unable to give consent for sexual behaviors. Anyone who touches her in a sexual way has committed a crime, technically a felony. When we as teachers have this information there are mandatory reporting requirements, because this is seen as a child endangerment issue. If we do not report we are also breaking the law."

I knew George did not want to hear this, and he certainly didn't want the police involved. I could see his agitation escalating at the very thought of this scandal hitting the press.

He shifted in his seat and then turned the focus on me. "What the hell were you thinking, leaving your classroom unlocked?" He was red in the face and leaning in towards me.

I sat there trying to think of how to respond, when Will came to my defense. "Come on, George. I already explained to you that Elise had agreed to let some students pray in her room because it was Ramadan. Let's stay focused on the real issues at hand. These kids were having sex all over campus and Elise's room was just one of the many places they frequented– like the bleachers in the football stadium. Where there's a will there's a way. These kids acted on an opportunity and in my mind, they took advantage of Elise," Will finished.

My heart was filled with gratitude. Will had backed me up. We sat in silence, waiting for George to respond.

After a moment, he stopped clasping and unclasping his hands. When he spoke his voice was calm and steady. "Let me be abundantly clear. You're not to discuss what happens in here today with anyone. And I mean *anyone*, including the police or child protective services or whoever they are. We will handle this internally because none of us want to invoke the big consequences, now do we?"

I knew this was not open for discussion or negotiation.

I also knew what the law said about mandatory reporting.

And then, as if we were discussing something routine, like a new textbook for my class, George let out a deep breath and passed me a bowl of multicolored Hershey kisses. A little sweetness delivered with the implied threat. What consequences was he threatening me with? I could only speculate.

"You have shared with us what you have been made privy to, and I appreciate that, I really do." He smiled to convey gratitude, but his hands were now clenched on either side of the conference table. Again he leaned towards me, and caught my gaze. He held it just a bit longer than I was comfortable with. I could hear his slow rhythmic breathing. The timbre of his voice, and his demeanor barely concealed a threat. "Now, let me put this in a broader context for you, so that you can understand the ramifications of this *dilemma*. Okay?"

My mind flashed back to a conference on ethics that I'd attended last summer. What was a *dilemma*? According to one of the speakers at the conference, a dilemma was when people were conflicted because the only choices available were either between competing goods or competing evils. And how one resolved the dilemma could be very revealing about their character.

George continued to lean towards me. I dropped my eyes from his face to his hands. It felt safer and yet his hands clenched the table. His fingernails were white and the blood vessels on the back of his chapped red hands were bulging, I felt an internal shudder. For God's sake what was going to happen here?

"Let me just lay out the dynamics of this situation, so you get the full impact of what's really at stake here," George said, his voice was cool. "First off, you do know that Brooklyn Powell is a triple legacy here. Right?" he asked.

I shook my head. "You had better start at the beginning. In my classroom, my students are known only by their first names. I have no idea who their families are and how they rank on the social register. It is irrelevant to how they perform and are treated in my classroom. The significance of *a triple legacy* is lost on me, perhaps you should assume that I know nothing."

George's expression went from cool to cold.

I sat up and straightened my spine. I was not about to apologize for trying to keep privilege out of my classroom.

When he spoke again it was with a tone of righteousness and arrogance. "Well, let's just say that *my* ability to keep this place afloat and pay your paycheck requires me to pay attention to that which *you* are able to ignore." I could tell already that it was unlikely he and I would see eye to eye on this.

George took a deep breath and I felt like a stranger in a strange land. I felt a little like I was just about to engage in a remedial reading program with a teacher who had little tolerance for who I was and what I knew, but only focused on my limitations.

"Okay, then let me try to enlighten you."

I could hardly stand it. He was such an arrogant prick. It was all I could do to keep from telling him so. His whole manner and tone of voice were condescending.

"Brooklyn Powell is the granddaughter of Beatrice Ward. Do you have any idea who she is?"

Again I shook my head, and kept my expression blank.

"You really don't know, do you?"

"No, should I?" This wasn't the first time I had been unaware of the pedigrees of one of my students. The fact was, I already knew more about many of the students than I cared to know.

Will had apparently decided to cut through some of the tension, and intervened. "Beatrice Ward is Rosalie Powell's mother and Brooklyn's maternal grandmother. Beatrice Ward is the heiress to the industrial conglomerate Ward Steel. She is legendary for ruling her family and her only daughter with absolute control. The Powells live on Riverside Drive in one of the turn of the century estates. They live there with Grandma Bea. The business, the mansion, and all the property belong to Grandma Bea– Mrs. Beatrice Ward."

Will paused for a moment as I tried to comprehend why all of this was significant and relevant.

"Mrs. Ward, the *grande dame*, is quite elderly and her daughter Rosalie Powell is her only heir. Beatrice Ward is a very big donor at the school and her late husband was an alumnus here and sat on the board in the '80s," George said with a tone that implied I was an imbecile not to know this.

"I guess that complicates things," I stated.

"Yes, it certainly does," and then again in a voice just above a whisper, he closed his eyes and said, "It *certainly* does."

But at least I had the wisdom not speak the rest of what I was thinking, *It complicates things for him, but not for me, and not for the students involved. Silly me, I thought this was supposed to be about the students.*

He continued, talking to me as if he was addressing a two-year-old. "I guess it goes without saying that you're probably unaware of the dynamics involved with the Hedges family either. The Big Ten signing day is next Wednesday. Evan is supposed to sign the commitment papers to accept a full four-year scholarship to play football at Ohio State. The timing of this allows no time to investigate the allegations made. There is little doubt that all offers of any athletic scholarships will be withdrawn if criminal charges are filed."

This much had not gone unnoticed on my part.

"Elise, there will be no further investigation or inquiry of Evan or any of the boys allegedly involved in this unfortunate debacle until after the signing. I can't have any of this leaked to the press. They would have a flippin' field day. Halcyon Heights would bear the brunt of this and I won't have it. Have I made myself clear?" George asked, but this was not a question. This had been commanded and I understood completely. I felt as if he was holding me completely responsible for the behavior of the students.

And with that George stood, smiled in a most disingenuous way, and extended his hand in my direction, "Thank you Elise. I need a few more minutes here with Will."

I was being dismissed. *Thank God*, I thought, *Get me the hell out of here.*

Just before lunch, Liz, Will's assistant, knocked on my classroom door while I was teaching. I stepped out to meet her in the hallway.

"Mr. Warwick wants to see you during first lunch in his office. Can you make it?" she asked.

Normally, I met with the Freshman Support Team on Mondays during lunch, but this meeting with Will would take precedent. "Sure, I'll be there as soon as class is finished," I said and stepped back into my classroom to pick up where I'd left off in my lesson.

When I reached Will's office thirty minutes later, his door was open and he was waiting for me. He gestured towards the chair and I knew I wouldn't be going anywhere anytime soon.

"We are going to open the inquiry in phases. Given the sensitive nature of the issues involved I really need you to be present," he said, in a way that sounded more like a request than a demand.

"Okay." I knew full well that refusing was not an option. "Where will we begin?"

"I think we should start with Brooklyn's parents. The purpose of the meeting will be to tell them about the allegations that have been made."

"Did security see anything on those security tapes?" I asked. "I certainly hope this doesn't come down to one person's word against another." I said as I again considered all the different ways this whole thing might unravel.

"Oh the *security tapes*– they show us almost nothing. Nothing to hold onto at all," Will scoffed. "In fact, I've just learned that most of our video surveillance system is just a hoax. The cameras have a light on, but they are incapable of filming anything. Apparently, we just want to give the students and their parents the impression that we're watching them. So if you want to commit some foul misdeed, just don't do it in the main lobby. Otherwise, you're good to go."

I got the impression that Will was pissed that he had been kept out of the loop on this. I couldn't blame him. The director of the upper school was the equivalent to the principal in a public school, the buck stopped with him. He quickly let this pass. We had other issues to discuss.

"If the meeting goes well, I'll have Liz go get Brooke. In her parents' presence I will confront her with what has been alleged about her sexual liaisons here at school." It was clear that Will and George had strategized how best to handle this.

"What will my role be?" I asked, hoping for clarification.

"You are to be my support person and a witness to what takes place, but mostly to be the calming influence that you always are," he said.

"I have to ask," I paused, wondering if I really wanted to know the answer. "I've been thinking about our meeting with George this morning and what you shared about the Powell family. Do you know *this* much about all the families?" It was really unsettling to think the administration was scrutinizing our students' families like this.

"Elise, don't be so naïve," Will replied. "Ever since they *retired* Jose, all his admissions' responsibilities were added to the Director's job, and it has become my responsibility to know who these people are and to manage their needs and expectations. There are days when I am really a glorified salesperson, keeping the seats filled, and keeping our customers happy."

Will was obviously disturbed by this frank admission. He had let his guard down and spoke with more candor than I was accustomed to.

My mind drifted and I thought about Elliott. I remembered him asking if I had a sign tattooed on my forehead that said: *tell me your story*. I think it was because I asked people the important questions, the questions about themselves and their lives, and then truly listened for the answers.

"Have any decisions been made about the consequences for the students involved?" I asked.

"It's a bit premature to think about the consequences. We need to perform our due diligence and first determine what happened," he said.

"Of course," I said. This was why he captained the ship. I was already onto the sentencing and there had yet to be a trial. I needed to remember not to rush to judgment. I trusted Will to do the right thing.

"Ultimately, once all the facts are in, George will make the decision." Will concluded.

I realized then that I had little or no faith in George Walker.

Just before I left Will's office, Elizabeth called to inform us that she had scheduled the first of multiple meetings. The meeting with Brooke's parents had been set for the next day at 3 PM during my free period.

Funny, I couldn't remember ever feeling less free. This was burdensome and the burden was mine to bear, whether I liked it or not. I was just glad I didn't have to bear it alone. Thank God for Will.

Catherine and Libby were waiting for me outside the clinic when I returned. I informed the girls that parent meetings were being scheduled and I advised them to lay low. They looked like a pair of little frightened bunnies clinging to one another. I think they were just beginning to grasp how divisive this whole thing might become.

"Girls please call me if you need to talk," I said in a low voice. "This could get ugly, real ugly. I don't think you should be seen hanging around the clinic or in the athletic corridor. As Mr. Warwick likes to say, '*We live in a fish bowl.*' It wouldn't require too much detective work for someone to figure out the source of these allegations." The girls agreed. I was sorry I couldn't give them the reassurance that they were so desperately looking for.

I could see in their faces they were frightened. They had followed their hearts and done what they felt was the right thing to do. Yet, if word got out about the role they had played in this, it would not go well for them. Kids could be so brutal to one another.

It was time to put this in the hands of the adults. At least that was what I thought at the time. I needed to do my part to protect the whistle blowers, these two innocent girls who had done nothing more than say, "Someone please put a stop to this. This is just not right."

I had missed lunch again. My dear colleague and confidant Joanne had run over to the dining room and brought me back a salad. I didn't have time to eat it then, as I needed to be in class. "I'll put it in the refrigerator for later," she said.

It's often the little acts of kindness and consideration that show the depth of one's character. I had people in my life that were so good, and so good to me. Joanne wanted to make certain that I didn't forget to eat. God bless her.

I would need more people like her in my camp very soon.

CHAPTER 9

February 2000

Since the Academy was a multicultural environment there were many different types of families. There were also many different attitudes about what constituted appropriate discipline. The meeting with Brooklyn's parents was scheduled for that afternoon. I could only imagine how they would react to their daughter's participating in this-- *sex-for-tutoring* exchange. The academic pressure from home had to be pretty high for a 14-year- old to exchange the use of her body for the promise of an A in chemistry.

There were those who truly believed that to spare the rod was to spoil the child.

How would the Powells react? Would they see Brooklyn as the victim or would they punish her for her participation or something in between?

There were parents who appeared to base their children's value solely on their achievements, because of the glory or the shame this brought to their family name. The pressure to perform academically for some of these kids was astronomical. So many of our students came from high-achieving parents– doctors, lawyers, and captains of industry.

The expectation was: if I was able to secure my place and position in this world then you should be able to do the same. This began with good grades at the best school, followed by an acceptance to the best colleges and universities. For those who endorsed this philosophy– this was only way to attain success.

My mind drifted as I thought about all I had encountered in my tenure at The Academy. I had seen some pretty out-of-the-box parental behavior, particularly where student grades were involved. Many parents were looking for a big return on their $25,000 annual investment. The student's quarterly statement, otherwise known as a report card, was the equivalent of a profit and loss statement on their academic portfolio.

One dad whipped his daughter with the end of an electrical cord, leaving bruises on her back and chest in the size and shape of the plug because she did poorly on an exam. When he was called in for a conference before we filed the report with Child Protective Services, he brought pictures from their trip to Paris with him. There was his daughter, her arms over-flowing with shopping bags *a la haute couture*. This was his proof to how much he loved his daughter.

It was a pretty good indication of how the conversation with a parent was going to go when the opening question was, "What grade did you *give* my child?"

As if grades were distributed like gifts rather than a reflection of the effort their child put into the class and the mastery their child showed of the material.

There was another mother who made an appointment to see me about the *B* I had *given* to her son. "There must be some mistake, Ari needs an *A* in this class." She wanted to know, "What can be done about this?" But what she really wanted to know was whether or not I could be persuaded to change her son's grade from a *B* to an *A*.

In response, I sat down with her and showed her Ari's grades. I wanted her to see that I hadn't looked out over my sea of students and somehow mis-categorized her stellar son as a *B* student when indeed in her mind he was clearly an *A* student.

So I showed her how I'd calculated the grades in my class based on the points her son *earned* on each assignment, multiplied by the weight given to the assignment, resulting in the total points *earned,* and then divided by the total points possible, and that Ari had *earned* an 87, thus a *B*.

She sat there for a moment, then got up and began to pace around my office. Her brow was creased as if she was doing some heavy thinking.

The quarter was over. The grades were in. I wondered what else we could possibly have to talk about, when she asked, "How about if we borrow three points from next semester? Give him a 90 so an *A* will show up on his Quarterly, and next semester he will need to earn a 93 or better to get the *A*."

Did she think I was a bank and she could simply take out a loan? If her kid wanted an *A*, he'd have to earn it just like everybody else.

"I'm sorry Mrs. Gottrocks, but I can't help you," I said, and stood to indicate this meeting was over.

She was incensed. "This is so *not* over. I will take this up with George," she said, indicating that she was on a first name basis with the headmaster.

Big fucking deal. I didn't say it, but I wanted to.

Gratefully, this day had been uneventful until at last it was 3:00 PM and time to meet with Mr. and Mrs. Powell.

I arrived in Will's office and took my seat. Then we waited in near silence for the Powells to arrive. The overhead lights had been turned off and the blinds had been drawn to keep the curious from minding someone else's business. Will had done all he could to assure privacy and confidentiality in this extremely difficult situation. A small light on the credenza cast a glow in the room on this gray February day. Then Liz knocked on the door, opened it and said, "Mr. Warwick ... Mr. and Mrs. Powell are here to see you."

Will stood and came around his desk to shake hands with Brooklyn's parents. "Thank you for coming," he said to the Powells. "Have you met Mrs. Duncan? She is our Director of Health."

I stood, smiled, and I extended my hand to meet theirs.

Brooke's mother was a beautiful woman. She looked younger than I expected, but I felt that way about many of my students' mothers. She was tall and lean with shoulder length auburn hair. I suspected she had a close and personal relationship with her plastic surgeon. No one who carried so little body fat had natural breasts as large as hers.

Her face was devoid of the tell tale signs of aging that usually grace the faces of women in their forties. Her brow was worriless and there were no smile lines around her eyes. I sensed she was an ice princess, and I'm generally a pretty good read of character.

She shook my hand, but neglected to make eye contact as she quickly turned back towards Will.

"Mrs. Duncan was also Brooke's health teacher last semester," Will said, completing the introductions.

"Yes, nice to see you," she mumbled.

Perhaps she had no smile lines on her face because she never smiled. Perhaps her life and very existence were without joy. If that were the case then this meeting would be yet another day in a long line of days that have stripped this woman of reason to rejoice and be glad.

Mrs. Powell was dressed in tight-fitting, camel-colored riding pants tucked into her dark brown leather riding boots and an ivory cashmere sweater. Her jewelry was substantial; gold necklace with a matching gold bracelet, and a diamond ring with the stone the size of my thumbnail. Her whole countenance spoke of old money.

Mr. Powell turned towards me as he took my hand, then wrapped his other hand over the top of mine. "Nice to see you again, Mrs. Duncan. I remember you from the Meet the Faculty Night and I know how much Brooke enjoyed your class."

He was about the same height as his wife. His hairline was receding and his smile was open, warm, and genuine, and so was his handshake. Maybe it was just my first impression or more likely it was my intuition, but I liked him.

Will gestured to the parents to be seated as he walked back behind his desk and sat down. We all took our seats. The Powells were on one side of his desk sitting close together. There was an empty chair between us and I sat two feet from them as we all faced Will.

"This is a difficult conversation to have with you," Will said as he addressed Brooke's parents. He paused and they nodded in his direction encouraging him to continue. "Just last Friday some of Brooke's classmates came to see Mrs. Duncan because they were concerned about your daughter. We have done some very preliminary investigation and we believe their concerns are justified and the allegations to be true." Will paused again and took a deep breath.

I knew that what came next would be very, very difficult for him to say, but not nearly as difficult as it would be for these parents to hear.

"Brooke has gotten herself involved with some of the upper classmen and we believe that she has been trading sexual behaviors for tutoring in her chemistry class and perhaps in other classes as well."

Brooke's father dropped his face into his hands and her mother was immediately defensive.

"Who's making this kind of allegation about my daughter? Who are the boys involved? What proof do you have? Where did this take place? How could you have let this happen to my daughter?" She spat the questions out indiscriminately like a rapid-fire machine gun. "Brooke is a brilliant student. Why in the world would she need to do this?"

William let her pour it all out and waited until she had finished before he began again.

I sat in silence and wondered how I would have responded if I had been in her shoes. I couldn't know for certain, but I doubted it would have been like this. My inner voice begged me to be still, for we all react differently when those we love are threatened. I felt a sickness in my belly; a mix of shame and heartbreak. I knew when this mother was provided with the detailed answers she was seeking, her anguish would only escalate.

I turned my face towards Brooke's father. He was wiping the tears that were slowly slipping from his eyes. I reached across Will's desk for a tissue and handed it to him. Will began laying out the allegations, as we understood them. "At this point we only have the word of a couple of other students that sex is being exchanged for tutoring, but we have been told that it has happened frequently throughout the fall and this winter. We have been told it's happening here on campus and that there has been more than one young man involved." Will continued, "Before we speak with any of the young men, we wanted to first speak with Brooke. Mrs. Duncan and I thought it would be in everyone's best interest if we had that conversation in your presence. I must tell you, I believe our source of information is credible. These people have nothing to gain by bringing this to our attention, but they are doing so because they fear for your daughter's safety as well as for her physical and emotional well being."

Next came the excruciating part.

Will turned and picked up the phone on his desk to call to his assistant, "Liz, would you please send Brooke in?" As we waited for Brooke to join us, Mr. Powell spoke quietly, "She's been irritable lately and overly concerned about invasions of her privacy. Every time her cell phone rings she bolts out of the room with great urgency and secrecy like she's just received a call from The President and is needed to consult on matters of national security. She never used to do that."

He stopped himself, considered, and then continued, "I thought it was just part of being a teenager." It was almost like he was talking to himself as he tried to come to terms with what he'd just heard.

"She plays this God awful rap and hip-hop music at all hours of the day and night, but my parents didn't like my music when I was her age either." He shook his head and chastised himself. "Oh dear God, I guess I should've been more attentive. I should've asked more questions."

His wife shot him a look and spoke in a tone of utmost disrespect, "Let's just wait for Brooke before we try and convict her without listening to what she has to say about this."

It was easy to see who wore the pants in this family. She had just openly emasculated her husband without a hint of remorse.

He closed his mouth, looked down at his lap where he clenched and unclenched his fists; his fingers were turning red with tension. There was a knock on the door, and Brooke entered.

Brooke was a very pretty girl. She stood about 5'5" and couldn't have weighed more than 110 pounds. She had narrow hips and was still relatively flat chested. I couldn't help but wonder if she'd even had her first menstrual period yet. It wasn't uncommon for thin girls to go through puberty later because they didn't have much body fat and thus low estrogen levels. This was my field of expertise, adolescent development.

Her shoulder length auburn hair was pulled back in a barrette at the nape of her neck, revealing diamond stud earrings. She had brilliant blue eyes and a smattering of freckles across her nose. She wore a retainer, indicating she'd probably had her braces removed in the last year. Her teeth were perfect, as were most of the students' at The Academy.

She wore her gray uniform skirt a full eight inches above her knees, shorter than the dress code dictated. It wasn't rolled; no, it had been professionally shortened, a sign that her mother was in agreement. The school rules were for someone else, the elite need not comply.

The sleeves of her white oxford cloth blouse were rolled to the elbow, revealing her classic Cartier watch. Brooke carried her school blazer and a Tory Burch messenger bag holding her books.

She looked confused in the dimly lit office. Again, Will stood up and extended his arm and open hand towards the only open chair in the room, the chair between the one I was seated in and the one her mother occupied. She looked to her parents, "What's going on?"

My heart went out to her. Poor dear, she must have been terribly troubled to see both of her parents and her former teacher gathered in the Director's office on a Tuesday afternoon in February.

"Maybe that is something you can shed some light on," her mother responded with an acrid tongue.

Will shot Mrs. Powell a look, as he exerted the control that his position allocated to him. "Brooke, please know that we are gathered here because we only have your best interests at heart. Last week, some unfortunate allegations were made concerning your sexual conduct on school grounds. I want you to listen to me before you respond." He was direct, but his voice was both fatherly and kind.

Brooklyn was already tearing up.

"A couple of students came to Mrs. Duncan because they care about you and are concerned about you," Will continued. "They feel you may have gotten yourself into a situation that has now gotten out of control. They said, that in exchange for tutoring in chemistry that you were providing some young men in the senior class with sexual favors, and now more boys are approaching you for sex."

He paused, and let the allegations hang there for a moment. "Before you answer, I need you to take a moment and think about the importance of telling the truth to me, to your parents, but mostly to yourself."

Fearing the truth, Mrs. Powell spoke first. "Brooke, don't say anything. We will deal with this at home," she commanded her daughter.

Brooke turned to her mother and glared at her in anger. "Maybe for once you should stop trying to tell me what to do."

Then, she turned to face Will and spoke in a most respectful tone. "Yes, Mr. Warwick, I had sexual encounters in exchange for some help in chemistry," she stopped and waited a moment, "and in pre-calc too." She responded like this was already a matter of fact. And yet, there was something akin to pride in her voice implying, she wasn't a little girl and didn't intend to be treated as such. "Is that all you need to know?" She asked, and without waiting for his answer she reiterated, "What you say is true."

"Thank you for being honest. I know this can't be easy." Will took a deep breath. I knew that this wasn't the response he thought he would get. We had already speculated about the outcome and had expected tears, shame, and denial— but not bravado, definitely not bravado.

"Brooke, I need to know the names of the boys involved," Will said. Everyone else in the room held their breath.

Tears were welling up in Brooke's eyes now, "I'm sorry, but I just can't tell you. I just can't."

But while we sat in silence, Brooke continued to speak in spite of her best intentions not to. The story she had been guarding for so long began to spill out.

Over the next few very painful minutes she gave up one boy's name and told of the places and details of the encounters.

I felt like a voyeur in the life of this young girl. I wanted to crawl under the carpet and hide. She bared her shame for all to hear and my heart broke for the obvious pain she was in.

Her tears were mixed with anger towards her mother. "It never would have come to this if you hadn't made me take two sciences *and* pre-calc this year. I just can't do it. What part of this is so difficult for you to understand? The classes are too hard for me. I should just be taking biology and geometry this year like every other freshman. But no, mother here, has me on the fast track to failure and a nervous breakdown. Are you happy now?"

She had directed the question towards her mother, and for a moment I thought maybe this storm might blow itself out. But she wasn't done yet. "I just don't have enough time to study. There is no time to meet with the teachers. I don't have a study hall, and I have practice and games until seven every night and you can never seem to get here to pick me up on time. It's always something. Even my best is never quite good enough."

The tears were flowing down Brooke's face and she made no attempt to wipe them away. I handed her a tissue, which she accepted with a cursory glance in my direction.

There clearly was a major rift in this mother-daughter relationship.

Again, in spite of her best efforts not to, she continued the story of how it all had begun innocently enough, in the stairwell one evening in October after practice.

"Mom was late again and I knew it would be after eight before I even got home to start my homework. I had a chemistry test in Stoichiometry. I had missed the class where Dr. Jones had taught the material because we were away at the field hockey tournament. So Evan offered to tutor me. He took chemistry last year as a junior. He's smart and sweet, and over the next few weeks we got really close. We really liked each other."

She turned away from her parents and turned her attention first to Will and then to me, in hopes that we might come to understand the predicament she had gotten herself into. She addressed us as if her mother and dad weren't even in the room.

He asked me to go to homecoming with him. I knew I could never say yes, no matter how much I wanted to. Evan knew why. My mother would have kittens if I was seen dating a black guy."

Mrs. Powell drew a sharp breath, but Brooke looked towards her mother and sneered, "You know it's true, Mom."

Then Brooke turned back towards Will. The tears poured down her face and I wanted to take her in my arms, hold her close, and tell her it would all be okay. But somehow I knew– this wasn't the case.

Where was her mother during Brooke's confession? Why was she not offering her daughter her unconditional love? Perhaps this mother's love was just that– *conditional.*

Brooke continued, "He was offended and said I was a racist. So I gave him oral to show him how much I appreciated all he had done for me and how much I really liked him. I didn't want him to call me a racist."

She was sobbing by then. "You're a racist, but I am not. I'm not a racist like you." She spat the words out at her mother. "So instead of going to homecoming we began to see each other at school. He would tutor me and I would say thank you in a way that pleased him," she wiped her eyes on her shirtsleeve, then smirked.

Shaking her head, she began to laugh. It was almost like the little girl who began this story was being circumvented by a callous, hard-heartedness as a way to protect her tender feelings. "At first it was just oral, not real sex or anything. But then he started losing interest in me, so I offered to go all the way. It was the first time for both of us. I thought he loved me. He said he did. I thought if I slept with him then maybe I could keep him. But now he's moved on. What difference does it make? I'd already given away the prize, *my sacred virginity*." She sat up straight and looked at her mother, "Isn't that what you called it, Mom, *my sacred virginity?*"

"Brooklyn stop. I think I've heard more than enough of this sordid tale." Mrs. Powell scowled and shifted her weight in the chair. She was clearly uncomfortable and ready to leave.

But Brooke wasn't finished. "So that's me, the dirty, nasty girl, the one who gave it all away. And now . . . well let's just say I have lots of boys who are tutoring me. The barter system is alive and well right here in our hallowed halls. But rest assured I'm getting all *A*s because . . . well, I know how important that is. Right, Mom?"

With this her mother changed her tactics. "Brooke you must tell us who has done this to you. I want names, goddamn it. There will be hell to pay."

Brooke turned towards her mother and snarled, "Names? Oh you want names. Let's just say they're all the star scholar athletes. That's right, Mother, they're all the black boys. You leave me here at school all hours of the day and night and there's only so much studying a girl can do, so I found other ways to entertain myself. I know what you're thinking, you and your cocktail party racism. You think they forced me. Well, no one forced me to do anything. It was just a bit of sexual commerce. You didn't seem too upset when I earned an A in chemistry. Well, that's how it was done. One hour of one-on-one tutoring gets you a blowjob. Do you want to know about the A in pre-calc? Well that was two hours of tutoring every week, bought and paid for with my own body. Where do you think I learned how to get what I want? Aren't you the one who always says that everyone and everything has a price? I guess I was just willing to pay the price to keep you off my back."

Brooke was raging, and there was no stopping her now. "I know how you parade my accomplishments out and about at the club. My dear Brookie this, and my dear Brookie that," she said mockingly. "I wonder what your high and mighty friends will think of your precious daughter now, once they learn just how it was I found my way on the fast-track to the Ivy League."

At long last Will spoke up, putting an end to this barrage of hostility this young lady had for her mother. "Okay Brooke, I think we've heard enough. I want your parents to take you home. This has been quite enough for one day. I need to give this some serious consideration and have a discussion with the headmaster. As of now you will be on an indefinite suspension until we can sort this out."

"What do you mean *she* is indefinitely suspended?" Mrs. Powell appeared confused and sought clarification. "How is she going to keep up with her schoolwork? She is the victim here. There needs to be a criminal prosecution. My daughter is only 14 years old. This happened here on school grounds. I am holding the school personally responsible for not protecting my child."

And then she turned on me, "And you, Mrs. Duncan, where were you when these black monkeys were screwing my daughter in your classroom? I want answers, and I will be getting them."

I might have felt more compassion towards Mrs. Powell if she had offered her daughter even a modicum of sympathy and understanding for the emotional turmoil she was in, rather than concerning herself with her daughter's missed classwork. I might've felt more compassion if she wasn't such an abysmal racist.

Mrs. Powell was the epitome of what disturbed me most about white, affluent anglophiles. I felt ashamed because I was one too. I could only imagine the disdain others must have for the likes of her. I hoped for mercy, and that I wouldn't be painted with the same broad brush.

Brooke turned and again scowled at her mother. "I'm not a child. Yes, we used Mrs. Duncan's room, but we were also in the stairwells, in the field house, and in the orchestra pit too. Are you going to threaten everyone or just the one person at this school who actually cares about me?"

Mrs. Powell was gearing up to respond when her husband finally intervened. "Rosalie, *stop talking.*"

His voice was powerful and strong. He stood up and walked in front of his raging wife and wrapped his arms around Brooke, who melted into the embrace of her father's chest. "I'm so sorry, darling. We will sort this out at home."

In that moment Brooke broke down and cried. The toughness she had displayed was washed away with her tears, and she was transformed into a little girl in her father's loving arms.

After a minute or two, Brooke reached down to grab her book bag. Mr. Powell took the bag from Brooke and hoisted it up and over his right shoulder while drawing her close under his left arm. She rested her head on his chest, still quietly sobbing.

"Mrs. Duncan, please know that in no way are we holding you responsible. I'm just glad the students feel there's someone in this school that they can trust. Thank you for caring enough to bring this to an end." For just a moment, Mr. Powell reached over and placed his hand on my shoulder. In that gesture, I felt the gratitude he was extending. "This will stop today before any more damage is done to my daughter. Mr. Warwick, we will wait for your call."

"Charles, Charles, please don't say anything to Grandy," Mrs. Powell begged. "We don't want to upset her. We need to think of a reason why Brookie is home and not in school . . . " Her voice trailed off as she followed her husband and her daughter out of Will's office.

"I'll be in touch," Will concluded, as he escorted them out the door.

When Will closed the door again, the academic corridors were deathly quiet. The outer office was empty, and school had been dismissed 40 minutes ago. It had been one very long afternoon.

I felt like I had been eating rocks. I was filled with undigested emotion with all that had been said, and all that had been left unsaid.

I remained in my seat while Will returned to his desk chair. We both needed to process what had just happened, before we could even begin to plan for or even speculate on what might happen next.

Will looked as pale and tired as I had ever seen him. He shifted his weight forward and placed his elbows on his desk. For a moment, I thought he might just put his head down and cry. He, too, was the father of an adolescent daughter, as well as an adolescent son.

It was hard not to personalize some of the situations we encountered. I couldn't help but feel that our understanding as parents added to our overall effectiveness or at least helped us bring some compassion to the table.

But as I had grown to expect, Will pulled himself together, took a deep breath with an audible sigh and straightened up. He carried the weight of all the students and their families on his shoulders, to say nothing of his love and concern for the faculty.

The look on his face and the way he turned his right palm up indicated he wanted me to go first. Maybe he just didn't trust himself to speak.

So I started, "Okay, let's unwind the tape. Let me guess– Grandy is Mrs. Beatrice Ward, the *grande dame.* Is that right?"

Will nodded and cleared his throat. "Clearly, Rosalie doesn't want her mother to know that she can't manage her own daughter. Perhaps Mrs. Powell is concerned that if her mother hears of this, then it may cast doubts on her ability to manage the family fortune."

Will shook his head and I began to see the ripple effect of this minor earthquake.

"Do you really think *that's* what she's thinking?" I asked incredulously. "I guess the rich have issues all their own," I couldn't begin to imagine how this would be her primary concern, but I'd been wrong before about these people.

Then I asked, "What is Mr. Powell's story?" There was a part of me that didn't really want to know. Yet, I suspected it might be relevant.

"Charles Powell? Oh, he's a kept man. No one in that entire household has a job. Not like any job you or I might ever hold anyway. Surely you could see that. I was really quite surprised he had enough testosterone to call the meeting off, just when his wife began to storm the gates. No doubt, there will be hell to pay for that move."

And without any more encouragement, the story just came forth.

"There certainly isn't any love lost between Mr. and Mrs. Powell. I think they tolerate one another, but they won't ever divorce. They're just keeping up appearances in order to keep the family fortune intact. They married when they were young. He had the right pedigree and social status, but all the money is held and controlled by the Ward Trust. It will pass from Beatrice to Rosalie and eventually to Brooklyn. It will stay in the hands of the women in the family. It has all been decreed by the Trust."

Will shook his head.

"How is it that you know all of this?" I asked.

"You can't believe how much of this information is shared when these women have a few drinks, and then it's shared again and again as little bits of social and political currency. It's sad, but life among the landed gentry isn't all that different from middle school. I've been here a long time. The kids trust you and tell you things because you're trustworthy; I guess some of the parents see me the same way. They tell me things that are really none of my business, but they tell me just the same," he said.

And then Will shifted gears again, "It's closing in on 5:00. I think we both have had enough for one day. It's time to go home."

I rose and walked to the door. "See you tomorrow. I hope you have a restful evening."

He winced, "Not very likely. I have to call George tonight at home, and fill him in on what has transpired. See me tomorrow and I'll let you know what has been decided and what we're going to do next. More than likely, we'll need to have another meeting with Brooke and her parents in the next few days. I'd like to have you there."

I nodded, "Okay."

"Thank you, Elise."

Again I nodded and whispered, "You're welcome."

So much had gone down, and sometimes words just got in the way.

The days and nights have all run together and now my memory is unclear as to how I processed what had happened that day in Will's office. But it was time for me to go home, so I'm certain I must've picked up my children from my parents' home. Days when I worked late my mom picked my kids up after school. She brought them to her house, where they would have a snack and start their homework. I'd pack a pair of sweats in their backpacks in the morning and my dear, sweet mother would wash their uniforms so they would be ready to go for the next day.

It was an hour's drive home amidst the evening rush hour, but it was long enough to hold my children captive and talk about their days, to sing with the songs on the radio, to tell a few stories, to laugh at some jokes, and to share the joys and sorrows of the day.

When I got my children home– they were mine, all mine. I treasured them for they were the real gold of my life. I did my best to leave my troubles at work.

Years later, I would recall that someone asked about my children and how I had raised two *out-of-the-box* kids in such a bourgeois community?

I think I shrugged my shoulders and was without an answer.

Elliot and I had consciously chosen to live in a little rural town, and away from what we saw as the detrimental influences of wealth. But perhaps they had grown to be the people that they were in some small part because of the lessons I had learned as a teacher at Halcyon Heights. As I saw it, when the pursuit and preservation of wealth had become the primary goal of one's very existence, too often it was purchased at the cost of their humanity.

I thought of Rosalie Powell and her lack of compassion for her fourteen-year-old daughter and the situation she found herself in. How was it possible that her primary concern was saving face with her mother and preserving her rights as the heiress to the family fortune? Indeed, it must have been a deal with the devil when the end result was to forsake one's own humanity and the dire needs of one's own child.

I may not have known exactly what I intended to teach my children, but I did know one thing, I did not covet my neighbors' lives. No, somewhere deep within I knew I was looking for something else. I guess my children knew this too.

What was meant by *out-of-the-box*? My once-small children would grow up to be creative, wise, compassionate, and progressive adults.

By the grace of God, the next three days we were encased in a blizzard. No one was going anywhere. On the first morning my kids and I made pancakes and hung out in our pajamas until long past noon. We spent the afternoons playing in the snow, watching movies, and reading. What an unexpected gift, a glorious, glorious gift.

When I arrived back at school on Monday morning I checked my email. There was a message from Will. It read: Please stop by my office this morning.

I picked up the phone on my desk to call and see if he was available. My voicemail indicated that I had two new messages. Both were from Will. Clearly, he needed to see me. Instead of calling I grabbed my pen and a notepad and headed for his office.

Again, the door was closed and the blinds were drawn. Light seeped out at the edges of the window. His lights were on. Will was already in his office, and likely in a conference. I waited a moment, deciding if I should knock or not when Liz came around the corner. "He's inside with the Powells, and they're waiting for you."

I took a deep breath. "Maybe you should call in."

She did, and then I knocked on the door and entered.

Everyone was in the same seats that we'd occupied the last time we had been together. Mine was vacant, so I sat down.

"Good morning," I said. "Long slow drive in from the country today. They seem to take their sweet time getting the roads plowed out where I live." I offered up an excuse, as I glanced at the clock on Will's desk. It was just 7:35 AM and I wasn't late, but I wondered how long these people had been here.

Will began, "Mr. and Mrs. Powell are here to talk about Brooke's future at Halcyon Heights. Let me briefly summarize our conversation and bring you up to speed, Brooke is not in school today because she has been suspended indefinitely."

This I knew. This was how things had been left last Thursday.

Will continued, "Mr. and Mrs. Powell have spent the last few days discussing their options with their daughter. Mr. Powell and Brooke feel it would be in her best interest to change schools. They want to do this immediately as the new semester has just begun here, as well as at other private schools in the area."

I looked over at Mr. Powell and he nodded in my direction indicating this was his position.

Will continued, "Mrs. Powell believes . . . "

"Mrs. Powell can speak for herself," Rosalie Powell interrupted. Will conceded the point and yielded the floor to her. She was obviously irritated and her tone was venomous.

Mrs. Powell turned to address me, "Charles and Brooke think that she should go to Marywood or Regina," she said through her hostility. "It's no secret that these schools are substandard when compared to The Academy. What chance does Brooklyn have of getting an early admission to one of the Ivy League schools with an accelerated six-year combined undergraduate-medical school if she graduates from a substandard high school?"

I was feeling a bit like Dorothy just dropped into Oz. I asked the first question that came to mind. "Brooke is 14 years old. Does she want to go to an accelerated medical school?"

I worked with 14-year-olds all day long. Most of the 14-year-old girls I knew were more concerned with what their girlfriends thought of their new haircut than where they would go to college, what they would study, and what they were going to be when they grew up. This was Rosalie Powell's issue and we had much bigger fish to fry here today.

Before allowing her to answer, I continued, "I've had Brooke in class. She's a smart girl and a hard worker, and she will be successful wherever she puts her efforts– be that here or at one of the other schools. I'm far more concerned about her emotional well being and quite frankly her safety when all of this unfolds, and the boys involved are brought to bear the consequences of their actions."

I took a breath and sat tall in my chair. These people had asked me for my opinion. They had asked for it, and I couldn't and wouldn't keep silent as I found the words for my nebulous state of anxiety and concern.

"I fear this will cause deep divisions in some rather tenuous alliances that we have tried to nurture here at school. I fear as we try to determine where to cast the blame that the students and their families will choose sides based on gender, age, or socio-economic class, and of course on race."

I let the power of my words settle in. Had this woman not considered how this might all play out? It could be mayhem. Their daughter's life plan wasn't the only thing in jeopardy here. There were probably half a dozen boys who could be facing criminal charges, loss of scholarships, and destruction of their goals and dreams. There was a great deal at stake. People would choose sides, people would cast blame, and this was not going to be pretty.

"I agree with you, Mr. Powell. For her own sake, Brooklyn needs to change schools. If she were to stay, she will always be the one who brought these boys down. The other students may not say anything unkind to her when she is in class, but there is so much more to high school than what happens in the classroom. We will not be able to protect her from the anger, rage, and all other forms of unkindness that may be directed towards her. If not for the fact that your daughter is only 14, she is no more innocent or guilty than any of the others involved but she is far more vulnerable."

"I need to think about this," Mrs. Powell said quietly.

Will took advantage of the change in her demeanor to ask, "Did Brooke give you the names of the other boys involved? I'll need those names so we can continue with this inquiry."

"At this point the only confirmed name we have is Evan Hedges. We don't know any more about the other boys involved than we knew before, only that the boys are black and Brooke described them as the star athletes," Mr. Powell said. "She's refusing to give us any of the names. You probably have a better idea of who these boys are than either my wife or I do."

Will replied, "Please be patient with us as we continue to investigate. I ask that you refrain from discussing any of this with anyone outside of this room. I fear it will hamper our investigation. Please let me know what decision you make about changing schools. If you decide to withdraw and enroll Brooke elsewhere, we will do everything in our power to help you facilitate that change," Will said. The great kindness and sympathy he felt for this family could be heard in his gentle voice.

Rosalie Powell glared at Will and then at me. "Trust me when I say that we haven't decided anything, Mr. Warwick. My father and his father were both legacies here. Apparently, you have no idea the amount of money that my family has donated to this institution over the years. The truth is that you, Mrs. Duncan, and the entire football team are far less important, and thus can be more easily dismissed than my daughter Miss Brooklyn Powell."

She was on a roll.

"Rosalie, please," her husband tried to stop her.

"Shut up, Charles," she snapped at him. "We will not go away quietly while you try to protect these child rapists. Just because *your* former President Bill Clinton was confused about what constitutes sex and my 14-year-old may be confused as to whether oral sex is indeed sex, the criminal justice system will not be." She snarled, raising the corner of her upper lip to show her perfect teeth.

Then she turned and said to me, "You must be one hell of a fine teacher, Mrs. Duncan. Just what are *you* teaching our children about sex?"

I blanched and my stomach clenched, feeling personally threatened by the power this woman yielded.

"Brooke may have been confused. She thought she was old enough to make her own decisions, but I suspect that the county Prosecutor will see this another way. In this county there are lines that are not to be crossed. The issues of right and wrong are very *black and white*," she said.

The racial implication was clear.

"I think you know what I mean. If you believe this is going to go away than you've underestimated me, and the power of the Powell family. Those young niggers put their cotton-pickin' hands on the wrong little white girl."

Will looked as stunned as I felt. This racial slur was so far beyond the boundaries of acceptability.

She continued unapologetically, "And yes, Mr. Warwick, we will let you know *our* plans– whether *we* plan to prosecute or not. So do your job and get me the names of the men involved. For that is what they are and that is how they will be tried– as adults."

Rosalie Powell stood. She grabbed her full-length sable coat and Prada handbag as she turned to her husband, "Get up Charles. We're leaving."

Then she walked out through the door without looking back. Charles stood and his lips moved to say, "I'm sorry," as he followed his wife into the outer office and down the hall.

"I need to see George," Will said, coming around from the back of his desk.

I was already standing. "Yes, and I have a class to teach," I responded.

"Hang in there," he said. "This is going to get rough."

We parted company as he turned towards the headmaster's office and I down the athletic corridor.

In the meantime, all of the other activities associated with the life of the school continued. There were classes to teach, tests to be given, and papers to grade. And of course, there was the ever-demanding push of the afterschool athletic program. The men's basketball team was also having a winning season. The talent pool was deep that year and those in the know thought The Academy was a contender for another state championship, this time in basketball.

Many of our student athletes were required to play three seasons of athletics as one the terms of their financial aid. Therefore, many of the boys who played football also played basketball. Behind the closed doors of the administrative offices there was speculation about the participants in what Will and George were now calling the *sex-for-tutoring scandal.*

But speculation was just that. Ten days after we had been put on notice that something untoward had happened under our watchful eye, we still had not approached any of the young men who might have been involved. The only name that had been verified was Evan Hedges.

When I passed Will in the hallway later that afternoon, he said, "He wants you to talk with the girls again."

Will didn't need to tell me who *he* was or who the *girls* were. I knew he had met with George earlier in the day and George wanted names.

"I'll ask," I agreed. "But they might not be interested in talking."

The girls were waiting outside my door on Tuesday morning. I quickly opened the door and let them inside the clinic. I had this pervasive fear. I didn't want anyone to see them with me. This was about to get ugly.

"Brooke's not in school again today," Libby said.

By the way she said this, I had a very distinct impression the girls didn't know that Brooke was on an indefinite suspension or that her parents were considering taking her out of The Academy. Perhaps no decision had been made yet.

I just listened. It wasn't my job to tell them anything.

"She called me last night when her parents were out of the house. They've confiscated her cell phone and have forbidden her to talk with anyone. She wants to know who talked. I lied to her, and she's one of my best friends." Libby began wiping the tears from her face. She was a good girl. "I'm not a liar, and now I'm lying to my friend. Maybe we never should have said anything."

I understood her regret. She had broken a confidence and then lied about it to a dear friend who had trusted her.

"I told her I didn't know anything about it. Brooke was sobbing through the whole conversation. She's afraid of what her mother will do," Libby finished and let out a deep sigh.

"Her mother has been listening to Brooke's messages, she's had lots of calls from a lot of guys looking to hook up. Some even left dirty messages and now her parents are really mad," Catherine added as she tried to retain her composure. Her eyes were red and swollen. I suspected she'd been crying earlier and hadn't slept well.

"They have phone numbers, but not names, at least not anyone's full name," she said before she took a slow deep breath. "Her dad hasn't decided if he wants to press criminal charges or not. But Rosalie's on a witch-hunt."

There was something about a 14-year-old referring to their friend's mother by her first name; these girls had little or no respect for Rosalie Powell.

"Sit down girls," I said. They sat side by side on the couch, leaning into one another for support and protection. "I don't want you to answer right away. I want you to think first. The headmaster has asked me, to ask if you know the names of the boys involved," I said, as softly and gently as I could.

In response, the girls turned and clung to one another, and began to sob.

The first bell rang. The first class would begin in five minutes. The hallway was crowded with students rushing to class so they wouldn't be marked tardy. Someone was knocking frantically outside the clinic door. In some ways, today would be like every other day at The Academy, but not for Libby and Catherine.

I grabbed a late pass for each of them and said, "Girls, take a few minutes and get yourselves together. Wait until the hallways have cleared before you go to class. I don't want either of you to be seen coming or going from here. You have my phone numbers. Call me tonight and let me know what you have decided. The headmaster has decided that nothing is going to happen to any of the boys until Thursday, until after Signing Day. So you have some time."

The girls stood up and each of them gave me a hug before they retreated to the private consultation room.

I went to open the clinic and in rushed three students, two girls looking for tampons, and another with a headache. By the time they had signed in and I'd attended to their needs, the final bell had rung and they hurried off to class. I went to hang up my coat, which was still folded over my desk chair. I plugged in my computer and opened my email to see if there was anything urgent that required my attention. When I looked up the librarian was standing in front of my desk.

This couldn't be good. I loathed this woman. Once upon a time we had been friends or at least friendly, but when I didn't seek out her wise counsel after Elliott passed, she turned on me for supposedly spurning her attempts at friendship.

I recalled how last spring she'd told me, "It's so much easier to be a widow than it is to be divorced. Everyone here feels sorry for you. You'd better get used to being alone. I haven't had a date in over ten years." That was no great surprise. I could hardly bear a ten-minute conversation with her, let alone an entire evening in her company. The last thing I wanted was this miserable old woman's pity.

"Hi Danielle," I said as politely as I could. "What can I do for you?" I hoped she needed a Band-Aid and would soon be on her way.

"I need to talk to you."

"Of course. Please sit down," I said.

"Privately," she added succinctly as if I should have known.

"Okay, give me just a minute." I said, as I walked over and knocked on the consultation room door. No answer. I opened the door. The girls had gone to class. They'd left out the backdoor that led into the hallway.

I breathed a sigh of relief. The last thing I needed was to have this busybody nosing around while the girls were here. Danielle followed me to the consultation room. I switched on the overhead light and held the door so she could enter. She sat on the couch and I took the chair across from her.

"What is on your mind?" I asked.

"It's your advisee. You know that little kid who carries the briefcase and looks like he belongs on Wall Street, " she laughed as she scoffed at him.

Was she ridiculing this freshman boy because he was small or because he was a late bloomer or because he was always in dress code and buttoned up tight? Great. If the librarian thought he was laughable I wondered how he was faring with those less mature, like the other freshman.

"Yes, his name is Theodore Rogers. He likes to be called Trip," I responded. I was already irritated.

"He's in the library every day during lunch. He stands in the stacks reading about the Civil War. He *never* goes to the dining room," she said, as if he had just been implicated in some horrendous war crime.

"I know he's very interested in history. He's always reading some historical tome when he comes to advisory too." We were a school after all. It was a good thing when students found something they were interested in, something they were passionate about. It was a good thing that he liked to read. Was this woman inventing problems?

I knew it couldn't have been easy to be Trip. He was an introvert in a world that valued the gifts of the extrovert.

"What exactly are your concerns?" I asked.

"I don't know, I just think he's . . . weird. You're on the crisis team, and I think you should do something about him." As usual she was being snappish.

"Are you saying that you are concerned with his social adjustment here at school?" I offered, as calling him weird wasn't particularly helpful.

"I don't know. Why doesn't he go to lunch? Why is he reading about the Civil War? He's just weird," she said again as if this illuminated the issue.

"I'll try and see him later today," I said. And in her usual abrupt manner, Danielle was up and out of the chair without even saying good bye.

I sat there for a moment. I liked Trip. He was polite, respectful, and smart. He was 14 years old. Some of the boys his age looked like full-grown men, but still acted and reasoned like 11-year-olds. Trip looked like an 11-year-old, but he was more respectful and intellectually mature than most of the students were when we sent them off to college. It couldn't be easy to be him.

Still I was concerned. Why was he not going to the dining room for lunch? Maybe he didn't have anyone to sit with or maybe he didn't want to endure the torment of the lowbrow boys who were known to bully anyone who they saw as different.

He would probably stop by either later today or tomorrow. We always had a short advisory meeting on Wednesdays. I decided not to pull him from class today just because Danielle thought he was weird. He would hate having all that undo attention brought upon him; no, I'd see Trip tomorrow morning.

Classes came and went that Tuesday in February. I was teaching cardio-pulmonary resuscitation or CPR and first aid. My students really took it seriously and I was proud of them. If they passed the skills test and earned an 80 or better on the written test then they would receive their certification, just like every other adult in the building. Everyone from the headmaster to the custodial staff was CPR and First Aid certified. And every two years they were required to go through a refresher course. Students wouldn't eligible for their driver's license until they turned 16, so some students carried their American Red Cross certification cards in their wallets right next to their school ID cards and their ATM and credit cards. It was a right of passage and their first real adult responsibility.

I wrapped things up early and was out the door by 4:00 PM, and happy to see that it was not yet dark. For months now it had been dark in the mornings when I arrived at school and dark in the evenings when I left for home. I felt a glimmer of optimism starting to build; perhaps spring was around the corner. The hardest part about winter for me wasn't the cold and snow. I actually liked winter. No, it was the darkness.

Months and months would pass and the only time I would see the sun, other than on the weekends, was on my way to lunch, and again on my way back. Both the clinic and my classroom were without windows.

But it was a beautiful day, and the sun was setting over the snow-covered hills. My kids had gone home with friends after school. They had gone sledding and then we'd planned to all go out for pizza.

The Foley's had a son Ian's age and a daughter a year older than Shea, and all the kids got along famously. Jennifer's husband traveled fairly frequently with his job so we started to see this family pretty regularly, at least when Rob was out of town. I'd known her for years before Elliot died, but we were never really close friends. In the eighteen months after Elliot died she had become my confidant and best friend. As I drove towards her house I thought I might feel better if I could talk through some of this craziness at school with her. But then there was that *gag order* set forth by the powers that be. However, Jen didn't hobnob socially with people at The Academy anymore than I did. Still . . . I would need to think about this.

When I arrived at Jennifer's, the kids were all still outside and they had no interest in going to dinner, at least not yet. Jennifer tossed me a swimsuit and said, "Put it on and join me in the hot tub. The wine is already poured and waiting for us."

I thought about saying no thanks, but only for a moment. I had been holding my breath and carrying this burden for the last few weeks, I needed someone to talk to.

Covering myself with her spa robe I went out onto the back deck. Jen was already in the hot tub. We could hear the children laughing in the distance as they climbed the hill and slid back down on sleds and saucers. The snow was gently falling in clusters of snowflakes as big as quarters.

I placed the robe on the back of a chair, reached for my glass of wine, took a sip, slipped into the hot tub, and exhaled. "Oh dear God, I don't know when the last time was that I felt this good." It's often the simple pleasures that are the most welcome. Jennifer was a stay-at-home mother. There were days, like this one, when I envied her. There are some secrets that one must take to the grave, but was this was one of those? I needed to let go of some of the fears that haunted me day and night, only to be repeated day after day and night after night. So when Jen asked, "How are you? You look like you are carrying the weight of the world. So spill."

Jen was absolutely trustworthy, but still there was so much at stake. I thought about telling her, but in the end I changed my mind, "I'd love to ... but I can't. Let's just say it was another day of high stakes drama at the palace. Some of the ruling royalty may be dethroned and heads are going to roll."

She raised her wine glass in my direction, "Here's to the loyal keeper of the secrets."

We clinked glasses, "Thanks, love. I'd love to tell you, but then, of course, I'd have to kill you," I said. And we laughed.

"What movie is that from?" Jen asked.

"Hell if I know," I said. "Sherlock Holmes if I were to venture a guess. All I do know for certain is that I must be a wicked old witch because I'm melting. And that is from the *Wizard of Oz*," I said, as I grabbed a towel and climbed out of the hot tub. Again, I wrapped myself in one of Jen's robes.

My body was relaxed, even if my brain was still spinning. As much as I wanted to talk this over with her, a misplaced confidence could have such dire consequences. I trusted her, but I couldn't risk it. I just couldn't.

By the time we had finished our soak it was dark, and I needed to get the kids home. "Let's order a pizza and have it delivered," I suggested, "And then we'll be on our way. I'm guessing these kids are going to be starving and exhausted from all those trips up and down the hill."

Jen was on it. I went to change back into my work clothes before heading for home. I would have loved to put on a nightgown, but I still needed to drive home, so instead I offered up a little gratitude for the fact that I was wearing pants instead of a dress and stockings, which last year's dress code required.

Before long, we had eaten and the kids and I were back in the car heading for the country. By the time we got home it was nearly 8:00 PM. The kids showered and got ready for bed. Our days started early. My alarm went off each morning at 5:30 and the kids were up by 5:45 AM. So as I'd expected they were tired from all the sledding and gave me no grief about going to bed earlier than usual.

Dear God, I loved my children. These were the golden days of childhood, and this afternoon and evening had been delightful. I offered up a prayer of thanksgiving. I knew in other households in our county that trouble was looming just over the horizon. Ian was just a couple years younger than Brooke, Libby, and Catherine, and six years younger than the boys. These families were about to have their worlds blown apart. I was certain they loved their boys every bit as much as I loved Ian. And yet if my dear, sweet daughter had been defiled, how would I feel? How would I cope? And how would they?

I lay down, but still couldn't rest. Who were the victims and who were the perpetrators? How the hell did I know?

I rolled over and looked at the clock, it was already after 11 PM. I wondered why had I been unable to talk this out with Jen? What was I afraid of? I think I kept quiet because we all lived directly in the shadow of The Academy and I know how people like to gossip about the lives of the rich and famous. I knew that Jen would never intentionally betray me, but still, she probably didn't keep secrets from her husband. It didn't take much imagination to figure that if she told him, and he told someone else, that this kind of carelessness could be like a match in the forest and start a wildfire. I trusted Jen, but the potential consequences of unburdening my heart to anyone in this community were way too great.

But maybe I could talk with my sister. She didn't know any of the people involved and she didn't live here. Even if she slipped up, as people do, the chance of a devastating disaster was just so much more unlikely. She lived in California, not here in Albemarle County, Virginia. I picked up the bedside phone and called my sister, Kay. She would still be up, as it was only 8 PM on the west coast.

"Hello," Kay answered.

"Hi, Honey. It's me. Can you talk?" I asked.

"Sure, this is late for you. Playing hooky tomorrow?" she asked.

"I wish," I said.

I needed to ask, "This has to be just between us, okay?"

"Of course," she said. In the past I would have talked this through with Elliott, but he wasn't here. I trusted Kay. I needed to. So, I provided a brief sketch of what had transpired in the *sex-for-tutoring scandal.*

I told her, "I felt like a voyeur as this girl confessed the details of these intimate behaviors to her parents, let alone the director of the school and her former teacher. It was awful. I felt her shame."

Kay just listened, for that is what good friends do. Kay was my sister, but she was also my closest friend.

"I've thought about how the judicial system routinely shames rape victims, where the victim is put on trial when they must confront the accused. If this goes to trial, I fear for this young girl's safety. I fear that she will lack the emotional fortitude to put this behind her if she's forced to endure any further humiliation. For God's sake she is only 14 years old."

"Do you think she should change schools?" Kay asked, getting to the heart of what might be best for this girl.

"Last I heard was that she wanted to leave the school. She's feeling ashamed. Her parents are still undecided if changing schools is the best course of action or if they are going to file criminal charges. I do know that the law in Virginia is clear. This girl is considered a child and at least one of the boys involved is over 18 and considered an adult. It's quite likely that all the boys are over 18. They could all be charged with statutory rape and that is a felony, punishable by at least two and up to ten years in prison," I filled her in on what I knew, and I went on to process it all one more time.

Sometimes it just helped to tell someone else. I guess this was why people went to therapists.

"This whole scenario hinges on the fact that she's considered a child. If these boys had been involved with an older girl, there would still be ramifications for having sex at school, but it wouldn't be criminal," I said.

"I feel sick to my stomach," she said. "I can't imagine how this is affecting you. Tell me about the boys. Did you have them in class? Do you know them?" she asked.

"Only one boy has been named and I have a hard time seeing this young man as a rapist or a sexual predator. He may be an opportunist, but not a rapist. I'd have a hard time convicting him based on what I know. Which at this point is only one person's side of the story and clearly that isn't enough. The director is supposed to interview him on Thursday."

"The school attorney has indicated that the boys, as well as this girl, may also be charged with prostitution. I don't know if he knows what he is talking about or if he is just trying to work the case and pad his wallet. Can it be prostitution if no money was exchanged?" I asked, again not expecting an answer.

"I don't know. This is a little beyond my area of expertise," Kay said, and we both laughed.

"No doubt your husband will be grateful to hear that," I added before continuing. "I did some research in the wee hours last night. Is it any surprise I can't sleep? According to Wikipedia, *a person commits prostitution if he or she engages in or offers to engage in or agrees to engage in sexual conduct with another person in exchange for something of value.* Sex-for-tutoring –sounds like it meets the definition of prostitution to me, at least this definition."

"Who does the attorney say they would charge, the 14-year-old girl?" Kay asked.

"I have no idea, I only met the guy once. I think he's a doofus, but that's just my clinical opinion," I said, and Kay laughed.

"To add to the drama the young man who's been named is the football star. Our school's team won the state championship in the fall. He and a couple other boys have been offered full scholarships to play football for the next four years. I guess a number of schools want him and tomorrow he's supposed to tell the world where he will play."

"What position does he play?" Kay asked.

"Really Kay?" I said. "This is me you're talking to here. You know I couldn't give a rat's ass about football."

"Sorry, I forgot for a moment. I'm actually surprised you know about the NCAA signing day," she said. Unlike me Kay actually liked football. She spoke the language and watched it on TV. Must have been all that testosterone in her house. She lived with her husband and my three nearly grown nephews.

"I don't know anything about the NCAA or signing day, except it's all everyone around here is talking about: '*Where is Evan going to sign?*' It may be a moot point, if criminal charges are filed. He will be dropped like a hot potato. It's a little hard to play football if you're serving time."

Then at long last I asked the question that had been left unasked, "Or is this just a private matter, a private contract made between the two parties involved? We are continually pressuring the kids to grow up, assume more responsibility, to do their best, to achieve and accomplish more, more, more, and then when they take their lives and personal decisions into their own hands the adults call *foul.* Oh God, I wish I knew the answer. I'm exasperated and exhausted from this never-ending cycle of circuitous thinking. Perhaps these are questions that have no answers, at least no good answers."

"I'm so sorry you're carrying all of this. I wish Elliott was here to help you sort this out," she said. "I know you aren't asking me for advice, so I hesitate to give it, but as I listened to you, the same thought played on and on in my head."

"Oh, and what was that?" I asked.

I felt the tears begin to well up in my eyes. I could hear Kay crying softly on the other end of the phone. "You are not the long arm of the law. That is not what you have signed up to do, and that is not what you were hired to do. No my dear, sweet sister, you are a healer."

"Thanks for reminding me of that and thank you for listening. It's after midnight now. I'd best get off to sleep," I said as I readjusted the pillow under my head.

"Sweet dreams, love. Call me tomorrow," she said.

"Love you," I said, and then she was gone.

∾

When I arrived at school on Wednesday morning there was a message on my phone from Rosalie Powell. "Mrs. Duncan, I need you to gather all of Brooke's books from her locker and contact her teachers. Tell them that Brooke will be out of school for the remainder of the week for a family emergency. And by all means, you are not to specify the nature of the emergency. Let Will Warwick know that as of today no decision has been made about where Brooke will be attending school. At this point we are keeping *all* of our options open. I will be in your office at noon today to collect Brooke's things." I listened to the message twice.

"At this point we are keeping *all* of our options open." There was something in her tone of voice that led me to believe they were still considering filing criminal charges.

I had a class to teach, I'd deal with this during my free period later that morning.

When I arrived in my classroom Trip Rogers was already there with a thick, hardcover book on the Civil War opened on his desk.

"Hey Trip, what are you reading?" I asked.

"Good Morning Mrs. Duncan. It's still the same book– *The Great Battles of the Civil War*," he said smiling. "I'm reading about battle strategies and the tactical moves of the North."

Trip was always the first one in class. He always chose the same seat, the first seat just inside the door with his back up against the wall.

In that instant my mind flashed to a scene from a movie. Didn't one of the characters in *The Godfather* always sit with his back to the wall? It was a defensive position so no one could sneak up behind him and hurt him.

I knew then and there that Trip was being bullied at school. I hadn't seen it, but all the signs were there. He wasn't going to lunch, he was the first one to class, and he carefully selected this particular seat. He didn't feel safe. He didn't feel safe in the dining room, he didn't feel safe in the hallways, and he was securing the safest position in the classroom– the one where his back was to the wall and closest to the exit.

The interest in battle strategies caused me concern.

It was February 2000. The massacre at Columbine High School had just taken place last April. It was less than ten months ago and everyone was still on high alert.

If it could happen there, could it happen here?

Trip was a smart, sweet kid. He was also small for his age and would have a hard time defending himself physically if he were to be targeted by a bully. I needed to talk with him.

I hated it when that busybody librarian was right, but this time she was. I needed to talk with Trip.

Other students were starting to file into the classroom. Trip wasn't going anywhere. I'd see him next hour during our Advisory, just before the weekly assembly. No worries, he was here with me now.

When I'd finished teaching my first class of the morning Trip offered to carry my books back down to the clinic where our Advisory met each week. It was hard to imagine a sweeter kid or anyone who was less of a threat to anyone. I trusted my intuition on this one, but still, that didn't mean he wasn't being threatened or bullied. I needed to follow up on this.

The others arrived and were raiding my cupboards and refrigerator for the snacks I always kept there: juice, string cheese sticks, and graham crackers. Today, I'd also brought a crate of tangerines. They ate like a pack of wild wolves. Growing teenagers can consume small mountains of food. A couple of the kids had brought chips and salsa from home. It was our weekly gathering and food fest. I had a few announcements to make, but mostly this was the time for the kids to reconnect with one another and share a little down time. Earlier in the year, I had thought of them as *the least, the lost, and the forgotten* of the school, but I was wrong. Now they were really bonded with one another. They'd let their guard down and were becoming friends. I listened while they spoke of their weekend plans, how they were doing in athletics, and shared a joke or two. These kids who'd been so socially isolated and disparate just 7 months ago were developing social skills that would serve them well in life.

The bell rang and the kids asked, "Can we leave our bags here?"

"Of course," I said. It was funny that after all these months they still asked. They didn't assume anything. Perhaps it was part and parcel of their upbringing. Their manners were impeccable. I liked these kids.

As they started to make their way out of the clinic *en masse*, I asked, "Trip, may I see you for a minute?"

He turned and looked at me quizzically, "Of course."

I shut the door behind him and he returned to his usual seat by the door with his back up against the wall. I took the seat across from him.

"Mrs. Budinski, the librarian, came to see me yesterday," I said. Trip rolled his eyes and I laughed. I realized that I'd never seen him do that before. Apparently, he felt the same way about her as I did. "She's concerned that you're not going to lunch."

"She concerns herself with things that are truly none of her concern," he said.

"There may be some truth to that," I smiled.

"It's the library and I'm in there reading. I don't know why she should have a problem with that."

He wasn't going to get off that easy. So I prodded him, "Can you tell me why you're not going to lunch?"

"Do you want the long list or the short list?" he asked.

I settled in. He was going to tell me what was going on. I just needed to let him.

"Well let's see– as you know the freshman eat with the seniors and we eat second lunch. The lines are so long to begin with, the seniors push the freshman out of the way, you know *Senior Privilege*, so by the time I reach the serving area the seniors are coming in for seconds, and most of the food I would even consider eating is already gone," he said. I could hear the frustration in his voice.

"Is there anything else?" I asked.

"By the time I've finished my lunch, that is if I even get my lunch, I'm late for my next class." He took a deep breath and pursed his lips together to keep from telling me any more.

"What do you mean– if you even get your lunch?" Again I prodded and waited for his response.

"Okay, there are a couple of kids who've taken to bumping into me and knocking my lunch tray out of my hands, accidently on purpose, of course," Trip said, and I could hear that he was starting to get choked up.

I knew if he continued to tell me any more, he might start to cry. He was doing everything in his power not to let that happen. My heart ached for him as I tried to imagine the humiliation. Could there really be any wonder that he'd sought refuge in the library?

I continued to talk. I wanted to give him a moment. He inhaled deeply as he tried to get himself back under control. "So let me see if I understand:

the lines are long, there isn't enough food that you like, the seniors are domineering, you're late to class, and there are a couple of jerks who've made a bad situation even worse."

Trip nodded his head, "That about sums it up."

By then he'd regained his composure. I didn't have a problem when boys cried and expressed their pent-up emotions, but I knew this young man would have been embarrassed. So for his sake, I was grateful.

"It's February, Trip. The seniors will be leaving at the end of April for their Senior Projects, and then the dining room will be much less crowded. We also have three weeks of vacation in the next three months. So we are talking about eight more weeks of school."

He quickly did the math, "Only about 40 more days of school while the seniors are still here. Not that I'm counting."

"In the meantime, would you like to pack a lunch and keep it here in the clinic refrigerator? You can come down and eat in here with Mrs. Wink," I suggested. "You wouldn't be alone. There are a lot of kids who hang out in here during lunch. Just another safe haven, in case Mrs. Budinski starts to hassle you."

"Thanks, Mrs. Duncan, I'll think about it," Trip said.

We were nearly done, but not quite. "Any chance you might want to tell me who knocked your lunch tray from your hands?" I asked.

He smiled a genuine smile, "Nope, not a chance."

"Okay," I said. I wasn't surprised. "I hope you know that I don't mean to pry, but I also need to know if you're planning to retaliate."

"Are you kidding, Mrs. Duncan? They'd wipe the floor with me," he said.

"Are you thinking about hurting yourself or anyone else?" I continued.

"No, I'm not going to hurt myself or anyone else. But I don't intend to put myself in harm's way either."

I'd asked and he'd answered.

"Trip, do you have access to weapons?" I asked.

"I shoot skeet with my father at the Hunt Club. Our guns are there, under lock and key," he said. "I don't even have a driving permit, it's too far to go on my bicycle and they would never let me take the guns out without my father being present. Mrs. Duncan, I'm not going to hurt myself or anyone else. Please don't worry about me."

"Okay, I hear you. Did you tell your parents about the incidents in the dining room?" I asked.

"I mentioned it, but that was before Christmas and I haven't been to lunch since."

"Okay. Are you making friends here at school?" I went slowly because I knew that making friends could be difficult for some kids, particularly those who were introverts or just plain shy.

"Actually I have. I met this girl. She's a sophomore. Do you know Winnie Fisher?" he asked.

"Of course," I said smiling. "Sweet girl."

He returned my smile. "We're both in Quiz Bowl and on the ski team. We're tied for last place in the Grand Slalom," he said with a laugh. "She's every bit as cautious as I am, but we show up so we'll earn our blue points."

With that the bell rang and the Wednesday Morning Assembly was over. We'd missed the whole thing. But I wouldn't have missed this conversation for the world. What a nice young man. "Trip, I'm going to give your mom and dad a call, just to bring them up to speed about this lunch time stuff. I want you to think about having lunch in here for the next couple months. Okay?" I said.

He stood and gathered up his book bag, "Thanks, Mrs. Duncan, I'll think about it."

I wondered who the bullies were and whom they were targeting now that Trip had taken himself out of the equation.

The next hour was my free period. I took a minute to pull the list of Brooke's teachers and then cross-referenced it with where they were teaching during Block 6 so I could find them. Brooke had access to her syllabi and the corresponding readings and assignments online, so she already knew what was being covered in each class every day. But she'd been gone from school for over a week now and she'd need her books if she were even thinking of coming back. I stopped by the academic office to get her locker number and combination.

By the time I'd met with all seven of her teachers and her advisor, the better part of my free period was over, and I still needed to go to Brooke's locker. Everyone had questions that I wasn't at liberty to answer. I skirted the issues as best I could before I went up to Brooke's locker in the science wing. There were a few folded pieces of loose-leaf paper that had been pushed through the vents at the top of her locker. I stacked them and put them all in the pocket of my blazer. Right or wrong, I intended to read these before I turned them over to anyone. I guess I was surprised that security hadn't been here already.

There were half a dozen books still in her locker, primarily paperbacks for freshman English. Most of the students carried all their books with them because the school was large and there was rarely enough time to go to your locker during the time allotted for passing.

There was a navy pea coat still hanging in her locker.

I put her books down on the floor.

I don't know why I thought to check her coat pockets, but I did. Just call it following my intuition. I usually honor other people's need for privacy and I honor their boundaries. I didn't know what I might find, but this girl was in big enough trouble already and I didn't intend to add to it through negligence.

There was a pair of leather gloves and a three pack of condoms in the pocket on the right and a small baggie of marijuana, some rolling papers, and a lighter in the pocket on the left.

If she hadn't been suspended already, she would have been suspended for this.

I put everything back in her coat pockets and folded the coat over my forearm. The tag at the back of the neck, as well as the signature plaid lining was exposed– it was a Burberry and probably cost over $1,000.

This hadn't been on Rosalie Powell's list of things to collect, but I brought it anyway. Before I headed back to the clinic I stopped in the restroom, the one reserved for the women faculty.

I pulled the folded notes from the pocket of my blazer, and looked at them. I had intended to read them, but they were not written to me. I thought about what my sister had said the night before, "You are not the long arm of the law. No you are a healer."

I feared that they might answer the unanswered question– *who were the other boys?*

I feared the fall-out and more broken lives. I tossed the folded notes, unread, into the trashcan. Next, I unloaded the pockets of Brooke's beautiful Burberry pea coat of everything except her leather gloves, into the trashcan too. She didn't need anymore trouble than she was already in.

Later this decision would haunt me.

I rounded the corner towards the performing arts center with my arms loaded down with her books and her coat, I could see that the circular drive in front of the school was full of TV news vans, reporters, and cameramen. They had gathered with their television cameras and microphones, in the lobby outside of the auditorium. It was the NCAA Signing Day.

I hurried back to the clinic to drop off Brooke's things before returning to the auditorium. Attendance was mandatory for the students and the faculty. I found all my advisees sitting in their assigned seats. I knew by the looks on their faces, they weren't the least bit interested. They just wanted this to be over so they could go to lunch.

Four of our student athletes had been actively recruited, and would be signing The National Collegiate Athletic Association letter of intent. These student athletes were committing to attend a designated college or university in exchange for academic scholarships.

One of the athletes was Evan Hedges. He was the most highly recruited student athlete that we'd had in years.

He was the reason the press was here.

Everyone wanted to know: *Where was Evan going to play next year?*

Well, almost everyone.

The boys on the stage were dressed in their color day attire. Gray dress slacks, white button down shirts, navy blazers with the school crest on the right chest pocket and a green and gold repp-striped tie, black belt, black socks, and black shoes.

All students were required to dress like this for formal occasions. Even the girls wore the same ties, with the same shirt, and blazer, but with gray pleated skirts and stockings rather than slacks. Often the students dressed to the letter of the law and still appeared disheveled. But today, all four of these boys being honored fully embodied the spirit of the law. They were polished and shined and all put together.

Evan stood on the stage, both tall and proud. He was well over 6 feet tall, strong and fit. This was apparent even as he was dressed in his color day attire. Today he looked like a junior executive headed for the boardroom or a partner in a law firm, rather than a young man with his sights set on a career in the NFL.

His hair was trimmed close to his head and his dark skin glowed under the lights on the stage. When he smiled, his perfect white teeth allowed you to think this young man could be anything he chose to be. He was the poster boy, demonstrating the best of what The Academy of Halcyon Heights had to offer.

The headmaster, the director, the coaches, the parents, and the college representatives were all present on the stage. The athletes sat at four individual tables that were covered with green tablecloths, each table was adorned with a vase of yellow roses, as well as a pen and a glass of water. Each of the four athletes had their moment of glory. The reporters took a moment to interview the athletes and get a two-minute sound bite that would air later on the evening news.

The signing was followed by a myriad of photographs so the day would be remembered for posterity.

Later, all the dignitaries enjoyed a slice of cake that was emblazoned with The Academy's crest, lest these privileged few forget where they'd come from.

By the time the assembly was over my stomach was upset. All the students were released for lunch and I made my way down the hallway towards my office. Evan had committed to play football at Ohio State University.

Ohio State had a very prestigious football program. They were in the Big Ten. Even I, someone who knew almost nothing about football, knew this.

Tomorrow, some of our great heroes would fall, and in the meantime a 14-year-old girl hid in shame, while the honors were bestowed upon the so-called conquerors.

Swept up in a herd of students making their way to the dining room, I released myself from the throngs of many. When I reached my office, Mrs. Powell was there waiting for me. She was beside herself and looked like she, was about to explode.

I turned to the students who had followed me into the clinic, "You all have to go. You cannot stay here. Come back later."

"But I just need ..."

"No exceptions. Everybody out." I cleared the clinic, because I knew that I couldn't speak to Rosalie Powell in the presence of the students. God only knows what she might've said.

The last kid finally left and the door swung closed. "Where is the justice here?" she spat the words at me. She no longer saw me as her daughter's lone protector. In her eyes I'd been transformed into a member of the school's establishment. I had become someone who was advocating for her daughter's dismissal from The Academy. A diatribe of racial and ethnic slurs ensued.

"Why should my child have to leave the school?" she asked, clearly not expecting a response. "She has gone to school here since pre-kindergarten. We have paid the full tuition from day one." She put her hands on her hips and her face reddened.

I didn't like where this was going. Once the hurtful, hateful words had been spoken they were impossible to retrieve. She was going to show me her true colors and I knew it wouldn't be pretty.

"Those black boys are all here on scholarship," she spoke the words as if she'd just tasted something offensive.

"They could never have gotten in here on their own. We fill the playing field with the intellectually inferior so the school can fill the gym with banners and flags. It's just a little hard to accept that my tuition dollars and donations are actually paying to bring those big black monkeys into our school to rape our daughters."

I took a deep breath. "Mrs. Powell, I understand that you are upset. But I don't think this kind of talk is going to help make you feel better. I'm certain you will not feel good about this conversation once you've had a chance to cool down." I spoke slowly and calmly, and tried not to inflame the situation any further.

Wow, she assumed that just because I was a white woman and stood up for her daughter that I shared her prejudices.

But she could not let it go.

"Now it is *my* daughter who is being forced to leave. *My daughter's tutor* indeed, I doubt if that gridiron protégée could think his way out of a paper bag. Just wondering, Mrs. Duncan, when do you think The Academy is going to honor my daughter and bring the press in and bake her a cake with the school's crest and logo? *A Strong Mind and A Screwed Body.* Maybe she could get some press if she decided to shine the light on this golden boy football star."

Her hands were trembling as she reached over to pick up the stack of books and the coat from my desk. She shook her head as she glared into my eyes. She held my gaze until I had to look away, and then she opened the door and walked out into the hallway.

I collapsed into the chair in front of my desk. My heart was racing and my hands were shaking too. I wrestled with this. How would I feel if this had happened to my child? I knew that I would be outraged. How could children be in danger in their own school? There was an implicit understanding that the teachers and administrators had an obligation to keep the students safe.

I understood the anger this woman felt. I felt it for her too.

But still, I couldn't imagine losing it like this mother just did.

The synchronicity of this young girl's dismissal and the young man's day of glory was not lost on me.

Still, the racial slurs spilled forth so freely from this mother's mouth, showing the depth of the prejudice that still lived just below the surface in this genteel community. I felt dirty and sullied by her comments.

Why? They had nothing to do with me.

Yet, somehow they degraded us all.

When the Signing Day celebration had ended, the press had gone, the cake had been eaten, and all the dignitaries had gone home, it was then that Will asked his assistant, Liz, to call and schedule an appointment with the Hedges.

I'd heard Liz schedule these meetings before. She exercised the height of discretion, never giving any indication of the purpose for the requested meeting. Interestingly enough in this community of high-powered parents she never seemed to have any difficulty getting people to rearrange their schedules to find time to meet with the director of The Academy.

～

I happened to be in the front hallway chatting with one of the deans when Evan's parents came through the front door the next afternoon. I'd seen them in the building the day before when they'd been at school for the NCAA signing, the press conference, and reception. I knew why they were here, but judging by the looks on their faces, they did not. I was certain that Liz had done her job well.

The Hedges appeared to glow with pride and delight as they stopped to shake hands with some of the students and faculty who took the time to congratulate them on Evan's scholarship and his position on the Ohio State roster for the upcoming fall.

There was something about Evan's father. He exuded warmth and charisma with his strong handshake and slow open smile. It was easy to see where Evan got his height and good looks. His father was well over 6 feet tall and his beautiful wife was nearly as tall with her three-inch heels. He wore an expensive suit. I'd worked here long enough to know. This suit was not purchased off the rack at Macy's, the quality of the fabric and the cut of the suit told me otherwise. His white shirt had been professionally laundered with extra starch, and his gold silk tie matched the fabric of his wife's suit. His fingernails were manicured and a gold watch could be seen as he extended his hand to one of the teachers he knew.

It has been said that you can tell a man's position in life by his shoes and his wristwatch, if that was the case then Mr. Hedges was doing all right for himself.

Mrs. Hedges stayed one step behind her husband while he smiled and shook hands with all those he knew. Evan's mother was tall, thin, and graceful. She looked like a runway model in her fitted golden suit. The skirt hit just above her knees revealing her long brown legs and expensive golden heels. Her hair was pulled back in a chignon emphasizing her long neck and beautiful face. She was adorned with substantial gold earrings and a matching necklace. They looked like dignitaries dressed to meet the President of the United States, rather than parents called in for a conference with the principal of their son's school.

My heart went out to these parents too. There was always such a heartfelt pain when one's children mess up and bring disgrace upon themselves and their families.

Sam Fraser reached out and shook his hand. "Reverend Hedges, looks like you'll be trading in the Green and Gold for Red and Gray."

Mrs. Hedges laughed, "I've always been rather partial to red. Looks like I'll need to update my wardrobe before Evan heads on over to Columbus."

I was standing there with Sam and so I also smiled. Mrs. Hedges looked as if she'd just stepped off the pages of a magazine. She was a beautiful woman and impeccably dressed.

"Don't you worry about us, our blood will always bleed green and gold," Reverend Hedges said as he promised their loyalty with the reference to The Academy's colors. They all laughed as Reverend Hedges placed the palm of his hand on the small of his wife's back and ushered her toward the academic offices where Mr. Warwick was waiting for them.

I shuddered to think about the news that awaited them. "Is Evan's dad a minister?" I asked Sam.

"Yep, he's the head pastor at Gethsemane First Baptist in East Richmond," he said with an assurance that I knew which church he was talking about.

I must have looked confused.

"You know that big Baptist Church on the corner of East Broad just south of Grace Drive."

"Actually I've no idea," I said. "No wait a minute I think I can visualize it. It's down by Holy Redeemer Jesuit, am I right?" I asked, still uncertain if I had the right church or not. "Is it one of those mega churches with thousands of members?"

Sam nodded.

"Is it one of those churches where services begin at 10:00 and go all afternoon?"

Sam nodded again. I wasn't certain if I knew exactly which church he was the pastor of, but I certainly knew the type.

I wondered if Will knew. No doubt he did. He had already proven to be very astute about the *Who's Who* at The Academy. I was the one who was perpetually in the dark. The parental pedigrees and positions had been lost on me. But I was guessing that this was going to be pretty tough on this man of the cloth, and on his pretty wife. I checked my watch. It was five minutes to one.

"I'd better fly, I'm teaching next period. We'll catch up later." I said to Sam as I headed down the hallway.

"Later," Sam smiled and turned toward his office.

As I passed the academic offices I saw Reverend and Mrs. Hedges sitting in the two chairs outside of Will's office. The shades were drawn, but fragments of light rimmed the edges of the window. I knew Will was waiting inside. Will was a good and holy man. Perhaps he had his head bowed and was asking for some divine assistance. I knew how he hated to be the bearer of bad news and it was bad news he would be delivering that day.

Off to class, I was on autopilot. I don't remember what I taught. I had been at this job so long now I could nearly give some of these lessons in my sleep. I know my head and my heart were with this family, and also with this young man. His behavior would bring shame and dishonor down upon his family.

Oh dear God, life could be so difficult at times.

And yet, I couldn't help but feel there were no innocent parties here. Were they just kids messing up and breaking the rules? Rules that had been made to protect the innocent. Yet, one by one, children grow up and must find a way to bridge that gap between childhood and adulthood.

As my students were writing in their journals I was thinking about Evan.

Evan had been in my health class. There was something about the way he'd been raised. He was humble, courteous, friendly, modest, and his impeccable manners had been deeply engrained into his very being.

When he spoke to me he always addressed me by my name, and added the appropriate, "yes ma'am or no ma'am," in deference to my age. It was always, "Hello Mrs. Duncan," and "Would it be possible for you to write me a pass to the library Mrs. Duncan?"

Evan reflected the best of southern manners. It shouldn't have surprised me that he came from a solid home. His Southern Baptist parents appeared to have taken their parental responsibilities seriously.

I knew it could all be just the window dressing. There certainly were the chameleon types where the charm and good manners were simply a cover for a nefarious interior. But over the years I had developed a pretty good schmooze detector and it had never gone off when I encountered Evan.

Maybe I was wrong, but I didn't think so.

Over the last few weeks I had plenty of time to think about Evan and replay all of my encounters with him. I could visualize him in the hallways of the school wearing his letter sweater decorated with patches and pins announcing his athletic ability as a three season athlete, state championships won, and arm bands proclaiming his leadership as the captain of the football team. He had been groomed for leadership.

I lived in the athletic corridor; my office, my classroom, and the clinic were all right there. I could hear everything when my door was open and it was almost always open. All too often I needed to be the enforcer when kids got out of hand. Usually, all I needed to do was stick my head out the door and someone would say, "I'm sorry, Mrs. Duncan." Then the other kids would laugh. Evan might be with them but he was never the instigator. I had never heard any street language from this young man.

He was a standard-bearer for our athletic program. He was the best example we had of what we hoped to teach through athletics.

My heart ached when I thought about the Hedges meeting with Will, the allegations made about his behavior, his upcoming suspension, and the yet-unsettled potential for criminal charges. This was going to be devastating for this family.

The remainder of the school day passed, and I tried to focus in on my classes. Teaching provided a welcome diversion from the onslaught of worry that plagued me.

After school I was at my desk reading and grading the research papers that my classes had submitted. Some of them were excellent and some were disastrous. All were a reflection of the student's middle school experience, the effort they'd put forth, and had little, if anything to do with their intellect or ability. The phone on my desk rang.

It was Liz, Will's assistant, "Mr. Warwick was wondering if you're free?"

"Of course, would he like me to come down?" I asked, as I stood and picked up a notepad and a pen.

"Please, he's waiting for you in his office. I'll tell him you're on your way," she said, and hung up the phone. She didn't sound like her usual cheerful self, rather her voice sounded ominous.

Will owed me no explanation. I held no power here. I wouldn't be charged with making any of the forth-coming decisions. I was simply the messenger and yet already in my heart I knew why I'd been summoned.

Will needed to process what had happened in the meeting and I knew in my heart it couldn't have been good.

When I arrived, all the color had blanched from Will's face. He was gray and visibly shaken. He looked like the whole thing had made him ill.

I took my usual seat. And without any need for preamble he launched into the story of what had taken place that afternoon. "This was one of the most difficult days of my entire career."

"I'm sorry, Will," I said gently.

"I can count on one hand the number of times that anything I've had to say has made a grown man cry. Today both of Evan's parents were in tears. Reverend Hedges tried to comfort his wife as she sat in the chair and silently sobbed. Her head was bowed so low. She wouldn't even make eye contact with me. She was silently bearing her son's shame," Will said, as he grabbed a tissue and wiped his own eyes and blew his nose.

"Reverend Hedges asked few questions, but most of his concern was for *the young lady* and how she was holding up. I explained that she and her family had made the decision that it was in her best interest to change schools and that she wouldn't be coming back to Halcyon Heights."

"I didn't know anything definitive had been decided," I said seeking clarification.

"Sorry, I thought you knew. I had a phone call yesterday afternoon with an irate Rosalie Powell. They're still considering sending her to Regina in Charlottesville or perhaps an all girls' boarding school in Switzerland. There are tentative plans for Brooke to leave next week," Will said.

"It was later in the meeting that Liz escorted Evan to the meeting, just like she did with Brooke." Will said. "There was little doubt in my mind that when Evan entered my office and looked into his parents' tear-stained faces, he knew what this meeting was about. When I started to explain to Evan what had been alleged about his role in the *Sex-for-Tutoring Scandal*, without hesitation Evan admitted his guilt. He took full responsibility for the entire escapade and cast no blame on Brooke. He cried, and asked his parents for their forgiveness. But at that point and time, their forgiveness was not being offered."

Will inhaled deeply and paused. "I know I should be outraged at Evan for his participation in this whole affair, but I must say that he really stood up and took it like a man. He owned what belonged to him, cast no blame on anyone else, and offered no excuses for his behavior, just a heart-felt apology to his parents and to me. As crazy as this may sound, in that moment my admiration for this young man grew. He was loving and respectful to his mother and his father. It was heartbreaking. I delineated the terms of the suspension, but I don't believe anyone comprehended or cared to comprehend. They were just so mired down in shame and disappointment." Will was still all choked up.

"What are the terms of the suspension?" I asked. I thought if we shifted the focus of this conversation to something more concrete it might ease the struggle Will was having keeping it together.

"Evan will be suspended for the next 30 days. He can't be on campus at all. There is a precedent for this kind of a suspension. Remember when the girls' basketball team was suspended after drinking and drug use in the hotel after states?"

"I heard about it, but that happened before I was here," I said.

"Evan will receive a 50 for all of the class work that he misses during the suspension. He will need to keep up on his own. If he does well on his assignments, he will still pass. As you know, a student only needs a 60 to pass a class. He's already in at Ohio State, so they will not need to see his last semester grades. All he needs to do is pass."

"So there's no need to inform the university," I stated, but Will knew that in truth this was a question.

"It has been discussed. When the college counseling office signed, dated, and submitted his application last fall, we had no knowledge of this. The decision has been made to keep quiet, unless we are specifically asked."

"Is that it?" I asked.

"No, he will also be suspended from the basketball team. No games and no practices, but he will be back in time for districts, regionals, and the state championship tournament, if they get that far." Will said.

"Really?" I said. I regretted my tone almost immediately. Will was looking for support and I was certain I sounded snarky. It was just that I knew Will pretty well, and I was surprised that securing another basketball championship was on his radar at this time and part of this conversation.

"I know you don't really care about our co-curricular athletic program, and you probably think these concessions are wrong," he was starting to get defensive. I could tell that there had already been plenty of discussion about the suspension that I'd not been privy to. He didn't need to explain himself to me, and yet he must have felt that he did.

"There are a lot of other boys who are counting on a good showing this season. There are boys on the team who are innocent of any wrongdoing. Their chance of securing college scholarships and even going to college will be hurt if Evan doesn't play his part on the team," he said emphatically.

I needed to remember that Will and I were on the same team. He was one of the *good guys*, even if we didn't always see things eye-to-eye. Yet, I still couldn't let it go, "So we know that these other young men are innocent of any wrong doing? Do we even have the names of the others involved?" I asked.

Will took a deep breath and I'm certain in that moment that he wished he'd called someone else to discuss this with.

Will didn't answer my question.

Instead he said, "I'm certain I'll be getting a phone call from Reverend Hedges tomorrow to repeat the terms of Evan's suspension."

"When you spoke to Rosalie Powell last night, did she say anything further about filing criminal charges?" I asked.

"She was so angry. She's still threatening to do so. I spoke with the Hedges about this. They understand that Brooklyn's only 14 and there's a possibility that the Powells would file criminal charges alleging statutory rape."

"How did the Hedges receive that news?" I asked hesitantly. I was uncertain if I really wanted to know, uncertain if I really wanted to walk that far into this family's nightmare.

"The parent in me can only imagine what they were feeling . . . I'm certain they were filled with fear and terror at the prospect of their only son going to trial, being branded as a pedophile, and facing up to ten years in prison. All I know is if my son was in Evan's place, I would be despondent," Will said with great compassion.

"I can only imagine how they're feeling and then I must stop myself for even in my imagination that pain is too great for me to even fathom," I said. I too was heartsick at the very thought of this.

I sat quietly and let Will talk as he filled me in on the details of the meeting while he remembered who said what, and how it had all unfolded. "There came a time when I had nothing else to say. This whole thing had become a family matter. I suggested they all go home and that we would speak again in a few days," Will said.

He looked exhausted. I thought he would probably like nothing better than to go home to his own family, maybe have a good, stiff drink, and try to think about better days, if that was even possible.

"And Elise, as to your earlier question about the other boys . . ."

"Yes," I waited for the other shoe to drop. What was going to come next?

"When I asked Evan to give me the names of the other boys involved, he sat in silence with his hands folded in his lap for a long time and then said, 'I'm sorry, sir.' And he would say nothing more. I've already spoken with the headmaster. Tomorrow I must begin the inquisition. Robo-Cop has been going through what videotapes we do have and he has identified about 5 upper classmen hanging around with Brooke. There's nothing inappropriate on the tapes, just two students walking and talking together. I will be talking to all of those boys over the next few days. George hopes that if we can handle this internally that maybe Rosalie Powell will not go to the District Attorney and make good on her threat to file criminal charges. You know who they are. Just like Catherine and Libby said, and Brooklyn confirmed, they're the African American seniors on the football team, and they're on the basketball team too."

"I don't want to know anything more," I said. "I'm sad and I want to go home. See you tomorrow," I picked up my notepad and started to leave.

"Elise . . ."

I paused and looked back over my shoulder. I too had started to cry. I tried to wipe my tears with the sleeve of my jacket, but they just kept coming.

"Not a word to anyone. Okay?" he asked.

But he didn't need to. "Whether I like it or not, I am the keeper of the secrets. Don't worry, I won't be saying anything to anyone." There was a part of me that was a little offended that he'd had to ask, but I understood Will's need for reassurance. God only knew I needed some reassurance too.

As I walked past the gymnasium the boys' basketball team was running drills. Their practice would be over in about 30 minutes. I didn't want to face these boys and pretend everything was all right. I wasn't that good of an actress. I intended to be in my car and long gone by then.

∾

The next morning the school was rumbling as the word got out. I was always amazed how rapidly things that were meant to be private became common knowledge. Perhaps when Evan didn't go to basketball practice after school or because Brooke hadn't been in class for the last week, some of the other boys involved in the scandal had begun to put two and two together.

There were plenty of people who'd been asking where Brooke was. Both boys and girls had tried to call her on her cell phone, but the phone went directly to voicemail both day and night.

The rumor mill was up and running and bits of gossip were being traded like stocks on Wall Street.

Will continued the investigation as more and more of the young black men on the athletic teams were called into his office. No one was talking. No one was admitting to anything. Until this was sorted out, anyone and everyone who was under suspicion was suspended.

I walked down the athletic corridor after lunch and the kids were clustered in groups by race. I was forever telling them that they needed to be quiet because the hallways were usually filled with raucous laughter, but now all I heard was the buzzing of whispered secrets, which grew silent until I'd passed.

The administration was saying nothing. It felt like some type of guerrilla warfare. All were left to wonder–*who was friend and who was foe?* No one knew anything definitive, except one day someone was in your class and the next day their desk was empty. Things were changing and changing quickly. I felt it in the hallways and I felt it in the dining room. The dining room was once integrated. Only yesterday kids ate with their classmates, their teammates and their friends. Now all the black kids sat together at the tables by the windows.

Trust had broken down.

The students were angry. They were operating on limited information, but then so were the adults. However, that didn't stop anyone and everyone from having an opinion about who was guilty and who was innocent.

Kids whispered to one another and occasionally to me. They wanted to know, "Would Evan still be going to Ohio State? Would he get to keep his scholarship? Were the Powells going to go to the police?"

I gave the pre-scripted response, "I'm sorry. I can't talk about this."

The law was clear on this: the school had a legal obligation to go to the police even if the Powells did not. The decision to inform the police was put on hold by the headmaster, until our own internal investigation had been completed. In the interim, Will tried to determine who was involved and what had actually happened.

In spite of pressure exerted by the headmaster, Will was true to his word. He never approached Libby or Catherine to pump them for information that they were unwilling to share.

Libby and Catherine had plenty of good reasons to keep quiet. I knew they weren't speaking to anyone, except maybe each other, about what had transpired, and they certainly were not talking about their role in any of it.

Catherine told her mother the whole story because it was just too much for her to bear on her own. Her mother had called me to say she was taking Catherine to Chicago to see a play and do some shopping. She wanted her daughter out of this mess, at least for the weekend. When Catherine returned to school she redoubled her academic efforts and spent every free minute she had working on her project for the Science Olympiad. This kept her up in the science wing and out of the fray.

Libby was less skilled at avoiding detection. She and Brooke were closer friends, and thus Libby was under a continual barrage of questions. People wanted to know: "Where is Brooke?" and "What's her family going to do?"

Both Catherine and Libby had gone silent. They had done what they had set out to do, and that was to protect their friend. They weren't going any further. They weren't going to implicate anyone else. The risks were way too great.

I didn't seek them out for I didn't want anyone to suspect the source of the information.

The school was restless.

Kent Shields, the security guard who the students called Robo-Cop, was spending hours and hours going through months and months of old security tapes to see who was leaving school with whom. He would've liked nothing better than to blow this whole scandal wide open by cracking the case and providing definitive proof. Maybe then The Academy could justify his salary, his position, and maybe they would even let him carry a little gun.

In the end, it was Rosalie Powell who seemed to be orchestrating this witch-hunt. She turned over Brooklyn's cell phone records and three more African American boys were identified as having placed phone calls to her daughter. The implication was that if Brooklyn spoke with them on the phone, then they must have had sex with her. Or so the allegations went.

But unlike Evan, who freely assumed responsibility for his wrongdoing, the other boys admitted nothing. They stood in silent solidarity.

There was no open forum for discussion. The gag order went out during the next faculty meeting. Will said, "This is being handled. This is not your business. Please respect the process. Under no circumstances is this to be discussed."

The headmaster was distancing himself from the whole scandal. Will had become the point person. If people didn't like how things were being handled, it was Will who would take the fall.

This was a hallmark move of the headmaster, and everyone knew it. Maybe if we don't talk about it then we could pretend it wasn't really happening. This was typical, and should've been the expected response.

The problem was the students didn't get the memo. So they weren't given the opportunity to listen to the wisdom of their teachers, for we feared that heads would roll, and jobs would be lost if the gag order was violated.

To even speak of this was to be disloyal to someone.

So it was that the students talked amongst themselves.

Unlike Brooke's parents, there were those who felt that in spite of her age, Brooklyn had been the instigator and that Evan and the other boys had been her prey.

One day the following week some of the girls on the basketball teams were in the clinic during their study hall. They spoke openly about Evan and how he was doing. I was sitting at my desk grading papers and there were times they seemed to forget that I was even there.

"Evan's mama is so angry with him. She has him on his knees for hours every day askin' God for forgiveness. The rest of the time he's just tryin' to stay ahead in the class work he's missin'. His mama won't even let him out of his room."

The kids talked freely about how they thought their mothers would've responded. Brooklyn's name was dragged through the mud. It was easy to see whom they thought was guilty and who was innocent. The black girls were outraged.

"*Little miss debutante,* she had her sights set on Evan from the day she walked in here."

"Just tryin' to get some attention from her own mama."

"Well she got that now, didn't she?"

"But what's he doin' messin' around with her?"

"She's just another piece of skinny little white ass."

"Givin' it away at school. That girl's got no shame."

"But he's gonna take the fall, while she skips off to Switzerland in her mama's jet plane."

It was time to put a stop to this. The kids were getting agitated and I could see that tempers were rising. I spoke up, "Girls, could you find something else to talk about?" I asked, but my tone was stern. They knew that I'd heard enough.

"Sorry, Mrs. Duncan."

"You know we love you, it's just that there's white folks and then there's *white folks.* And we know the difference and so do you."

"Besides, it's just about time for lunch."

Then this small gathering of girls decided to leave the clinic.

The freshmen and the seniors shared a lunch period. At one point in time the faculty thought this was a good way to limit the large number of people trying to get their lunch at the same time. The senior class had the smallest number of students and the freshman class had the largest number. This decision had proven disastrous because there was a big difference between freshmen and seniors.

A small group of freshmen girls remained behind and talked quietly amongst themselves. They had been privy to too much information.

Some of the girls took Brooklyn's side and thought she must've been manipulated and forced into doing something she never would've chosen to do on her own. Those that knew her well, continued to see her as the victim.

The senior athletes, both male and female, saw this as a private matter between the girl and whomever she chose to share her body with. They thought this was none of the school's business. Other loyalties divided along race and class lines.

Some of the students felt that if the boys involved had been wealthy white boys the whole issue would be seen as appropriate sexual commerce where everyone was getting what they needed and familial alliances would be formed, and future dynasties created.

I couldn't help but wonder if this was true.

But this wasn't the case.

The fact was that all the boys were over 18 and the girl was only 14 and this type of sexual commerce was against the law.

Pandora's box had been opened and the demons had been released ... the law, the issues of sexual predators and children, of gender, race, class, wealth, privilege, privacy, parental codes of ethics, and academic expectations had all been rolled out to be examined. The students, the faculty, and the parents, *our customers*, to whom we had sold the promise of a world-class education and protection from the underbelly of life, all had different ideas about who had been victimized and who should be punished.

The parents whispered over cocktails and after tennis at *the club*. They whispered in the bleachers at the basketball game, and in the narthex of their churches after Sunday services. The lines had been drawn and fingers pointed. Who was guilty? And who was innocent? These were the questions left unanswered. Lives would be changed and futures altered depending on how this all unfolded.

In the midst of all this turmoil, Brooklyn's mother petitioned the school for readmission for her daughter. She was certain things had blown over, but instead, things were just coming to a boil. She still hadn't decided if she was going to bring the police into this or not.

Brooke had gone to Regina, an all girls' Catholic school to see if she wanted to transfer there, and she did. But Rosalie Powell thought the math and science programs were substandard or equally likely, she may have found the other families there weren't quite to her social standards.

I can't really say what happened or what was being promised, and to whom. The administration had taken over the investigation, and I was no longer in the loop or privy to any information. I did know that the police had not been called and no charges had been filed. I wondered if the school would also assume the role of judge and jury?

In the long, cold nights of that February winter, I wrestled with this. My late husband Elliott had held a prominent position for over twenty years in the District Attorney's office. I had dear friends who were attorneys there. I knew what the law said. The law was clear on this. As a teacher I had a legal, as well as a moral responsibility, to report issues of child endangerment.

I also knew I had passed this responsibility onto my supervisor when I told Will, and he had passed the responsibility on to his supervisor when he informed the headmaster. But did this really let me off the hook when I knew that they had not honored their legal obligations?

I tossed and turned in bed. I justified my silence with the knowledge that Brooke was no longer in *danger*. She was no longer at school. She was no longer in contact with the boys involved. Then just as I was about to drift off into sleep, I found myself struggling with this notion of danger. Had she ever really been in *danger*? Or was she just another young woman exploring her sexuality?

Was the real problem that she had chosen the forbidden fruit? She was involved with older black boys, which was forbidden by culture and law. Was this Biblical justice? Perhaps she was the temptress and her inability to control her own sexual desires was the reason she must be cast out of this Garden of Eden? My dreams turned to nightmares as the old and gray headmaster played the role of the angry Creator, deciding the fates of these students.

I awoke with the sound of my alarm clock in a cold sweat. 5:30 AM. I hit the snooze. I'd had an awful night's sleep.

I'd been dreaming–

I was on the witness stand. The prosecutor badgered me with questions that I was unable to answer. Why had I kept my mouth shut? Why did I not come forward? Why had I broken the law? I had been tongue-tied and in tears. I was unable to provide any reasonable justification for doing nothing.

My dreams had become disturbing. As I lay there in that dreamy state between sleep and wake, my subconscious voiced the questions that begged to be looked at.

Who would be my judge and who would be my jury?

To whom must I justify my choices?

Could I continue to work in a place where my choices were to break the law or lose my job?

Could I work where the goals and wishes of the parents dictated policy?

Did the wealthy parents truly have this power because they provided all the revenue and funding for the school?

When power and money talked did truth keep its mouth shut?

Was I naïve to think that this wouldn't happen here?

Was the purpose of the school to keep the money flowing in? Or was it to provide a safe place for children to learn and grow into the people they'd been created to be?

Who was captaining this ship?

There were issues of leadership and governance that I needed to think about.

TGIF. It was Friday. One more day and we would be off for a week. It was our mid-winter break and it was never more welcome than it was that year. At the close of the school day all the students would be released for a week.

If we could only get through the day, and get out of here, and off on our mid-winter break perhaps time and space would relieve some of the hostility the students were feeling towards one another, towards their teachers, and the administration. Maybe then this great racial divide could begin to mend and heal.

Valentine's Day would fall on Monday and all the students would be on break and not at school. So, the student council had planned their annual Valentine's Day flower sale and fundraiser for the week before the break. The flowers were distributed on that Friday, February 11th during the second period class.

Over a hundred flowers had been purchased and were delivered for Brooke in her math class. But since Brooke wasn't in school, her math teacher took Brooke's flowers to the academic office. Each carnation was tagged with a heart cut out of construction paper. On one side was the recipient's name, on the other students typically wrote a note or signed their name or both. The cards on Brooke's flowers said things like: cunt, whore and slut. The flowers had been sent anonymously, but it was widely known that the girls on the basketball team had orchestrated the prank. They were sending a message. They were standing with the boys.

∾

Thank God for the break. My kids didn't have the same vacation time as I did since they attended a different school. It didn't matter; I took them out of school anyway. Saturday morning we loaded up the car and headed to Florida. I needed a break from the cold. I needed a break from the drama of my everyday life. So we went to visit some friends on Sanibel Island. I hadn't seen the Maxwells since Elliott's funeral. They had kids about the same age as mine. We sat on the beach, the kids played in the ocean, I read a couple of books, we talked until there was nothing left to say, and I drank a rum punch that was appropriately called *a painkiller*. We weren't in the islands, but close enough. A good time was had by all and by the end of the week we were going home– ready or not.

It was nearly a 14-hour drive each way and fortunately my kids were good travelers. While I drove, Ian read aloud to us from one of the Harry Potter books. The time went quickly, for every time he was ready to call it quits, Shea would beg him to read another chapter, and willingly he complied with her requests.

We arrived home late Sunday night. Thank goodness it was Presidents' Day weekend and we had all been blessed with another day of vacation. Tomorrow I would attack the laundry, get some groceries, and clean the house. But not tonight, I was tired. Tomorrow would be payback time for the kids too. They had missed three days of school last week and had homework to make up. Still, this little trip had been a great diversion.

I went upstairs to make certain all the lights were out and that my kids were safely tucked into their beds. Old habits are hard to break. I'd been doing this since they were infants. I guess this was just part of my bedtime routine. They were both already asleep, their faces tanned, and each of them had a sprinkling of new freckles across their noses. I pulled up their covers and kissed their foreheads. I savored the sweetness for I knew these days were fleeting.

The kids had been in bed for about an hour and I was in my bed reading. A few more pages and then lights out. My cell phone rang at about 11:00 PM. This was late for me. I looked at my phone, but didn't recognize the number. "Hello?" My voice trailed up at the end for I had no idea who might be on the other end.

"Elise, it's Sean Brogan," the voice was solid and strong coming through the receiver.

"Sean," was as much as I could come up with. Why was the football coach calling me at 11:00 at night?

"Sorry to call you so late. I got your number from Will and he thought I should call you."

"What's going on?" I asked. I had a sense of foreboding. Something bad had happened or he wouldn't be calling me. I swung my legs over the edge of the bed and reached for my robe.

"Evan's mother committed suicide this afternoon," he said. I could hear the great sadness in his voice as he tried to be as gentle with me as possible.

"Oh my God. Oh no. Oh Sean." I tried to wrap my head around what he had just told me. My eyes filled with tears as the reality of this senseless tragedy took form in my mind.

"There's more, Elise. I didn't want you to hear about this at school and be unprepared."

"What?" I asked.

"While Evan was home this afternoon, she loaded up her car with all of his stuffed animals from his childhood and drove to a park where she used to take him as a child. She lit a match and dropped it into a gas can– she blew herself up," he said as calmly as he was able.

"What! Oh dear God. No!" I was nearly shouting into the phone.

"The police said she died instantly. When they finally got the fire out she was burnt beyond recognition," he said, and then paused for me to process this horrific news.

This was more than I could deal with. More than I needed to know. The images burned in my brain.

Through my horror and my tears I asked, "How is Evan?"

In response Sean told me, "The boys from the football and basketball teams are over at the house right now. I went over for about an hour tonight, but didn't get a chance to speak with Evan or his dad. The members of their church were hovering close, forming a protective shield."

"Oh Sean. I feel so terrible." My whole body was shaking and I was dizzy. I needed to sit back down for I feared I might collapse.

"Will asked if you would call the girls and their parents tonight." He didn't need to say who the girls were. I knew whom he meant. "He doesn't want them to be blindsided when they return to school."

"I understand," I reached across my bedside stand for an envelope and a pen, turning the envelope over I asked, "Do you have their phone numbers?"

"I have them right here. Are you ready?" he asked.

"Go ahead," I said, and he recited the numbers to me.

"Thanks for calling, Sean," I said. I knew this couldn't have been easy for him either.

"One more thing ..." he said.

"Yes," I heard myself say. What now ... Dear God, what now?

All I wanted to do was get off the phone. Right then. Right that very instant. I didn't want to hear one more thing, from one more person. I was barely holding it together.

"Will wants to meet with us tomorrow at 10:00 AM in his office," he said.

"I'll be there," I said, realizing that I'd hung up the phone without even saying good bye.

I dropped to my knees and cried. I couldn't get the image of this beautiful woman and devoted mother blowing herself up out of my head. Blowing herself up by her own hand, in her own car, taking all the remnants of her beloved son's childhood with her.

How could she have?
How could this have happened?
How could she have done this?
How would Evan ever get past this?

As I looked up from my bedroom floor, my daughter Shea was standing in the doorway rubbing her eyes. She was in her pink flannel nightgown with her pale blonde hair sticking up in all directions. "I heard someone crying," she said. "Mommy, are you okay?" she asked.

I raised myself up on my knees and opened my arms to receive her sweet embrace. "Yes darling. I'll be okay. I just heard some sad news about a boy at my school," I told her.

"I'm sorry Mommy. Do you want me to sleep with you?" she asked.

I couldn't help but smile at my dear little daughter. She always wanted me to sleep with her after she had a bad dream, and now she was offering me the same comfort.

"That would be so nice," I said, as I pulled back my blankets and tucked my 10- year-old into my bed. "I need to make a couple of phone calls before I come back to bed," I told her as I kissed her forehead. "I'll be back in just a few minutes," I said, and I turned out the light on the bedside table. I think she was sound asleep before I was even out of the room.

I walked towards the kitchen with the envelope in my hand. I caught myself thinking that there was a big difference between a 10-year-old and a 14-year-old. And if this line of thinking was valid and I believed it was, than there was also a big difference between a 14-year-old and an 18-year-old too.

It was closing in on midnight when I called all three of the girls' homes. In each instance one of their parents answered the phone. Apparently, the student hotline had outpaced the school's for all three families had received the news a couple of hours ago. All of the parents were comforting their daughters and they thanked me for my phone call and concern.

When I returned to my bedroom Shea was sound asleep. I crawled into bed and wrapped my arms around my little girl while I pondered the big question: what was our responsibility as parents and as adults? Perhaps our greatest responsibility was to protect the innocents and provide shelter from the storm. I closed my eyes in prayer as I asked God to bless and protect Evan, and his mother, and his father, and Brooke, and her parents, and Catherine and Libby, and all the boys who had been implicated, and all of the kids who had taken sides, and for Will, and the coaches, and for me, and for mine, and the list went on and on and on until at last I was blessed with sleep.

∾

Ian was sleeping in. Shea got up and turned some cartoons on the television. This was a luxury she rarely had the opportunity to indulge in. I could be overly restrictive when it came to television. My kids liked to quote me, "Garbage in, garbage out."

Today I let it slide. I needed to go into school for the meeting. I called my next-door neighbor Jody. "Sure, send them over, my kids are just hanging out at home today," she said.

"Thanks love," I said. "I shouldn't be too long. Ian may choose to stay home and work on his homework."

"I'll call him over when lunch is ready," she said.

What a love. I had great neighbors.

This was still supposed to be a vacation day. Sean Brogan had said something about Will wanting to meet with *us*. I didn't know who *us* was. As much as I would've loved to wear a pair of jeans, I thought better of that. I dressed in a long skirt, sweater, and a pair of riding boots. It wasn't exactly within the confines of the faculty dress code, but at least I'd be warm. I brushed my hair, pulled it back, and was out the door by 8:30. This wasn't exactly what I'd had in mind for my day off, but I knew I wasn't alone in that.

I grabbed a cup of coffee in the faculty workroom and made my way towards Will's office. Liz was already in. She had a sadness in her eyes as she told me, "You're meeting in the boardroom this morning."

When I arrived I was glad to see that Will and George had also foregone their suits and were dressed in matching navy cashmere sweaters. Sean Brogan was also there. The mood was somber. Will said, "We're just waiting for Lamar."

Lamar Alexander was the men's basketball coach. I had been wondering who was invited to this meeting. Perhaps summoned was a better word. While we waited, the room was uncharacteristically silent.

I was pretty certain we were not being brought together to support one another and process our grief, nor to collaborate and share our opinions on the best way to proceed. No, I was pretty certain those decisions had already been made, and we were just there to be informed. This wasn't a democracy, it never had been.

The word would be pronounced from on high. Like it, live with it or leave. Those would be the options. I took a deep breath as I tried to quiet my own mind and not try to predict the future. It would all be revealed in a matter of moments.

Lamar arrived and slipped into the chair next to me. "Sorry I'm late," he offered his apology to the group. "I had a phone call from Reverend Hedges as I was heading out the door."

He looked shaken. I reached over and gave him a squeeze on the forearm and he turned and smiled. No doubt, he had been picking up the pieces of broken lives since all of this scandal had come to light.

George was seated at the head of the table. This was his chair. He was the headmaster and this was his meeting. He assumed the persona of the benevolent dictator.

"A terrible tragedy has come to pass for the Halcyon Heights family. As we all know, Mrs. Carmella Hedges took her own life yesterday. I understand that she has battled with depression over the years. In light of this tragedy we have decided it is in Evan's best interest to be back in school. We feel it would be too much for him to serve the remainder of his suspension at home alone. We are going to give him credit for time served." He paused momentarily before continuing.

"Visiting hours will be all day tomorrow at the Franklin Funeral Home on Broad Street and the funeral is scheduled for Wednesday morning at 10:00 AM at Gethsemane Baptist Church. A colleague of Reverend Hedges that he has known since seminary will preside over the services. I fully expect that many of our students will be in attendance at the funeral home tomorrow and at the funeral on Wednesday." He finished talking about the funeral arrangements, before he addressed the re-entry plan for Evan. "Evan will return to school on Thursday morning and resume his place on the basketball team on Thursday afternoon."

As I had predicted, the decisions had been made. The tone of George's voice and his delivery did not invite any discussion or any questions.

"You may be interested to know that Brooklyn Powell has been withdrawn from The Academy and is leaving for Switzerland this morning. She has accepted a position as a boarding student at the Montreux School for Girls. It has a wonderful international reputation in the areas of both math and science."

George took a deep breath and smiled.

Did he think this answered all the questions, solved all the issues, and wrapped up all the loose ends? There were times when wisdom should prevail;

perhaps this was a time when I should have known enough to keep my mouth closed. But I did not. "What has been decided about filing a police report?" I asked, knowing full well that I was opening up this can of worms.

George stood up and placed both his palms on the table, leaning forward he stared down the long mahogany table at me. I met his gaze and held it. He wasn't happy with me. His scowl told me so.

This was a question that needed to be addressed. This was a private meeting, not a public forum. If this couldn't be addressed here, I knew it would not be addressed or at least not in my presence. Yet, I was someone who had been asked to wait and trust the process. I was one of the people who had abandoned my legal responsibility. I knew that I could still be held accountable and this man would be the first to throw me under the bus if it ever came to that. I was merely a functionary. I was expendable. Rosalie Powell had told me so, and I knew she was right.

As George held my gaze and tried to decide how to answer me, I posed the question again, "What about the criminal charges?"

"Really, Elise, don't you think this boy has suffered enough? Can you not find it in your heart to forgive him? If the Powells can forgive him, surely you can let this go," George said.

It was in that moment it dawned on me that maybe this was a gender issue. I was the lone woman in this sea of testosterone.

"Please don't misunderstand. I'm just asking the questions. I'm not suggesting that I know the answer.

But this is truly an ethical dilemma. Our students aren't the only ones who are ill-equipped to decide between competing goods or lesser evils."

I needed to talk about this. No matter what was ultimately decided I felt we should look at the issues. Pulling forth all the courage I could muster I continued. "I'm hesitant to say, I am not altogether comfortable with this. I feel a great deal of compassion for Evan and for his father. I can't begin to imagine the kind of pain they are all in, but let us not forget that Brooklyn is a child of 14. The mother in me feels a need to protect her and all the young girls we are here to educate and protect. I can't help but feel she has been preyed upon. She is being sent off to boarding school and these young men return to campus. I'm asking you, does this solve the problem? Do we even know if Brooke was the only girl involved? Isn't it possible that there were others? Does this solution re-establish a sense of safety? Has justice been served? I have been privy to some of the details of this situation and I don't feel I have a clear perspective on who victimized whom, but I do know that our students are watching to see what, if anything, we will do. Will we obey the law? Or are we above the law? Perhaps this is why we have a judicial system?" I said. As I was gathering my thoughts to continue, George interrupted me.

"Elise," he spoke my name harshly. "The Powells have decided not to press charges. Brooke will leave the country tomorrow morning. Now there is no one here who can or will substantiate her claim that these boys took advantage of her." He spoke with the authority that accompanied his position. "This subject is closed. You are not to speak of this again . . . to anyone. Do I make myself clear?" George held my gaze until I looked away.

"Yes sir," I said, and swallowed hard. I didn't want to cry. I had spoken my mind and had just been shut down.

The threat was implied. I got the message loud and clear.

∾

But just because I couldn't talk about it, didn't mean I didn't think about it.

No, fifteen years later I was still thinking about it and wondering if indeed justice had been served.

Many of our black students were out of school the next day as they sat with Evan at the funeral home. Some of the kids went for a little while and then returned to attend the classes that they felt they couldn't miss. But the black students, and only the black students returned from the funeral home wearing black armbands over their dress shirts. They were in mourning and in solidarity.

The following morning was the funeral for Mrs. Hedges. Many students, their parents, and members of the faculty attended the funeral. The Gethsemane Baptist Church was filled with people of all races, creeds, and ethnicities. The administrators from The Academy were all in attendance.

Later in the afternoon, I passed Sam Fraser in the hallway. "Did you go to the funeral?" I asked. He was dressed in his Sunday best.

He nodded.

"How was it?" I asked.

"The church was packed. Reverend Hedges sat up front with Evan and Carmella's elderly parents. The choir sang Gospel music, and everyone was pretty broken up. The clergyman who eulogized Carmella spoke on the relentless torment of depression and the need for unlimited compassion for those who suffer."

Then Sam lowered his voice and turned to face me. He clearly didn't want anyone else to hear what he had to say, and he looked me in the eye before continuing. "We're both on the crisis team. We deal with kids with depression all the time. You know, the ones who come to school without bathing or washing their hair, the ones who can't get to class or finish their homework because they're either sleeping all the time or not sleeping at all. You were with me in the hall last week when I introduced you to Reverend and Mrs. Hedges. Give me your professional opinion– did Carmella Hedges look depressed to you?"

I shook my head. "I don't know Sam. I don't know anything about the woman. The whole thing is just so heart-wrenching."

"Well, I coached Evan and the offensive line for three years. I know these people. If Carmella suffered from depression, I never saw it," he said definitively.

Sam looked over his shoulder to be certain he wouldn't be overheard. "Was this just a *big fuck you* to Evan for messing up? Or was it just that she couldn't deal with the shame and embarrassment he brought on his family and his community? Or was it something else?" he asked, not really looking for an answer.

I knew that I didn't have one. I couldn't begin to fathom what could possibly have motivated someone to take their own life and in such a dramatic way. Perhaps Sam was right, perhaps this was just a *big fuck you*.

Again, I tried to put myself in Carmella's position. I tried to understand her motivation.

Sam continued, "I sat in that Southern Baptist Church today and thought about our own Catholic rituals and prayers. You know the one, *Lamb of God who takes away the sins of the world …*"

Again I nodded.

"Do you think there was any way she took her own life, just like Jesus, to take away Evan's sins, and to decrease the punishment for her son's transgressions?" He paused a moment before continuing. "I don't know. Just think about it."

Again I felt my stomach tighten. I didn't know. I didn't want to know. I didn't want to think about this anymore. I just wanted to wake up from this nightmare.

"If that was her intention, then it worked. How many times has someone whispered, 'don't you think he's suffered enough?' So I ask you, was Carmella Hedges a monster of a mother or was she the sacrificial lamb? I mean, look how quickly everyone is moving to forgive and forget Evan's transgressions. Her death bought that forgiveness."

Sam turned both of his hands up towards the ceiling and turned to walk away.

I didn't know what the gesture meant and Samuel didn't stick around long enough to offer any explanation, but I felt that in that moment he was submitting to the will of The Almighty.

Later that afternoon, all the students were back in school for their afterschool athletic practices, including Evan. I caught sight of him as I was leaving for the day and he was heading for the gym. He was dressed in his practice jersey, basketball shorts, and basketball shoes. He was also wearing the black armband on his right upper arm.

I don't know if he knew of my involvement or not. I had been dreading this moment, but here it was. We were face-to-face.

Evan paused for a moment and we looked at each other. I gave him a slow sad smile and said, "I'm so sorry."

Evan nodded and said, "Thank you, Mrs. Duncan. Me too." Then he went on into the gym for practice.

He looked so sad.

My heart was breaking for him. This had been the right decision. This boy needed to be with his friends and his teammates now. God only knew how this would have played out if he had too much time alone to wallow in the tragedy.

The basketball game was held as scheduled on Friday night in the gym at Halcyon Heights. Our boys were still wearing their armbands, and so were many of the black students who filled the spectator stands, when our team defeated the opposing team.

115 to 84

CHAPTER 10

March 2000

The weather in March seemed to mirror everyone's spirits. One day it was cold and overcast and threatened to snow. The winter was petering out as the skies only gave a dusting of fresh snow. There was just enough to make everyone cold and miserable, but not enough to cover the dirty, slushy snow that rimmed the edges of the roadways. Then the next day, it would rain all day before the temperature would drop at night covering the roads with ice, making them dangerous.

That was how it felt-- cold, dirty, miserable, and dangerous.

We once had been a bastion of hope and a model of an ethnically diverse community. If children from all these diverse backgrounds and cultures could learn to get along then maybe, just maybe, there was hope for the rest of the world.

In the weeks that followed the sex-for-tutoring scandal and Carmella Hedges' horrific suicide, the school continued to feel the racial divide; it hadn't felt like this before. There was a pervasive sadness that the students just couldn't seem to shake, and neither could the faculty and staff.

The men's basketball team had been touted to take it all, by those who made it their business to speculate on high school athletics. But the boys from Halcyon Heights fell apart in the regionals, and lost to a team they had beaten handily earlier in the season. They'd lost their fire. Their hearts were just not in it. The media was left to scratch their heads about what had happened, but it wasn't a surprise to anyone who knew the inside story.

Somehow, we all muddled through the next few weeks and to our collective relief it was time for spring break.

Praise be to God.

CHAPTER 11

April 2000

Easter would be late in April that year. My children attended a parochial school and thus, their spring break was always tied to Easter.

So while my kids were in school, I spent my days doing some spring-cleaning, first in the house, and then in the gardens. This was my annual ritual. It was with great satisfaction that I put away the winter clothes, opened the windows, and blew out the stale air of winter. I packed up the clothing the kids had outgrown and cleaned out my closets of things I no longer needed or wanted. Some things were threadbare or stained, and ready for the trash or the ragbag and other things with a bit of life left in them were sent off to Goodwill.

I cleaned and swept out the garage. It was amazing how much junk had accumulated there over the course of the long winter. The floor was gritty with dirt from the road as well as salt. I hosed it down.

When the first beautiful sunny day arrived I decided to tackle the gardens. Cleaning the house was necessary, but cleaning the garden was pure pleasure. The days were getting longer and the gardens were just starting to come back to life. I crawled around on my hands and knees, wearing garden gloves as I used my fingers as a rake to remove leaves and sticks. I needed to be careful not to disturb the little crocuses, tulips, and daffodils that were pushing their way out of the darkness of the earth towards the warmth of the sunshine.

All of this was pretty mindless work. As I picked up the sticks that had fallen from the trees during the last winter storm, I found that at long last I had time to wander around in my own head. I thought about the sorting and cleaning, and the small mountain of things I had gotten rid of. Since these last few months had taken their toll on me, maybe I also needed to sort through some of the fallout and residual debris from this latest storm at The Academy. I knew, I needed to look at it, before I could let it go and get rid of it.

There were things about my job I found deeply unsettling. It was stressful. That was all that I could say. And *stress* was a garbage can diagnosis if ever there was one. So many people talked about stress. I was one of them. It was even one of the in-class writing assignments I had my students do every semester. They had to write three paragraphs about what caused them stress, how they knew they were under stress, and how they dealt with it. When my students wrote about this, they uncovered a number of things about themselves. The writing assignment often opened the floodgates of emotion. I kept my own journal and frequently wrote on the same topics I'd asked my students to write about.

What caused me stress? My job was one thing, and it was a big one. But what was it about my job? Could I be more specific? Certainly there were things about my job that I loved.

One thing, was that I was the secret keeper. It was a big responsibility to carry another person's most closely guarded secrets. In some way, I felt a sense of responsibility for opening the door and shining the light on the *sex-for-tutoring scandal*. I couldn't let it go. What had my role been in this last disaster?

I knew I was stressed by this thought. What did it feel like in my body? My sleep was disturbed. I could usually fall asleep, but sometimes I had nightmares, and bits and pieces of the unresolved issues of the day would cause me to wake in a panic. I couldn't let go of the image of this beautiful woman in a car full of stuffed animals bursting into flames.

Then in the daytime I ruminated over the issues. How could this mother have been that unforgiving of her only son's very human failing? From a biological perspective he was a grown man who acted on his sexual desires with a girl 4 years his junior. Had he been 20 and she 16 no crime would've been committed. But had he been 20 he would've been in college and these two wouldn't have been in such close proximity on a day-to-day basis.

If they both had been black or both been white or
if they hadn't crossed that indeterminate boundary of
social class and social status, would people have seen
this differently? Surely, there were senior boys who
were sexually involved with freshman girls. This wasn't
the first time and it certainly wouldn't be the last.

Again and again my thoughts turned to Carmella
Hedges. I was also a mother and I couldn't fathom a
more unlikely response than this. I was certain she felt
shame, and undoubtedly fear, with the threat of legal
repercussions. But most mothers would feel instantly
protective of her children, right or wrong. This was
when most families pulled together.

Was there something more to this story, which I
was not privy to?

The question haunted me. Why had this mother
decided to take her own life?

I wasn't a Baptist and I didn't have an understanding
of their teachings on suicide or on salvation.

I struggled.

There was much that remained unresolved.

I needed to find a way to let this go.

Throughout the winter I'd felt that I was all too
often at cross-purposes with my employer. My employer
was savvy enough not to speak the words, but still the
threat was implied. I knew if I filed a police report or
contacted child protective services that I would not be
offered a contract for the next year.

Yet, I had abdicated my responsibility as a
mandatory reporter. I had broken the law. Why did this
disturb me so? I certainly didn't call the police when I
knew that someone had too much to drink and drove

themselves home. I didn't call the police whenever someone ran a red light or smoked marijuana. I wasn't proud of it, but the truth was that I too had done all those things on occasion.

This disturbed my sleep and I just couldn't let it go. I wished for Elliott's wise counsel, but he was gone and I was left to sort this out for myself.

Was I naïve enough to think I was the only teacher who had ever been put in a situation like this?

The voice of wisdom spoke–

No way you're not alone.
You are just a torchbearer.
One among many who light the way.
You must speak up.

I balked.
Did I *need* to stand up and make a fuss?

Oh dear one, you ask much of me.

I wondered how the other teachers responded. I understood the golden handcuffs. There were perks, financial, and otherwise to being a team player. And yet I wondered– if I stayed, what else would I be asked to ignore? When would I be asked again to look the other way?

This didn't feel good. I felt compromised as a human being. I felt my personal integrity had been undermined.

I wondered if I had enough security to walk away. And if I left where would I go? And for God's sake, what would I do?

I thought about the school's ideology of success and it was so often in conflict with my own spiritual understanding of morality and what was right.

Going to The Academy was like driving a Mercedes or having a degree from an Ivy League school or belonging to the right country club. Names were dropped in the right company, so the right people would know that you belonged, that you were one of them and not the other. You were worthy of respect for you had made it. You had achieved power, prestige, position, and privilege.

Sending a child to a school like this was only in part what it would do for the child, but also how it elevated the status of the parent. Sending one's children to The Academy of Halcyon Heights was just another piece of the portfolio.

The headmaster could talk equally well out of both sides of his mouth, depending who held the biggest gold coin. I had seen and heard it. He lacked the moral fiber that was so needed for the job or at least to do the job well. The old boys' club and the board of trustees only needed to look over the rims of their glasses for George to remember who buttered his bread, and how quickly it could all go away lest he forgot. I was certain that compromises had been made when the house on the hill and the membership to the country club hung in the balance.

Dear old Headmaster Walker had long ago given up the struggle with right and wrong.

What was my real issue with this? The students were watching and taking notice. What were they learning? What were the consequences for our young people if they learned that the rules of life didn't apply to them? Were we really doing these kids any favors when well-meaning adults covered up their mistakes again and again and the students were never brought to bear the cost of their errors? I feared the mistakes would only become larger and larger, and the consequences more dire.

There were teachers and administrators who towed the party line, kept their mouths shut and their heads down for fear the ax would fall and their positions would be cut. But there were other teachers, who understood that their real job was not to teach for the test, but to teach the child. No matter how much these teenagers might look like adults, they were still learning, and sometimes life's most difficult lessons were the ones that absolutely must be learned. The real preparation for life, I knew, had nothing to do with which college you were accepted to. Some teachers knew this and some never would.

Images of Brooklyn Powell, sent away and locked up in an all girls' boarding school in the Alps, removed from her family and her friends, also invaded my thoughts. Was she feeling responsible? Was she guilt-ridden, and if so, for what reason? Who would dry her tears and offer comfort as she tried to understand how all of this had come to pass? Was she not just a young girl exploring her God-given sexuality? Was she doing anything different than teenagers across the globe were doing in one way or another? She was challenging her parent's values. Any psychologist who was worth his or her salt would tell you it's a critical developmental task of adolescence to break away from one's parents. It is absolutely necessary so they can move forward into their independent adult lives. Brooke had been making her own decisions and arguably her own mistakes. That is what we do as human beings– we make mistakes.

I thought about all those labels that had been cast upon her with those Valentine's Day flowers. How quickly people had been to change sides, and cast blame on her like she was some kind of social pariah.

I had long thought that age was just a number; that maturity and wisdom weren't tied to one's chronological age. Was the only issue here one of her age? In some cultures, including the white European culture of old, once a girl reached womanhood, and had her first menses, she could be married off to anyone of her parents' choosing. Daughters were chattel. Even today, in many states, parents can legally give consent for their underage teenage daughters to marry.

Was the current law really written for the protection of virginity, as if this was a prize and gift to be bestowed at marriage to someone who paid the bride price?

I wrestled with the issues. What was really at stake here and for whom?

The teachers, students and even the parents knew that this topic was off limits. We had been banned from speaking of the scandal. Still, there were whisperings and everyone had their own opinion about who were the victims and who were the perpetrators. Again, I thought about the definition of politics given by one of my professors in graduate school. Politics: who gets what from whom?

This young woman offered her body to others in return for tutoring. Heaven knows that people are involved in sexual commerce all the time: love is exchanged for the promise of sex and sex is exchanged for the promise of love. And frequently, sex is exchanged for far less: for the promise of companionship or a few kind words, a drink at the bar or dinner and a movie, and sometimes sex is just exchanged for sex.

What was being said about this young woman's use of, and control over, her own body? I wondered how my feminist sisters would weigh in on this one?

Clearly, Evan was the standard bearer in his community. He carried the hopes and dreams of the racially oppressed. He had been groomed to make it in the white man's world of privilege. This was an overwhelming responsibility for a young person to shoulder. The assumption was that if he could make it, he would pave the path for others. Any human slip up or foible was a catastrophe. So much had been riding on his success.

Perhaps it was more than his mother could bear.

Then there was Brooklyn's rich, white mother seeking revenge. Prior to the suicide explosion she had been planning a witch trial. Everyone involved with the fall of her defiled virgin princess was going to be exposed and burned at the stake in the court of popular opinion. The gossip was rampant and the guilt and innocence had already been determined.

People had chosen sides before the evidence had been presented. A trial had not been necessary. The Academy of Halcyon Heights had played the role of judge and jury– the sentences had been handed down. The once cohesive nature of the school was coming unraveled. Personal reputations had been destroyed. Evan's mother had paid for her only son's release with her life and Brooklyn had been banished to a far-away land for safekeeping.

I felt like I was trapped in a time warp. Was this just a modern-day, misconstrued version of a Grimms' Fairy Tale?

Except for one thing– where was the part where they all lived happily ever after?

Time would tell.

I couldn't let this rest.

The questions remained unanswered and unanswerable.

What responsibility did I bear in the outcome of this tragedy? I was one of the adults involved.

The collective *we* determined that students' behavior had transgressed an unwritten social contract.

Social contracts require that individuals relinquish certain personal freedoms and submit to a higher authority in exchange for certain privileges.

But who had determined this social contract? Was this something we just expected the students to know– that it was wrong to have sex at school? Clearly, this wasn't something we had spelled out in the student handbook. There was a morality clause in the handbook, but it was not explicit. So the question was-- by whose account was this deemed morally reprehensible?

Did they know they had transgressed? Of course they did. But people have sexual interludes in inappropriate places all the time. Perhaps it was the thrill of the taboo or the fear of getting caught that enhanced the experience. For God's sake, I had friends with professional positions, who boasted to being members of the Mile High Club. We had laughed at the shenanigans involved with getting two people in the restroom on an airplane while a line formed down the aisle.

I thought of all the movies my students were seeing. They were filled with sexual innuendo and with teenagers having sex. Their parents and the school may have been telling them that it was best to wait, but the media projected a very different message, which was that everyone was having sex and if you weren't, well then there was something wrong with you.

But then there was the legal transgression. According to Virginia law anyone under the age of 16 could not legally give their consent to any sexual behavior. The law stated that those under 16 were deemed children.

I struggled with the issues of justice and fairness.

When should the law be taken into one's own hands? The school had taken the law into its own hands for a myriad of reasons. I wondered if we could have expected a fairer verdict from the court system.

I wondered if it was always best to insist on transparency. Or by exposing all decisions to the light of day did we sometimes do more harm than good?

Rather then turning this over to a lawyer, maybe it was better that people who actually had a day-to-day understanding of the issues of adolescence, act as the judge and jury. Perhaps they were just better qualified.

And yet I couldn't help but wonder if this entire tragedy could've been prevented if the adults had just stayed out of it?

Then my circuitous thinking began all over again. Were we right? Were we wrong?

Mea culpa
Mea culpa
Mea maxima culpa

I still felt bewildered no matter how I examined the issues.

I wanted to be let off the hook.

There had been unforeseen consequences by following the rules.

In a word, the outcome had been tragic.

Justified or not, the guilt haunted me.

᷈

At the end of my two-week vacation, the house and the gardens were immaculate and ready to burst forth in an array of springtime loveliness. Over the break, I had re-engaged my daily practice of yoga, and I was working on letting go. I felt like I had made some headway. Unfortunately, my spirit was still weighed down with some of the accumulated darkness. I knew I would need to be patient with myself as this was going to take some time to shake.

When we all returned to school, many of the students were sporting a tan from their trips out west for some spring skiing or from a lavish trip to the Caribbean or Hawaii. The mood about the school had grown lighter as the weather changed and the days got longer as well as brighter. The two weeks away had done most of us a world of good.

During our spring break, the admissions offices of colleges and universities across the country made their final decisions. Offers of admission had been extended and students had until the end of the month to decide where they would be attending. Once the seniors had their college admission all sewn up it was next to impossible to keep them in class, let alone to see that they learned anything. They were done.

So someone in their infinite wisdom had decided that during the month of May all senior students in good standing should go on *Senior Project.*

The advanced placement exams were taken the last week in April and any senior who had a C or better in any class was exempt from taking final exams. The colleges didn't need them and therefore they were not mandated. Things were winding down.

The last weekend in April was the Senior Prom. It was a dinner dance hosted by the junior class for the seniors. The Senior Prom was always held at *The Park*, which was the most exclusive hotel in the area. It was renown for its beautiful ballroom and exquisite dining. The Academy had been hosting the Senior

Prom there for over the last 100 years. Girls made appointments back in September to have manicures and pedicures and their hair done at the hotel spa. Parents had reserved rooms at the hotel for their children months ago. During the month of April the buzz around school was all about who was going to be going with whom. Girls brought in pictures of their dresses and asked me for my opinion, "Do you like the tea length dress or the strapless green one better?" Some of the dresses they were considering were well over $1,000. I was astounded to think that they were spending so much money on a gown for this little soirée.

I was just so tired of all of the hoopla. After all the drama of the year, this seemed like much ado about nothing.

One of the senior boys that I had grown fond of needed a date for the prom. So he created an application for girls who might be interested in going with him. He made an envelope for the applications and adhered it to the door of the clinic with a sign that read:

Opportunity of a Lifetime
Go to Prom with Jeremy Lee
Applications Available Here

Jeremy was as sweet as pie and so funny. About half a dozen girls filled out applications. It was all done in good fun. In the end, he asked one of the girls and his other dateless buddies were matched up with the other applicants, and they all went together in a couple of limousines. They referred to themselves as *the late great dateless wonders.*

The Senior Prom was on Friday night and on Saturday night The Academy hosted the annual auction on campus. The auction was the biggest and most successful fundraiser of the year. The auction committee had been hard at work transforming the school into a pre-Civil War plantation. They were throwing a garden party à la Scarlett O'Hara and *Gone with the Wind.*

I couldn't help but think that this was terribly inappropriate given the racial turmoil that hallmarked the last winter. But I guess they were too far along in the planning to change the theme. Rumor had it they had already changed the theme once. They had planned a James Bond Theme, but given the massacre at Columbine High School last spring the planning committee thought better of it.

Freshman and sophomore students often worked at the auction as a way to earn their community service hours. This year they dressed as pre-Civil War butlers and housemaids, and helped in various capacities at the auction. Some acted as cocktail servers and others ran the bids during the live auction. From the stories I heard, I don't know if there was more drinking at the post prom parties, or by the parents at the auction.

I guess this was another law that didn't apply to Halcyon Heights as we had our 14, 15, and 16-year-old students serving alcohol. So much for the last six weeks I had spent on substance abuse education. This was one hornet's nest I was not going to put a stick in. Again, I had the opportunity to practice– just let it go.

I do know that both parties had been deemed a great success.

CHAPTER 12

May 2000

When I returned to the clinic on Monday morning it was apparent that one of the beds had been used for a little sexual interlude. The bedding was rumpled and soiled, and two half empty cocktail glasses and a condom wrapper were still on the bedside stand.

Really? Who'd been in here, students or their parents? Either way, I stripped the bed and took the dirty laundry across the hall to Bart in *The Cage*.

He looked confused. "I washed the linens on Friday afternoon," he said.

"Looks like there was one helluva wing-ding here this weekend," I said as I placed the dirty bed linens on the counter.

"Humph, no kidding?" he said, as it dawned on him why I was bringing them back to be re-washed.

"Thanks Bart," I said with a smile.

He shook his head and returned my smile.

There were still trays of dirty wine glasses on one of the benches in the hallway.

"Looks like they had a few too many ladies on the flower arranging committee, and not enough on clean-up," he said.

I nodded as I picked up the tray and carried it back to the lobby where other abandoned dishes were finding a home. As I walked down the hallway I couldn't help but wonder who had unlocked the door to the clinic.

By noon that day the photographs of all the couples that had attended the prom graced the windows of the library. There was a photograph of Evan and a beautiful African American girl who didn't attend The Academy. She was smiling sweetly as she clung to his arm. He looked so handsome in his tuxedo. But there was sadness in his eyes. Maybe it was just this photo, but I didn't think so. I was surprised to see how long his hair had grown. He'd always worn it short before. I couldn't help but wonder if that had been at his mother's insistence.

And so it was that the seniors departed for their Senior Projects. We wouldn't see most of them until graduation. They left for work in doctors' offices, in art galleries, in small businesses, as horse trainers, and across the country in a diverse array of unpaid employment. I'm certain they all learned something, even if it was that they never wanted to work in that particular field again.

Classes would be over in a couple of weeks. Everyone was counting the days, including the teachers. It was just before lunch and I was showing my class how to apply a roller bandage if someone had arterial bleeding. It was a component of their first aid class when there was a knock on my classroom door. Leah Foster stuck her head inside the room. She looked like she was about to break into tears.

"Mrs. Duncan, may I see you for a moment?" she asked.

"Of course," I said. "I'll be right with you."

I turned my attention back to my class. "Practice this with your partners. See if you can locate the brachial artery, put pressure on it, and elevate their arm above the level of their heart. I want to check your bandaging when I return." I went into the hallway to meet Leah.

"What's going on?" I asked. I noticed she was trembling as a piece of paper shook in her extended hand. I took it from her. It was Benson Bell's math test. It had been graded and marked with a *50* in red marking pencil. I knew Benson. I'd had him in class two years before. Apparently, now he was a student in Leah's remedial Algebra II class. This wasn't a real surprise to me. I recalled that Benson had done poorly in my class too.

"Turn it over," she said. She wiped the tears from her face with the back of her hand.

On the back of his failed test he had drawn a picture of a smoking handgun. His drawing made it look like it had just been fired.

Leah was visibly frightened.

I reached out and held her hand. "Where is Benson right now?" I asked.

"He's in my office," she said, and I heard the quiver in her voice. "Samuel is keeping an eye on him. I told him I was coming to get you," she said as she wiped her face of tears.

"Okay," I said. I took a deep breath. I was on autopilot. I'd been down this road before. "Give me a second."

I opened the door to my classroom to peals of laughter. It looked like they were making a movie–*Revenge of the Mummies*. The students had wrapped each other from head to toe in gauze.

"You've never looked better. We will have to finish this up tomorrow. Clean up, and then, and only then you may head over to the dining room for an early lunch."

I walked with Leah back down the hall. She was doing her best to keep her tears under control. Things changed so quickly around here. It was truly just a microcosm of a bigger world. One moment was filled with laughter and the next with tears. Comedy and tragedy were so often two sides of the same coin.

Leah unlocked the door to her office and let me in. I sat in her chair and she left for lunch, as I settled in to have a little chat with Benson.

"Ms. Foster gave me your math test," I said.

No response. Benson looked down at the ground and shuffled his feet as if he was trying to untie his shoelaces, by stepping his right foot over the laces of his left shoe.

We sat there in silence for about a minute. "Yeah, I forgot to study," he mumbled, still looking down.

"I see," I said, acknowledging that he'd done poorly on the test. "Can you tell me a little something about the picture you have drawn on the back?" I asked, shifting the focus off his poor performance to the real reason for this conversation. I turned the paper over and showed him the drawing.

"It's a Beretta Px4 Storm Compact," he said. His voice was flat and registered no emotion. He dropped his head again, and continued to look down at his shoelaces.

"You've drawn the gun with a good bit of detail. Have you ever seen one?" I asked.

"Yes, my dad has one in his collection," he said with pride in his voice.

"Collection? He has other guns too?" I asked.

"He has dozens of guns. He collects them."

Benson looked up briefly, but his face registered no concern, and he offered no explanation as to why he might be drawing detailed pictures of guns on the back of his failed math test.

I continued, "Does he keep his guns at home?"

"Yes ma'am," he said.

I found this terrifying. But then I remembered something that Elliott had so often said. "Most people in this world do not think about things the same way that you do."

"Are they locked up?" I asked consciously, trying to keep any fear or judgment out of my voice. I knew this would be critical if I wanted him to continue to talk, and I did.

"Some of them are, but this one's in the drawer in the kitchen," Benson confided. He appeared to be feeling more comfortable with me. He sat back in his chair and had started to look me in the face as we talked.

"Why did you feel the need to draw a picture of it on the back of your math test today?" I asked. I needed to understand what was behind this, and the only way I was going to find out was if Benson would tell me.

"I was just so mad at Ms. Foster. Math is really hard for me. I was barely hanging on in that class, and now she gave me an F." Again, he dropped his head in shame.

I waited in silence for him to continue and then a moment later he was angry. He made a tight fist and slammed it into the open palm of his other hand. "Now I'm going to have to go to summer school and I won't be able to go to camp. I was supposed to be a Junior Counselor this summer. Now she's ruined everything." His face was red. He shook out his fist as it most certainly hurt from the force of the punch he'd just thrown.

I took a deep breath and proceeded with caution.

"How do you feel about Ms. Foster?" I asked, and then paused.

"Oh, I hate her. She can't teach and she knew I had to pass her class, and she failed me. God, I hate her." His words spewed forth venomous and uncensored.

He was blaming her. I understood why she was fearful. He was on a roll and I let him continue, as I wanted to see where this might lead.

"And I hate all those suck-ups in that class. I can't learn this stuff with all those little morons masturbating in there. I don't belong in *that* class with *them*. I took this class last year. This is already the second time I'm taking it. I just can't take it again. I need a different teacher. She's a fucking idiot."

He was on a rant now. He had crossed a threshold and had begun to use profanity. He was losing it. And he had access to weapons.

"Did you see her? She was crying. She's afraid of me and she should be. You'll see her brains splattered all over that dry erase board before you'll see me in summer school," he said. Now he was openly defiant and glaring at me.

I had heard enough. I picked up the phone and called Sam who was waiting in the office next door. He didn't answer the phone. He just opened the door and walked in before I'd even replaced the phone on the receiver.

Benson said, "I'm not talking to him."

I stood up and Sam took my seat. "No problem, you don't have to. But you're not going anywhere either."

"Benson, I need to talk to Mr. Warwick and your mom and dad. Why don't you use this time to get some work done? Final exams are less than a week away." I said.

"How about we just forget about all of this and I go get my lunch?" Benson suggested as he started to get up.

"Sit down. I'll order you a tray," Sam said. He was a mountain of a man. He was truly a gentle giant, but he had a very commanding presence.

Benson sat back down. He was smoldering now.

I left and went to find Will.

I had earned a reputation for not shying away from the big issues. I was the public health official and coordinator of the crisis team for the school. Every student as well as every adult employed in the building was required to take my CPR and First Aid class. Everyone had heard the lesson: there are secrets that you just can't keep. When someone is a danger to themselves or to others this must be reported. Usually, it was reported to me.

I could see it clearly now. I had brought this upon myself by caring for the well being of others, and not just my job, I had become the depository for any and all information that might put anyone's health or safety at risk. Over the years there were times when the consequences of this teaching would rope me into some pretty sticky entanglements. It wasn't uncommon for me to be at odds with parents, students, and other members of the faculty with how any given situation should be handled. I would err on the side of safety, come what may. I wanted to be certain I didn't lose anyone because I misjudged the seriousness of the threats that were made.

I found Will in the dining room having a leisurely lunch with some of our colleagues. He looked up as he saw me approach. "Let me guess. Is this about young Mr. Bell?"

"I'm afraid so," I said. "I assume you've already had a conversation with Leah."

Will nodded, picked up his napkin from his lap and wiped his mouth.

I walked with Will towards his office. We walked rapidly and with purpose, yet neither of us said anything. There were far too many people just hanging around looking to pick up a loose thread of information, which they might spin into a tale.

When the door was closed in his office I recounted the conversation I'd had with Benson. Will said, "This is a no-brainer. We need to follow our protocol. There's a reason we have one. Benson is out of school immediately for a psychiatric evaluation. This has been a rough year for both of us. I've got this one. I'll call Mrs. Bell and have her pick him up."

"Thanks," I said. I was emotionally fragile. This kid scared me. "I have to teach next block, but I'll stop by after class to see how it went," I said. I knew this wasn't going to be an easy conversation for Will, but I was glad to be let off the hook.

After class, I walked back towards the academic office to see how the meeting had gone with Mrs. Bell; as I rounded the corner I saw Benson and his mother. They were still in the front lobby. Her back was to me and I could see Benson's face. She was in an intense discussion with her son. Both of her hands were crammed into the front pockets of her designer jeans as she leaned in and growled angrily at her 17-year-old son. He must have told her that I was behind her as she turned on a dime and asked, "Are you Mrs. Duncan?"

I looked into her angry eyes and said, "Yes."

"Take this, Mrs. Duncan," she said as she drew her hands from her pants pockets. Both of her index fingers pointed at me as if her hands were guns.

"Takka takka takka takka takka."

She ruffled her tongue across the roof of her mouth to sound like a machine gun. And then she laughed a loud laugh that sent chills down my spine.

"Are you afraid of me too?" she snarled. "Or are you just afraid of the students?"

I was shaking like a leaf. I kept one eye on her and as calmly as I was able, I walked over to the receptionist who was sitting at her desk in the lobby. "Mary, call security," I directed.

Do not engage with this crazy woman. Do not engage with this crazy woman.

In a blink of an eye, Robo-Cop was in the lobby and so was Will.

Perhaps it was the intensity and seriousness of the morning's encounter followed by this unexpected response from this raging woman, but it was as if somewhere inside of me a switch had been flipped and I broke.

My emotional fortitude was shattered, and I was openly sobbing as Will escorted me back to his office while the security officer attempted to escort Mrs. Bell and her son out of the building and off campus. But I could still hear her raised voice and angry protests from behind the closed door of Will's office.

I tried to describe the encounter to Will, but I had difficulty speaking because by then I was sobbing uncontrollably. He did his best to reassure me that Benson and his mother had left campus. Another security officer joined us to complete the incident report. Rationally, I knew I'd never been in any real danger. Still, I couldn't get the images out of my mind. I couldn't help but think how quickly this woman could have shot me had that been her intent. She was out of control, angry, and crazy. And she had access to weapons. She was bat-shit crazy. I was afraid of her, and of her son too.

Had Elliot still been alive I would've been able to talk this through with him and release my fears. But he was gone. And the truth was I no longer felt safe and protected. Crazy shit happened every day and I felt unbelievably vulnerable. I was a single mother now. What if something happened to me? Who would raise my children?

When we had finished with the incident report the security officer escorted me back to my office. He did everything in his power to reassure me that neither Mrs. Bell nor Benson would be allowed on campus for the remainder of the school year. Somehow, this didn't do much to alleviate my fears. School wouldn't be over for another twenty minutes. I didn't care. I was leaving. So I grabbed my purse from my desk and the security guard walked me to my car.

"Thank you, Kent," I said as I closed the car door and then locked it. This was all I could manage. I was going home.

The days had grown longer and it was a beautiful spring evening. Both Ian and Shea had finished their spring sports and wanted nothing better than to just go home, ride their bikes, and play with the other kids in our neighborhood. I busied myself with the tasks of domesticity, tidied up the house, did a load of wash, and started dinner before I poured myself a glass of wine, and went out to sit on the back deck. The sun was just beginning to set. I sat in the warm glow of the sunset and counted my blessings. I had some serious thinking to do.

I wasn't sure how it had all evolved. Over the course of the last few years I'd begun taking on more and more of the responsibility to assure the safety and well being of everyone at the school. I noticed that no one else had volunteered to take on the cause. No one wanted the responsibility, and yet, the news continued to report on violent crimes and shootings in schools across the country. Countless tragedies had ensued when the warning signs had been sloughed off and not taken seriously. If any one of these kids were coming back to school after making a threat to hurt themselves or someone else, it wasn't going to be on my say-so alone. I had read the academic literature and the newspapers since the tragedy at Columbine. I understood that plenty of kids have access to weapons and deep-seeded reasons to want to hurt themselves or someone else. I wasn't going to bear the full responsibility for saying one of these young misanthropes wasn't a danger to themselves or someone else.

My responsibility was to keep the school environment safe. Like it or not, if they wanted to return to school, it would be only after a full psychological evaluation. Very few students were happy about it, and even fewer parents.

In the years I'd taught at The Academy, more than 2500 students passed through the school. We never lost a student. This was a record that I took great pride in, but perhaps that pride was misplaced; perhaps we were nothing more than just lucky.

When I returned to school after the weekend, Will asked me to stop by his office.

"The men's varsity lacrosse team won districts over the weekend, but just barely," Will said.

I smiled. "And this concerns me how?"

"The coach, Owen Schmidt, called me at home this weekend. He thinks they may have a chance at States. You may not know this, but Benson Bell is the back-up goalie. Owen thinks they're going to need Benson if they're going to stand a chance," Will said–and then he paused as the magnitude of what he was saying hung there in the space between us.

"You're kidding, right?" I asked. I was hoping that this was some kind of a sick joke. Was he really thinking about allowing this boy back into school? This boy who only last week said we would find his math teacher's brains splattered on the white board in her classroom. Was he asking me to give this my blessing?

"Elise, I'm getting a great deal of pressure on this from Charles," Will said.

"Charles Elder, the Director of Finance?" I asked, seeking clarification.

"You know that the headmaster is well past retirement age. Clearly, you are not so insular, as not to know that the Board of Directors has already tapped Charles as his replacement. It's all done, but the announcements. In this economic climate there's a great deal of pressure to operate The Academy more like a business and winning teams are good for business." Will looked across his desk at me.

He didn't need my permission to do anything.

"When did you drink the Kool-Aid?" I asked.

Will just shook his head.

But I was on a roll. I had played the role of the obedient employee long enough, and I couldn't let this pass. "I wonder if a school shooting would be good for business?" I said. I'd lost my temper, and it was in my words and in my tone. "Perhaps you can ask Charles. Or maybe we should consult the math department to see if there's a greater probability of Leah Foster's brains being splattered across the white board in her classroom or of the men's lacrosse team from the illustrious Academy of Halcyon Heights winning the State Championship?" I stood up and walked towards the door.

"Elise ..." Will's voice trailed off.

"Sorry, Will. I cannot and will not give you my blessing on this. No way." I walked out the door and again my tears began to fall. I wiped them away with the sleeve of my navy blue blazer. They could dress the women up like men here, but it was all for show. I still cried like a little girl.

The winds of change were blowing. The headmaster was indeed long past retirement age and he had much more interest in working on his golf game and bouncing his grandchildren on his knee than he had in the drama and trauma of this affluent suburban college prep school. George had given the faculty and administration a great deal of flexibility to do their jobs, and with few exceptions people had risen to the challenge and took that trust seriously.

However, the heir apparent had a different management style. Charles had begun to speak of our students as our customers. Our objectives were shifting from helping students to grow up and into their own personal potential, to that of assuring a legacy for The Academy of Halcyon Heights. The goal was to develop students for the honor and glory of the institution, where they would acquire power, prestige, and position, and in gratitude contribute substantially to the ongoing development fund of their alma mater.

Charles liked to refer us as The Academy Family. I couldn't help but remember that the Mafia also referred to itself as a family. This was not my family and it never would be. I had love and loyalty to the members of my own family.

This was my job and I had a job to do. I intended to do the best I could to keep the school a safe place, but it didn't take a wizard to see that the up and coming headmaster and I were already at cross-purposes.

I think it was at the awards assembly the week before graduation when I knew for certain that this would be my last year at The Academy of Halcyon Heights. So much had happened over the course of the last year that weighed so heavily on my heart. But as it so often is– it's the little things that break the camel's back and I knew I couldn't stay.

The assembly took the entire morning as students processed across the stage of the performing arts center to receive one award or another. George was announcing the names of all the students who had attained *Summa Cum Laude* as they had received the highest honors or all A's. I sat up and took notice when they called his name– Ari Gottrocks.

I recalled that particularly nasty conversation I'd had with Ari's mother last fall and how she had wanted to borrow a couple of points from the next semester so that her son would have all A's. I had refused. I knew that boy had earned a B in my class. I remembered because I remembered his pushy mother.

When the assembly was over I went to the academic office and pulled his transcript.

First semester ... Health Education ... *90*.

Someone had changed his grade, and it wasn't me.

Later, the same day, Benson Bell was declared psychologically fit. No longer was he a danger to himself or others. He returned to school to take his final exams, but they were taken in the academic conference room while Robo-Cop sat guard outside the door. He also joined the other members of the men's lacrosse team and they progressed to the final four in the State Championships. The men's team came in third that year. People said that Benson's game was off. He missed a couple of shots on goal that he should have had. Such is life.

Benson was already away at summer camp when the final grades were released. Summer school started without him. At Will's insistence Ben was asked to seek a new school for the fall. He had failed Algebra II twice and therefore it would be impossible for him to successfully complete the math requirements for graduation from Halcyon Heights.

The end of the year faculty meetings went off without a hitch. I packed up my desk and my personal things before I went on summer vacation.

My contract was left unsigned on my desktop.

Before I closed the door for the last time, I looked at a poster that still hung on the bulletin board behind my desk. I had painted it a couple of years ago during one of our many advisory meetings. It said:

What other people think of me is really none of my business
What I think of myself is what is paramount
—unknown

Epilogue

Fifteen years later this still burdens my heart.
If I have learned anything from my personal practice
of yoga it is this—

I must learn to let go.

The twists and turns of life have moved all of
the characters from this long-ago drama out on the
trajectory of their own lives.

I kept track of some of the kids through my friends
and former colleagues at The Academy. I saw very little
of Catherine that spring. She became more and more
involved in her academics and spent almost all of her
time up in the science wing. By the end of her senior
year Catherine was a science and math virtuoso and
was heavily courted by some of the most prestigious

universities in the country. When her years at The Academy of Halcyon Heights had ended, she went to California to attend CalTech in Pasadena.

In the spring of that year, Libby and her parents decided that maybe The Academy wasn't the right school for her and she transferred to Regina, the all-girls' Catholic School. I followed her progress through some of the faculty I knew through the Independent Schools Association. They were pleased to report that our former student had transitioned well. She was happy, she'd made friends, and was doing very well academically.

The years have passed, and I've heard no mention of Brooklyn Powell. It was almost as if she had vanished. I can only hope that she is somewhere living a happy life of her own choosing. Occasionally, when I'm at the hair salon I will see a photograph of her parents, gracing the pages of *Town and Country Magazine*, attending some high-profile philanthropic event.

I did see in *The Richmond Press* that Mrs. Beatrice Ward passed away and that her daughter Rosaline Powell was appointed Chair of the Board at Ward International Industries.

Evan went on to play football at Ohio State. I can't tell you what position he played, as I never really paid much attention to the game. I do know that he sustained a career-ending knee injury in his junior year. After graduation he went onto Southern Baptist Theological Seminary in Louisville and is now employed as a youth pastor at a mega-church somewhere in Texas.

I have tried to put this out of my mind and let this go. The news about pedophilia in the clergy brings a gnawing irritation in my belly and the stories can wake me from my sleep. I hope and pray that Evan no longer desires the sexual company of adolescent girls.

There was a time when I felt that Will had betrayed me. I felt that he had abdicated his responsibility to assure the safety of all the students and employees in the school when he allowed Benson Bell to return. I now choose to see his decision with greater understanding and compassion. He wasn't doing anything different than I had done.

His compromise had been an act of self-protection as had mine. I had so often turned to him and he had been stalwart. But the truth was, he was not my protector and never had been, no, he was a husband and a father, and his greatest responsibility was to his own family, and they needed him to do his job, to protect them, and to provide for them. He had compromised and bent where he could and stood strong where he needed to.

During the height of this ethical dilemma I had been conflicted about what the best course of action was and in the end I chose to obey the directives of my employer and I did not call Child Protective Services as I was required to by law. I too, had chosen self-protection for the same reasons Will had. My responsibility was to my own family and they also needed me to protect and provide for them.

How could I expect him to cross a boundary I was unwilling to cross myself?

Within a year, Will also chose to leave The Academy. I didn't know the reasons surrounding his decision, as we no longer kept in touch. Perhaps it was simply the kind of opportunity he couldn't pass up. Will is now the headmaster at a Christian prep school in Seattle. He is a good and wise person and I wish him well.

I have thought about what it means to be privileged. Clearly, the privileged have been spared injustice or benefited from unjust enrichment. Over and over again, the privileged have been the beneficiaries of courtesy and deference, as well as given access to the best schools, the wherewithal to participate in the abundance of all that life has to offer, as well as leniency by the judicial system. And that is just the short list.

Elite, private schools labor to protect and promote privilege. The Academy was indeed an elite private school and the training ground for the children of the most privileged. One of the goals of The Academy was to set the expectations of the *good life*, and through rigor and competition to show our students just how that *good life* was secured, all the while upholding the status quo. Our students and their families were led to believe the rigor of an education at The Academy was unmatched, that through our tutelage they had been infused with a moral superiority and sophistication, and the social competency to compete with anyone, for anything, anywhere in the world. There were students that truly believed that their privilege was justified and had been *earned* by the strength of their merit. However, what was never acknowledged were the unearned assets that had brought them to The Academy in the first place or the extensive scaffolding of support that held up this meritocracy. It was privilege that was being sold by The Academy and it was privilege their parents were purchasing.

The Academy was an institution that espoused the virtues of promoting equity and fairness in a multicultural environment. But institutions are not people, but rather a community of people. Sometimes, we were successful and unfortunately sometimes, we missed the mark. I had seen it happen all too often, decisions were made at The Academy that had nothing to do with equity or fairness, but rather were made to protect and promote the health and well being of the institution.

Our students were watching and learning– when privilege talked, truth kept its mouth shut.

There are many people who believe if they had been born into a wealthy family their lives would have been better. No doubt, their lives would have been different, but I am not convinced that they would necessarily be better. My years at The Academy have shown that the privileged have issues all their own. Not one of us gets a pass when it comes to suffering. We all will have some pain and suffering in our lives, the privileged are not immune. Everything and everyone that we identify with is indeed impermanent and imperfect– and so we suffer. This is the nature of life.

I could be critical of the privileged and of the institutions that serve them. But I am not. Having wealth, power and position in and of itself is neither good nor bad, but it can create a chasm and a great divide that keeps people from acknowledging our common humanity.

In my years at The Academy, I saw how right and wrong were bought and sold to the highest bidder and also how every decision carried unforeseen consequences.

To those on the outside looking in, I caution you to be careful what you wish for.

As for my own life, my children are grown and living independent lives. Shea is a cultural anthropologist and is archiving the stories of the native people in South America. My son Ian is a graphic artist in Chicago.

Last fall I was visiting Ian at his apartment in Chicago when out of the blue he asked me, "Do you know someone named Catherine. She's a couple years older than I am and went to The Academy. She's Euro-Asian."

"I know who you mean, but it's been years since I've seen her. She was such a smart and beautiful girl," I said, as my mind drifted back to my years at The Academy.

"I guess she's pretty enough, but I wouldn't even think about getting close to her. She's an emotional train wreck and a rabid feminist," he said.

I paused to look at him. He was raised by a single mother and had a smart and capable sister. He'd never had any problem holding his own with strong women.

"How do you know Catherine?" I asked.

"She's a friend of Lillian's. I've met her a few times at various work-related events and we've even hung out together. She didn't know that you were my mother until she saw us when we were out for dinner last night," he said.

Lillian was Ian's colleague. I'd met her just the day before when she had joined us for sushi.

"Really?" I said. I was mulling over the coincidence of her resurfacing in my life through a colleague of my son's. We were miles and miles away from Richmond and this whole incident was from another lifetime.

"I don't recall seeing her at the restaurant."

"You might not have recognized her, but I guess she recognized you," Ian said.

"Lilly sent me a text at work today. She said Catherine wanted to get a message to you." Ian said, looking a little perplexed.

"Okay," I said. Now I was worried. What did she want to tell me that she couldn't have told me at the restaurant last night?

"She said to tell you she was raped by her tutor when she was 14. She said you'd understand."

I dropped my head into my hands, my stomach lurched and I thought I might be sick.

"Mom, are you okay? What does this mean?" My son looked across the table with love and concern radiating from his very being.

It was there and then that I first gave words to this story that I had carried silently for all these years.

Eventually, I would get to the heart of his question– *what did it all mean?*

I cannot say for certain, but I believe it meant that Brooke was indeed a victim. Were there other young girls, who had gotten caught up in the *sex-for-tutoring scandal?* I now believe that there were at least two 14-year-old innocents who were sexually abused, and possibly more. These girls were now edging in towards thirty and still carrying those emotional wounds. I worried about the long-term consequences of this wounding?

Once again, I was left to question my role in all of this.

Catherine had trusted me.

Had I indeed failed her?

Years later it still burdened my heart.

I was indeed a wounded healer.

Somehow those words seemed to resonate with me.

I had come to see myself as a *wounded healer.*

After learning this from Ian, I spent a great deal of time in reflection. What had it all meant? When my mind idled there were a few nagging questions from that astrology class I'd taken. How much of our lives was predestined and truly written in the stars? What was the significance of the placement of Chiron, the wounded healer in my chart?

On the date, place and time of my birth the comet Chiron was in my first house. What did this mean? Because the question kept resurfacing, I did some research to determine the significance of having Chiron– the wounded healer in my first house.

I was skeptical, would I learn anything relevant?

What I learned shifted my perception of astrology.

Chiron shows how our woundedness will be manifest.

Chiron is in my first house:

You attract people who are in need of healing
You are a wise counselor especially in health matters
You can be a gifted teacher
You must be careful not to lose yourself in attempts to help them
You have difficulty taking your own sage advice
Once your woundedness is acknowledged your energy is free for more creative pursuits

It is the sign we find Chiron in that indicates how we are to be healed.
In my natal chart Chiron is in Pisces:

You must make an extra effort to get rid of your unearned guilt
You may use your energy for imaginative and creative pursuits
This is the antidote for freeing yourself of the unearned guilt

In my natal chart Chiron aspects or is geometrically significant to the sun:

You need to learn to let go

So then I saw that if I was to heal myself that I must take some time to look at what it was that still caused these wounds to fester. They had become like abscesses and pockets of infection. Clearly, they needed to be lanced and opened up. The wounds must be cleaned out of the old necrotic debris and infection. This wound needed to be exposed to the light of day, if it was to heal from the inside out. As a nurse and a healer I knew that deep wounds fester if they are closed over prematurely.

Shifting back through all these details I have come to believe that the life lessons here may not actually have been for me. I played a minor role. A role that could have been played by anyone, if the girls had sought out another teacher to share their secrets with. I'd played through this story like an old vinyl record and it was time to move the needle and listen to another.

Perhaps the young people involved in this tragedy were playing out some karmic interaction, and working through past injustices.

And what about Mrs. Hedges? Perhaps her grief was just more than she could bear. I choose to see her as the sacrificial lamb that laid down her life for her son's transgressions.

None of this could have been predicted. If this same scenario had been played out a thousand other times, the end result would never have looked like this. The only person responsible for Mrs. Hedges' demise was Mrs. Hedges.

I needed to find a way to let myself off the hook.

Was this the unearned guilt that had been forecasted in my astrological chart?

Her death had nothing to do with me.

I was an observer when this story unfolded, just an observer.

The guilt I carried was unearned.

Now, I am the storyteller.

Now, I am the narrator.

What possible good could come from the retelling of this story? Perhaps it is merely the antidote to my unearned guilt. Or perhaps it will allow us momentarily to walk in the shoes of another. Perhaps if we can place ourselves in the role of victim and then in the role of perpetrator we may come to realize that often the lines are blurred.

Yet, I am left to wonder why I became entangled in this dilemma at a time in my life when I was so vulnerable?

Was there a reason or was it just happenstance?

The truth is– I just don't know.

There are times, when life presents complicated ethical dilemmas, where all the choices available leave us morally conflicted. Sometimes there just aren't any perfect solutions. So we do the best we can with the light and understanding we carry at the time.

Who does what to whom?

Who gets what from whom?

I guess we all just play the roles we are cast in, and do the best that we are able.

Hopefully in the end, it will be good enough.

My final prayer is this:

May all be blessed with healing
May all bask in God's grace, love, and forgiveness
Myself included

Namaste– the light in me sees and honors the light in you.

Jeanne Selander Miller has worked as a registered nurse in a major urban trauma center, as a hospital administrator, and as a high school health teacher.

She now runs a farm-to-table restaurant with her sister in the Adirondack Mountains of New York from the months of May to October. The rest of the year, she can be found writing in Vero Beach, Florida.

Jeanne Selander Miller's first three books are memoirs. *A Breath Away*, *A Million Miles from Home*, and *The Healing Path Home* were honored at the London Book Festival, the Paris International Book Festival, and the New York Book Festival.